THE LULLABY MAN

ANNI TAYLOR

THE LULLABY MAN: Copyright © September 2020 Anni Taylor

All rights reserved. No part of this book may be reproduced in any form or by any electronic or mechanical means, including information storage and retrieval systems, without written permission from the author, except for the use of brief quotations in a book review. This is a work of fiction. Names, characters, businesses, places, events, locales, and incidents are either the products of the author's imagination or used in a fictitious manner. Any resemblance to actual persons, living or dead, or actual events is purely coincidental.

Cover design copyright © 2020 Alexandre Rito.

978-0-6484380-2-1

PART I

PRESENT DAY

1

KATE

"I need to tell you what I've been keeping secret for the past ten years. But once you know, people are going to get hurt. Because this can never just be a talk between a mother and daughter. You're the *police*. You'll have to act upon what I tell you." Abby struck a rigid pose as she eyed the wind whipping up the water into small peaks. It was spring, but a cold snap had descended, as if the weather had decided to cling fast to winter.

A fearful drumbeat started inside my chest. I touched Abby's arm. "Whatever it is, you know it'll be okay. No matter what."

We were standing at the edge of Coldwater Lake. We'd just scattered stargazer lilies in memory of my mother, who'd died two months earlier. The pink flowers bobbed and spun, carried away by the current. The sun hovered just above the horizon, staining the sky and water in shades of deepest amber.

Abby had recently chopped her long locks to shoulder length, her thick curtains of hair falling around her face and accentuating her delicate features.

Ten years ago, Abby had been just fourteen. It was the year that my relationship with her had taken a sudden dark turn. She'd completely closed herself off. It had seemed to me that she'd begun hating me. It'd been a constant heartache in my life.

Wrestling with my thoughts, I drew a deep breath of the chilly air. "Abby, just tell me straight. Whatever it is, we'll get through it. I promise."

"I've wanted to tell you so many times. But it's like the words get caught in my throat. And then my mind shuts like a trap. I just can't—"

"Just... breathe...."

She jammed her eyes shut. "Here goes... Mum... when I was fourteen, I fell in love with someone."

I didn't know what I'd expected her to say, but that wasn't it. Instantly, images of boys she'd known flashed through my mind. Abby hadn't even had a real boyfriend until she was eighteen—had she?

"Who was it?" I asked.

"He was someone I never should have fallen for. It was all kinds of wrong. And he did some very... strange things. Things that are hard to speak about. I let it happen. I just... let it all happen—"

"Take a breath, honey. Slow down—"

"He pulled me in, day by day. Until I barely knew who I was anymore. He wouldn't allow anyone else to come near me. He even fought another man because of me."

"Did you just say, *another* man?" I breathed. "Does that mean that this person was a man... not a boy?"

"Yes," she answered. "He was my teacher."

Her words hung in the darkening air.

Bird calls echoed across the sky. The wind and current pushed the lilies out so far that they merged with the dim horizon.

2

KATE

The temperature seemed to have dropped a couple of degrees since we first arrived.

The sun was all but gone. Just a faint glow marking the spot where it had been.

Confusion and anger rattled through me.

Who was the teacher? How was it possible that she'd had a relationship with him? And how on earth had she kept it hidden from me?

But I had to wait for the answers to come from Abby.

I hugged her, holding her close, trying to be patient. She shivered in my arms.

"Mum..." she said. "It was Mr Eisen."

The cold air iced my lungs. I was glad she couldn't see my expression. "*Mr Eisen?*"

"Yes. *Him.*"

Thoughts raced through my mind, pulling me back ten years into the past.

I knew all about Emmet Eisen. I knew the details of his life because of something that had happened to him.

Emmet drowned in Coldwater Lake. The same lake that Abby and

I were standing at right now. He'd just been twenty-three. One night, when he'd been drinking heavily, he made the fateful decision to go out on his boat. Somehow, he'd ended up falling into the water.

Emmet had been a young teacher at Abby's school, Valley Grammar. His parents were Alex and Louisa Eisen, who'd moved here from Germany when Emmet was thirteen.

"I've been holding onto something else," Abby told me. "The day Mr Eisen had the fight with the other man is the same day he died. I should have told. But I couldn't have told without having to explain... *everything.*"

I hugged her closer.

It was me who'd led the investigation into Emmet's death. It'd been a short, routine investigation that hadn't been expected to reveal any foul play. The coroner had ruled that the drowning was accidental.

But now I knew there'd been a fight that day. That opened the possibility that the other man had pursued Emmet and had been involved in the drowning. Emmet's body had displayed a number of bruises, about which the forensics report had been inconclusive.

With unfocused eyes, I watched the wind whip its way through the tall grasses and reeds along the lake bank. My daughter was right. These revelations were going to tear some ugly wounds into this town.

Where did that leave us now? Reopening the case? And also putting my daughter through renewed trauma in telling all she knew in a court of law?

Right now, I could barely think. My mother instincts crushed my instincts as a detective. I felt fiercely protective of Abby.

I moved back to face her, gently holding her arms. "I'm so sorry... so very sorry that all this happened. You were so young and dealing with it all alone."

Tears bubbled in her eyes. "You knew something was wrong. Because I was tired all the time. What you didn't know was that I'd been staying up all night long to talk with Mr Eisen, sometimes until two or three in the morning."

The pieces came together in my mind—sharp, jagged little pieces.

Abby ran her bottom lip through her teeth, her expression tightening with pain and regret. "I'd drag myself out of bed every morning and get myself ready for school. It was like I was on a treadmill. But I... I thought I loved him."

"Oh, honey, I wish you'd talked to me. I tried... so many times."

Abby sucked in a breath and released it slowly. "I know. But I knew that if I told, my relationship with Mr Eisen would end. You ended up grounding me, and you took my phone and the internet away. I was so angry with you. And then... Emmet drowned. I thought if only I'd been able to talk with him... on the phone or at the parties... then he would have been okay. He wouldn't have gone out on his boat drinking that night. He wouldn't have drowned. *I hated you.*"

Tears rolled down my face, instantly cold on my skin. "It hurts just to hear you say that."

"None of it was your fault. But back then... I guess I was blinded... by love and grief. I thought my life was over."

"It wasn't your fault, either. You were a child. But, Abby, what parties are you talking about? You barely went to any parties when you were fourteen."

"Yes, I did. I didn't want to tell you any of this when Nan was still alive. It would have really hurt her. But on all the weekends that I was staying over at her house, I was sneaking out to go to parties with Layla."

I tried not to look shocked. But I *was* shocked. Abby used to stay at her grandmother's house a lot when she was that age. I'd thought it was the one good thing at the time, that the two of them had a close relationship.

Layla had been Abby's best friend. She'd left town when she was fourteen, and I hadn't heard her name since then.

"Where were these parties at?" I asked.

"At the Eisens' house. They had parties all the time. That whole summer."

"I had no idea."

"I know. I feel so awful," Abby whispered. "But I deserve it. For keeping all these secrets hidden away for so long."

"No, you don't. Abby, you deserve all the good things."

"You won't think that when you hear the rest of my story. I want to tell you... because it's been eating me up all these years. But it's so hard. Every time I even think back on that time, my skin crawls and I want to vomit everything inside me."

"You poor girl. Have you mentioned anything to Dr Quinley about feeling this way?"

Abby had been seeing a psychiatrist for the past two months.

"Yes," Abby said. "I told Dr Quinley how I've been feeling. He said I'm having anxiety attacks. He gave me some exercises to do when this happens. Mindfulness and being present—that kind of thing. I try. But I can't seem to get on top of it."

"Okay. Have you told him anything about what you just told me—about Mr Eisen?"

"I've started a few times. Dr Quinley tries to encourage me. But I know that if I tell him, he'll be obliged to contact the police. And well, that's *you*. So, I might as well just tell you. I don't know if I can get through my story once, let alone twice."

"Is there anything I can do to make it easier for you?"

"I don't know. I just feel... so much shame. When I told you all that I did just now, that's what I felt. Shame."

"I have a thought. At my job, I've sometimes had people tell me things via a psychiatrist. And it can be very helpful. I sit in on the session and just listen. How would you feel about that?"

As a homicide detective, I'd often seen people just after the worst possible thing had happened to them. Usually the murder of a family member. Sometimes, they'd even witnessed it happening. Often, they wanted to tell me what they'd seen, but they just couldn't manage to speak. In those circumstances, I'd used a psychiatrist as a go-between.

"Would a psychiatrist agree to that?" Abby said dubiously.

"Some would. Dr Quinley might. First, how are things going with your therapy in general? Are you happy with Dr Quinley?"

"Yes. I guess so. He seems to go the extra distance to make me feel comfortable."

"Okay. What if we do it that way? If Dr Quinley agrees, he could lead the session, and I'd just sit in?"

Her taut expression seemed to relax at the edges. "Okay, I'll ask him."

"Good. We'll try that. For now, we'd better get you home. You look like you're freezing, poor thing."

We walked back to my car, wind eddying around us.

Abby seemed to not want to talk as we drove away. She'd used up all her reserves to tell me as much as she had.

I switched on the car's heater, swept up in a maelstrom of thoughts.

3

KATE

I can't pinpoint the moment my daughter started hating me, but I know the image that comes up in my mind. I know that image clearly.

I picture a door.

Abby's bedroom door.

Because the year she turned against me was the year she started keeping her door firmly shut.

It was the year she turned fourteen. Before that year, she and I had been close. We'd go clothes shopping together and stop off for ice-cream, and we'd sit and giggle like friends would. At home on the weekends, we'd watch movies together, wrapped up snug in the one blanket. I'd helped train her soccer team—my husband Pete and I would take the whole team running up and down mountain tracks.

Abby had been an active child, her bedroom filled with her sporting equipment and dance costumes. I don't know what I'd imagined her teenage years would be like, exactly, but I'd expected she'd continue to blossom.

But during her fourteenth year, the lights went out. She became almost like a stranger to her father and me.

The way it started was that she became restless, always wanting to be out of the house. And when she was at home, she was always in her room, with the door shut. She'd lost interest in her sport and dancing. At the same time, she had days where she was deliriously happy—and I had no idea why.

When I'd asked for advice among my friends who had teenage daughters, the answers were always the same: *That's just what teenage girls are like. Girls are moody. Girls are hormonal. Girls test the boundaries. It's just a phase. It'll soon pass.*

I'd tried hard to hang in there, but it was difficult for me to understand. I hadn't been that kind of teenager myself. But I was trying my heart out to understand Abby.

Still, something felt wrong.

Then Abby's moods took a darker turn. She became angry with me. I felt seething anger in her every word and glance and gesture. When I'd ask her what was wrong, she'd insist she wasn't upset with me. At the time, I became so concerned that I spoke with a couple of her teachers and the school guidance counsellor. They'd noticed she'd become especially quiet, but nothing more than that.

In desperation, I'd taken Abby to see a child psychologist. But Abby refused to talk.

I remember nights after work where I'd sit outside the house alone, nursing a coffee, gazing out at the lights over the park that lay beyond our yard. I'd be trying to figure out what I did or said to Abby, what I did or didn't do.

How did I hurt her? What did I do wrong? What did she need?

More than a few times, I'd gone upstairs and stood outside her bedroom, facing that closed door. I wanted to plead for her to tell me what was wrong.

One night—eventually—everything I'd been holding back rose up to boiling point. I stormed in and demanded she talk to me. I raged at her. It wasn't my finest hour.

I'd expected that she'd say what she usually said and tell me that I was being crazy and that everything was fine. But she'd burst into tears. She had sobbed like she'd never stop.

But still, she refused to say a word.

Ashamed of myself and emotionally bruised, I'd driven to the other end of town, to my mother's house.

My mother had sat me down and made me tea. She'd let me talk and cry.

When I returned home, I apologised to my daughter for my behaviour. I never talked to her about it again.

Abby's outward anger towards me subsided, but she was never again like the person she was before her fourteenth year. Instead, she was either anxious, annoyed, or aloof.

Abby moved out of home at age eighteen, and the next thing her father and I knew, she was pregnant. The relationship didn't work out, but she kept the baby.

I'd ended up deciding that the grudges Abby held against me must be to do with my job. I'd been too occupied with the heavy workload required of a senior homicide detective. Somehow, I'd missed noticing important things. And I'd paid the price.

But now I knew there had been another person wrapped up in all of this.

The dead teacher, Mr Emmet Eisen.

4

ABBY

My heart raced.

I wanted to vomit.

I'd just told my mother what happened back when I was fourteen.

I'd told her about Emmet.

I wanted to explain to her how I got pulled into the world that I did, but I didn't know how. How could I explain something like that?

It started with the parties that Emmet's parents held all summer long at their house.

And of course, Emmet was at all those parties.

He was magical and amazing and terrifying. He held me in the palm of his hand, like a magician performing tricks. I was the trick—the rabbit in the hat, the vanishing bird trick, the *saw-the-girl-in-half* illusion.

I'd go to school and watch Emmet teach our science class, holding the knowledge of who he really was deep inside me. All the things he said to me would be spinning through my head. All the things he'd wanted me to do.

I'd talk to him all night long on the phone, until I'd fall into a heavy, dreamless sleep.

And on the weekends, I'd go to the parties.

To an inexperienced fourteen-year-old, the parties were intoxicating.

As a ruse, I would stay at my grandmother's house. And bake pies with her. She'd tuck me into bed like I was a little kid, and then she'd head off to her room and go to sleep. Then I'd change out of my pyjamas and into party clothes, and I'd leave the house. Nan wouldn't hear a thing.

And I'd go meet up with Layla, in the dark.

We'd go together to the parties at the Eisens' house.

The Eisens lived next to a forest, right on the lake.

Barefoot people in party clothes would be dancing beneath coloured lights that were strung from tree to tree. They'd bring chairs and small tables right down to the lake edge. Music would pump all night long.

Layla and I would dance for hours and hours, sneaking small drinks of vodka and whiskey. Sometimes, Emmet's friends from university would come along. Layla and I would dance with them, in one big group. It was... *tribal*.

There was always lots of singing and guitar and Conga drums. Lots of dancing. Lots of drumming. They'd all drink a lot, and smoke, and talk. They all had stories about the places they'd been. Portugal, Barbados, the Canary Islands, Mexico.... To me, it all sounded so... exotic.

Sometimes, Emmet would even perform magic tricks for the partygoers. He was *good*. He mesmerised me. Everyone would clap and beg him for more.

That part of the lake edge was like a little secret pocket, kept buttoned up from the rest of the world. On the party nights, people would drift in by boat. Others seemed to drift in on the night air.

During summer, the temperature would be hot enough to make you sweat, but cool breezes would skim the lake and make you feel alive.

Everything was complicit in this world. All the people and the landscape and the night itself. Even the straight, soldier-like ghost gums that stood guard and the night birds that crooned in the unseen parts of the lake were part of this.

Emmet's father, Alex, would sit reciting from his novels—written by authors I had never heard of. Jack Kerouac and Ernest Hemingway. Stories of road trips and drinking and restless men and women. The characters in those books were always restless.

My parents had a pretty busy social life, too, but nothing like the Eisens' party life. Most of Mum's friends were cops, and most of Dad's friends were financial analysts, like him. As a young teenager, I'd felt the weight of all that authority around me. Cops and analysts.

I'd felt the pressure to be smart, to be clever, to be *good*. I hadn't known if I would ever live up to all of that.

When I was down at the lake, the pressure was off. The adults there were always talking about living in the moment, and they were always quoting from books about deeply flawed people.

At age fourteen, that had spoken to me.

And then there was Emmet.

He enveloped me as if by a magician's cape—taking me from one world into another.

And I was never the same.

5

KATE

The morning dawned with a thin cloud cover and enough sunlight filtering through to look pleasant. But after what Abby had told me yesterday, a grey veil seemed to hang over everything.

I walked out to the back deck to have my morning coffee. Normally, I'd grab a coffee once I arrived at work at the station. This morning, I needed to talk with Pete. He was out on an early morning run.

There hadn't been time to talk to him last night. We had a busy household. Besides Pete and me, there was Abby and her partner of one year, Logan, their baby, Jasper, and Abby's six-year-old daughter, Ivy. We'd recently bought a large house on some land. Pete and Logan had been busily painting and fixing up our former house so that Abby and her family could move in there and have their own space.

Last night, Pete had come in late from painting the ceilings at the old house—exhausted and just wanting dinner and bed.

I sipped my coffee, bracing at the morning chill. The clothes I'd dressed myself in for work just weren't warm enough. Mist hung at the distant fence line. I could hear the chickens clucking and pecking in their coop.

Two large dogs bounded out of the mist—looking almost ghostly with their white fur. Our Maremma dogs—Elsa and Snowdrop. They raced to the deck and leapt up beside me, demanding to be patted.

Bending, I hugged each of them and stroked their heads. Their fur was beautifully soft.

They'd been doing a wonderful job of keeping the chickens safe. Pete had bought six chickens as soon as we moved into this new house, just a month ago. In truth, the chickens were more for the Maremmas than anything—dogs of that breed needed something to guard or they'd go crazy.

My husband came jogging through the open gate and along the wide gravel road that led to our house.

The dogs bounded up to Pete, seeming happy that one of their flock had returned to the safety of the boundary fence.

When Pete saw me on the deck, he cut diagonally across the land.

"Hey," he breathed, as he ran up the steps. "Good morning. It's a cold one out there."

"Freezing," I agreed. "I'm going to have to get used to living out here. Seems a couple of degrees colder than in town."

He smiled. "You need to come for a run with me in the mornings and warm up."

Pete was a die-hard runner who thought running was the answer to most of life's ills. I used to go for a lot more runs. Lately, I'd been slowing down. To be fair, Pete had more spare time than I did. In his late sixties, he was a little older than me and already retired.

Right now, he had that distinct glow and alert look in his eyes that he always had after a run. He was as handsome to me as the day I'd met him.

"Pete...." I gathered my breath. "I've got something to tell you. Something difficult."

Deep creases appeared in his forehead. "Okay?"

It hurt me to see a sudden pain enter his eyes. The past few years had been devastating for our family. We'd had one tragedy after the other. It'd seemed that finally, life had settled into an easy pace. A crime that had been committed against our family had been solved. I'd found acceptance after my mother passed away. And Pete and I had moved to the kind of large property we'd long dreamed of. Everything seemed to have smoothed out. Even the rift between Abby and me had finally been healing.

But that peace was about to be shattered.

"I don't know how to tell you," I began. "It's about Abby. Last night, when we were down at the lake, she told me what she'd been keeping from us all these years."

"Sounds more serious than what we were expecting?"

"It is."

I glanced back at the house. All was quiet. Logan had gone to work to the mechanic's shop earlier. Abby and the kids were asleep. It was safe to talk.

I explained to Pete what Abby had told me.

His face crumpled. "If Eisen were alive, I'd go punch his face."

"Me, too. Well, I'd want to."

"What did Abby mean, exactly, when she said he did *strange* things?"

"She didn't give details. But she'll need to talk it out. The whole thing has affected her life in the worst way."

Pete cursed under his breath. "How did we not know this was going on?"

"You know all those weekends she stayed with my mother? She was apparently sneaking out to see Emmet once Mum was asleep. And she was talking with him via text. Pete, that's why she was so angry with me. Do you remember when I grounded her and took away her internet access? That's around the time that Emmet drowned. She hadn't been able to contact him. And, in her mind, it left him all alone. She blamed me for his death."

"That's... crazy. It wasn't your fault."

"She was fourteen and had a huge crush on her teacher. She wasn't thinking straight."

"Yeah, true. She was just a kid. This explains so damned much."

"She's got more to tell. But I think she might have a trauma disorder

—like PTSD. She just can't seem to get the words out. I suggested that she tell her story in her usual sessions with her psychiatrist, and I'd sit in. I don't know if he'll agree."

"Good idea. Let me know what the psych says."

"I will. Pete, the other part of this is Eisen's death. I can't be certain now if it was accidental."

"It was no loss," Pete growled.

"I know exactly what you mean. I'm sorely tempted to let it go, myself. But if someone killed Eisen, that person could be as bad as Eisen was. And, the thing is, there could be a murderer out there in our town."

"Or," Pete countered, "the other person might have had good reason to attack Eisen. Who knows if Eisen played his dirty tricks on other young girls, just like Abby? Could have been an angry father."

"Maybe. Maybe not. You're a good man, Pete. But everyone isn't *good*."

Pete shut his eyes tightly. "I'm talking like an enraged father. Which is what I am right now. I just can't believe our little girl went through all this."

Reaching out, I held his hand. "We'll get through this. Abby will be better for it once she's got it all off her chest and starts the road to healing."

The dogs stood, letting out warning barks as a police vehicle came through the gates. They charged towards the car. They were fluffy, energetic freight trains, wanting to know who'd come onto their property and what they were doing. The Maremmas were like that.

Detective Sergeant Jace Franco stepped from the car.

He cupped his hands around his mouth. "Call off your bloodthirsty hounds!"

I kissed Pete goodbye. "Franco's early for once." I called out to the dogs. "Elsa! Snowdrop! It's okay. It's just Franco."

The dogs retreated, but just a little. They were only friendly to people once I'd told them that everything was all right. The Maremmas were new to our family, and I was still learning about them.

"Hey," Franco protested. "I'm not *just Franco*. My mother thinks highly of me, I'll have you know." He grinned widely as I walked across the grounds.

"You keep telling that story," I joked. "Someday, someone will believe it."

Franco squatted to pat the dogs, who were now eager for his attention.

Just before I stepped into the car, I glanced back at Pete. Standing there on the deck, he looked as lost as I felt.

6

KATE

Detective Franco drove along the dirt road that led away from my house. Normally, I'd drive myself into the station. But Franco and I had planned to speak with a murder suspect first thing this morning, so it made sense to go together.

"Misty old morning," Franco remarked.

"Yes. We're lucky we're on a hill. If we were down low, it might get damp in the house in winter."

"My house gets damp as a squid, being at the bottom of a damned mountain. I need to crank up the heat at night and cook the whole place, just to keep it clear of mould."

"I've been telling you for years you should move. That house has a lot of problems."

"Yeah. But I'm used to it. And it's used to me. I don't want to have to introduce myself to another house and start all over again."

"Don't ever stop being weird."

"Thanks." He steered the car around a bend. "So, you're all prepared for this shindig with Coraline Fernsby? We've got to put the pressure on her, right? I mean, we know she did it."

Franco and I had a pretty good idea that Coraline had killed a nursing home resident. The bed-bound resident had been suffocated with a pillow. What made it hard was that Coraline was also a resident of the home, and last time we'd spoken with her, she'd pretended to be forgetful, almost to the point of having Alzheimer's. But the nursing staff had informed us that Coraline's mind was as sharp as a pin. Franco and I needed to force her to drop the act.

I tried to recall the conversation we'd had with her last week, but my mind was blanking. "Franco, would you mind going over the key points again?"

He side-eyed me. "You seem a bit distracted. Something happening with you?"

"Yeah. Family crisis."

"Ah. Family stuff can really get you in the feels."

"You said it. This goes quite a bit further than the ordinary, though. At the moment, I can't talk about it. I need to get some facts straight. But when I do... I'd like to talk it over with you."

"Are you saying it could be a police matter?"

"It's possible."

"Damn. That's the last thing you need."

"Yeah. It's the last thing *all of us* need."

"Well, you let me know when you need old Franco. I'm here for you. You know that."

I smiled. "Thanks, Franco."

Franco had been referring to himself as *old* ever since he turned forty. He probably pictured himself that way because his father had died at age forty-eight, of a heart attack. Franco was turning forty-eight in a few days' time. I guessed he thought he was looking down the same barrel as his dad. It didn't have to be that way, although I worried that he tended to go through bouts where he drank too much and ate too much junk.

His eyes were a little dark and sunken underneath. I'd been too caught up in my own thoughts to notice before.

"You feeling okay?" I asked him.

"Nothing I can't medicate myself for. I've got a bottle of bourbon at home with my name on it."

"Sounds like a plan," I said wryly.

"Yep," he responded. "A curvy bottle of Booker's is my idea of a hot date these days."

I knew he was under strain. His latest relationship had hit the dust. And then there was that whole thing for him about turning forty-eight.

He was my work partner, but I hadn't been there to share the workload recently. I'd had a month off before and after my mother's death. I hadn't even been certain if I'd return to work at the homicide division at all. I'd be sixty-five on my next birthday. I'd given my working life to this job, and it seemed it was time for a new phase.

But during the time I'd had off work, I'd realised I wasn't ready. I had more to do.

I made a mental note to organise a little birthday party for Franco down at the station. He'd like that.

Franco drove past Echo Point, then got stuck behind a line of buses filled with tourists. Echo Point was always full of tourists, from dawn to dusk. The scene of the mountains from the viewing platforms drew people from everywhere.

"Ugh," he said. "Should have gone the other way." He leaned his head back, rubbing his forehead.

After a minute, he got past the banked-up tourist buses and headed to the nursing home.

A staff member showed us through to Coraline's room.

Coraline was eighty years of age. With her soft, rounded body and sparkling blue eyes, she looked every inch the loving grandmother type. But as far as I knew, her family refused to visit her. Normally, it would seem an awful thing to leave an elderly family member all alone. But Coraline was not all that she seemed.

"Oh... lovely," exclaimed Coraline as Franco and I sat in the room with her. "I do like visits."

"Hello, Coraline," I said. "You remember Detective Sergeant Franco and me—DS Wakeland—from two weeks ago? We came to talk with you. We've been doing some investigating since then. And today, we'd like to talk with you again. This time, we'll be recording the interview. I have to tell you that anything you say can and might be used against you in a court of law. Do you understand?"

She smiled. "You're going to do a recording? Will someone be singing? I used to like The Andrews Sisters when I was a teenager. I loved that big-band sound. There's never been anyone like them since."

Franco exchanged a glance with me. "No, Coraline. We're the police and we'll be recording everything you tell us."

"Oh dear. The police? Is something wrong?" She opened her eyes innocently.

Today, I had no patience for her. "You're a few years too young to have been a fan of the Andrews Sisters, Coraline. And I'll tell you what's wrong. On June the sixth, you walked into Meredith Willet's room while she was sleeping, and you placed a pillow over her face. Meredith died by suffocation, due to you keeping the pillow there until she was dead."

Coraline gasped. "Meredith is dead? Why didn't anyone tell me?"

Franco sighed. "Cut it out, Coraline. We know all about the things you've done in the past. Let's say you've had an *interesting* life. We also know that you said to another resident that you wanted Meredith's room because it had a better view and that she was taking too long to kick the bucket."

The distant look vanished from Coraline's eyes.

"She couldn't even see the garden," Coraline whimpered. "Just lying there in bed all day—as she did. But the staff refused to swap me with her. *The bitches.*"

Franco and I were able to pry a confession from Coraline there and then. Neither of us had thought she'd crumble so easily.

After the interview with Coraline, we headed to the station to work on two open homicide cases. The case of Meredith Willet's murder could now be closed.

At 3:30 in the afternoon, I started on a late lunch. I realised I'd forgotten to eat all day.

Abby called as I was taking the third bite of my sandwich.

"I finally got through to Dr Quinley," she told me. "At first, he was a bit dubious about you sitting in at the sessions. But he came around. My next appointment with him is actually this afternoon. I'd totally forgotten. This isn't enough notice for you, right?"

"What time?"

"Four. Logan will be home in a few minutes to watch the kids."

"I'll be there."

7

KATE

Franco gave me a lift across town so that I could make it for Abby's appointment. My car was at home, but if Franco drove me there first, I'd lose too much time.

A bundle of nerves gathered in my chest. It was good news that Dr Quinley had agreed to my request. But I was still terrified about what further secrets Abby might reveal.

Franco parked the car outside Close Quarters. *Close Quarters* was an enormous development that dominated Tallman's Valley. Built in recent years, it had changed the entire face of this sleepy town. It consisted of a hospital, a university, a tech sector and a retail sector.

"It's not my business," said Franco. "But does your daughter's psych appointment have something to do with your family crisis?"

"It could have."

"Well, take it one day at a time, okay? No rushing at it like a bull in a China shop."

"Got it."

Franco knew me too well. We'd been partners for just over a decade.

I headed for the retail sector of Close Quarters. The psychiatrist's office was on the top floor, in a quiet area reserved for offices.

Dr Quinley was a Sydney psychiatrist who'd only started seeing clients in Tallman's Valley for the past few months, splitting his time between Sydney and the valley. By all accounts, he was very good. Abby had been lucky to secure him as her therapist.

Two middle-aged people sat patiently in the waiting room of his office, both in business suits.

Quinley's receptionist showed me through. There were three rooms down a short corridor—with the names of different psychiatrists in gold lettering on the doors.

The receptionist tapped on the door that displayed the name, Dr Gordon Quinley, and then opened it.

The first thing that I noticed were large windows that allowed broad sweeps of daylight into the room. Tall, potted plants occupied each corner. A painting hung between the windows—a painting of Coldwater Lake. It was depicted in silky, pastel-blue colours, with mist sitting at the horizon.

The room felt perfectly balanced. I guessed that was deliberate.

As I stepped inside the L-shaped room, I saw a man sitting with Abby in a pair of plush leather chairs.

He rose and came to greet me. "Detective Kate Wakeland, it's good to meet you."

"And you, too. Thank you for agreeing to this. I know it's irregular."

He offered a kind smile. "If it helps Abby's progress, I'm all for it." The doctor looked to be in his fifties—his silvery hair offset by a dark blue sports jacket, retro watch and loafers.

The receptionist beamed and closed the door behind me.

I gave Abby a hug. She felt tense, her back a fraction too straight.

"Hi," she whispered.

Selecting a chair at the back of the room, I went to it. It was out of the way, next to one of the potted plants. I gestured to Dr Quinley. "Am I okay to sit here?"

"Yes, that looks like a good spot," the doctor said.

From where I was, I had a side view of Abby and the psychiatrist, with the drooping leaves of a Devil's Ivy plant filtering the view.

"Are you ready to start, Abby?" Dr Quinley asked.

"Yes. I'm ready to do this." She didn't sound ready at all.

"Good," he replied. "Now, I understand that there are events from the year you turned fourteen that you wish to talk about today. Do I have that right?"

"Yes," she said. "It's time that my mother knows... everything that I've been keeping from her."

"I sense a great deal of strain in your voice," Dr Quinley noted. "What is it that you're finding the most difficult right at this moment?"

"It's just... there's so much to tell, and I don't know where to start, and my throat feels like it's seizing up, and—"

"Okay, Abby," he broke in. "I want you to stop there. What I want you to do is to close your eyes and imagine a tree. It's a fruit tree. Tell me, what fruit is on that tree?"

She let her eyelids drift downwards. "Pear."

"All right, it's a pear tree," he said. "Imagine the tree. It's standing on a grassy hill. The day is warm. You're safe. Everything is well. You're holding a basket and you want to fill it with pears. That's very good news for the tree because it's heavy with fruit. Far too heavy. The tree needs some of its weight released. Each piece of fruit is ripe and ready to be picked. Can you see this tree, Abby?"

"Yes, I can see it." Her voice was so small.

"Well done," he said. "Now, this is a very special pear tree. It holds all your memories. From the time you were a baby until now. Each piece of fruit is a memory. You're walking up that hill, towards the tree. You will go to the part of the tree that holds all your memories from when you were fourteen. And you will pick a memory. How do you feel about that?"

"I feel... okay. I'm okay."

"Good. Now, most of the pears are too high for you to reach. You would need a ladder for that, and you don't have one... not yet. Don't worry, I'll give you a ladder when you're ready. But right now, there are

28

pears that are well-within your reach. Can you picture the low-hanging fruit?"

"Yes."

"You're doing well. You're going to pick one small, contained memory from the pieces that are well-within your reach. A memory from before everything that hurt you began. Are you ready to do that?"

She nodded.

"Good. Please tell me about the piece of memory you've chosen?"

"Layla. It's a memory of Layla."

"Okay. Now, who is Layla? A family member? A friend?"

"She used to be my best friend. This day is where it all starts, because it's when I met *her*. My story starts and ends with her."

"Tell me about that memory."

Abby went quiet for a few moments before she began speaking. "I'd been at my grandmother's house with my parents. I got bored and went out for a run. And I found a girl with frizzy blonde hair at the lake. She told me her mother had died, and she'd come to live with her aunt Nina. We were both thirteen. I thought her accent was strange—she was Scottish. She told me she knew we'd become good friends."

"That's a fine memory, Abby," Dr Quinley remarked. "Full of childhood innocence. Please... take another pear from the tree. What do you see?"

Abby nodded. "It's April. I see Layla on her bike, riding to school. It's her first day at Valley Grammar. She's got her long hair back in a ponytail, with six hair ties, all different colours. I remember thinking that was endlessly cool. And she ends up being in all my classes. I'm happy about that."

"Thank you," Dr Quinley said. "Feel free to pick another memory."

"It's October. The day after the spring break. There's a new teacher at school. His name is Mr Eisen. He's a science teacher. We learn about clouds in his first class. About cloud shapes and what they mean."

"This obviously made an impression on you. What are you thinking at the time?"

"I'm thinking that I love this lesson. I love learning about clouds. He makes it all sound so amazing."

"And what else?" asked Dr Quinley.

"Layla and I think Mr Eisen is the most beautiful man we've ever seen."

I listened, trying not to let my thoughts run wild. I wished that this were just about an innocent schoolgirl crush. But I already knew the story was going to go much, much further.

"It sounds like you were very fond of your teacher," Dr Quinley commented.

"Yes," Abby breathed. "I loved him. No. I just thought I did."

"I see," Dr Quinley said. "Well, we'll be exploring that. In time, of course. Not all at once. That's your third pear, Abby. You have three memories in your basket now. Well done. Was that okay?"

"Yes, it was," she answered.

"Time to choose another pear from the tree," he told her. "Perhaps another memory of Layla?"

Her breaths quickened. "I see her... standing in the boat shed at the back of the Eisens' property. This is... many months later. It's the end of January, the next year. Layla and I are now fourteen and a half. She's in the boat house with Emmet. He's *Emmet* to me now, not Mr Eisen. Because I know him... much more intimately. Layla is shouting at him. Telling him over and over: *this isn't right, this isn't right. You've got to do something about it. Right now. If you don't, I will.*"

Abby shook her head. "Emmet is just... drunk and not talking. Layla pushes me out of the boat house. Tells me she knows things about Emmet I don't. She tells me he doesn't love me. And she's wearing a necklace—a necklace with a pendant that looks like a tiny birdcage. It's the exact same kind of necklace Emmet gave me. I run back home, lock myself in the bathroom, and cry my eyes out."

"Abby," said Dr Quinley quietly. "I'll stop you there."

She nodded, breathing hard.

"It seems that your memories of that year keep circling back to the teacher," he told her. "It will make your therapy more difficult if you do that. It's like jumping into the deep end of the pool."

"It's hard," Abby responded. "Because Layla reminds me of him. And he reminds me of Layla. It's all wrapped up together."

"I see. Well, then try to find a happy memory that involves him. Are you okay to do that?"

"I'll try. Okay, I'm picking a memory. I remember... being in his boat. He was asleep. I was lying... on his chest, watching the clouds, knowing exactly what kind of clouds they were. They were cirrus. The highest kind of clouds."

My lungs squeezed tight. She'd been in his boat? Lying on his chest like they were lovers? What had he done to my daughter? Again, I wondered why I hadn't guessed that this was going on. And what had Layla been arguing with Emmet about in the boat shed?

"You're doing well, Abby," came Dr Quinley's calming voice. "That's five memories in your basket. The tree is feeling lighter. Please, choose another."

"Okay," she said. "Just before we went out on the boat that time, Emmet had drawn my name in the sand. I wanted it to stay there in the sand forever. But the next day... it had sunk away to nothing. The sand was too wet to hold it." Her voice rose in pitch, stretching out as thin as elastic. "Nothing that's good ever stays. Something always comes and snatches it away. Nothing is ever—"

"Abby," Dr Quinley interrupted. "I want you to return to the pear tree. Take a breath. Feel the sun on your face. Feel a warm breeze. I want you to reach out and touch the tree. Hold the trunk. Can you feel it? It's solid. It's been growing on that hill for a long time."

"Yes," she breathed. "I'm at the tree. I'm holding on."

"Good. Remember, you can walk away from the tree any time you choose."

She nodded, her head bent low.

"If you feel strong enough," he said. "try picking another memory."

"I'm... I'm blanking."

"That's okay," he replied. "That's to be expected. Perhaps you could tell what happened the day after Mr Eisen wrote your name in the sand? Sometimes it helps to soften a difficult memory by remembering the day that happened just after it. It can reassure us that life does go on."

I watched her hands grip the armrests of her chair. I wanted to jump up and tell her to stop.

But I had to trust that the doctor would guide her.

"The day after he wrote my name," Abby continued, "I... I found...." She halted.

"We seem to have hit upon a painful memory," Dr Quinley cautioned. "Let's leave that one for now. Choose something else, something easier to tell."

But her knuckles strained beneath her skin and she was breathing so hard that I could hear it.

"Abby," said Dr Quinley quietly. "I want you to return to the tree now. Hold onto the trunk. See the branches stretching out above you? You're safe, protected. Slow your breaths."

But I could tell that Abby was no longer listening.

She seemed locked inside her memory, speaking in a voice that now sounded so much younger.

PART II

A DECADE EARLIER

8

ABBY

The boat was sinking.

I jammed a bare foot over each rusted hole, swearing my lungs out. My back burned with the strain of paddling the oars while trying to keep the holes plugged.

But the water kept leaking in.

Damn. In my rush earlier, I'd taken the wrong boat out. Of all the old boats and kayaks along the lake's edge, I had to go and choose the one with the rusted bottom.

In a brief moment of clarity, I saw the ludicrous side of it. I was a schoolgirl out searching for her drunk science teacher, to make sure he made it to school on time.

Sweat trickled beneath my school dress and made the thin fabric stick to my skin. Thick clouds held the world down tight. Even though it was just eight in the morning, it was so hot I could almost hear the air crackling.

Whipping my head around, I searched for the closest point that I could swim to. But if I jumped in and swam, my school uniform would get soaked. I'd have to go home and get changed, and I'd be late for school.

Water trickled down the length of the boat's floor.

It was Cooper who'd told me about Emmet going out drunk on his boat last night. He lived a few doors up from Emmet. I didn't know if I could trust Cooper, though. Cooper was my age, and he used to have a thing for me. He knew I was in a relationship with my teacher, and he sent me taunting texts now and then.

When I rode down on my bike this morning, I'd expected to see Emmet's boat in its usual place along the shore. But it hadn't been there. That meant Cooper was telling the truth, and that Emmet was still out on the lake. *Somewhere.*

Water covered my feet, trickling over my toes and lapping at my ankles.

Kookaburras chortled in the far trees, laughing at the girl with the sinking boat.

I'd show them. I'd make it around the next bend, and I'd get close enough to shore to jump on the gum tree. It had branches that hung far out over the shore. Layla and I had spent many afternoons climbing out on those branches and jumping into the water.

With an effort that made me groan out loud, I steered the boat closer to shore and around the curve of the land. Here, the landscape was still trapped in the darkness of early morning. Stands of soaring, dead-straight ghost gums glowed ominously.

A boat drifted on the water, trapped in the reeds, just beneath the tree with the overhanging branches.

Relief washed through me. I'd found what I'd come out here for.

The faded lettering, *Lovecraft*, on the side confirmed it as Emmet's boat.

He'd called it after one of the authors who'd been his favourites when he was a teenager. H.P. Lovecraft.

I steered closer, not even feeling the strain of rowing now.

When I reached the boat, I knew I'd find Emmet lying on the bottom of it, drunk and asleep. Just like the other times.

Emmet would take bottles of whiskey and wine with him onto the boat at night and drink himself stupid. And then he'd sleep so late that his skin would redden and blister under the summer sun.

I'd never told anyone about those times. I'd never betray him like that.

He was a teacher. He needed his job.

Lately, he'd just been... depressed. But he'd get better. I knew he would. Emmet was a special person who made the world a better place. He loved astronomy and animals and the tiniest flowers that grew along the lake edge.

And he loved a fourteen-year-old girl named Abby Wakeland.

I was sure of that.

Over the past months, he'd become everything to me—trips together out on his boat and secret late-night phone conversations in which we talked about everything.

Of course, there was the strange stuff, the terrible stuff that I couldn't begin to understand. All the things he'd asked me to do.

But he had some kind of hurt deep inside him, and that had twisted him. It'd be okay. Love could get anyone through anything. I just had to love him harder.

He was twenty-three, which made him nine years older than me. That wasn't too much. When I was twenty, he'd be twenty-nine. No one would bat an eyelid then.

Any minute now, I'd be jumping from this sinking boat onto his. And I'd paddle it back to shore. I'd wake him up, help him to his house. If his parents weren't home, then I'd even tuck him up in bed. And then head off to school.

I'd rescue him. Because that's what love was all about.

I drew closer to the *Lovecraft*, close enough to see inside.

Emmet wasn't there.

Bottles of alcohol rolled listlessly on the floor, making ominous rumbling sounds. Emmet's bucket hat was lying crumpled on the seat.

Was Emmet already at home, sleeping off the alcohol from the night before? Or had he already sobered up enough to get himself off to work?

No, something was wrong.

He'd never let his boat drift about on the lake. He'd had that boat since he was thirteen. He took good care of it.

Was he hurt? Had he been forced to take his boat to shore and jump out?

I scanned the shoreline.

When I turned back to Emmet's boat, I watched it pull loose of the reeds and drift away on the current. I guessed that my boat coming near had loosened the reeds' hold.

Water swirled in the bottom of the boat in which I stood. I had minutes before the boat sank.

Jumping up onto the bench seat, I calculated how high I'd have to jump to reach a tree branch.

I made the leap, making a desperate grab for the branch. My feet dangled over the water as I moved along, hand over fist, to the other end of the branch.

Before I'd even made it to shore, the boat had almost completely submerged.

9

ABBY

As I dropped to the ground, sticky mud swallowed my feet.

Racing about, I looked for his footprints, searching for any clue he'd come to shore here last night. But I found nothing.

As I ran, I called his name—just loud enough so that he could hear me if he were close by.

Emmet... Emmet...

There had to be an explanation. He might have stumbled from his boat last night, and he'd been too drunk to pull it into shore. Then the boat had simply drifted away.

Yes, that sounded right. He was probably at school right now, getting lessons ready for the day.

When I got to school, I'd have to pretend that I didn't come looking for him. I'd seem like a naive schoolgirl. And I didn't want to look like that in his eyes.

Now, I needed to get myself to school.

I'd been late too many times lately. I was out of excuses.

My mother was already watching me closely. And Mum was not the kind of parent who'd easily swallow excuses. She dissected everything.

Being the only child of a detective wasn't easy.

I'd been clever so far. I left no trail behind of my texts with Emmet. I stayed at my grandmother's house on Friday and Saturday nights and snuck out when she was asleep.

I couldn't risk being found out.

No one would understand what Emmet and I had together. They'd turn it into something dirty and wrong.

I ran all the way back to where I'd hidden my bike.

The hem of my school dress was damp, but it'd dry by the time I rode to school. The smell of the lake mud might be harder to explain. I made a mental note to spray myself with the deodorant I kept in my backpack.

But I needed to wash my feet clear of the mud first. I reached the spot where the shoreline turned to sand instead of mud.

It was close to the houses here, but still, no one could see me. The curve in the lake's edge kept me just out of eyesight. Jogging down to the water, I bent to grab a handful of sand, and I scrubbed the thick mud from my feet and between my toes.

Something white and filmy billowed in the water. At first, I thought it was a piece of lost or discarded clothing. A shirt or a dress.

My muscles froze.

I stood.

It was a man. The body of a man. Face down.

He floated on the current, resting in the reeds and yellow bladder-wort. His white shirt rippled on the water's surface.

It was Emmet.

Dead.

It was unmistakably him.

The slim body with the wide shoulders. The dark hair jutting just past his collar and his business shirt half hanging out past his woven, suede belt.

He looked like something that belonged to the lake, almost completely submerged in it. His legs trailed listlessly, and his head had plunged beneath the water, as if he were staring at the bottom of the lake.

A swathe of horror and revulsion moved up from my stomach and into my throat.

I vomited. My legs buckled, and I fell to my knees.

A silver necklace swung loose from the collar of my dress. Sunlight glistened on the pendant—a tiny bird inside a tiny birdcage.

Emmet had given it to me. He'd said it meant that I was his forever.

My back froze stiff then, as I heard someone calling Emmet's name. I couldn't let anyone see me here.

I turned to look.

Emmet's mother was walking down to the lake, her hands cupped over her lower face, calling his name. "Emmet! Emmet!"

I crawled away to where the tall grass would hide me, tucking the pendant back into my collar.

When Mrs Eisen stopped at the lake and her knees and shoulders sagged, I knew she'd found her son.

Her shrill scream shattered the air—a scream that made the brolgas near the shore pirouette. The brolgas flew away across the lake, flapping their enormous grey wings.

Keeping low, I made my way back to the spot where I'd hidden my bike. When I forced myself to turn my head, I could tell that Mrs Eisen hadn't seen me. She was already splashing into the water and dragging Emmet to shore.

10

ABBY

Wheeling my bike out from the thicket of trees, I jumped onto the seat. My hands shook so badly I could scarcely hold the handlebars. I couldn't breathe.

My hands, my mind—everything was shaking and whirling. Like all the times I'd touched a daddy-long-legs spider and made it go into a frantic spin.

The word *dead* repeated in my mind. Caught up in the senseless spin.

Dead, dead, dead.

How could Emmet be out there in the lake—just... floating?

I didn't know what to do or where to go.

How could I live when Emmet was *dead?* How could our *forever* be gone like that?

As I steered the bike out onto the road, the clouds finally broke their banks. Fat, warm raindrops fell on my bare arms and face.

Right then, I knew exactly what I needed to do next.

My heart pumped with terror at the thought of it.

But there was no way out. If I didn't do it, people would find out about the things that I could never, ever let anyone know. Yes, Emmet had done strange and frightening things. But he'd just needed help, that was all. With love, he would have changed. I was sure of that.

But now, he'd never get that chance.

All I could do was to make sure no one found out about him.

I retrieved a raincoat that I had at the bottom of my school bag. Mum always insisted that I take it. It'd been there for two years or more without me ever once using it. But today, I was thankful for it. I pulled the coat on over my back and schoolbag, then put my helmet on.

Riding away, I threaded in and out of the trees that lined the streets.

"Goodbye, Mr Lullaby," I whispered.

11

KATE

Inspector Jiro Shintani was on the phone.

"Kate," he said, "this might be one for you. We've got a drowning victim out at Coldwater. A young man. Nothing suspicious so far. I've got forensics on their way."

"Who made the call to police?"

"His mother. As far as I understand, she's the one who found him."

"Oh, harsh...."

"Yeah. He died close to home, too. Number one, Bellbird Drive in the valley."

"I know the house. My daughter's teacher lives there." I paused. "Oh, no... does that mean the man who drowned is Emmet Eisen?"

"Yes, that's the name."

"He's Abby's science teacher... *was* her science teacher."

"I'm sorry to hear that."

"Me too."

After ending the call, I angled my head around to Franco. Seated a few feet away from me at his desk, he was eating a late breakfast.

He lifted his eyebrows, his mouth full of sesame seed bagel. "What's up?"

"A drowning at Coldwater. A young teacher."

He swallowed. "Not good news. Are we handling it?"

"Yes. Shintani gave it to us."

"If it's an accidental drowning, that shouldn't take long. If it ends up being anything more, we couldn't take it on... could we? We've got a lot of cases on the books right now."

"That's true. But I'd want to take it on anyway. He was Abby's favourite teacher."

"Ah. That changes things. You know that if it's personal to you, then I'm all in."

"You're good people, Franco."

He stood, turning his face to hide a grin as he packed up the rest of his lunch in a paper bag. "Don't tell anyone that."

Detective Franco was a fairly recent recruit to homicide. A year ago, he'd been working in the fraud squad. When he expressed an interest in swapping to homicide, I'd taken him under my wing. So far, it was working out well—better than I'd expected. Just eight years earlier, he'd been a farmhand on his family's flower farm. He wasn't the most experienced cop around, but he was one of the most dedicated. He'd progressed quickly up the ranks.

Outside, the heavy rain we'd had earlier had completely subsided. Instead of relieving the heat, the downpour had made the air feel sticky and superheated, like steam coming off a kettle.

Franco tugged at his collar as we walked to the car. "Must be forty degrees."

"At least."

I drove the car while Franco finished his bagel. He was normally talkative, but not while he was eating. Eating was a serious business for Franco.

People in light summer clothing streamed up and down the streets. Mothers pushing prams. Shop owners opening up their businesses. Retirees doing a bit of early morning shopping before the temperature reached its full, blistering height. By the end of today, they'd all know that one of their own had drowned in the lake. Many of them would know Emmet and the Eisen family. His death would hit the community hard.

Even with the air conditioning going at full pelt, the car's interior felt oppressive. The vehicle had been baking in the street outside the station all morning. Also, I suspected that Franco had driven the car recently with the window down while it was raining. He had a nasty habit of doing that. The air had a wet, musty odour in here.

I drove along the long, twisting road that led to the lake and onto Bellbird Drive.

The Eisens' house was the last one on the street, next to a forest. The sharp curve of the road gave the property the look of being all on its own. The house was large and two-storey, with a design that I thought of as *Brady Bunch* architecture. It was a ranch style that had been popular in the seventies, with lots of stone and wood. Bougainvillea spilled over the top balcony. In its day, it would have been a glamorous house.

An ambulance was parked in the home's driveway.

Without warning, the rain returned, lashing the windscreen as I parked.

Heavy rain was bad news at an outdoor investigation site. It had the potential to wash so much evidence away. At least this was not a murder investigation—it sounded like a sad but straightforward drowning.

A van pulled up beside us, with the lettering FSG on its side. The Forensic Services Group.

We called out a quick greeting to each other above the heavy patter of rain. They'd come well-prepared—they had their wet weather gear with them.

Franco grabbed the only protection we had—a single umbrella.

We all headed in one group along the sodden dirt track that led to the lake. Mud oozed around my shoes.

Two paramedics—both women—walked towards us from the opposite end of the track, carrying medical kits.

"The mother called us out in a panic," one of them told us. "I'd say the victim has been dead for hours, probably since last night."

I nodded at her. "Thanks."

We continued along the track.

A forlorn couple stood down near the shore. They didn't run for cover the way people normally did during a downpour, instead remaining huddled close together, seemingly fixed to the spot. With a sinking heart, I knew they had to be Emmet's parents. I'd only met them once. I remembered that their names were Alex and Louisa. I guessed that their son's body must be close by the spot where they were standing.

Franco and I walked across the heathland to the couple. They were both soaked to the skin and looking very different to the people I'd met many months before. Their faces were white and drained, hair plastered to their heads and their expressions shell-shocked.

"This is just devastating. I'm so sorry," I said. My words were half washed away by the heavy downpour. But no words were adequate anyway. There was nothing I could say to make things better.

"How?" Louisa said, barely keeping her voice under control. "I don't understand *how*. How does a boy who used to be a champion swimmer end up... *that way...?*"

Alex placed an arm around his wife. "What I want to know is how he even ended up in the water. He went out on his boat, for Christ's sake. He should have been safe."

"We hope to have some answers for you soon," Franco told them.

Less than two metres away, the body lay on the ground. He'd been dragged out of the water, the drag lines still visible in the mud. His young body looked strong and wiry beneath the wet clothing, as if he should be able to rise from the ground and walk away. But the heavy rain falling on his face told a different story. He no longer felt the rain, nor the ooze of the mud in which he lay, nor the oppressive heat of the morning. His eyes were closed—one eye with a dark bruise beneath it, spanning across to his temple.

"We should go find shelter and let the forensics do what they need to do," I said to Alex and Louisa, offering a small, tight smile.

They seemed reluctant to leave him, staring blankly as the forensics team gathered around the body. That was natural. It often took many hours—or days—for a family to even come to terms with the fact that their loved one had died.

But then Alex guided his wife away. They walked alongside Franco and me to a stand of trees. I'd chosen a location that was out of the rain and out of sight of Emmet's body. It would be doubly distressing for them to see the forensics people poking and prodding at him.

"He should be at the school right now," Louisa told me in a lost voice. "Standing before his class, teaching the kids their lesson…. He loved science. Always such a clever boy, interested in everything. I just can't—" She broke off.

"He was a wonderful teacher," I said in a firm voice. "I know that the kids loved him, including my daughter."

"You're Abby's mother…" Louisa stared at me, blinking. "Of course you are. I remember you now."

"Your son had Abby enjoying science class for the first time," I told her. "This will devastate the students. A huge loss."

Her expression crumbled. "It was his first teaching position. He had so much to give."

"This is damned cruel." Alex sighed heavily, taking his wife's hand in his.

"So, your son went out on his boat—last night?" Franco asked Alex.

"Yes," Alex replied. "That's something he often did. He just liked going off by himself, pottering around the lake."

Franco nodded. "He was alone?"

Alex pushed wet hair back from his face. "Last time we saw him, he was. I need to go find his boat. That might tell us something. I don't know how he got separated from it."

"I'll get police out on that job, Mr Eisen," Franco said. "If it didn't sink, they'll find it."

Alex took a step away. "I can go. It'll give me something to do."

Franco grasped his arm. "It's better you let the police do it. I've already called out a team. They can check it for anything unusual."

Alex's shoulders sagged. "Yeah, okay. I just feel damned useless. Something happened out there to Emmet, and I want to find out what it was."

Franco dropped his hold. "Mate, I understand."

I turned to Louisa. "I was told that you were the one to find Emmet?"

She nodded, splaying a hand across her throat.

"Can I ask why you were looking for him down at the lake this morning?" I said. "How did you know he hadn't come back from his boating trip? I'm sorry to ask these questions. I just want to establish a timeline."

"Because he wasn't in his room," Louisa told me. "And he wasn't downstairs making himself breakfast. He always eats a lot for breakfast. And his briefcase was still in his room. He needs that for school. I thought maybe he'd gone for a run or something. But the time got later, and he should have left to go to the school. So, I decided to check if his boat was back inside the boat house. It wasn't."

"Had he ever stayed out on the boat overnight before?" Franco asked.

"Only a few times, when he'd been drinking—" Louisa seemed to stop herself from saying more.

Franco glanced from Louisa to Alex. "Do you think he might have been drinking last night?"

"He was young," said Alex. "Young people like to have a few drinks now and then. It was nothing."

Louisa closed her eyes tightly. "He's been a bit down lately. So, he was drinking more than usual." Her eyes widened, and she waved her hands as if brushing a thought away. "This wasn't a suicide."

"I noticed a bruise on your son's face," I said. "Just below his eye. Do you know if he had that before he went out on the boat, or—"

"That's what *I* want to know," Louisa snapped. "I have no idea how he got that."

"Do you know who he was with or what he was doing yesterday?" I asked.

Louisa glanced at her husband, then shook her head. "No. He often went off by himself on the weekends. We just... we wouldn't see him at all."

"Do you mind if we take a quick look in the boat shed?" Franco said. "We won't go inside and disturb anything. We'll leave that for forensics."

"Go ahead," Alex told him.

The boat shed was only a few metres away. We walked through the rain to the small, covered porch.

Franco and I peered inside. On one side of the shed was an empty space that I guessed was for the boat and trailer. Boat oars were stacked in brackets on the wall. On the other side was a small sitting area, with two sofas, a table and a bar fridge. Empty bottles of beer and wine sat on the floor here and there.

A piece of crumpled foolscap paper was lying behind a sofa, right next to the door.

"Would you mind if we see that?" I said to the Eisens.

"It might be something personal of Emmet's," Louisa protested.

"It will either be forensics or us who picks it up," Franco told her gently.

I slipped on gloves and reached in, picking up the ball of paper and placing it in a zip-lock bag.

I wanted to have more of a look around, but Franco and I would just spray rainwater everywhere.

Alex bit down on his lip. "What happens now, with our son?"

Franco told the couple what the next steps would be and who would be taking Emmet's body away. It was never a pleasant conversation to have with a family.

I touched Louisa's arm. "The best thing to do now might be to have showers and get into some dry clothing. Then you might want to call family, or anyone you'd usually lean on for support."

She and Alex nodded with numb expressions.

Franco and I watched the Eisen couple head towards their house, their shoulders bent and footsteps heavy.

12

ABBY

There were whispers at school about Mr Eisen not showing up for his science class this morning. Two of the boys said he must be passed out cold somewhere. Word had been getting around about him drinking heavily on the weekends and after work.

I hated hearing it.

None of them knew Emmet like I did.

And none of them knew—yet—that he would never come back to the school. He would never teach another class.

But how long would any of them even care that he was dead? Probably just minutes. Then they'd be carrying on as usual. Laughing and shoving each other in the hallways, stealing behind trees at the back of the playground to sneak a quick cigarette, gossiping about who got with whom at the last party.

I was different to them. Emmet had seen something special in me.

I had to keep all the secrets tucked away. I had to pretend I didn't just find him floating face-down on Coldwater Lake.

At school, he'd been strictly Mr Eisen, my teacher. He'd instructed me to never, ever talk to him the way we talked via text or when we were alone.

When he'd been down at the lake, he'd simply been Emmet. I pictured him sitting on his deck chair on the shore—his feet in the water, his shirt unbuttoned, and his belt unbuckled. He'd sit and drink after school, and watch the sun go down.

The rest of the time, he was *Mr Lullaby*.

The darker things about Emmet crowded into my mind again. I tried to push those thoughts out. I never wanted to think about them again.

I barely heard a word the teachers said all morning. All I could see and hear was Emmet. He was the only man I would ever love—I was certain of that.

The birdcage pendant swung between my breasts as I picked up my books and slung my backpack over my shoulders. I headed out of class. My backpack was weighed down with the item belonging to Emmet that I'd picked up just before riding to school. I couldn't allow anyone to know what was inside my bag.

It was time for lunch. But I couldn't eat and even less wanted to talk to anyone. I decided to hang out in the library.

A blond, older boy I'd once liked walked past in the corridor, carrying a baseball bat and gloves. Logan Norwood. He was two years older than me. Once, that had seemed *so* much older. But it wasn't. Age didn't matter. Emmet had taught me that.

I wasn't interested in Logan anymore—not that he'd ever noticed me.

Over the past months, my life had become all about my relationship with my teacher. It had been exhilarating and disturbing and terrifying.

That was love. At least, it was the kind of love that Emmet and I had shared.

After lunch, when I was walking back from the library, my friends circled me like sharks.

It was like that sometimes. Girls had sharp eyes and ears.

"Where were you?" Chelsea demanded. Chelsea Dawson always wanted to know everything. I had to be careful.

"Oh, I had a stupid history assignment to finish." I made a show of rolling my eyes and sighing. History was the only class that none of my friends were in. They wouldn't know there were no history assignments due.

Lianna blew me a kiss of commiseration. "Sucks to be you."

I laughed. The laugh sounded flat, like it'd rolled off my tongue and fallen with a clunk to the floor.

My stomach was turning itself inside out. That sick feeling rolled around in my stomach the rest of the day. A few times, I almost asked the teacher if I could run to the bathroom.

But I held myself back, pretending I didn't taste bile in my throat. I couldn't be seen looking ill on the day Mr Eisen died. I couldn't allow anyone to suspect anything.

Finally, the home bell echoed through the halls.

I had indoor soccer practice after school, but today, I wouldn't be going there. I had something else to do. One last thing for Emmet.

13

KATE

After our trip out to the lake to investigate Emmet's drowning, Franco and I headed back to the station.

Seeing the young teacher dead on the lake shore—plus the heat, humidity, and the musty smell in the police vehicle—were all combining to make my head throb.

I sat at my desk, drinking down a long glass of cool water.

Franco walked over, munching on an apple. "Anything on that bit of paper we found, Wakeland?"

"Forgot to look, to tell you the truth."

I retrieved the zip-lock bag from my inside jacket pocket. Taking out two sets of plastic tweezers from a drawer, I gently pulled the bunched-up paper straight.

"Whoa. Love letter," said Franco. "Now, that's sad."

Quickly, I scanned the letter:

Emmet,

I need you to know something. No one will ever love you in the way I do. I love you to the moon and stars.

It's killing me inside to live this lie. And it's killing me that you won't talk to me.

We were meant to be together. You know that.

I'm coming to see you later. We need to talk. Please, just open your mind and heart and you'll see that I'm right.

All my love, always and always.

I sat back in my chair. "Okay. Well, it would be nice if whoever wrote that had signed it."

"Damn. Wish someone would write *me* a letter like that."

"Looks like Emmet wasn't happy about it. He screwed it up and threw it away."

"Some guys don't know how lucky they are." Franco took another bite of his apple.

"The letter is a bit dramatic, don't you think? *To the moon and stars?*"

He shrugged. "I think it's sweet. You just don't have a romantic bone in your body, Wakeland."

"That's not true. I'm just not going to... beg someone to love me."

"That's how I get *all* my girlfriends." He winked and made a cheesy grin.

"Lucky women," I said dryly.

"Seriously, I think the letter is sweet. You're going to make fun of me for being a romantic, right?"

"I want to, but I can't think of anything clever to say. So, it's a missed opportunity."

"Hilarious, Wakeland."

I smiled. "Well, we'd better get this fingerprinted. And then find out who this mystery woman of Emmet's is."

I spent the next half hour writing up notes about what we'd witnessed at the scene this morning. Franco and I then headed to the school to inform them of Eisen's death and ask them if any of the teachers had noticed anything unusual about Emmet over the past few days.

All day long, the intense heat didn't let up. Rain poured down on and off.

I drove home after work in a mood that descended like a heavy cloud. It had been one of those emotionally exhausting days. Talking with Alex and Louisa Eisen this morning about their dead son had wrung all my energy from me. I was devastated for them. Losing a child in that way was horrific.

Emmet Eisen's body had been taken to a dedicated facility in Sydney to conduct the post-mortem. From there, the coroner would decide on whether an inquest was warranted. It could be a long process that took weeks or months. The forensic pathologist would conduct the autopsy and might call on the expertise of specialists such as technicians, radiologists and DNA biologists. Emmet's toxicology report alone could involve the taking of many samples, including taking blood from different areas of the body and tissue samples from the liver, brain, eyes, stomach and kidneys.

I tried to lift my mood as I walked into my house. All the years I'd worked as a detective, I'd always tried not to bring my work mood home with me. But it wasn't always easy.

No one was home. That was a good thing. It would give me time to unwind.

I walked through to the kitchen and put the kettle on. I stared at the view beyond the kitchen window—a circular park. Children raced about like small dynamos in the playground.

A crashing sound echoed from downstairs in the basement.

I heard Pete curse loudly.

"Pete!" I rushed to the basement.

I expected to find him fallen from a ladder. Instead, a stack of boxes had fallen, but not Pete himself.

Pete was standing there looking pleased. He'd cleared away all the junk we'd been storing down there, suddenly making the space look twice as big. Pete always had a project on the go. It was just how he was wired.

I caught my breath. "Thought you'd hurt yourself."

"Me? Never." He glanced around the basement. "What do you think?"

"Looks... great. So much space. But why?"

Pete grinned, spreading his arms out wide. "Two words. *Home. Gym.*"

"Really?"

"Yeah, really. Why not? We've got to keep up the strong bones. Especially you, so you can chase after the baddies."

"I don't chase them anymore. I make the young 'uns do that."

He picked up the fallen boxes and pushed them against a wall. "Well, pumping up your muscles will come in handy when you get someone resisting arrest."

"True. I could look more intimidating," I joked.

Maybe Pete was right. The two of us went on runs each week, but we didn't do a lot in terms of weightlifting. I needed to work on my upper-body strength. I had a gym membership, but like a lot of people, I found it hard to squeeze in the time.

"What are you putting in?" I asked him.

"Hmmm, haven't thought that far ahead yet. I guess a weight bench... a multi station... a rack for the dumbbells. A few other thingamajigs."

"Sounds like a plan. I know you've always wanted more space for that kind of stuff."

"One day, Mrs Wakeland, we'll get a property. With a house on a hill. A big vegie patch. Room for everything."

"Nice dream, Pete."

"It doesn't have to be. It's something we can work towards."

Pete was right. We both had good jobs. Pete was a financial analyst on a good wage. My wage wasn't as high as Pete's, but it was still decent. But we'd left it so long to make a move to a property that land prices had soared. Besides, from here, on our suburban block, Abby could ride her bike to and from school and to her friends' houses. She wouldn't be able to do that if we moved out to a property. Abby was already irritable and angry all the time. I couldn't imagine moving her away from here.

"Want some help to clear the rest of the stuff away?" I offered to Pete.

"Nah, I'm fine," he said. "Got it under control."

I sat on a box filled with Pete's old finance textbooks, resting my forehead in my hands.

Pete glanced at me. "Rough day?"

"A difficult one. One of the teachers from Abby's school died. He drowned in the lake. It was Mr Eisen."

"Oh. Not good. He was her science teacher, right?"

"Yes."

"How did it happen?"

"That's what we've got to figure out. It seems it was an accident. Apparently, he'd been drinking. He might have just lost his footing and fallen in, and then been too inebriated to find his way back to the boat."

Pete sighed, crinkling his brow. "Whatever way it happened, it's a waste. He looked like not much more than a kid. He was fresh out of university, right?"

"Just a year. He was twenty-three."

Pete jerked his head up at the sound of the front door closing. He frowned. "Doesn't Abby have soccer practice on Thursday afternoons?"

I nodded. "Maybe she didn't feel like it. The kids were told about Mr Eisen's death in the afternoon. I think he was one of her favourite teachers."

"Poor kid." Pete cupped his hands around his mouth. "Abby, we're in the basement."

Abby's long, slim legs appeared on the basement stairs. There was a large scrape on her knee. She stooped low to peer down at us. "What're you two doing down here?"

"Your dad's putting in a home gym," I told her. "Hey... come down here a minute?"

She took a few more steps but seemed reluctant to venture any further.

"You didn't go to soccer?" I asked.

"I have a sore stomach," she said.

"That's no good." I drew my lips in. "Abby, I know your class was told about Mr Eisen today. I'm so sorry. It's extremely sad."

"Yeah... we were told. They said he drowned?"

"Yes, he did," I said. "Are you okay?"

She half-shrugged, half-nodded.

Pete gestured towards her knee. "Did you have a fall? Your leg looks pretty scratched up."

She glanced downwards, seeming surprised by the injury. "Ohhh... yeah. Yes, I did. I came off my bike. A car was coming around a bend and I... miscalculated."

Pete puffed up his cheeks and blew out a tight breath. "Be careful, honey. We want you in one piece."

"I will. I'll be careful. I'm going to go lie down. I'm not feeling good."

She'd turned and jogged back up the stairs before we had a chance to say anything else.

"She seems okay about her teacher, at least," Pete said, turning to me.

"Yes, she does." I chewed my lip, thinking. She seemed a little odd. She'd been quiet and moody for months now, but this was different. It was almost as if she were trying to hide something.

No, I was reading too much into it.

Perhaps hearing about Mr Eisen and then the near car accident had rattled her. Her best friend, Layla, had recently left town, too. She'd returned to live with her grandfather in the city. I knew that she and Abby had fallen out with each other just beforehand, but I didn't have the faintest clue what that was about.

I decided to go up and talk with Abby later—I needed to try to reconnect.

I'd grounded her weeks earlier. I'd stopped her from being able to chat with her friends at night on her phone or use the internet. I was only allowing her to use the computer downstairs for her homework— where Pete and I could see what she was doing.

I'd hated taking those extreme steps, but Abby had become addicted to late night chats, and at the same time, she'd become a very different girl. Sullen and tired and even jumpy.

As a parent, it was my job to guide her through her teenage years. But I had to admit, I was completely lost.

14

KATE

I pulled up outside the house that was next door to Alex and Louisa Eisen.

Number three, Bellbird Drive.

It'd been two days since Emmet died. Franco and I were trying to establish the circumstances of his death and anything unusual in the days leading up to it. Franco was interviewing some friends of Emmet's today. I was interviewing his neighbours. I'd already talked with Emmet's parents for the second time, getting an official statement from them.

Nina and Scott DeCoursey lived here at number three. I'd called them earlier to ask if I could come down and have a chat about Emmet Eisen. They were both criminal defence lawyers—I'd seen them around the court system for years.

Nina was also the aunt of a good friend of Abby's—Layla.

Over the past months, Abby would often ride down here after school to spend time with Layla. And on weekends, Abby would stay with her grandmother, and then come down to the lake to see Layla during the day.

It was sad that Layla was gone now. It seemed like the end of an era in Abby's life. But if Layla had been part of the reason that Abby had been so moody for months, then perhaps it was for the best.

I walked along the front path, the golden cane palm trees sprinkling water on my head. The day had been stormy, but the rain had eased.

I'd had a few brief conversations with Nina and Scott DeCoursey down by the lakeside during times when I'd come to pick Abby up, but nothing more than that. Nina was originally from Scotland, and still had a faint accent.

Nina welcomed me in at the front door, offering tea and scones.

There were few things as welcoming on a rainy day as tea and scones.

I accepted gladly and walked with her through a hall that was decorated with tasteful black and white photos of the couple.

The interior of their house matched my concept of what a house owned by two lawyers would look like—everything very neat and orderly and somehow *solved*. Each room I saw on my way to the kitchen was an equation of well-chosen furnishings and colours in shades of grey and warm whites.

In the kitchen, a large rectangular pane of glass presented a picture-perfect view of the lake. Scott DeCoursey was seated on a kitchen stool, sipping tea while studying an open file. He wore a business shirt and tailored pants.

"Detective Wakeland," he said, glancing up. "You're looking well."

"Thank you. You're looking dapper for a Saturday morning."

"No rest for the wicked." He grinned, walking across to shake my hand. "By the way, sorry for getting Mr Camacho off on the murder charge."

Franco and I had solved a cold case last month, in which we were certain that the offender—Camacho—would get the maximum sentence for the crime of killing his brother. Instead, Scott DeCoursey had convinced the jury that Camacho was only guilty of manslaughter.

I half-shrugged, hiding the burn I felt inside. "You put forward a good case."

"Camacho wasn't even grateful," Scott replied, shaking his head incredulously. "He expected I could get him off on all charges."

In court, Scott DeCoursey had taken full advantage of every avenue of law he could muster. He was as cool as a cucumber, cutting a polished figure with his immaculate grooming and steady voice. The jury had bought his performance hook, line and sinker.

I couldn't help but notice that Scott's face looked untouched by time, even though he was the same age as his wife. In the wedding pictures I'd seen of them in their hallway, they'd both been baby-faced twenty-somethings when they married. They were in their forties now.

It figured that Scott had unlined skin. He probably went through life in a happy-go-lucky mood. He didn't strike me as the type to care deeply about his clients' problems.

In contrast to Scott, Nina looked a lot more natural, with her messy waves of hair, casual clothing and tired eyes. Even her Scottish accent sounded a lot more earnest somehow than Scott's smooth, polished tones.

Nina guided me towards a stool, brushing errant strands of hair back from her face. "Have a seat, Kate. I'm about to get a batch of scones out of the oven."

She fetched a tray of hot scones and set them down on the kitchen bench. "These didn't turn out too bad."

"They're lovely," I said.

Nina's eyes saddened. "It's so awful about Emmet. I can't believe it. Just can't believe it."

"It *is* awful," I agreed. "He was so young."

"Louisa told me he had a bruise on his face," she said angrily. "Who did that to him?"

"That's what I'm trying to get to the bottom of," I said. "So, neither of you have any idea?"

Nina shook her head, frowning.

Scott rubbed his chin. "No... but the kid had been drinking pretty heavily over the past couple of months. He might have gotten into some stupid fight. Nina and I saw him get a bit shouty a few times."

"Shouty? In what way?" I asked.

Scott shrugged. "Just... yelling at his father. In a kind of rage. Don't know what about."

The Eisens hadn't mentioned anything about their son having arguments with his father. They'd painted a picture of domestic calm. But it was natural for families to talk about their recently deceased members in the best possible light.

Scott helped himself to two scones, heaping on the cream. "Am I still needed here? Or will I just get in the way? I've been buried under an avalanche of work lately, and I doubt I've seen anything else that's useful."

"If it's okay," I answered, "I just have a couple more questions, and I'd like you both here."

"Go for it," Scott said.

"Okay," I started, "did either of you happen to see Emmet about on the day he died?"

"I don't remember seeing him at all," said Nina. "Did you, Scott?"

"Nope. Sorry."

"Thanks," I said. "Okay, thinking about the past few months, have you seen Emmet about with a girlfriend at all?"

"A girlfriend?" said Nina curiously. "Did he have a girlfriend? News to me."

"We found a letter," I said. "A romantic kind of letter."

She shrugged. "Could have been from a lovelorn student, maybe?"

"Maybe," I replied. "Okay, did either of you have any conversations with Emmet recently?"

"Not real conversations," Nina told me. "I spoke with him a couple of times. You know, just hello and how are you—that kind of thing."

"Come to think of it," Scott said, "you've jogged my memory. There was one conversation that was a bit curious."

"Oh?" I took a scone and placed it on my plate.

"He asked me about a case I'd recently taken to court. The case concerned the historical sexual abuse of a minor."

"What did he want to know, specifically?" I asked.

Scott grabbed another scone and proceeded to spoon a mound of cream on it. "About how I'd managed to get the alleged offender out of the charges. I only defended that case because I believed the allegations were baseless. It was a custody case. Nina was there when Emmet was questioning me. Did you think it was a bit odd, hon?"

Nina placed a couple of scones on her plate. "He *was* kind of intense. But that was Emmet. He was an intense sort of person. He asked me all kinds of questions about my work, too. I think he just liked to know things. Just like when he was a child. He was in a hurry to know everything about everything. No wonder he studied science when he grew up."

Nina scowled at the now-empty bowl of cream. "Scott, you could have paced yourself!"

He winked. "I'll go grab some more and then remove myself from the kitchen. I'm obviously being a nuisance. I'll even make you girls tea to make up for my indulgences." After replenishing the bowl with cream and making tea for Nina and me, he collected his file. "Got to get to work. I've got a client who's up on charges of stealing from his company. Can anyone say *extenuating circumstances?*" With a brief smile, he stepped away down the hallway, humming as he went.

Nina sighed, stirring her tea. "I'm a bit conflicted about what Scott does, to be honest. In one way, I'm damned proud of him for being so good at his job. In another way, I find it disturbing when he keeps bad people out of jail. He and I work in very different circles. My clients generally haven't had much of a chance in life."

"Your job must be rewarding," I commented.

"Yes, it is. Most days. Not every day. Got to go to court first thing tomorrow. For a seventeen-year-old kid who got caught climbing a phone tower. For the fifth time."

"Frustrating."

"Tell me about it. Sometimes, you have a good day and make a difference. Other days, you feel like you're in that movie. What is it? *Groundhog Day*. Yeah, just like that."

"How is Layla doing?" I asked. "Does she know the news about Mr Eisen?"

"Yes, I sent her a text to let her know. She replied to say she was sorry. She really liked her science teacher."

"So, has she gone back to her old school in Sydney?"

Nina's eyes creased with a hurt look. "Not yet. I'm not sure what's going on with her. She insisted she wanted to go back and live with her grandfather again. But now, she's gotten in touch with her father. And she's gone to stay with him for a while. Heaven only knows why. Seems she just can't settle anywhere."

"Oh, dear. I'm sorry to hear that."

"I'm trying to convince her to at least come back to her grandfather's house. So far, she's refusing. She's so... strongminded."

"I wish I had some sage advice for you. But I don't. Abby has been really moody these past few months. It's driving me a little crazy." I hadn't meant to admit that, but it had just burst from me, unguarded.

"You, too?" sighed Nina. "Perhaps it's the age they're at."

"Well, I hope Layla changes her mind and returns to the valley."

"I hope so. I've tried my level best to do as my sister would have wanted. I don't think Kirsten would have wanted Layla to go off with damned Rusty."

"So, Rusty is Layla's father? Did he and Layla have a close relationship?"

"Close?" Nina scoffed. "No. But it seems they started making contact again after Kirsten died. I used to tell Kirsten it was all my fault that she met him. If not for me, she never would have laid eyes on him."

"I'm sure she didn't see it that way," I said kindly.

Nina pressed her lips together in a sad, wistful expression. "It's true though. That's what life is like. Moments made up of sliding doors. My family is from Scotland, as you know. Sixteen years ago, I met a handsome Australian tourist who was backpacking his way through Europe. Scott DeCoursey. We got married and moved out to Australia. Then Kirsten came to visit me. While she was here, she met a man. *Rusty*. It was just a silly fling. But she ended up pregnant. She and Rusty had a bit of a long-distance relationship thing going for a while. Rusty would fly to Scotland and then Kirsten would fly to Australia. Layla was born in Australia during one of those trips. And then when Layla was nine years old, Kirsten decided to move out here to Australia, bringing our father with her."

Nina expelled a tight breath of air. "They got a government housing place in Sydney—right in the city, close to where Rusty was living. But things quickly fell apart between Rusty and her. Then Kristin contracted stomach cancer. She died just months later."

"I'm so sorry. How tragic. I didn't know how your sister died."

"It happened so quick. It wasn't that long after she'd gotten the diagnosis. I miss her so much. And now I'm missing her daughter, too. Layla and I had become so close-knit. Like two peas in a pod. She's a lovely girl. I just hope she sees reason and comes back to us."

I turned to look out the window. The rain had stopped, and the sun was peeking through the clouds again and making the water glisten.

I pictured Layla and Abby as they were the last time I'd seen them together at the lake. There was Abby, with her flowing, dark hair and long, lanky legs beneath her short summer dress. And there was Layla, with her kinky blonde hair spilling over her shoulders. She was very pretty with her milky-blue eyes and dimples. She wore denim shorts and a paisley print handkerchief top, a camera slung on a strap around her neck. Layla had been taking photographs of black swans. Layla had told me she had to be quick to get the photos, because things that were there one minute might not come back again.

"I hope Layla changes her mind," I told Nina. "Well, I'd better go now. Lots more people to interview."

15

KATE

I continued up the street, talking with each neighbour who answered their door. I noted the door knocks that went unanswered. I'd have to go back to those houses on another day.

Everyone I spoke to was very sorry about the drowning of the young teacher. But no one had seen anything.

There was only one lot of neighbours who didn't seem all that sorry. The Tecklenburg family. I only knew of them vaguely. Abby and Layla had once been friends with two of the boys. I'd never met the parents.

The Tecklenburgs were a wild-looking family of seven kids. All of them with faded tee-shirts with motifs that ranged from crass slogans to rock bands—even the toddler. The kids uniformly had shaggy hair with blonde streaks.

The father had been out the front, digging what he said was going to be a pond. He'd been friendly enough, showing me through to the backyard.

I found the mother of the unruly tribe sitting on the steps of her back deck—a deck that was crammed full of toys and junk. She was smoking a cigarette. She wore a pink tank top with an image of a princess doll sticking up its rude finger.

After a minute's conversation with the woman and her husband, I had the distinct impression that they didn't like anyone else on the street.

"Our neighbours just can't handle people who do their own thing," Mrs Tecklenburg informed me, ashing her cigarette on the step. "We let the kids make mistakes. We don't wrap 'em up in cotton wool like some people do. That gets us a bad rep around the neighborhood. But, screw 'em."

"Well, your kids look like they're thriving," I remarked.

It was a true statement. The kids all seemed to be happy and healthy. The seven of them were outside, in the enormous yard that led down to the lake shore. They were all busy. Hammering things, fixing things, climbing, and running about. The children had made all manner of things—makeshift chairs, swings, go-carts and playhouses.

"Yeah, they're thriving all right," said Mr Tecklenburg with pride puffing up in his voice and chest. "Young lions, they are."

I smiled. "Can I ask you both a few questions about Emmet Eisen?"

"Shoot," the man told me.

"Okay, did either of you see Mr Eisen about on the day that he died?" I asked. "And did you happen to see him go out on his boat?"

The woman shrugged. "Can't remember."

Her husband flicked the stub of his cigarette onto the ground. "I didn't notice nothin'." He called out to one of his children. "Hey, Coop, you were out on the lake the night the teacher drowned. Did ya see him that night?"

A boy of about fourteen stopped tinkering with his dirt bike and walked over. "Yeah, I saw him. Wish I saw him the next morning though, floatin' on the water."

"Cooper!" his father admonished. "That's enough o'that."

The boy shrugged, unrepentant. "Couldn't stand 'im. He used to tell me off all the time for disturbing the wildlife. The wanker. Just because my tinny has a motor."

I glanced at the small tin boat that was sitting near the shore. "So, you were out in your boat when you saw him?"

Cooper nodded. "Yup. Doing some fishin'. Didn't catch nothing though."

"What time was that?" I asked him.

"Just on twilight," the boy answered.

"Was the teacher with anyone or was he alone?"

"Alone," Cooper said confidently. "Who'd wanna hang with him, anyway?"

I gave him a sardonic smile. "When you saw him, where was he going?"

"Down the other end, where he always goes. We don't go down there, 'cos he'll yell at us."

"You mean that way?" I pointed to the right, which was past the Eisens' house, where the land was all forest.

"Yeah. He thought he owned the whole place. Wouldn't shut up about the frogs and the birds."

"Did you see anyone else out on the lake that night?" I asked. "Anyone at all?"

"Nah. Don't think so."

"So, you go out on your boat a lot?" I asked him.

"Nah," he replied. "Got better things to do. I go up in the mountains on my 350. Saving up for a 450. I need more grunt." He grimaced suddenly, his eyes popping. "Oh crap, you're a *cop*. I only ride where I'm allowed to. Honest."

I knew that some kids rode their dirt bikes illegally. Sometimes Pete and I encountered them on our runs in the mountains.

"That's okay, Cooper," I said. "I'm not *that* kind of cop."

The kid puffed up his cheeks and blew out a breath. "You're all right, you know that? Thought you were gonna blast me. Those snotty girls at the lake tell me off for disturbing the wildlife, too." He stared at me then. "Oh, I know who you are, lady. You're Abby's mother."

I nodded. "That's right."

"Sorry for calling her snotty. But she is. She used to be cool. But then she started sticking up for that teacher dude and she got weird."

"That's okay, Cooper. Maybe she *was* being snotty. If you remember anything else about that night, be sure to let me know. Thank you for talking with me. You've been a big help."

The boy beamed, looking proud of himself.

I handed Mr Tecklenburg my card. "I'll see myself out."

As I walked back to the street, I mused that there was a lot I didn't know about Abby's life down here at the lake. And it *had* been a big part of her life for the past year.

Cooper Tecklenburg was the first person I'd spoken to who had seen Emmet go out on his boat that night. He was just a child, but he'd been very certain.

At the very least, I could now assume that Emmet had gone out on his boat alone, and there had been no one else out boating near him at that time. That didn't mean that someone hadn't gone after Emmet later in the night, though.

I hoped the autopsy could fill in the question marks about the bruising on his body.

16

KATE

Tonight was our night to have dinner at my mother's house. We tried to have dinner at her house on at least one night per week. It'd been the routine ever since my father had died.

I didn't like Mum being alone so much. Pete and I had tried hard to talk her into moving in with us, but she maintained that she preferred her independence.

And so, the best we could do was to stick to a routine of seeing her as much as we could manage. Abby had also been spending almost every weekend at Mum's house for the past few months. The two of them had a much better relationship than did Abby and me.

Mum had made a light soup and bread for dinner. She made good soup, my mother.

After dinner, we stepped out to the balcony to take in the vista of trees and filtered glimpses of water. It was summer, and the days didn't dip into darkness until after nine at night. The last of a rich, golden sunset blazed in the sky.

Mum, Abby and I sat on Mum's vintage cast-iron chairs, iced teas in hand. Pete had gone to fix one of Mum's leaking pipes in the bathroom downstairs.

"I never tire of that view, Mum," I commented.

"It is nice," she agreed. "Your house has a lovely view, too, looking out over the park."

"It was great when Abby was younger. But she's fourteen now, and too big for the playground." I shot Abby a smile that wasn't returned. "Pete keeps talking about getting a house on a big property."

"Oh," said Mum, "your husband always has a hundred plans on the go. Never known a man so busy as yours."

I sipped my tea, then chuckled. "That's Pete in a nutshell."

Mum turned her head to Abby and patted her hand. "How about you, love? Would you like to go live on some land? Perhaps you could even convince your parents to get you a horse."

Mum winked at me when I gasped.

"Don't give Pete any ideas," I said. "He would love to have a menagerie."

Abby managed a small smile at her grandmother, but she seemed somehow distant.

"How are you doing at school, Abby?" my mother asked her.

Abby rubbed her arms, though it wasn't at all cold. "I'm doing okay, I guess."

"I was very sorry to hear about your teacher," Mum said. "A dreadful thing to happen."

Biting down on her lip, Abby simply nodded.

I wondered if Mr Eisen's death had affected Abby more than she was saying.

"Abby, are you okay?" I asked. "You seem very quiet tonight."

"I'm fine. I've got an assignment to do later. I was just caught up thinking about that."

Abby shot me the strangest look. My mum didn't see it.

It took my breath away. She often gave me looks of annoyance, but this seemed like a look of pure... *hate*.

"What kind of assignment is it, Abby?" Mum asked.

A mask came over Abby's face when she turned to her grandmother. "History. World War Two. All about war strategies. It's tedious."

"History used to give me the willies," Mum told her. "All of those lessons about the wars and such. It wasn't until I left school that I realised I'd lived through a war that would become history itself. Of course, you don't think that when you're living it. It's just life. And that made me realise that history was about real people living real lives."

"It doesn't feel like real life the way it's taught," Abby complained. "It's just about armies and who won what battle."

Mum pressed her lips together. "Can I tell you a little story about my young years during the last world war? That might help make it more real for you?"

"Of course you can, Nan," Abby told her.

"I was born just before the war began. World War Two, that was," Mum said. "And I started school before it ended. But I didn't stay at school very long. I was sent away."

Abby mixed the ice around in her tea with a spoon. "Why were you sent away?"

"The government," Mum answered. "It was a very frightening, confusing time. I lived in London with my mother and grandparents. My father had gone to war. The government sent me away, alongside thousands of other children, all the way to the countryside. To live with strangers."

Abby screwed up her face in puzzlement. "What? Why would they do that?"

"Because they were worried about London being bombed and losing all the children," said Mum. "It was thought the countryside was safer. I was put with a family that had three children. The Southmores. The two boys were eighteen and twenty, and they'd gone off to fight in the war. And they had two daughters, Beryl and Sadie, both older than me. The girls and I became as close as sisters. But it was a tough time. Their parents were very strict. And their house was very cold. Freezing, in fact. The only warmth in the entire house was the stove. The girls and I had to run across a field every morning to fetch water. My fingers would be so cold I could barely hold the bucket. It was terrifying to lie in bed at night and hear the German planes coming in. I would pray to God that my mother and grandparents wouldn't get bombed. And that my father wouldn't get shot at. I'd have nightmares in which all of London's buildings were flattened and all the people were dead, and my father would be lying on a battlefield somewhere. I'd worry that everyone in the whole world would soon be dead, because we'd all have killed each other. And this little house in the field would be the only one left with anyone alive in it. Those were terrible dreams."

"What happened?" Abby asked Mum. "Did you go back home when the war ended?"

"Yes and no. I never went back to our house, because it was destroyed in the bombing. But my mother and grandparents survived, which is the most important thing. People usually went to shelter in bunkers when the German planes were coming. They didn't stay at home."

"What about your dad?"

"He came home, too. We were very, very fortunate."

"Did you ever see Beryl and Sadie again?" Abby paused. "That's one good thing you had, at least. You had sisters for a while."

That stung me. I knew that Abby had wanted a sibling for a long time. But I'd already been forty when I had her. Pete and I had spoken about having another. But the years slipped past. And we didn't have another child.

Abby hadn't seemed to form any very close bonds with her friends —until Layla. But Layla was gone. My heart ached for Abby. I was glad she was having this little chat with her grandmother. Mum didn't often talk about the war years, but she seemed to have won Abby's interest with this story.

My mother's eyes were bright as she nodded at Abby. "Yes, I did see the girls again. Their family was on the same ship as my family when we migrated to Australia."

"Oh wow, did you get to see them much?" Abby asked.

"Yes. You've actually met them. The Southmore family bought

some land in the same place as my family did—in Tallman's Valley. I still remember them as those young girls who held my hands when the enemy planes went overhead." My mother's eyes grew watery. "One thing in my life has held true over the years. We can always find a way to some measure of happiness when everything goes dark."

Setting down her drink, Abby leaned across to hug her grandmother, and she held on for quite a while.

It was one of those precious moments I knew would stay with me. At the same time, I worried that Abby wasn't telling us what she was feeling inside.

We stayed at my mother's house for another hour before heading home.

It was pitch dark by the time we parked in our driveway.

The second after Pete opened the front door and took a step inside, he backed out—his arms stretched wide to hold Abby and me back. "Wait," he said in a warning tone.

"Pete," I breathed, "what is it?"

"We've been robbed," he said from between gritted teeth. "I'm gonna check if anyone's still in there."

He ran into the house.

I wanted to go in there with him, but I couldn't leave Abby out here alone. I called the station and then waited with her.

Pete emerged from the front door two minutes later, puffing and panting. "Checked every room. I think they're gone. But be careful."

Inside, everything had been tipped out and upended.

Abby stepped in through the door and looked around with wide eyes.

"Honey...." I went to put an arm around her, but she ran from me and up the stairs. I heard her slam her bedroom door.

I followed her. It wasn't certain that the thief wasn't still in the house. They could be hiding, waiting for their chance to escape.

I recoiled as I opened her door. Abby's room had been shredded— there was no other word for it. Every drawer had been pulled clean out of the wardrobe. Every book and board game had been scattered around the room. Thousands of polystyrene beads from Abby's two beanbags had been spilled out. The thieves had even torn her mattress from the base and thrown it onto the floor, with the contents of Abby's schoolbag emptied out on top of it.

Abby fetched a blanket from the tangled mess and wrapped it around herself. "Why would someone do this?"

Pete walked in, cursing. "They got in through the back of the house. The puzzle is how they got past our security system. They were damned thorough—they smashed the security cameras, too."

"Not an amateur on their first run," I remarked.

He stared around Abby's room. "Hell, they really ran riot in here."

We both looked across to Abby. With the blanket still pulled tightly around herself, she'd stepped across to the window and was staring out at the night.

17

KATE

A month flipped past.

A lot of it was spent repairing or replacing our household items that had been damaged in the robbery.

Abby was still cold to me and she still wouldn't talk. I arranged a meeting with a child psychologist, but it didn't help matters. My daughter had become unreachable. After the meeting, the psychologist spoke with me privately. She explained that Abby had been through a lot of changes, and she would grow out of it. I wanted to believe that, but I didn't know if I could. Day by day, Abby was slipping through my fingers.

I was surprised to receive a call from the forensics team that had been working on Emmet Eisen's autopsy. The call was from Luke Miller. I'd known Miller for years—he'd carried out the forensic work on many of my cases.

"Kate," Miller told me, "as far as we can assess, the death was accidental. The position of the body in the water gave every sign of an accidental drowning. The family told us he was face down when they found him, his head low in the water. And our tests correlate with that. The timing of the body rising to the water's surface is early for an accidental drowning, but it's most possibly due to the warmer temperature of the lake this time of year and the fact that he was in shallow water close to shore."

I breathed silently, listening. The only good news about a death was when it was found not to be a murder. The characteristics of an accidental drowning were often pretty clear. A body floating face down could be indicative of an accidental drowning. A body floating on its back was more indicative of a murder victim. The time in which a body took to float to the surface helped tell how long since death had occurred.

"Thanks, Luke. What about the bruising on the victim's body? What were your findings on that?"

"The bruises on the face and torso could have come from a fall," he said. "There was no indication of fist marks. The bruising appears to have been present for at least eighteen hours earlier than when the body was discovered. If he only went out on the boat at night-time, then the bruises didn't happen on the boat."

"Okay, thank you. That tells me a lot. Was there anything else that you discovered?"

"The toxicology tests showed no drugs in his system, apart from alcohol. He did have a heavy concentration of alcohol in his blood. I'll send you the full report and bloodwork."

"I'd appreciate it," I said. "Thanks for the call."

"Cheers."

He ended the conversation. Luke Miller was always sharp and to the point, saying exactly what needed to be said and no more.

Franco and I had spent the past weeks investigating what might have happened the night that Emmet died. We'd interviewed everyone possible. All we had at the end of all of that was the testimony of fourteen-year-old Cooper Tecklenburg that Emmet had gone out on his boat alone that night.

But the evidence seemed clear enough. The bruises didn't happen on the boat. Emmet's death was a sad accident.

Emmet's parents had wanted updates every step of the way,

including about the autopsy. Most families didn't ask and didn't want to know about the autopsy processes that their loved one was undergoing. I much preferred it when the family didn't want to know.

I mentally prepared myself for a call to the Eisens to tell them the news about the final autopsy outcome.

PART III

PRESENT DAY

18

KATE

I sat in Dr Quinley's office, listening with growing horror to Abby's revelations from the year when she was just fourteen years' old.

Her stories had returned me to the past, too. I'd remembered my side of things with the investigation into Emmet's death. Back then, it had seemed like the tragic death of a wonderful, talented young teacher. Now, I was repulsed by the thought of him.

Abby was sitting there without speaking, her eyes closed, breathing in gasps.

"Dr Quinley!" I cried in alarm.

He nodded at me, then turned to Abby. "Abby, listen to me. You can walk away from the tree of memories any time you want. I want you to walk away right now. Down the hill and into the sunshine. Everything is all right. You are here in my office with your mother."

Abby's eyes snapped open.

It had been a rough first session for her.

Dr Quinley had asked her to imagine a tree of memories. He'd guided her to pick one memory at a time.

She'd told him some of her memories. It'd started well, but it'd quickly gotten out of hand.

I ran through her memories in my mind, to commit them to my own memory:

The day Abby had become friends with Layla.

The day that Abby and Layla had met their new science teacher.

An incident at the end of January 2010, when Layla had been arguing with Emmet in the boat shed.

Emmet giving both girls necklaces with birdcage pendants.

Abby being on the boat with Emmet.

Emmet drawing her name in the sand.

Abby finding Emmet's body in the water.

And then there was the part that terrified me most of all. Abby had called Emmet *Mr Lullaby.*

Why did she call him that? What had he done to her? Who had Emmet Eisen been, really?

Dr Quinley checked his watch. "We're only half an hour in. But I think we'd best leave it there today, Abby. You did well. We lost you for a while there, but that's natural for a first session into a subject that is so intense."

"I don't know what happened," she said. "I was trying to tell you what I was remembering, but then it was like I was back there, and I just couldn't force the words out."

"And that's perfectly okay," he answered. "We'll get there. How are you feeling?"

"Kind of like I've just turned myself inside out."

"It will get easier with each appointment," he told her warmly. "This was a strong start. You should be proud of yourself."

Abby looked and sounded drained.

All I could do until her next appointment was to try to support her as best I could.

After we'd left the psychiatrist's office, I hugged her. "You did so well, honey. I could see that it was taking everything you had to tell what you did."

She nodded, a deep sigh making her body shudder. "Mum, let's go home."

I walked with her to her car.

"Do you want me to drive?" I offered.

"But then you'd have to leave your car here, wouldn't you?"

I smiled. "No, Franco dropped me here so I could make it in time."

She nodded. "Then, yes. My hands are still shaky. All of me is."

"You should have a nice warm bath when we get home and try to relax."

Abby switched on the car's warm air-conditioning as we drove away. "I can't imagine what you think of me, now that you've heard what you did."

"Oh, Abby, I just feel... so very sad. Sad that I didn't see what was happening to you. Sad that you've had to deal with it all this time. I just... it's hard for me to get my head around. It makes sense now. How you were back then."

"I behaved terribly."

"You were just a kid. Don't be hard on yourself." I glanced her way. She had her thick hair tucked behind her ear, exposing a face in profile that was pale and drawn. "I didn't know that you and Layla had a big argument just before she left town. I knew that your friendship had cooled, but that was all."

"I'll tell you what happened between Layla and me... soon."

"Did you ever get back into contact with her, after she left town?"

Abby shook her head. "I tried once or twice, but she never answered my messages."

"Oh, what a shame."

We travelled in silence for a few minutes before I asked her if she wanted me to tell her father about today's session with Dr Quinley.

"Yes," she said in a voice that was both certain and shaken. "He should know. I was an absolute horror to both of you when I was a teenager. This is my start to try to fix things. Just... maybe wait until tomorrow to tell him. I think, tonight, I need to decompress... or something."

"I can understand that. Especially seeing as we're all living in the one house right now. What about Logan? Does he know what's going on with you?"

"No, he doesn't know anything. I'm waiting for the right time. But he wasn't around back then. He's not the one I have to make amends to."

I drove in through our gate and then along the dirt road that led to our house.

Logan walked out of the house holding the baby.

My granddaughter skipped beside him, a paper kite trailing behind her.

Abby left the car and ran to hug and kiss the baby and Ivy. Then she hugged Logan, clinging to him. Logan looked surprised and shot me a questioning glance.

I gave him a reassuring smile.

Ivy ran up to me. "I made a kite with Logan. He cut it out, and I coloured it in."

"It's beautiful, sweetie. The best kite ever."

"Can you fly it with me?"

All I wanted to do was to head inside, grab a coffee and sink into the lounge. The sun was low, about to set. The nights pulled in just after six this time of year.

But it was Ivy asking—Ivy with her sweet, six-year-old face upturned and large, serious eyes.

"Of course, Ivy," I told her. "A kite as wonderful as this just has to be flown."

Taking her hand, I walked with her across the field and up the nearest hill.

Ready to fly.

19

KATE

The morning was chilly.

I drove along roads that were heavily shaded by the mountains on my way into the station.

As soon as I was at my desk, I settled in and wrote myself a list of things I needed to complete today. I was in the habit of doing that. On days where it felt like I was spinning my wheels, I could at least look back on my checked-off list and realise that I'd done all I could do.

The first thing on my list was to talk with the inspector of our homicide division.

I walked to his office and rapped lightly on his open door. "Jiro? Can I have a minute?"

"Come on in, Kate."

Jiro Shintani was one of the few people at the station who called me by my first name. I'd never been certain if that was due to his Japanese background or just old-fashioned traditions.

I sat on the chair on the other side of his desk. "I have a dilemma."

"I can see that by the expression on your face."

"A decade ago, there was a teacher who drowned in the lake. His name was Emmet Eisen."

"The name doesn't ring a bell."

"I'm not surprised. It wasn't a homicide. The coroner ruled no foul play. His body had bruising, but forensics couldn't determine anything conclusive."

"Hmmm. So, have you found something to the contrary?"

"I have a witness—she was a teenager at the time—who says she saw bruising on Emmet's face the day he died. He told her he had a fight with another man."

"And your dilemma is?"

"Emmet had an inappropriate relationship with this girl. She was just fourteen at the time. And it seems that the fight was because of her."

"Ah. There's the wrinkle in the fabric."

"Yes. The other man might have had something to do with Eisen's drowning. I can't rule that out." My chest tightened. "But if I reopen the case, then I'll be putting the girl through trauma—and Emmet's parents, too. And maybe for no good reason."

Shintani went quiet for a few moments. "Well, Kate, I think you know there is only one path here."

"I thought you'd say that. I guess I just needed confirmation." I slowly exhaled.

I stepped from his office, apprehension needling the back of my neck. I hadn't told him who the girl was. But if I'd told him, the most likely result would have been that I couldn't take the case on. But if I didn't, who would? No one, not right now, anyway. Our homicide team had a full caseload. Worse, if one of our team did take it on, it could be a rushed investigation.

This case involved my daughter. I wanted to see it through—as long as I could, anyway. It would mean walking a tightrope. And I had no idea what I'd find at the other end of that tightrope. I could well be walking into a lions' cage.

I steeled my backbone for my first stop on this investigation— visiting Emmet's parents to tell them that the case was about to be reopened.

I drove down to the lake and parked outside the Eisens' house.

Their house exterior looked much the same as it had ten years ago. It still had that distinctive *Brady Bunch* look. Nothing had been updated.

I tapped lightly on their front door.

Louisa Eisen opened the door. I hadn't seen her in years, not face-to-face. I'd noticed her around town, but we'd never come close enough to exchange greetings.

She kept her former shoulder-length hair in a short style these days. Her eyes were hooded and tired, and they held a searching expression.

I guessed that she could tell I was here on official police business, because she hesitated before offering a vague smile. "Kate?"

"Hello, Louisa. Is it possible that I could set up a time in which I could speak with you and Alex?"

"Alex has gone away for a few days—for work."

"Oh... I can come back when he's here. This concerns your son, Emmet."

Her jaw went slack. "Emmet? Oh.... Well, you can tell *me*."

"You're sure?"

"Of course. Come on in."

I followed her inside.

Just like the exterior, the internal décor seemed not to have changed since I was here last.

Steps led down from the entry into the cavernous sunken living room. The same semi-circular corduroy lounge faced the fireplace and the high brick wall. The bar still stood in its niche—but it didn't look like it'd been used for a long time. More steps led up to three open arches, through which I could see the same twelve-seater dining table that the Eisens used to have, and then a further set of arched windows and the view of the lake.

"Take a seat," Louisa said, gesturing towards the lounge. "Can I get you a coffee or tea?"

"I'm okay thanks, Louisa."

I sat on the corduroy lounge, glancing about at the photographs on the brick wall. The photographs were new. I guessed that the Eisens had the photographs enlarged and framed after Emmet's drowning, as a way of helping keep the memories alive.

There was a picture of a young Louisa and a pre-teen Emmet standing in front of a place I recognised as the Brandenburg Gate in Berlin, Germany. They were dressed in winter clothing, the sky heavy with grey clouds behind the gate. Emmet looked about twelve in that photograph. I knew that the family had come out to Australia when Emmet was close to that age, so that might have been one of the last photos taken in their native Germany. There was another picture of the three of them—Alex, Louisa, and Emmet—down at the lake here. The day was sunny, and they were all in swimsuits. Emmet, who looked about thirteen, was sitting in a boat—his parents standing on the sand beside him. They all looked happy.

My heart felt heavy as I braced myself for what I'd come here to say.

Louisa sat opposite me, frowning now as she studied my face. "What's this about?"

"Louisa, due to new information coming to light, Emmet's case is being reopened."

"Reopened?"

"Yes. The decision was made earlier today."

"Does that mean... my son's death wasn't an accident?"

"We're uncertain. We've spoken to someone who knows that Emmet was in an altercation earlier that day. It seems that's how he ended up with the marks on his face and body. We're trying to find out the identity of the other man."

Louisa turned her head slightly, not before I saw a tear tracking down her cheek. She breathed deeply. "I... don't know what to say. Alex and I thought those bruises might have been caused by someone, but the police investigation found nothing."

"I know. We found nothing. But someone has come forward, and we know a little more, now."

She faced me. "Who? Who's come forward?"

"I can't say at this point in time."

She was silent for a few moments before speaking again, wiping at her tear with the back of her fingers. "Look... in all honesty, I don't know if anything can be achieved by this. Ten years ago, Alex and I would have been very grateful to know if someone had been responsible for our son's death. But now.... Well, it's just been so long, and it'd really just bring all the trauma of that time back."

"I knew this would be difficult for you. It's worth pursuing though, for the sake of justice for Emmet."

"He deserves justice. But... I have a question, Kate."

"Of course. Go ahead."

"Once I talk with Alex, if he and I decide we don't want the case reopened, what happens then? It's *our* son we're talking about. Can we make that decision?"

Her question took me by surprise. "I'm sorry, but no, you can't do that. Once new information comes in, we're obliged to consider it. In this case, the information is quite compelling."

"But it's not going to bring Emmet back."

"I know. The other side of this is, if this other person did do something that led to your son's death, then it could be a risk to have them out there in the community."

She nodded, looking down at her hands now, anxiously stretching out her fingers.

I understood her reasons for not wanting the case re-examined, but I'd hoped that at least this could be something I could offer her and Alex—the prospect of finding out if someone was responsible for Emmet's death. Because what was to come after that would not be pleasant for them. At some point, I'd have to tell them about Emmet's abusive relationship with Abby. But I wouldn't tell them yet. I'd let them get used to the idea of the case being reopened first.

I raised my eyes to the photographs again, a new and terrible thought circling in my mind.

At some point after the case was closed, did Louisa and Alex find out something about their son—something they didn't want anyone else to know?

20

KATE

After leaving the Eisens' house, I headed back to the station.

The next thing on my list was to locate Layla Maddox and set up an interview with her. I needed to know what her argument with Emmet had been about and what she knew.

Before I did that, I wanted to let Abby know that the case was now open again. This case was inextricably wrapped up with her, and every move I made would affect her.

Abby answered the phone with a puffing breath. "I just took Ivy and Jasper for a walk to see the horses down the road. Long walk! And Jasper's getting *so* heavy."

"I bet the kids loved the horses."

"They did. It's freezing out there though."

"Very bitter. Abby, I have to tell you something. The case has just been reopened."

"Okay... thanks for letting me know." Her voice sounded strained.

"I also wanted to let you know that the first person I'll be talking to is Layla."

"I can't even imagine what she's like now. I keep wondering what she's doing. Maybe she's even had a kid of her own."

"When I talk to her, if she asks if she can contact you, what would you like me to say?"

The line went quiet for a second. "Tell her... tell her I'd like to talk to her," Abby said finally.

"I'll do that," I said gently. "Now, go warm up in front of the fireplace. Maybe make some hot chocolate for you and Ivy. I think there might be marshmallows in the cupboard."

"Sounds lovely. I'll do that."

"Abby, you said the other day that you haven't spoken to Layla since the day before she left town, right?"

"That's right."

"Okay, just checking. I'm sure she won't be too hard to find."

I soon discovered that I was wrong. Layla Maddox proved to be very, very hard to find. She didn't have a landline or mobile phone number listed. I couldn't see her on social media either, not under her real name, anyway.

Perhaps she'd gotten married and changed her name by deed poll. I tried the Births, Deaths and Marriages register. I did find her birth certificate and a record of her Australian citizenship, but there was no record of her name being changed.

It frustrated me to the point that a headache began to twinge in my temples.

I'd have to call Layla's aunt—Nina DeCoursey. She should have Layla's contact details. I'd hoped to talk with Layla without anyone else knowing that I was looking for her. But now, I couldn't do that.

"Nina, it's Kate," I said, when she answered the phone. "Detective Kate Wakeland. Abby's mother." It'd been ten years since I'd spoken with her, apart from a quick hello in court or in the street.

"Oh, yes," came the reply. "Hello, Kate. It's been a long time! Is there something I can help with?"

"I'd like to catch up with Layla. It concerns a police matter."

"Layla? Oh no, what's wrong?"

"I want to assure you that she hasn't done anything wrong. I just have a few questions for her."

"I see. Well, to be honest, Kate, I don't have so much as a phone number of hers. I wish I did. She hasn't been in contact with me at all. It's heartbreaking."

"When was the last time you heard from her?"

"Maybe a year after she left."

I concealed a gasp. "You mean, the year after she left *Tallman's Valley*? You haven't heard from her in *nine* years?"

"Yes, not in all those years."

"My goodness. How sad for you, Nina." I paused. "I remember you saying that Layla went to live with her father after leaving the valley. Would he have her phone number?"

"If you can find him, he might."

"Okay, you don't have a contact number for him?"

"No, nothing. It would have been nice if Rusty had called once in a while to give me updates on where they were and how Layla was."

"Well, I'll try looking for him. So, his name is Rusty? Rusty *Maddox*?"

"No, my sister wasn't silly enough to marry him. His last name is Zamano."

"All right, *Rusty Zamano*." I noted the name down. "Is Rusty a nickname?"

"I'm afraid I don't know. That's all I knew him as. Let me know if you find him. I had no luck at all. I actually went to the police weeks after Layla first went away with him. I just didn't like the set-up. He was going to homeschool her on the road. I couldn't even imagine it. Rusty was always such a drifter. But the police told me that if Layla's mother was dead and Rusty was her father, then he had the right to have custody of her. They told me to back off, basically."

"Oh dear. If I have trouble locating Rusty, is it possible that I could speak with Layla's grandfather? She stayed there just before leaving with Rusty, right?"

"Yes. But I'm not sure that's the best idea. He's in a nursing home—in Sydney—and he's in poor health. This will really upset him. And he doesn't hear well at all over the phone. Could you give me even a clue to what this is about?"

"I understand. I can let you know a little, but I have to ask for strict confidentiality. I don't want word about this getting out—to anyone."

"Of course. I won't tell a soul."

"The reason I want to talk with her is that she might have information about a possible crime that occurred a decade ago. The crime is of a serious nature."

"Oh... okay. Wow."

"I'm just at the first stages of this investigation."

"Well, I can certainly pass on some questions about Layla to my father. I was going there next Wednesday, when I have a day off work."

"If you don't mind, I'd rather go personally. Don't worry, I have a good manner with elderly people. I'll be gentle. And look, if I find Rusty first and he has information about where I can find Layla, then I might not need to go see your father at all."

"I hope you don't need to. My father is very fragile, and he'll be going into hospital for a procedure soon. He's all I've got left of my family. I don't want him upset."

She gave me the details of the nursing home, and I wrote them down.

His name was Ernest Maddox, and he was a resident of the Lavender View nursing home, in Lavender Bay, Sydney.

An awful feeling nagged at me after I ended the call. Abby had grown distant and difficult when she began her relationship with Emmet Eisen. Could Emmet be behind Layla's decision to leave town?

I was anxious to find her and get answers to the questions that were running wild in my mind.

21

KATE

Rusty Zamano proved to be almost as difficult as his daughter to locate. There were a few fragments of him here and there online, but no fixed address and no phone number.

Rusty didn't have a criminal history. What he *did* have was a long series of failed businesses, and consumer complaints about those businesses.

With the help of Franco, I went through the list of Rusty's old companies, trying to find clues as to his present location. Most of his early businesses had to do with money management and investing.

But we couldn't pin him down. Franco pulled up Zamano's most recent driver's licence, but it was fifteen years old. If Rusty Zamano had been driving around Australia during the past ten years, then he'd been driving unlicenced.

With Zamano nowhere to be found, that left me with no option but to go and see Layla's grandfather. I knew Nina wouldn't be happy about that.

I called the Lavender View nursing home. Mr Maddox was due for surgery on his hip, but I could see him if I came down tomorrow. And I could only come in the morning. Mr Maddox apparently became too tired for visitors in the afternoons.

I headed home through rainy streets at 6:30 at night, my head heavy and weary.

I walked into the house to see Pete and Logan cooking up a storm. Abby and the kids were at the table—Ivy drawing pictures of kites and Jasper in his highchair, banging on his plate with a spoon.

I loved this—us all being together. I had to keep reminding myself that these were good days. Abby would be okay. She had her family surrounding her, and together, we were strong.

The next morning dawned clear and crisp. No rain. No fog. And much warmer than the days preceding it.

I padded downstairs in my pyjamas. The scent of freshly brewed coffee saturated the air. Pete was in the kitchen.

The view through the kitchen window caught my attention. The early morning sun lit the slopes and hills of our land with gold.

"It's so beautiful," I said.

"I'm never gonna tire of that view," said Pete, sipping his coffee. "Hey, it's Saturday. And you have a rostered day off today, right? We can go to the local markets and buy up some seedlings for the garden? Then lunch and a walk in the sun after?"

I felt my shoulders hunching. "I have a thing I have to do this morning."

"A thing?"

"An interview. Layla's grandfather. He lives in the city, unfortunately."

"Say what? You mean the friend Abby used to have?"

I turned to face Pete. "Yes, that Layla. I'm sorry, I forgot to tell you. It seems that Layla might have been the last one to talk with Emmet. She had some kind of argument with him. But I can't find her. Her aunt Nina lost contact with her years ago. I can't find her father, either. So, that leaves the grandfather. And, unfortunately, he's going to have a hip replacement in a couple of days. If I want to see him, I have to do it today."

"Bummer. But I get it."

"You could come in with me, if you want? We could grab lunch in the city somewhere?"

A deep wrinkle appeared between his eyes. "Maybe not. I'll go grab the plants and do some work on the garden."

I knew Pete wasn't a fan of the city. He'd worked in Sydney for years as a financial analyst, back when I was also working there in the state homicide squad. We'd been part of the Sydney rat race. He'd never been happier since when we moved back to the mountains.

"Okay," I said with an apologetic smile. "I'm sorry."

I had to make this up to him when I could.

Two hours later, I was driving across the Sydney Harbour Bridge, and then down past Luna Park. I could see Luna Park's giant Ferris wheel spinning and the broad expanse of water beyond it. Lavender Bay was just around the corner from here.

Once I'd arrived at the Lavender View nursing home, one of the staff members pointed me to an area outside on the lawn. Ernest Maddox sat on a plastic outdoor chair, along with three other people from the home. The group seemed to be just enjoying the sunshine and each other's company. Oak trees provided dappled shade, new spring growth decorating their thick, gnarled branches.

The scene reminded me of all the times I'd been to visit my mother at the hospice back at Tallman's Valley, in her last months. I'd always find her outside. Tears pricked my eyes. She'd been gone for two whole months now.

I dried my eyes with a clean handkerchief and then ventured across to Mr Maddox.

His grey hair was still thick, and it looked freshly washed. He wore a yellow floral shirt and white rimmed sunglasses, as if this nursing home were a resort.

"Hello, Mr Maddox?" I said.

He looked up at me. "Who might you be?" He had a much thicker Scottish accent than his daughter, Nina.

"I'm with the police. I'm Detective Kate Wakeland. Could I have a private word with you?"

One of the women cackled, a lady with grey hair dyed a bright red colour. "Have you been up to mischief, Ernie?"

I laughed. "No, sorry to disappoint. He hasn't been up to any mischief."

The woman chuckled. "Stick around long enough, lovey, and you'll see plenty of mischief here."

"Well," said Ernest to me, "I'd better go with you. When a good-looking girl comes calling, you don't turn her down." He winked at the others, and they tittered in response.

He pulled himself up from the chair unsteadily and then walked with me to a more secluded spot inside an ivy-covered gazebo.

"Have a seat, Detective Wakeland. I'm going to need to sit down myself. My legs aren't much good." He puffed up his cheeks and blew out a breath several times as he attempted to sit. I understood that the effort caused him pain.

He pulled the sunglasses from his eyes, blinking in the sudden deeper shade of the gazebo. His eye colour was a similar clear blue that I remembered Layla having.

"Thank you," I said. "Did the staff tell you I was coming today?"

"Yes, they did. I remember now. Sorry, it had slipped my mind."

"That's okay, Mr Maddox. I'm here because I was hoping you might be able to help me. I've been trying to find your granddaughter, Layla. So far, I've been unsuccessful."

"Layla...?" An immediate look of surprise and sadness entered his eyes. "Is she in trouble?"

"No, not at all. She's not in trouble. I just have a few things I'm following up on. About things that occurred ten years ago."

"Ten years ago? That's a long time." He thought for a few seconds. "That would be about the time I last saw her. If you do find her, tell her that her old granddad would like a visit. She'd be all grown-up now."

"You haven't seen her in ten years?" I chewed my lip. That wasn't what I wanted to hear. "Could you tell me when you last saw her?"

"It was when she came back to stay with me. She'd been living with my other daughter, Nina, for a year or so. I don't know why she came back, exactly. She wouldn't say. But her mother, Kirsten, was a head-strong woman. She got that from her."

"And then Layla left again?"

"Yes," he said with a sigh. "She got in contact with her father and then she went with him. She didn't give me a chance to talk her out of it. All she left me was a note."

"Do you still have it—the note?"

"Yes, I do. But please don't take it. It's all I've got."

"I might just need it for a short while. But I'll keep it safe. Did anything unusual happen on the day Layla left with her dad?"

"No, not that I can recall. We had breakfast together, and then I took her to lunch at a café down the road. She went out sometime in the afternoon when I was having a nap."

"Did you hear from Layla at all after that day?"

"No. She never called. And I've never had a mobile phone, so she couldn't send me any messages." His eyes glistened with tears.

He shook his head regretfully. "You know, Layla lived with me from the time she was a wee baby. She was born here in Sydney, but then Kirsten brought her back to Scotland. Sometimes, the noise would get to me, but most of the time, I was very glad to have that little girl there in the house. She made every day worth getting up for."

I nodded, smiling. "I know what you mean. Six years ago, my daughter brought her first baby back to live with my husband and me. I loved it. My daughter—Abby—was actually good friends with Layla. When they were both fourteen."

He crinkled his eyes. "Ah, so you would have known my Layla personally, then?"

"Yes, I did. She's a lovely girl. Sounds like the two of you were very close."

"She was my best little buddy. It didn't take much to make her smile. Her whole face would light up with that gap-toothed grin of hers. I'd take her for walks to the park and to school. She was real interested in the small things. Ants crossing the path. Caterpillars on people's roses. And then, as she grew older, she'd just walk beside me and tell me about her day. A real chatterbox, that one."

His eyes grew watery again. "And then my Kirsten got sick and passed away. It was so quick. She'd only just gotten the diagnosis four months earlier. She wasn't supposed to die. Her doctors were supposed to treat her and make her better. She was just thirty-nine years old." He sighed deeply. "I'm eighty-four now. How is that I get to live to this age, and she doesn't even get to live to half of it? It wasn't fair."

"No, it wasn't fair. I'm sixty-four. If there's one thing I've learned so far in life, is that it doesn't always go the way we hope and plan for. Some people deserve so much more than what they get. Others get away with far too much."

He eyed me with a critical glance. "Sixty-four, eh? You've kept yourself together well, hen. And you've still got a long way to go. You're going to see a lot more injustices between now and when you get to my age."

"I'm sure I will. I'll try to even out the injustices score as much as I can along the way."

"Good. Someone needs to get them bad ones off the streets."

The conversation paused as an elderly man shuffled past, a worker by his side. He wore a dark red dressing gown, his white hair forming a crescent around the back of his bald scalp. As if he were a king stepping through his ruined kingdom. I guessed the walk was his daily exercise.

I turned back to Mr Maddox. "How well did you know Layla's father?"

"Rusty?" Mr Maddox scowled. "Glad to see the back of him when he and Kirsten broke it off. They were engaged for a while there. But he was bad news."

"Did he spend much time with Layla after he and Kirsten broke up?"

Mr Maddox lifted his bony shoulders. "No. Not at all. He came one Christmas with some toys for Layla. Dolls and such. Trouble was, she was ten and she wasn't playing with dolls anymore. Even *I* knew that."

"So, it's true to say that Layla barely knew him?"

"Aye. He was not much more than a stranger to her."

"You said before that she didn't tell you why she decided to go with him?"

"That's right. I don't know why. She was in a bit of mental turmoil when she came here. That's all I know. I'd never seen her quite like that before. Like I told you, she was a sunny little girl."

"She didn't give any clue as to why?"

"I should have asked her. But I didn't. I'm not so good with young lasses. It was Kirsten who raised her, and she did a damned good job. I just helped out where I could."

"Was Layla like that the whole two weeks she was with you?"

"Yes. She was like a foal I had as a boy—skittish and at unease with the world."

"Hmmm, that's not good. So, was Rusty hanging around a bit before Layla went with him?"

"Not that I saw. He didn't so much as show his face. Typical. He would have known he'd get an earful from me."

The man in the king-like robes walked past again with his trademark shuffle.

Mr Maddox fixed his eyes on me. "I'm glad you came today. No one else has been interested in finding Layla. Apart from me and Nina, that is. Nina tried. Even went to the police. But it seems Layla didn't want to be found." His shoulders trembled. "It'd mean a lot to see her again."

A breeze swept through the oak trees. Raising his head, he watched the leaves fluttering.

"Can I ask you something?" I said gently. "Would you have any idea where I can find Rusty? I'm not having much luck tracking him down."

"I'm not surprised. He's a real slippery one. I don't know where he is. He used to big note himself and say he was a big shot businessman. He'd start a business, then not bother to turn up for the jobs he'd booked. It frustrated the hell out of my Kirsten. He used to use the same daft photo for all his businesses—one of himself standing in front of a canary yellow Lamborghini. He was such a tosser."

"Thanks. I just have one last question. Did Layla leave anything behind at all? Anything you might have kept?"

"No, I'm afraid not. She came with just a bag of clothes, and that's what she left with. All I have of hers is a book. Kirsten gave it to her. It used to be Kirsten's. Layla wasn't much into reading. It's where I keep the note she left me."

"Could I see it?" I hid the fact that I felt deflated. I didn't know what I was hoping for, but a book and a note wasn't going to tell me much.

I walked with him into the aged care home and along dim corridors that smelled of cleaning fluid and fresh flowers. His room was neat, without many possessions.

He pointed at the wardrobe. "Would you mind opening the bottom drawer? I can't get down that far anymore."

"Of course." I knelt to slide open the heavy wooden drawer. Among the folded blankets was a novel with yellowed pages. There was a photo of a blonde girl dressed in early 1900s clothing on the cover. The book was an Australian classic, *Picnic at Hanging Rock*. Holding the spine, I flicked through the pages.

A creased note fell out—the one he'd told me about.

I read it quickly:

Poppy,

I'm going away with my dad. Don't worry about me. We're going to be travelling on the road a lot. It'll be fun. Love you and I'll miss you,

Big hugs and kisses,

Layla

There was nothing else in the book.

I raised my face to Mr Maddox. "Thank you. Good book. I read this when I was a teenager. Of course, back then, it had just been newly released. I remember being disappointed with the ending. I wanted the mystery solved, all the ends tied up in a neat bow. But the book ended soon after the girls walked into the cave at Hanging Rock."

"Spoken like a true detective," he said, winking.

With a laugh, I closed the drawer and rose to my feet. "Yes, I think you're right there. That would explain my disappointment. I'm too pragmatic for my own good."

"Me, too. The dreamers hear music that people like us never can."

"True." I smiled. "I'll take the note, okay? But I'll return it, I promise."

"I'll hold you to that."

"Thank you so much for talking with me today. I'll be in touch."

As I went to shake his hand, he surprised me by holding on tightly. "Please... find Layla."

22

KATE

I headed out of the Lavender View nursing home, mentally trying to sort through all that Ernest Maddox had told me.

One thing stood out. It was just a small detail, but an important one.

Rusty Zamano had been using a photo of himself and a yellow Lamborghini to advertise his businesses. Mr Maddox had remembered it because it had annoyed him. But it could prove to be the needle in the haystack.

I sat in my car, taking out my computer tablet and browsing to the list of defunct businesses of Mr Zamano's that Franco and I had found yesterday. I conducted an image search of the old businesses, hoping to find a picture of the Lamborghini.

I found one—a picture of a yellow Lamborghini Gallardo, with a proud man in a too-tight business suit standing in front of it.

There was no name to go with the man, but I was almost certain that I was looking at Rusty Zamano.

I enlarged his face, then checked that against the image I had of him on his last driver's licence. He was sporting a thick beard on his driver's licence photograph. But the two images were a match.

Next, I did a reverse-image search on the Lamborghini photo.

I found a recent lawn mowing business called *Green Thumbs R Us*.

The *About Us* page of the website bore the slogan: *Let Rus make all your gardening dreams come true*. And there was the photo of good old Rusty next to the yellow Lamborghini.

I was in luck. There was an address listed. It was only a forty-minute drive away from here, in one of Sydney's outlying suburbs. I might as well try heading there now.

I drove away.

The landscape quickly became flat and featureless. That was the part that I found the most difficult about most parts of Sydney—how flat it was. The land to the south and west of Sydney Harbour had no mountains or valleys to break up the never-ending march of houses.

The years that I'd lived in the city, I'd keenly missed my mountain home. There'd been upsides, though. What many Sydney suburbs lacked in geographical features, they made up for with their food and culture. Different suburbs had clusters of people with family backgrounds from Asia, Lebanon, Greece, Italy, Vietnam and others. That was the side of Sydney I'd enjoyed.

My stomach was grumbling right now. I stopped off at a little café for a Lebanese Fattoush salad. I finished off the meal with a slice of baklava and a coffee. Baklava was a weakness of mine.

Rusty Zamano lived just a few streets away from the café—at least, I hoped he did. Getting back in the car, I drove to a street filled with single-storey houses that all looked as if they'd been built in the sixties. All red brick with red roofs, apart from a few that had bad render jobs.

Rows of jacaranda trees on either side of the street carried masses of lilac blooms.

A woman aged somewhere in her mid-thirties was sweeping the wilted leaves of the jacarandas from a path—right outside the house I was looking for. I hurried to park my car and run across to her.

"Hello," I called in a friendly tone. "Could I have a minute of your time?"

The woman kept sweeping for a few moments, with long slow flicks of her broom. Finally, she stopped and looked me over. "Why?"

"I'm Detective Kate Wakeland. I'm looking for Rusty Zamano."

"I know him."

"Great. Can you tell me where I can find him?"

"Inside."

She was very economical with her words. And she made no offer to show me into her house or introduce me to Rusty.

I decided to go it on my own. I walked up the path and knocked on the front door. The woman watched on while she continued to sweep.

No one came to the door.

Children's squeals came from the backyard. Perhaps Mr Zamano was out there.

When no one answered the front door after a minute, I turned to the woman. "Is it okay to go around to the back?"

"We've got dogs."

I assumed that the dogs must be aggressive. Then again, if there were children in the yard, perhaps the dogs weren't too manic.

"Okay, would you mind getting Rusty for me?" I asked.

"I'm pretty busy out here."

No, you're not, I thought. *At that glacial speed, you'll take a week to sweep those leaves. Might as well go and get Rusty for me.*

But I didn't want to antagonise her in case I needed to ask her questions later.

"All right, then," I said. "I'll just head around to the back yard myself?"

She shrugged.

I had to stop myself from shaking my head in annoyance. I made my way around to the side gate. The gate was a high one. Did that mean the dogs were large?

Gritting my teeth, I pulled at a vine that completely covered the latch. The vine was passionfruit, its fruit rotting away on the ground. No one at this house was a fan of passionfruit, it seemed.

As I pushed the gate open, I called out, "Mr Zamano?"

If there were dogs in the yard, my voice should have them racing towards me. If they seemed at all aggressive, at least I'd get a chance to rush back and shut the gate.

Three dogs bounded in my direction. A dachshund cross, a Staffordshire bull terrier and a portly beagle. All of them wagging their tails.

I scooted through the gate and closed the latch, then crouched to pat each one of them. Their paws were muddy, but if that was going to be the worst thing about the trio, it was a good day.

"Hello? Mr Zamano, are you there?" I said, continuing down the side of the house to the yard.

Two steps more and I had a clear view of the yard.

A blond man was sitting on a low stack of bricks, watching two toddlers as they rode their three-wheeler bicycles. Both girls.

The man looked over at me in surprise but didn't rise from his seat. He was the man I was looking for.

"Mr Zamano, I'm Detective Kate Wake—"

"Careful of the dog's tail," he snapped at one of the children.

The child, to her credit, obediently rode the bike around the sitting dog, giving it a wide berth.

Mr Zamano turned his attention back to me. "You're a cop, did you say?"

"Yes. I'm looking for Layla."

He frowned. "Who?"

"Your *daughter*. Layla Maddox."

"Oh. Is this about old child support debt? Didn't know they sent cops out for that."

"No, it isn't. I just need to know where she is."

"Well, you're looking in the wrong place. Her mother died when she was a kid. She went to live with her Aunt Nina. Blue Mountains. You can start by looking there. But who knows—Layla could be anywhere by now? She'd be all grown up." He closed his eyes, lips moving as if he were silently counting. "She'd be, uh, twenty or so now?"

"Twenty-four," I told him. "Mr Zamano, the information I have is that, yes, Layla was living with her aunt in the Blue Mountains. But when she was fourteen, she returned to live with her grandfather, in Sydney. Two weeks after that, she left his house and went travelling with her father. *You.*"

His eyes widened and he shook his head emphatically. "Nope. Didn't happen. Who told you that?"

"As far as I know, you were seen leaving the grandfather's house with Layla." That was a bold-faced lie. I hoped it would force him to tell the truth.

"Well, whoever thinks they saw me must need glasses."

I showed him the note I'd gotten from Layla's grandfather.

He went bug-eyed as he read it, shaking his head again. "What the? Well, Layla must of been up to some shenanigans. Maybe she went off with a boyfriend and didn't want anyone to know."

"When did you last see her?"

"She was about ten years old. I bought her a present for Christmas. But I got it all wrong. She was too big for what I bought her. I felt real bad about that. I knew I'd been a shit father to her. And then I turned up with the wrong present, like a big stupid goat."

His expression seemed authentic.

"Are you sure about that, Mr Zamano? Layla sent messages to both her grandfather and Aunt Nina that stated she went with you."

"Well, I can't explain that. Anyway, doesn't Nina have Layla's phone number? Why'd ya come looking for me?"

"Nina hasn't heard from Layla since the year after she left her house."

His face paled. "Oh, jeez. Not in all those years? What's the reason you're looking for her? Something bad happen?"

"There are a few reasons that we need to catch up with her. She hasn't done anything wrong. We'd just like to talk with her."

"Well, I'd help you if I could. But I can't."

I glanced around at the tiny children who were still riding about on their bikes, oblivious to my presence in their yard. The dogs were happily chasing them.

"Are these children yours, Mr Zamano?"

"Nah. They belong to my girlfriend."

"I met her out the front. How long have you two been together?"

"About eight months, give or take."

"Can I ask what you've been doing for the past ten years?"

That got him to his feet. He put up the palms of both hands. "Whoa there. What are you trying to say? If Layla is missing, I've got nothing to do with it. Hear me?"

What Rusty had just said brought something into sharp focus.

Layla was missing.

I'd been so intent on finding her so that I could talk with her, I'd lost sight of the fact that she seemed to have vanished.

A chill passed down my spine. No one had seen her. And if I could believe Zamano—she hadn't gone travelling with him at all. But I needed to be certain of that.

I crossed my arms, guarding against Zamano reading my thoughts. "I'd simply like to know, for my records."

"There's no point."

"Okay. But I'd still like to know."

"I've been travelling about," he replied reluctantly. "It's what I do. I don't like staying in the one place too long."

"Thinking back to January and February of 2010—what were you doing, then?"

"Say *what* lady? How am I going to remember back that far? Is this a trick question? Are you going to haul me off to the cop shop if I give you a wrong answer? I didn't hurt my daughter, if that's what you're thinking. I'd never do something like that."

"Mr Zamano, the only thing I'm interested in is locating Layla. I realise that might have been a difficult question. Look, I'll give you my card, and I'll ask you to try to remember what you were doing around that time. Call me and let me know. If I don't hear back within a couple of days, I'll call you."

"Right, okay. I'll see what I can come up with. Not going to be easy, though. I mean, do you remember what you were doing a decade ago, in February?" He lifted his eyebrows.

"Yes, I do. But, to be fair, if you asked me that question about most months, I couldn't tell you off the top of my head. But if I sat down and thought about it, I could. What will help is if you look back on what age you were that year and what you did the Christmas just before those months."

He gave me a wary look, but he nodded. "I'll give it a try."

"Thank you. I'd appreciate it."

I wasn't going to admit it openly, but I was already leaning towards believing him. In my job, people who lied to me often had a ready answer to questions about what they were doing at certain times, even it was years ago. They just made up an alibi on the spot. Zamano hadn't done that. But I remained cautious. Until I knew for certain where Layla was, I'd keep an open mind.

The smallest of the girls fell from her bike on the concrete path and started bawling.

Zamano was quick to step across and pick her up. "You okay, lil' darlin'? Let me see that knee. Awww, that'll hurt for a couple of minutes and then you'll be 'right as rain."

The girl's sobs stopped like he'd flicked a switch.

"Mr Zamano," I said, "would you mind showing me out? I'd rather not go through the side gate. I'm worried about letting your dogs out."

It was just an excuse to see inside his house. Now that I'd come all this way, I wanted to be certain that Layla wasn't actually still living with him. The possibility was remote, though.

"No one goes through the side gate," Zamano said. "Yeah, I'll show you out."

Still carrying the little girl, he walked inside. "Come on, Mackenzie," he called to the other child.

I followed them in. The house was small, with the bedrooms leading off the kitchen and living areas. All the doors were open. There were three bedrooms, two of them filled with pink toddler girl things.

The third bedroom had a queen size bed and fishing rods against the wall, which I assumed was shared by Zamano and the girls' mother.

Layla didn't live here.

Mr Zamano's girlfriend was still sweeping the path when I walked outside. It must be a joyless exercise, with stray leaves constantly spiralling down from the large jacarandas that occupied the nature strip of the street. I knew that jacarandas dropped their leaves in early spring, just before blooming in late spring. This woman must have been out here sweeping for weeks. And she must be beside herself in the summer months, when she'd have thousands of dropped flowers to contend with.

I doubted that Zamano would stay with her for very long. He seemed genuinely fond of the two little girls, but I guessed that he wasn't invested in the relationship with their mother. Zamano was a drifter.

It made no sense that a drifter like him would have persuaded fourteen-year-old Layla to come travelling with him. She would have needed schooling and clothing and food—and he would have had to supply all that.

This visit with Rusty Zamano had started a gnawing worry inside me.

Where on earth was Layla?

And who had she left her grandfather's house with?

23

KATE

I called in on Nina and Scott DeCoursey on my way home from Rusty Zamano's house.

Sitting down with them in their kitchen, I explained that I'd been to see both Nina's father and grandfather.

Nina's mouth opened in surprise. "You actually tracked down *Rusty?*"

"Yes. He was living with a woman and two little girls. The relationship was pretty new—just a few months."

"Sounds like Rusty," she said. "One woman after the other. Did he tell you where Layla is?"

"I'm afraid not," I told her. "He didn't know. I've got something difficult to tell you."

Scott put his arm around his wife's shoulders. "About Layla?"

I nodded. "Rusty claimed not to have seen Layla since she was ten years old."

The DeCourseys turned to stare at each other, worry clearly stamped in their eyes.

Nina looked as if she were about to faint. "He's lying. He has to be.

Because if he isn't, then where did she go, and who—?" Her voice cracked.

Scott kissed his wife's head. "Don't get upset, honey." He turned to face me. "We know the guy's a liar. I only spoke to him a few times, and even I can tell you that much."

"I'm going to be checking into what he told me," I said. "As much as I can, anyway. The problem is the passage of time. It makes things difficult to follow up on."

Nina stood. "I'll get you my old phone. It's no good anymore, but I kept it because it's got Layla's messages on it."

She left the room, disappearing into the hallway.

Scott fixed his eyes on me. When he spoke, he spoke in a tone just above a whisper. "I don't want to say this in front of Nina, but I worried a lot about Layla going away with her father. I really didn't trust him. And I thought something was a bit... *off*... about the messages Layla was sending us. They just didn't sound like her."

"Oh?" I said.

"Yeah. It's like Rusty was telling her what to say. And I thought it was odd that Layla didn't answer any of the messages I sent her. She and I had a bit of a special relationship—at least, I thought so. I really liked the kid."

"Did you tell Nina that at the time—that the messages sounded off?"

"No, I didn't want to worry her. She was already crying every night about Layla leaving. She'd been to the police in Sydney, and they told her they couldn't do anything. Unless she could prove that Layla was in danger, they couldn't act. So, what I ended up doing was to send out my own private investigator to look for Rusty and Layla." Scott sighed. "But he didn't find either of them."

"That's a shame."

"Yes, it is," he said. "It would mean a lot for us to see her again. I wish she'd at least taken the camera with her, so she'd have the pictures to remember us by. All the photos she took are still on the card. It was my camera, but I said she could have it."

I gave him a smile. "I'm sure she remembers you and Nina."

Nina returned with the phone. "I recharged it the other night, after you called me to ask about Layla. I just wanted to look at her last messages to me again. I miss her so much."

"Great," I said. "Let's take a look."

There weren't many messages on the phone. Only eight in all.

The messages began in February 2010:

Aunt Nina, I know you're sad about me leaving, but I just didn't fit into Tallman's Valley. I've been talking with my dad since Mum died. I've decided to go and live with him. He's leaving tonight, so I had to make a quick decision. Don't worry, this is what I want to do. Love to you, Layla.

The other seven of her messages from the months after that were even briefer, just talking about doing her schoolwork on the road or sights she'd seen.

In between Layla's messages were Nina's frantic replies, asking repeatedly for Layla to come back home and demanding that Rusty call her. Layla's messages became less and less frequent, until they stopped altogether.

After seeing Rusty in person today, this message exchange was chilling.

Could he be lying, after all?

I needed to find out exactly what he'd been doing at the start of 2010.

24

KATE

I drove home from the DeCourseys' house and spent what was left of my Saturday at home with my family.

Sunday was another pleasant spring day. We had a picnic out on the grass, finishing off the lunch with apple pies that Abby had baked. The pies were a lot like the pies my mother used to make. Mum must have taught Abby how to make them during the weekends when she used to stay with her as a teenager.

Baby Jasper rolled about on the rug, gabbling to the sky. Ivy flew a new kite that she and Logan had made.

Ivy was still getting used to Logan.

In truth, she was still getting used to all of us. In a harrowing incident, she'd been stolen away from us when she was just three years old. I'd tracked down the person who took her when she was six—but by then, she barely knew any of us. Ivy had even been shy of Abby—her own mother. During the last year that Ivy was gone, Abby had met Logan, and she'd become pregnant with Jasper. Ivy had had to get used to the fact she had a new brother, too. The incident had struck a deep wound in our family. We were very fortunate to have her back.

But today was a good day. I had to remember to collect such days in my memory and keep them in a jar—to shield against the days that weren't so good. I could tell that Pete felt the same way. He went totally snap-happy, taking enough pictures to fill a photograph album.

Before I knew it, it was twilight.

We moved inside and played boardgames with Ivy.

The weekend had passed with the snap of the fingers.

On Monday morning, I headed down to the station in a sombre mood. I was no closer to locating Layla.

It was time to pull out the case notes for Emmet Eisen. It wasn't an extensive file. The investigation had been over and done with quickly.

Together, Franco and I re-examined our notes about the people we'd spoken to and what they'd said.

"Hey," said Franco as he picked up a handwritten letter. "I remember this. We never did find out who wrote it."

Frowning, I looked across at the crumpled piece of paper. "Oh... yes... the love letter."

Franco scratched his chin. "Hmmm. It's not your daughter's writing, is it?"

"No, it's definitely not Abby's. But I've got something—a note that Layla wrote to her grandfather. I went to see him on the weekend."

"Oh yeah?"

"Yep. I need to catch you up."

I told Franco all about the conversation with Mr Maddox and then about Rusty Zamano insisting that he hadn't seen his daughter since she was ten.

"Right," he said at the end of it. "I don't like the fact that no one has heard from Layla in so long."

"Yes. It's worrying me, too."

I drew Layla's note out of my briefcase and placed it against the love letter.

Franco whistled. "It's a match."

I eyed the two samples of handwriting. "Okay, so... Layla was in love with Emmet. Just like Abby."

"But he rejected her. He'd thrown the letter away."

"Yes, it would seem so."

"Could that be why Layla left town, then? The scumbag teacher seduced her and then tossed her aside for Abby? Could have been a very painful experience for a fourteen-year-old kid."

I nodded. "A very painful and confusing experience. I guess it could partly have been what she and Emmet were arguing about in his boat shed. It was the day that she left town. It all fits."

"Okay. Do we assume it's the reason why she was telling your daughter that she had to end the relationship with Emmet? Because she was in love with him?"

"Wraps up neatly," I agreed.

A cold sensation passed through my chest, then. A terrible thought had pushed its way into my mind.

"Except," I said, "some parts of this don't wrap up neatly at all. We don't know exactly what happened when Layla left her grandfather's house, never to be heard from again. That's not normal. What if she met with foul play? I mean, not in the years after she left Tallman's Valley, but directly after. If so, then someone could have forced her to write the letter and note."

Franco stared back at me. "Emmet Eisen. *He* could have forced her to write them."

"Yes. He could have. If he did that, then he might have done something to Layla two weeks after she left Tallman's Valley. Because she was at her grandfather's that long. That only leaves a day or two between that time frame and when Emmet died. It's a tight timeframe."

He nodded. "And how does the other guy fit into this—the guy Emmet had a fight with? And do we know for certain that Layla even wrote the letter and note? I mean, Emmet could have written them himself, as a cover up."

"Well, I can find out about one of those things. I'll call Layla's aunt and get some more samples of Layla's writing. Then we'll know if it's hers, at least."

I walked to my desk to call Nina DeCoursey. She was at work and sounded stressed and busy when she answered.

"I'll be quick, Nina," I said. "I'd like to ask a small favour. We need some pieces of Layla's handwriting."

"Oh... okay, let me think... You know what? I actually don't think we have anything. She was only here for a few months in total. I held onto her schoolbooks for years. For sentimental reasons, I guess. But eventually, we had to clean out her room. Scott wanted to use that space as an office. It was a sad day, but you can't hold on forever."

"No," I agreed. "You can't. What about birthday cards and things like that?"

"Hmmm. I can't remember her ever giving us any cards. She gave us little presents, but not birthday cards. I'll ask Scott if he can think of anything her writing might be on—but I doubt he would."

"I'd appreciate it."

"Kate, can I ask why you need this?"

"We found a letter... in the Eisens' boat shed, ten years ago. We just want to check if Layla wrote it."

She went quiet for a moment. "So, this is part of your investigation—the letter? What kind of letter was it?"

"It's a love letter."

"To whom?"

"I'd rather not say."

"You know, Kate, I'm starting to feel uneasy about this whole thing. I'm not sure what Layla is being dragged into. She's my niece. Family. And she's not here to defend herself."

"I understand."

"I just feel very protective of her. And you know what my job is—I protect young people who are in trouble with the law all day long."

"It's just a routine check. We also have the note that Layla wrote to her grandfather. The handwriting on the note matches with the letter. But we're just being thorough."

"He still had the note?"

"Yes."

"Well, that's something, at least. But I can't help but think that you're not being entirely honest with me, Kate. Look, I know that you're investigating the death of Emmet Eisen again. Louisa told me. If Layla was a witness to anything that went on, well, to be honest, I don't want to be the one who throws her into the frying pan."

"I can assure you, she's not in any trouble."

"I hope not. I don't want to inadvertently cause problems for her. I'm guessing she finds her past painful—with the death of her mother and then the loss of her friendship with Abby when she lived here in the valley. Maybe she just needed to let it all go and start again."

I hoped that Nina was right, and Layla was happy and just hiding from her past. But a niggling sense told me that something was wrong. Very wrong.

25

KATE

After ending the conversation with Nina, I called Abby—asking if she happened to have anything that Layla wrote.

She didn't. She wasn't sure about the sample of handwriting I sent her, either. It had been ten years. She didn't remember what her friend's handwriting had looked like.

I had an idea. Layla's old school might have kept some of her work. It wasn't likely, but in the off-chance that they did, I'd get the handwriting sample I was seeking.

Leaving Franco to work on another of our open cases, I drove across to Abby's old school.

Abby had graduated from Valley Grammar in 2012. In the dim light of the heavy, overcast day, the building looked every inch of its one hundred odd years, with its Federation Queen Anne brickwork and arches, tiny windowpanes, and steps everywhere in sight.

I headed in.

The students had all gone home, and it was quiet inside.

It felt strange to walk inside those school halls now.

I could picture Abby and Layla stepping just ahead of me, in their school dresses and school socks, sharing jokes and girlish chatter with each other—Abby with her thick dark hair and Layla with her blonde tresses.

An immense sadness overcame me.

Because now I knew what Abby had been through at school here when she was fourteen. I knew terrible things about the school's science teacher, Mr Eisen. I didn't know the full story yet, but I knew enough to be horrified.

I walked past the room in which Mr Eisen had taught science to Abby's class. There must have been days in which Abby came to school here just after a night in which she'd been with Eisen, and she'd had to pretend to just be another one of his students. I could almost sense Abby's confusion and dread still lingering here in the dim corridor.

The assistant principal met with me in her office. Her name was Evelyn Mitchell, and she had a somewhat snooty appearance, with her hair in a perfect bun and eyebrows that resembled the twin arches of a bridge. Her voice was quick and efficient.

"How are you, Detective Wakeland?" she said. "How's your family?"

"We're all well, thank you."

Everyone in the valley knew about the trauma my family had been through in recent times after Ivy was abducted.

She nodded with a warm smile on her face. "How can I help you?"

"This is a long shot. If possible, I'd like to see a sample of work from a student of yours who was here years ago. A handwriting sample."

"What was his or her name?"

"Layla Maddox."

I could see that she didn't recognise the name.

"She was at the school for less than a year," I explained. "During 2009. She was a friend of my daughter's."

"Hmmm. Well, I'm afraid we wouldn't have kept anything from that far back. If we kept work from all our students, we'd end up stacked to the rafters. The only thing I can do is to contact the teachers who were there at the school when she was a student. Perhaps one or two of them happened to take photographs of their students' work. What grade was she in when she was here?"

"She was in Year 9."

"Okay, leave it with me." Her eyes crinkled with curiosity. "It might be helpful to know the reason why you need the handwriting sample?"

"Sorry, I really can't say."

"No problem. I'll do my best to get you that sample. But I warn you, I don't like my chances."

I thanked her and walked out of the school again.

Back at the station, I tried other avenues to gain samples of her handwriting. I called her old school in Sydney. And I asked Abby if Layla had ever written her a card or anything. There was nothing. I knew that Layla's grandfather hadn't kept anything of hers except for the note. I looked up his old address. His previous house, in which Layla had once lived, had been taken back by the government housing board and given to another family in need.

Layla would have gone to school in Scotland before she came to Australia, but I'd probably only run into the same problem—the school wouldn't have kept any of her work. And even if they had, her writing might have changed a lot between when she lived there and when she was nine and fourteen years of age.

Everywhere I looked for Layla, I kept running into roadblocks.

26

KATE

First thing in the morning, I attended a regular meeting with Franco, Shintani and our homicide group.

After that, I headed across to see the detective who headed our local missing persons division. Detective Sergeant Reagan Grimshaw.

I found her sitting at her desk, a glum look on her face. In her lunch box, she had a measure of boiled chicken, some limp cooked beans and a small rice salad.

"That doesn't look too appetising," I remarked.

"Doctors' orders," Grimshaw said. "First, they came for the fried food, then they came for the full-fat dairy, then they came for the bagels."

"High cholesterol?"

She nodded, sighing. "Yup. Luckily, I can do without the dairy. Gives me gas. But I do miss my poppy seed bagels."

"Enjoy," I said, eyeing the anaemic-looking meal.

"So, why are you here, Wakeland?" she said, in her usual abrasive tone.

"I'd like some advice."

"Right. Well, I don't give that out for free, you know. Next time I've got a case that I could use your eyes on, I want more police hours from homicide than you lot currently give me."

"Deal."

I smiled sardonically. I knew that she was only half-joking. Every police area command had the same problem. We were all overworked with not enough police for the cases at hand. If a local missing person case required our homicide team, we were there on the spot, and we worked feverishly alongside the missing persons team for those first hours and days—hoping to recover the missing person alive. But as those cases wore on without resolution, we were forced to step back.

Grimshaw speared her beans and ate a bunch of them. "So, who's missing?"

"I can't find a girl who lived here at Tallman's Valley ten years ago. Her name is Layla Maddox."

Briefly, I explained the circumstances under which Layla had left town, and my recent efforts to find her.

"Lemme take a little look," Grimshaw said. She began tapping at her computer. "Right, so there is a record about a Layla Maddox at an inner-city police station. The record was placed by a Detective Trent Gilroy. It appears that Layla's aunt—a Mrs Nina DeCoursey—came in to ask about putting in a missing person's report. Subsequently, she told them that Layla had left a note and messages about going away with her father. There is nothing more here. A missing person's report wasn't filed."

"Nina said the police told her that the father had the right of custody of Layla."

"Well, perhaps he did. Depending on circumstances, he had more rights than the aunt did."

"But it's strange that Layla hasn't resurfaced in all this time."

"Sounds to me like she doesn't want to be found."

"That's possible. But I need to be sure."

"Ah, the old famous Wakeland intuition." She smirked.

Grimshaw and I had long been at odds with each other in our

policing methods. She wasn't fond of chasing things up purely on the sense that something was wrong.

"I guess I'm just looking for another perspective on how I can find this girl. Perhaps I'm missing something."

"Well," she said, "people who don't want to be found can make things damned difficult. I can run some checks for you, but I don't like my chances, because of how many years have passed. She could be anywhere. Living overseas even."

"Yes, she could well be living overseas. But some things are bugging me. The way in which she left and the fact that her father claims not to have seen her since she was ten. And there are a few more factors involved with this. Two weeks after Layla left town, a young male teacher died. This teacher had been having a relationship with the best friend of the girl who's missing. He'd also had a punch-up with another man because of that girl."

I didn't want to give Grimshaw the names of the teacher and my daughter. Not yet, anyway.

She stabbed a piece of pallid chicken. "Do you think your dead teacher might have had something to do with Layla going missing? Is that what you're saying?"

"Maybe."

"When and where did the teacher die?"

"February 2010. He died here in Tallman's Valley."

"Well, I can see from the record from Detective Gilroy that Layla was at her grandfather's house in the city that month."

"That's correct. But I just feel that this teacher and Layla are linked and that he might be the reason she left town."

She eyed me sceptically. "But if he *was* the reason she left town... why didn't she come back after he was dead? Why would she feel the need to hide herself away? Not making a lot of sense, Wakeland."

Grimshaw was always the curmudgeon, but her lunch today seemed to be making her especially grumpy. She chewed a mouthful of food and swallowed.

"I know," I said. "It doesn't make sense. But I don't have all the pieces to this yet. The teacher was into some disturbing stuff. The girl he was having the relationship with is telling me her story slowly, via sessions with a psychiatrist. She was only fourteen back then—as was Layla. Apparently, this teacher called himself *Mr Lullaby*."

Grimshaw stopped chewing. "Mr Lullaby? Ugh, losing my appetite for lunch. Even more than before." She pushed her lunchbox away. "You know what, Wakeland?"

"What's that?"

"What if there's a second one?"

"A second what?"

"A second Mr Lullaby. If Layla felt the need to stay away, maybe the danger wasn't over for her."

I frowned at her, thinking. "You know what, that's a good suggestion."

"Yes, it is a good suggestion. Because it doesn't sound like a bog-standard case of a slimy teacher pursuing a student. This guy was into disturbing stuff, and he had an odd name for himself. I mean, Mr Lullaby? Creepy. Those are the hallmarks of a paedophile who is a serial child abuser. And lots of those guys join up with others."

"Thanks. That's given me something to chew over."

"Anytime. I'd hate to think of someone like that still out there, getting away with what they've been doing. If it helps, I'll take a good look at our cases of missing girls and see if I can pinpoint any connection. Might take me a couple of weeks. I'm swamped."

"I'd really appreciate that."

I walked away from her desk with thoughts of a second Lullaby Man running through my head. If there *was* a second one, who was he?

27

ABBY

I sat Jasper in his highchair and gave him some home-cooked custard and stewed pears. His face lit up with a big smile. That was his favourite food.

Within a minute, he had custard smeared in his hair. I wet a cloth in warm water in the sink and then dabbed away at the sticky substance on Jasper's head.

Jasper's hair had grown so much over the past month, from barely covering his scalp to a thick, silky blond that was almost white. Logan had hair this colour when he was small—I'd coaxed a couple of his childhood photos from him. His hair was more of a dark sandy shade now.

I carried Jasper to a rug on the living room floor and then sank into a lounge chair. He'd had an unsettled night. I was exhausted. I reflected that there was no other job that required you to be working during the night and then get up and do it all again during the day.

Jasper crawled to pick up an object off the floor. It was a pencil. I rushed to take the pencil from him. I'd told Ivy not to leave anything around that Jasper might find, but she was still learning. I had to be patient with her. Ivy had only known she had a baby brother for the past two months. She wasn't used to having to be careful where she put things. I'd been trying hard to get Ivy used to being part of her family again. After being away from us for so long, she wasn't about to get used to everyone again overnight. Logan had been gently trying to build a relationship with her, but she was still so shy around him.

Predictably, Jasper began bawling. All of my efforts to replace the pencil with a rattle or toy car were rejected. Jasper hurled the offending items across the room.

Scooping Jasper up from the floor, I began pacing the room.

I held him close, singing.

He struggled and screamed for the next five minutes, his tiny body rigid with anger, before finally wearing himself out and succumbing to sleep.

I laid him down in his cot and tiptoed from the room. My head felt as if it had been sand-blasted by Jasper's screams.

Stepping out to the kitchen, I went to grab myself a juice, but every part of me felt dizzy and tired. I laid my forehead down on the cool stone of the kitchen bench top.

Dad often walked around the property with Jasper during the day, and I didn't realise how much I'd come to rely on this.

It wasn't just Jasper who was wearing me out. It was my sessions with Dr Quinley. I'd thought the sessions would go slower, but they were like steam trains.

It was my fault. Once I started remembering things, I couldn't stop. Scenes rushed at me, and it would be like I was living them all over again.

I heard the front door swing open. Logan came in from work, his expression tired but his blue eyes as bright as always.

"Uh oh," he said. "Did Jasper give you a hard time of it?"

"Yeah. He fought sleep like a demon."

"He's a little fighter all right."

I just smiled. Logan didn't really understand, and I didn't try to explain. It was too hard to explain the minute-by-minute strain of caring for a small baby who wasn't a good sleeper. No one understood, unless they were in the thick of it.

He hugged me. The smells of grease and engine oil hung on his clothing. Logan always brought those odours home with him from the car repair garage.

"Hey, how's pizza and wine sound?" he said. "We can put on a movie and relax together later."

"Sure."

"What's Ivy doing?"

"She's with Charlotte—at Lori Hinton's house. Play date."

"Okay. How about I get you that wine now? Just wait, I'll go jump in the shower first. I'm probably giving you head spins from the stink of grease." He headed away out of the kitchen.

I went to lie down on the lounge, praying that the sound of Logan having a shower didn't wake Jasper.

Ten minutes later, Logan emerged, with fresh clothes and wet hair. He poured me a glass of wine and himself a beer.

Logan sat next to me while I positioned myself to rest my head on his lap.

"Hey," he said softly, stroking my head. "How are you doing with the psych?"

"It's been... strange. I guess the whole thing was a strange episode, so it can't be anything else."

He fell silent for a moment. "One day soon... you're going to have to tell it all to me. I should know."

"I will. I promise. Once I've got it all straight in my head." I sighed heavily. "I've got another appointment with him this afternoon."

Logan finished his glass of beer and leaned across me to set the glass down on the coffee table. He brushed my hair back from my face. I could tell he was thinking hard about something.

"Do you still think about Emmet Eisen?" he said. "I mean, do you miss him? That sounds really messed up. You were fourteen. He was your teacher. But... do you miss him?"

I chewed my lip, deciding whether to answer honestly. I decided to be honest. "There is always going to be a part of me that misses him."

"Ever since you told your secret about Emmet... it's been like, I don't know what to think. I feel like maybe I'm not going to measure up —to him."

"Don't think that. Back when I was fourteen, I thought I'd be spending my life with him. But, I grew up. I got a lot wiser." I turned my head to look up at Logan, touching his chin. "*You* are my future. And I'm very, very glad about that."

A grin spread across his face. "I should give you wine more often."

I returned the smile. "It's not the wine. I'm sorry if I've been distant lately. I've just had too much on my mind. Once I'm done with the sessions with Dr Quinley, we can start moving towards a normal life. Jasper will get better with his sleeping. Maybe he's picking up on my anxiety and getting unsettled himself."

"Hey, I'm on baby watch tonight, okay? If Jasper wakes, I'm the one to get up."

"But you've got to get up for work."

"So do you. You're the full-time carer of a tiny tyrant."

I nodded. Maybe Logan did understand how tiring Jasper was, after all. Or he was trying hard to understand, at least.

The wine had made me sleepy. I felt myself drifting.

It hadn't occurred to me that Logan would worry about my feelings for Emmet. It was all so far away and in the past. Like a murky dream. Even back then, I had never felt as if I were walking on solid ground with Emmet.

In contrast, what I had with Logan felt real.

The day I met Logan, I'd been in a pitch-dark state of mind. Ivy had been missing for about two years. I was caught up in a spiralling whirlpool, pushed down to a place where it was always dark and bone-cold, a place where I had no fight left in me.

I'd left Tallman's Valley and moved to Sydney. I couldn't bear it there any longer.

The only work I could find was in a small bar. I was wasting all my money on alcohol and drugs, trying to erase myself. I'd already attempted suicide once, and I was a hair's breadth away from trying it again. At the time, I was sharing a unit with a girl I barely knew—a girl who'd been two years above me in school. Collette. Collette was in a band, and she did small gigs in bars around the city.

I used to go along to some of the gigs—when I wasn't working or sleeping off the drugs I'd taken the night before. One night, Collette's band played with a drummer friend of hers. I knew his face.

He was Logan Norwood. Like Collette, he was two years older than me and had gone to the same school I had. At school, I'd thought he was cute.

That night, Logan had walked into the gig wearing a white T-shirt and faded blue jeans, his pale hair tousled and his eyes very blue.

I'd never been a fan of blond men. I liked dark hair and eyes, and preferably olive skin. Like Emmet Eisen.

But one look at Logan changed everything. In an instant. The cute teenage boy I'd known had become a man of twenty-five, with an angled jaw and rugged edges.

And Logan had seemed smitten as soon as Collette introduced us to each other.

For the first time in a long time, life had almost become salvageable. Almost. It was still a life without Ivy. Which was unbearable.

I hadn't meant to get pregnant to Logan. I'd had a stomach bug and my contraception failed.

Logan was overjoyed by the prospect of a baby. I wasn't.

I didn't want a baby in case something ever happened to it. Because of Ivy, I knew what it was to have your heart torn from your chest.

Logan talked me around. Slowly, step-by-step, I began catching sight of glimmers of sunlight. A way back to having a life.

I gave birth to Jasper when I was eight months pregnant.

Logan and I decided to move back to the Blue Mountains, so that Jasper could get to know his family who were there. I'd had to find a way to reconnect with my parents. They hadn't seen or heard from me in a long time.

Logan and I had no money. I hadn't been working for months. Logan's drumming gigs hadn't paid much. The only place that Logan could afford was a room in a share house.

Soon after my return to the mountains, Mum figured out who had abducted Ivy and she'd gotten her back.

Everything was okay now.

All I needed now was to sign off on my past—my lost teenage years.

I didn't know what was coming next.

And I didn't know exactly what I wanted. If anything, I guessed I wanted a thing that Emmet and I had spoken about once: *absolution*.

I half-sat up, rising from Logan's lap and checking my watch. It was time to go and see Dr Quinley.

28

ABBY

Mum met with me at Dr Quinley's office.

I felt both comforted and horrified that she was listening to my stories. I still felt just so ashamed. The therapy wasn't working so far to make me feel any better about myself. But maybe that wasn't why I needed to tell what happened. I needed to tell it to let the truth come out.

Dr Quinley engaged in small talk with Mum and me for a few minutes, while his receptionist fetched us coffee. And then he asked if I was ready to start.

I said that I was—as ready as I could be, anyway.

"Abby," he said. "I want you to sit back, get comfortable. Let your eyes close. You will see the pear tree in your mind. You're standing beneath it."

His voice was so soothing that it pulled me straight in. "I can see it."

"Good," he said. "Is there something in particular you want to tell me about today?"

"I'm ready to tell you about what Emmet did. And what I did, too."

"Are you sure you feel ready for that?" Dr Quinley sounded concerned.

"No... But I want to get it out from inside me. I need to."

"Then you can go ahead. And, Abby, I want you to feel like you can tell me anything."

I nodded, closing my eyes, still nursing my coffee cup.

I saw myself, on a sunny day, walking up the grassy hill to the pear tree. It was *my* tree. As Dr Quinley had told me, it had been growing there since the day I was born. Its branches were weighed down with ripe fruit. Each piece of fruit was transparent, with moving images within it.

All my memories.

It was beautiful.

And ugly.

And terrifying. All at once.

I concentrated on my breathing.

It was time to tell about the bizarre side of Emmet Eisen.

"It was a rainy day in November 2009," I started, "when Emmet first asked me to go somewhere private with him. I was at home, doing a school assignment. I'd been talking with Emmet for months. At first, there had just been a message from him here and there. But then we started talking every night. When he told me he wanted to meet someplace where we could be alone, I thought he would get us a hotel room. I was scared, but I thought I'd lose him if I didn't agree."

"Remember, Abby," said Dr Quinley in a tender tone. "You need not justify yourself."

I nodded. "Okay."

"Just let yourself tell the story. No one here is judging you."

I took a few moments to breathe.

A scene opened up in my mind.

PART IV

A DECADE EARLIER

29

ABBY

I was at the desk in my bedroom, bored and trying to slog through a geography assignment. Rain slashed continuously against my window.

A text came through on my phone. From Emmet.

At first, he was a welcome distraction. And as always, his name on the message was *Mr Lullaby*.

I loved it that he called himself that. It was like a secret code between us that no one else knew. Mr Eisen, the science teacher, was Mr Lullaby. I'd been nursing that secret for months.

What are you doing, Birdie? came his first text. I also loved it when he called me Birdie. It was his special name for me.

A stupid assignment, I replied. *Geography.*

Can you come out for a while?

I wish. I gotta get this done. Besides, it's raining. Where would we go?

I've got somewhere special.

I felt a blush of warmth deep within me. He wanted us to go somewhere to be alone? He'd never outright invited me somewhere like that before. It had always just happened.

You do? I texted back. *Like, your boat house?*

No, not there.

Okay, then where?

Somewhere new. I can tell you, but you've got to promise me you'll come.

I held my breath. This proved he was taking our relationship seriously. At the same time, sharp warning signals embedded themselves in my mind.

Abby? What's your answer?

My dad's here. He won't let me go out in the rain.

Is the library off-limits?

I guess not. But if I go out, I won't get my assignment done.

I'll do it for you. I'm a teacher. I'll murder your assignment.

You'd do that for me?

For you, anything. What's the assignment question?

It's boring. We have to explain the collision between the landforms we now know as North America and Africa, from about three hundred million years ago.

No problem, he replied. *So... are you ready?*

Again, warning signals prickled me. If I turned him down, he might not ask me again. Maybe he'd think me too young and silly and he'd shut me out of his life. The thought of that made a dark veil fall, making everything go dark. Panic tapped in my chest, so hard I could almost hear it.

Birdie?

I'm not sure.

I thought you were. Guess I was wrong.

Rising from my chair, I walked across to my window and gazed out at the rain. I couldn't think. Didn't want to let myself think. Because if I stopped to think, I might tell him no.

I looked at my phone again.

He hadn't sent another message.

Panicking, I typed out a text. *Are you there?*

The screen remained blank for seven full terrifying seconds.

Then an address appeared.

Don't write it down, he texted. *Just remember it. It's the old funfair on Lancaster Road.*

A funfair?

Don't worry. It's been closed down for a long time. It will just be you and me. I will wait for you for one hour. If you're not there by then, I'll know you're not coming.

Nerves raced up and down my body.

But as I started getting ready, the nerves vanished, and I just felt robotic.

I changed all my clothes, from the skin out. I had no clue what to wear. After four wardrobe changes, I ended up deciding on my newest jeans, a denim jacket and a cute long-sleeved top. It was the best I could do. I brushed my teeth, combed my hair back into a ponytail, and then applied lip gloss and mascara. Not too much, though, because Dad would notice it.

Then I headed downstairs.

Mum had gone out to take Nan to do her grocery shopping. Dad was in the kitchen chopping vegetables to make soup.

I snatched up a piece of celery from his chopping board and ate it. "Dad, I need a couple of books for my geography essay. I'm going down to the library."

"It's raining out. Couldn't you just Google it?"

"I tried. No luck. But Mr Seagrove gave us a list of books we can grab from the library."

"I'll drive you down."

"You're busy making lunch for everyone. The rain won't hurt me. I can ride down to the library and take my notes. The rain'll probably stop before I've even finished doing that."

He made a half-exasperated sound from between his teeth. "Yeah, okay, honey. Wear a raincoat."

"I will."

I rushed away before he had a chance to change his mind, grabbing my raincoat from the cupboard next to the front door.

Outside, the downpour sloshed down as if coming from a big

bucket. Everything looked dull and greyish. It seemed the wrong kind of day for what was about to happen.

Not that I had a clear idea of what was going to happen. But I could guess that before the hour was out, I'd have joined the ranks of girls at school who'd proudly announced they'd lost their virginity.

Only, I wouldn't be telling anyone.

Would people guess what I'd done?

Some of the boys at school claimed they knew the difference just by looking at a girl. Once, kids had shared around pictures of a naked girl from our class—a boy had snapped it while the girl was sleeping. In everyone's eyes, being naked or having sex made a girl dirty. But not boys. Never boys. It was hard to figure out.

We'd had a sex ed speaker come to the school last month. She'd told us that there was no importance in the actual mechanics of sex. It was all about how you felt, whether you were old enough, and whether it was consensual.

But the lines and rules were blurred with Emmet and me. And how did you know if you were ready? When it came to Mr Lullaby—Emmet —I just didn't know.

At least he was outside of the toxic teenage grapevine at my school. He was a teacher, not a student.

I rode across town to where the suburbs gave way to larger blocks of land, with empty lots in between. My socks and shoes were getting soaked, rain dripping from the hood of my raincoat and dribbling down my neck and inside my tee-shirt.

The road I was on was a long one, sparsely punctuated with houses, until there were no houses at all. I turned onto Lancaster Road.

A metal chain-link fence encircled a huge, empty field. Threatening-looking barbed wire ran along the top of the fence.

Surely, I had the address wrong. Emmet had mentioned a funfair. But there was no funfair here.

I couldn't check the address on my phone. Emmet used an app in which the messages deleted themselves five minutes after they were sent. To protect both of us, he'd said.

I kept cycling along the road.

There it was—the sign that Emmet had told me about. A sign that announced *private property*. That was where I was supposed to enter.

Sliding my bike in behind the sign, I looked for the way in. I found it where he said it would be. A hole in the fence.

Bending my head, I wriggled in through the space.

For a minute, the field ahead seemed like a war zone, a minefield.

But that was silly.

I raced across the field, worried that someone would drive past and see me. I shouldn't have worried, because I hadn't even seen a car for the past fifteen minutes or so. And the trees that dotted the field would hide me.

Across the field, buildings emerged from between the trees and undergrowth. Glad for a chance to get out of the rain but afraid at what lay ahead, I ran towards the buildings.

The first of the buildings looked like a set of offices. Ducking low beneath overhanging morning glory vines, I walked along a cracked concrete pathway. The windows had all been boarded up. I peered in through a small space of window where the board had disintegrated. Old desks, chairs and filing cabinets occupied the floor. Part of the roof was sagging, vines bursting in and claiming the room. The carpet looked dried out and brittle, like a living thing that had died.

Emmet had told me to keep following the path.

To one side I could see a giant Ferris wheel that had been turned over on its side, collapsed like a fallen dinosaur—with weeds growing through its bones.

The path wound around to a single building that spread out squat and wide. It carried a faded sign: *House of Fun*. The sign was one of the few things that told a story about this place having once been a carnival.

I found the door and pushed it open. Immediately, I recoiled at the sight of an almost pitch-dark, cavernous space. It was not the kind of building I'd ever choose to go into on my own.

My phone buzzed with a message.

I looked at the screen.

Come on in. Go to the left and to the left again, came his message.

Instantly, I felt better. Because he was here.

Where are you? I texted anxiously.

Just trust me, he replied.

After shrugging off my raincoat, I stepped inside and left it on a countertop. I squinted, adjusting my eyesight in the dark light. A large rink looked like it used to be for bumper cars. One of the bumper cars sat in a corner.

I walked to the left, as instructed.

Dead ahead, a corridor loomed, at the end of which was a tall mirror.

I stared at myself. I no longer looked as put-together as I had when I left home. I looked like a bedraggled, skinny teenager with a nervous expression. Straightening myself, I practised a smile.

To the left was an archway that led to another large space. Around the archway stretched the words, Hall of Mirrors.

I could hear flutters of music.

With the deepest breath I could muster, I headed down the corridor.

30

ABBY

Keeping my phone in hand, I stepped inside the archway that led to the Hall of Mirrors.

Images leapt out at me.

I saw... everything. All at once.

Mirrors all over the walls. Birdcage hanging by a chain from the ceiling. Bed in the middle of the floor. Fairy lights everywhere.

My stomach hit the back of my throat.

There were corridors of mirrors leading off from the room. Most of the funhouse mirrors were gone, replaced by yet more framed mirrors of all shapes and sizes.

It felt like a trap, an ambush.

My knees went to jelly. I was about to flee when my phone sounded again.

I've got something for you, the message said. *Go to the dressing table.*

The dressing table was over by the wall—a retro dressing table with a round mirror and a stool in front.

There were lots of items arranged on it. Trinkets. Hair clips with jewelled butterflies and birds. A pair of scissors with handles in the shape of birds' heads. And a jewellery box.

With trembling fingers, I opened the box.

Inside the velvet casing lay a necklace. The necklace's pendant was a tiny, delicate silver birdcage. I lifted the necklace from the box, examining it closely. Inside the birdcage was the tiniest bird on a delicate swing.

Put it on, he told me.

Seating myself on the stool, I put my phone down on the tabletop and did as he asked.

"I didn't know you were going to give me something." My voice sounded desolate in my ears. I had no clue that people gave each other gifts at a time like this.

"I wanted you to have this," he said. "It means you're mine."

I studied how the silver necklace looked against my neck and tee-shirt. A vein was jumping in my throat. "I love the necklace," I said tentatively.

"Now, you can give me something," he said.

"What can I give you?"

"Take the scissors and cut a lock of your hair. I want to keep it."

"You want my *hair?*"

"Yes."

I cut a small lock from underneath my ponytail and put the lock of hair and the scissors on the tabletop.

"Now, I want you to look nice for me," he said. "You can brush your hair and use the things I bought for you."

I pulled my damp hair from its hair tie. It really was a mess. I ran the brush through my hair, then slid the hair clips in. A smile stole onto my face as I gazed at my reflection.

He'd given me all these things. I should be happy—or grateful—or something.

"Do you like how you look?" he said.

I nodded.

"Okay, now that I've given you my gifts, I'd like you to do something for me."

"What is it?"

"I want to see you."

I laughed nervously. "I'm right here."

"I want to see all of you."

"What do you mean, Emmet?"

"Call me Mr Lullaby. I want you to take off your jacket and jeans. And your tee-shirt."

"What? It's cold."

"You'll be fine. You'll see."

My gaze slid towards the bed. Did he mean I'd be fine because I'd soon be in bed with him?

Of course that was what he meant. I was being stupid.

It was happening.

And this was how Emmet wanted it to happen.

Still sitting on the stool, I slid my jacket from my shoulders. My arms instantly chilled. I let the jacket drop to the ground.

My breath caught fast as I tugged my jeans down and removed my shoes.

Again, that strange robotic feeling took over. I was drifting… in a strange space I didn't have the language for. I pulled my tee-shirt over my head.

"Now what?" I said, nerves sending my voice high and shivery.

"Dance," he said.

"*Dance?* You want me to dance?"

"Yes. Like you do in ballet class. You've done it before for me."

Yes, I had danced for him before. But in my bedroom, in a dance costume.

"Not in my *underwear*," I told him.

"It's no different to wearing a swimsuit. I want to see you. You're the star of the show. It's all about you, little bird."

I stood. Apart from the tremors running down my back, I'd stopped feeling anything.

And so, I danced. In my socks, I performed the Dance of the Sugar Plum Fairy from Nutcracker.

I could see myself in all the mirrors. My hair fanning out around me. I felt stupid and awkward and weird.

When I was done, he clapped. The claps echoed everywhere through the dark spaces.

I stood there, out of breath. A wave of embarrassment hit me again and I folded my arms across my body, returning to the stool at the dressing table.

"Mr Lullaby? Is that what you wanted?"

"Thank you. You're beautiful. You can go home now."

"Go home?"

"Yes, Birdie. Fly home. Leave the hair clips here. But take the necklace. The necklace means you're mine. Just make sure that no one ever sees it. Can you promise me that?"

"Yes, I promise."

I dressed quickly and ran out of there.

All the way home, my fingers were gripping the handlebars so tightly that they shook.

When I got to the house, my mum's car was in the driveway. That meant that she was inside now with Nan.

I couldn't talk to them. Couldn't face them.

I stole inside and up the stairs.

Locking myself in the bathroom, I sat on the floor and sobbed.

I didn't understand a minute of what had just happened.

Not one single minute.

31

ABBY

One last message came through from Emmet that day.

I grabbed my phone as soon as it buzzed, hoping that it would be something that would help me make sense of what he'd asked me to do at the carnival. Maybe some words of love to make me feel better. And I really, really needed to feel better.

But all that there was on my phone's screen was just a single link. I copied it and pasted it into Google.

It was my geography assignment.

In the time I'd taken to ride to and from the old carnival, he'd done the whole thing and uploaded it to an online site.

Emmet's brand of love was so strange. He cared so tenderly for me, but then he'd just asked me to do something that I never could have imagined.

Two weeks went by before I spoke in private to him again. I was going crazy wondering what was wrong. I'd done what he wanted.

Part of me was glad I didn't have to talk to him. Another part of me craved an explanation. I had to go to school every day and see his face, knowing about the funfair and how he'd seen me dance there. Nothing ever showed in his expression. He was never Mr Lullaby at school.

When he did finally contact me again, I asked him about the mirror room. He just explained that adults sometimes enjoyed watching each other. He also said he wanted to take things slow with me.

He asked me back there.

Tomorrow.

I didn't want to ever go back there.

I told him I wanted a day to think.

He'd said he'd call me the next day, after school.

I stared at him the whole way through our science class. Watching him help the students with their experiments on the Bunsen burners. Taking in the curve of his cheek and the shape of his back and the way his dark hair splayed over the collar of his shirt.

During class, I loved him all over again.

After school, I sat in my bedroom. The door closed. Mum brought up some fruit cake she'd made—fruit cake was the only kind of cake she made. I took it and slammed the door shut again. I felt bad as soon as I'd done that. But I was filled with fear and tension, and I needed a quiet place in which to calm myself.

I stared at my phone, waiting for the call.

I wished that I could look back at Emmet's messages to me—all the sweet things he'd said. I needed to see the sweet things. But there was not a single record of anything he'd said to me. He made it all vanish, as if by magic. Of course, it was the app he was using that made the text vanish, but it all added to the mystery that was Emmet. I could almost believe that the whole thing had been imaginary.

A text popped up.

It was Layla.

Can Abby come out and play? The text said.

Not this afternoon, I texted back. *Have to catch up on homework.*

Too bad. Hey, you were kind of jumpy at school today.

Not enough sleep, I told her.

Too much Mr Eisen, she replied, including a row of kisses and love heart emojis.

Haha very funny, I texted back.

She was the only person who knew about Emmet and me. But she had no idea how far it had gone.

Another text came through. This one was from Emmet.

Got to go, I told Layla.

Come back to me, said Emmet's text.

Come back where? I said. But my heart was already pumping. I knew exactly where.

See you in twenty, he said. Then he was gone again.

A flood of anxiety washed through me.

My feet were no longer on the ground. I was floating, taken away on the current.

If I didn't go, he might never want to see me again. And the thought of that was bleaker than the old Hall of Mirrors.

I changed from my school uniform into jeans and a hoodie. This time, I didn't take care over what I wore.

"Going to Layla's," I called to Mum as I headed out.

"Be back before dark," she called back.

It took me a full twenty minutes to ride over to the abandoned carnival. He'd have to know how long it would take me. Even so, I worried he'd give up and go home.

As I stepped inside the House of Fun for the second time, a message came through from him: *Got a surprise for you.*

What is it? I texted.

Come and see, he texted back.

I didn't want any more surprises. What I wanted was for him to hold me. Because, so far, there'd been no hugs, no kisses.

I crossed the massive floor where the bumper cars were and then into the mirror room.

Something was behind a black curtain. Something large.

"Sit on the bed," he instructed. "And do your hair."

There were brushes and hair clips already on the bed.

My breaths were shallow as I walked to the bed, sat on it, and began brushing my hair. I slid the jewelled hair clips in.

"No clothes," he said.

"I'm not doing that," I shot back, trying to make myself feel bold.

"You're not as pretty with clothes on," he responded.

He slid the curtain back.

A bell-shaped, metal birdcage stood behind the curtain. A little taller than I was. A swing suspended from its ceiling. Two doors—both open.

"It's an old fixture from the gondola ride," he explained. "There used to be a water ride here, and this was one of the decorations. I found it and knew you'd like it."

I didn't like it.

It made my stomach clench.

But I did as he asked. Because I was in some altered space in which he had all the control and I had none. He was the teacher, I was the student.

And so, I swung on the ornate metal swing, inside the rusted metal birdcage, in and out of the front and back doors.

My clothes and underwear sat in a neat, folded pile on the bed. The girl on the swing reflected back to me in all the mirrors.

She wasn't me. I'd disconnected myself from the girl on the swing. If Emmet could be Mr Lullaby here, then I could just be *the girl*.

A lullaby tinkled and echoed in all the dead, dark reaches of the room.

32

ABBY

It went on like that. All through November, December, and January. Mr Lullaby would have surprises for me in the mirror room.

And each time, I'd grow more and more disgusted with myself. And then he wouldn't talk to me for days, until I was desperate to hear from him again.

It was a pattern. I see it now. I didn't see it then.

And then Layla left town.

She left at the end of January, in the middle of a blistering heatwave.

At the time, I was glad she'd gone.

Because when Mum grounded me and took my phone, Layla took her chance to make a move on Emmet. She'd betrayed me.

I didn't hear from Emmet at all after the end of January—not in private, anyway. I only saw him at school.

By mid-February, I couldn't bear it any longer. Despite myself, I was missing Layla. And I was missing something with Emmet that had never even been quite real—our relationship.

I needed to see him—in person. I needed to see his face in the daylight. Let the sunshine bleach away the strange episodes at the funfair.

I stole away from my house, flouting Mum's rules about being grounded.

Her rules had caused Emmet to turn away from me and seek out Layla. I wasn't going to obey her stupid rules.

I rode my bike down to the lake, hoping to find Emmet there.

He was sitting on a deck chair, facing the shore, his feet skimming the water. His drink of choice today was wine. He had a bottle and a glass of wine in his hands.

In every way, he was different to the boys at the parties I'd been to. Those boys drank beer or mixed spirits in with cans of cola. And when they got drunk, they'd stumble about and spit when they spoke, and then they'd vomit like cruise passengers in rough seas.

But on the other hand, Emmet was much harder to understand. His moods and the things he'd wanted me to do were so alien.

Emmet raised his glass to me as I approached. "Well, aren't you a scarlet robin in your red dress? Here's to you, Miss Abby Wakeland."

I knew that there were tiny birds called scarlet robins here. Emmet had shown one to me, once. They had dark heads and bright red breasts. My dress was new. A short dress with spaghetti straps. I'd begged Mum for it weeks ago, but I hadn't worn it until today.

Emmet frowned at me, then shrugged. "I'd offer you a drink... but I can't. You're a kid, and kids don't drink."

Tucking the hem of my dress between my thighs and upper calves, I seated myself on the sand beside him.

Sometimes—often—Emmet was awkward to talk to in person.

I ignored him calling me a kid. He didn't see me that way—I knew he didn't. It was just the alcohol talking. That was a saying I'd heard come out of my grandmother's mouth once, back when my grandfather was still alive.

Now, sitting next to the drunken Emmet Eisen, I didn't know whether to agree with Nan. I wanted to be patient with him, like Nan had been with my granddad, but something inside my chest pushed upward like a fist.

He should appreciate me more. I'd done everything he wanted. Wasn't that enough? And I was the one who cared about him the most in the world. Twice, I'd even gone looking for him after he'd been out drinking on his boat. Each time, I'd paddled around the lake until I'd found him, and I'd covered his sunburnt face and rowed him to a shady spot along the shore.

He had problems, and he needed me. Sometimes I was the adult and he the damaged child. Other times he was the adult and I his student. It wasn't the usual type of relationship, but it could work. *It would work.*

I attempted a conversation with him. "How's work been?"

He laughed. "Great. It's great. It's a wonder they don't fire me. Helps to have an old man who's put good money into that school."

When he turned his face, I saw that it was bruised.

"What happened to you?"

"It's okay."

"It's not okay. Who did that to you?"

"It was a guy who needed a belting. But I came out worse."

"Whoever it was, I hate him."

"I'll survive."

"Who was it?"

"No one. Caught him creeping on you."

"What?"

"Just go on home. Don't hang around here. Don't come to the parties."

"I'm not going home."

Despite the bruising on his face, his eyes were so beautiful they put a lump in my throat. Deep, dark brown eyes. Eyes to lose myself in. The same colour as his hair. The colour of forests.

His eyes looked a little odd though. His pupils were large, as if we were in the dark. But the day was bright.

"You're a good teacher," I told him, keeping my thoughts to myself.

"That's why they're keeping you in the job." I hoped that'd sounded like something an adult would say.

"Is that right?" He stretched his arms. "And how are you doing at school, Abby?"

"I'm okay. Thanks for your help with my assignments. I'm getting top marks."

"Is that right? Glad I could help."

"I've got an art project to do this weekend. I have to write my name in a decorative font that I design myself. I'm not good with drawing. Everything I try looks like something a five-year-old would do."

"Hmmm." He studied my face. "I see your name like you dance—in leaps and loops. That's how I see your name."

Blushing and struck silent, I looked away. Was that how he saw me when I danced for him?

He rose unsteadily from his chair. "This is how I'd write your name." Crouching, he picked up a stick and scratched my name out in the hard, damp sand. A-b-b-y. All in trailing loops and extravagant curves.

"I love it," I said, trying not to sound half as impressed as I really was. In my mind, I imagined another name beside it. Eisen. *Abby Eisen.* One day, that would be me.

He dusted his hands clean of sand. "I'm going out for a paddle."

I suppressed the delighted grin that tugged at the sides of my mouth. There was nothing more I wanted—ever—than to go out on his boat with him. Because when we were out on the lake, it was like we'd entered our own little world, far away from the world of people who would judge us.

I followed him along a short track, to the spot where he had his boat. He pushed the boat out onto the surface of the sparkling water. I wished he'd left the bottle of wine behind, but he'd brought it along.

Awkwardly, I realised he wasn't waiting for me. I didn't know what I'd expected—but I'd hoped he'd hold out his hand for me. Like in some old-fashioned movie. It was then I realised he hadn't exactly invited me onto his boat.

Kicking off my sandals, I splashed through the water to the boat.

There was no delicate way of getting in while wearing a short dress. I tried angling myself sideways as I lifted my legs over.

Did he see my underwear?

Did it even matter?

He'd seen me in and out of my underwear.

Anyway, we were a couple. It was silly for me to get shy.

He rowed the boat away.

"Where are we going?" I asked. In all truth, I didn't care. We were alone together.

"Around and about," he said.

He kept rowing towards the wildest part of the lake, as he always did. Where there were no houses at all. Just forest. Then he put the oars on the bottom of the boat and let the boat drift.

I hoped he'd start a conversation. Instead, he started drinking again.

"I have a question," I said.

"This isn't a classroom. You don't have to ask permission to speak."

"Okay... Where do you see yourself in the future? I mean, like, in two years' time?"

I hoped I wasn't being too obvious. In two years, I'd be sixteen, and old enough to be with him.

He laughed. "What kind of question is that? And in whose world is two years *the future*? Uh, I have no plans. Except for some half-cocked idea about making enough cash to go backpacking. Maybe for a few years, until the cash runs out."

"You'd go away for *that* long?"

"Maybe longer. I'd like to disappear. Dive into the blue."

My heart stopped and started and thumped. As if he'd taken hold of it with his fist.

I'd dreamed that the two of us could have a house together and he would work while I continued my studies. Frantically, I searched for an alternative future.

I'd go with him—like an adventure. I'd adapt to whatever he wanted.

"How much money do you need to do that?" My voice came out harsher than I'd intended.

He grinned drunkenly. "How much money does anyone need? Money is just shells on the beach. It's not life, love or liberty."

"Can I ask a quest—" I stopped, lest he admonish me again for asking permission to ask a question. "I mean, would you go away alone, or take someone?"

Emmet crinkled his brow. "Whoa. Rapid-fire questions. I don't know. I don't have anyone to take."

He was teasing me. He knew he had me. He was just scared.

He settled back low on the seat, with his arms stretched out behind his head.

I ached to be invited to sit with him, with those arms encircling me.

He mumbled something. I listened closely. I realised he was singing something. Only I didn't know the lyrics. He knew lots of songs I didn't and singers that I'd never heard of. And he was fond of lullabies.

Within minutes, he was asleep.

For a while, I watched him.

Then, like an explorer charting a land, I crept closer and closer. I examined every centimetre of his face. His skin was a light, even olive all over. Not a single freckle or mole. But he had the bruise and a small, angry rash of pimples on his right forehead. His eyelashes were short, and they were blond on the tips. The stubble on his chin was a much lighter tone than the hair on his head, more of a pale gold-brown.

I realised I must have been staring at him for at least fifteen minutes. Like some kind of crazed stalker.

Stretching my spine, I forced myself to move away from him.

The boat had drifted alongside the shore.

Sunlight bounced off the wine bottle. There was about a quarter of the wine left. I picked up the bottle. It was hot. No one wanted to drink hot wine. Even I knew that. And plus, he'd had enough.

Without giving it much thought, I pulled out the stopper and tipped the wine out over the side of the boat. Deep red liquid spurted into the lake. For a moment, it looked like blood in the shallow water, until the current took it away.

Was he going to be angry with me?

I pressed my lips together, strengthening my resolve. This was something I could do for him. Manage his drinking. Just like Nan had managed Granddad's drinking. That was love.

Mum was wrong. Love could overcome anything.

Feeling daring, I settled in beside him on the seat, nestling my head on his chest. His heartbeat echoed in my ear. The sound was a thing of wonderment to me. I'd never heard anyone's heartbeat before.

Cirrus clouds moved in long white wisps across the sky, like ghosts on their way up to heaven. The quick speed of the clouds meant that there were high jet streams of wind.

Emmet had taught me how to tell all the different clouds apart by the patterns they made. In truth, he'd taught the whole class, but in those lessons, it'd seemed like he was talking just to me.

Cirrus clouds were made of ice and they formed wispy ghosts. Cumulus clouds were little powder puffs that reminded me of cotton. Altocumulus clouds turned the sky into a mess of grey blobs. If you saw them on a humid morning, you knew that rain was building. My favourite clouds were lenticular. They formed just over the mountains and looked like spaceships.

I wanted Emmet to wake so he could watch the clouds with me. But he was softly snoring now.

I closed my eyes and rested with him. In the future, the two of us could sleep like this every day, every night. Because I'd be living with him. I couldn't quite grasp the concept of living with a man, but I'd soon learn.

He needed me. Maybe that was enough. He just needed to wait until I was at least sixteen.

Bubbles of panic rose in my stomach. Would he wait?

I worried on that thought for several minutes, until the gentle rock of the boat had me dozing off.

I let myself fall into a heavy sleep.

The two of us snapped awake when the boat hit rocks on the shore. I felt Emmet's body jolt.

"Hey," he slurred. "There's no one steering this boat."

"We were both sleeping." I hesitated then, before saying, "I tipped your wine out."

"Oh, you did?"

I nodded, waiting for his response.

His eyes were unfocused. "Why did you do that?"

"It got too hot, and it was no good, *Mr Lullaby*." The name had slipped out. He'd told me never to call him that except on the phone.

He frowned. Then, he leaned forward, and I thought he was going to whisper something.

But he kissed me. On the mouth.

In shock, I recoiled.

My lips felt hot and somehow swollen, and my head was buzzing.

He scowled at me and swore, as if I'd done something wrong.

Snatching up the oars, he shoved the tips in the water and began rowing like his life depended on it.

PART V

PRESENT DAY

33

KATE

Thoughts spun on a wheel in my mind.

Sunshine spilled in through the windows of Dr Quinley's office, but the feeling inside me was intensely bleak.

I could barely wrap my head around the events that Abby had just told to Dr Quinley.

For the first time, she'd told about the place to which Emmet had been luring her. The old funfair on Lancaster Road. It had been called Tallman's Funfair.

I didn't know how to make sense of what Emmet had made Abby do.

Was there something about the funfair that excited him and led him to want to indulge in his dark side there?

I hadn't thought about that funfair in decades. I didn't even know any of it was still standing. I only recalled seeing a large block of trees and shrubbery whenever I'd reason to drive down that way.

Dr Quinley spoke quietly with Abby for a while, slowly bringing her out of her memories.

After he ended the session, I asked if I could speak with him alone.

"Of course," he replied.

First, I went to cradle Abby. "I'm so proud of you," I whispered.

"I'm sorry you have to hear all of this," she said, her cheeks tear stained.

"You don't ever need to be sorry." I kissed her cheek. "I'll be out in just a minute."

Abby hugged her handbag to her chest and walked out, closing the door behind her.

Dr Quinley studied my face. "How are you dealing with this, Detective?"

"I'm... to be honest... I don't know. I knew Abby was going to be telling about some difficult events, and I tried to prepare myself. But I just never could have imagined the awful things that actually happened."

"I can understand how you're feeling. Some parts of the human psyche can be disturbing to encounter. Did you need to debrief about today's session?"

"Not so much a debriefing as your professional opinion as a psychiatrist."

"If I can, I'll certainly provide that. Remember, I cannot cross client privacy boundaries. I can't discuss Abby without her being here and consenting to the discussion."

"This isn't about Abby. It's about Emmet. I just... I can't get a handle on him."

"The things Abby just disclosed were certainly out of the ordinary. Of course, we have only Abby's recollections to go by."

"You think she might remember the events differently to how they occurred?"

He smiled thinly. "We all remember incidences a little—or a lot—differently to how they actually occurred. You, as a detective, would have come across that many times."

I nodded. "Yes, that's true. Indeed, I have."

"Abby's doing very well in general," Dr Quinley said. "She seems to recall days and events in good detail. But it is possible that she's romanticising things somewhat. On the other hand, perhaps things did unravel in exactly the way she told it. I would need many more sessions with her to get more of a sense of that."

"What do you think about Emmet? The way he kept the Mr Lullaby side of himself completely separate to everyday life. Almost like a... split personality or something. What do you think?"

"In psychiatry, we'd call that a dissociative identity disorder. It is a rare but interesting disorder. It's been found that during such change of personalities, blood flow to the brain can alter. I'd need to hear more of Abby's experiences with Emmet in order to form a better opinion."

"If he did happen to have that illness, what might cause such a thing? His parents seem to be reasonable, loving people—at least, from what I've observed. Could something have happened that they didn't know about? Something connected with funfairs, for instance?"

"You're correct—the things that occur in our formative years do shape us. With the dissociative disorder, a person might feel that each of their personalities has a separate set of memories, with different emotions and opinions. Yes, there *could* be an aspect of funfairs that Emmet formed a strong attachment to."

"Thank you. I know that you're busy. I'd better go, or I'll make you late for your next appointment."

"I'm happy to have had this little chat. I think Abby is making good progress. I've been careful to keep centring her in present time after each session, so she doesn't get caught up in her past. The pear tree is a technique to keep things under her control, to ensure she doesn't become re-traumatised. She is still in a very delicate frame of mind."

"I appreciate what you're doing for her, Dr Quinley. This is her chance to recover and heal."

I said my goodbyes and left his office.

Logan was coming to pick Abby up today. I walked with her out to the atrium area of Close Quarters to wait for him. It was a beautiful outdoor space with hanging plants and a large koi pond. It was what we both needed after Abby's harrowing revelations about Emmet Eisen.

I intentionally kept the conversation light. I sensed that Abby didn't want to discuss what she'd spoken about in Dr Quinley's office.

And it seemed best to leave things the way we'd been doing them. Abby was unfolding everything at her own pace, under Quinley's guidance.

Logan walked in with Ivy and Jasper. The baby squealed with delight when he caught sight of his mother.

The little family of four went off together, to have pancakes at one of the food stalls.

It was almost five in the afternoon now—close to dark.

I had one thing on my mind.

The funfair.

I'd intended heading home after the psychiatrist's session.

But my stomach was churning now.

I drove straight to the station.

After stepping into the police supply room, I started putting together a kit. Plastic specimen bags, gloves, and tactical LED searchlights.

Franco stuck his head in around the door frame. "Wakeland, thought I heard you come back. Whoa, that's some serious gear you're packing there. What's happening?"

I looked back over my shoulder. "I just came from the psychiatrist's session with Abby. She told Dr Quinley that Emmet Eisen lured her out to an old funfair here in town. He had it all set up—with furniture and a big birdcage and a damned bed. It was a difficult story to sit through."

He whistled. "Insane. There wouldn't be much left of it to see though."

"I know. I remember when they came and dismantled all the rides. I thought the whole place got bulldozed. But there are apparently a few buildings left."

"No, that's not what I mean. There was a fire out there some years back. I know that because I'd not long come off the fraud squad. I was still in touch with those guys."

A head-high wave of disappointment washed over me. I'd wanted to see the things that Abby had been describing. If no one else had been in the mirror room all this time, then it should have still been exactly as she'd said.

"Do you remember how long ago that fire was?" I asked him.

"Yeah. It would have been about three months after I left the fraud squad. I'd been making loud noises about wanting to join homicide. You know how it is—they stick all baby detectives in theft and fraud first. You'd invited me to train under your wing. So, lemme see... that's a decade ago, give or take."

"Really? Which month?"

"Would have to have been in February. Hey, I remember. It was the night before Emmet Eisen was found drowned in the lake."

"Wow. *That night?* What did the fraud squad find out?"

"Nothing much. It wasn't an insurance job. The owners didn't even have insurance on it anymore. The squad ended up deciding that it must have been a pack of bored kids. The fire was started with a cigarette lighter. They didn't even try to hide how it got started."

"I know who the owners are—or were," I mused. "Harold and Beatrix Mulden. It gives me a sick feeling just knowing that the Muldens owned the place."

The Mulden family had owned a massive acreage in the mountain area of Tallman's Valley. It had been a compound that'd consisted of several different families. The compound had been raided due to criminal activities—at which time, the carnival had closed down.

"The Muldens?" Franco queried. "I didn't know that they owned the funfair."

"The fire being on the same night Emmet died is interesting. I don't know if there's a connection or not, but it's certainly given me something to chew over. See you in the morning, Franco." I slung the backpack that I'd filled with gear over my shoulder.

He stared at me. "You're not thinking of going there *now*, are you? In the dark? Oh, wait, yes—yes you are. I can see it on your face. Well, I'm coming with you."

"You don't have to do that. As you said, there's nothing left to see. I guess I just need to go there. For my own sake."

He grinned. "You still standing there talking? Let's go."

Ten minutes later, I was driving down to the funfair with Franco.

I called Pete to let him know I'd be late. I didn't tell him what I was doing or why. It wasn't the kind of conversation you could hold over the phone.

It was darkest twilight by the time I parked my car on Lancaster Road.

Franco stared up at the imposing-looking chain-link fence. "Right. How do we get in?"

"Abby mentioned a sign that said *private property*. There was a hole in the fence behind it. Ten years ago, there was, anyway."

"I don't like your chances. After the fire, the council would have made the owners secure the boundary, so that more kids didn't get in there and start fires. Or, if they couldn't find the owners, they would have repaired it themselves."

We exited the car and examined the fence. As Franco had thought, the hole behind the sign had been repaired.

I breathed out a sigh of frustration. "I didn't even consider the fencing. My head is in a spin after the things Abby told."

Franco opened his jacket. Next to his gun and handcuffs was a small handheld bolt cutter.

"You take that with you *everywhere* you go?" I said lightly. I knew that he must have grabbed it before leaving the supply room.

"Used to be a boy scout."

"Yay for the scouts."

We were in luck—the wire that had been used to repair the hole was much thinner than that used on the rest of the metal fencing, and the job had been sloppily done. Franco cut through it within minutes.

The land on the other side of the fence was overgrown with lantana and ferns, with bare spots around the multitude of trees. Before I was born, most of the trees had been chopped down to make way for the funfair. But after its decades of operation, the funfair had closed down. And trees had sprung up again.

Franco and I threaded our way through, moving quickly. The light was fast disappearing.

Hidden from view was a brick office block. And then to one side, a massive circular structure that must have been the Ferris wheel, only it was now lying on its side. We kept making our way through the ferns and bushes, to the main building of the funfair. The charred sign read *House of Fun.*

It looked macabre in this deep light.

We stepped in through an open doorway.

34

KATE

Franco and I switched on our LED searchlights. The searchlights were powerful, handheld torches that could light up a room.

To the right, half of the roof had caved in, just above where the dodgem car rink used to be. I remembered riding in those bumper cars with my father.

Vines spilled down from the massive hole. Ferns grew from inside a scorched bumper car.

What remained of the building was a scene of charred destruction. Fire had burned the wooden panelling to shades of black and grey. The only bright colour remaining in the room were plastic, red ticket booths and yellow police tape lying about.

The air smelled of wet ash and dirt and rotting plant matter.

I picked my way around the bits of plaster and small plants that were growing on the floor.

Abby had said the mirror room was to the left.

I could easily picture this whole place in my mind, as it had been fifty years ago. All of us kids crashing the cars in the rink, just as hard as we could go, despite repeatedly being told to go around in an orderly circle. The clown head machines, where you paid ten cents to pop balls into their mouths, hoping to win a prize. And the Hall of Mirrors, where you lost yourself in the maze and giggled at your distorted reflection.

"Better keep moving, Wakeland," said Franco in a reassuring tone.

I hadn't realised I'd stopped still.

The left-hand side of the building was still standing firm.

I walked down a hallway with Franco. The mirror on the wall ahead had gone completely black. It was eerie.

We walked through an archway and inside the old Hall of Mirrors.

Apart from a few cracked and blackened mirrors, the room was empty. The floor was littered with broken mirrors and thick, whitish ash.

"There was supposed to be furniture in here," I said. "A bed. A dressing table. A small and large birdcage. Things like that."

He shrugged. "Maybe the owners started cleaning this place, and they got rid of the old furniture. It's pretty dangerous in here. Needs knocking down." He walked around, kicking at bits of mirror.

I didn't know why I felt so disappointed. The furniture still being here would have changed nothing. Perhaps Abby would feel better knowing it was gone.

Franco crouched to the floor. He tugged a small chain out from between the floorboards. Holding the chain up, he blew on it to remove the white dust.

I stepped across the room, shards of mirror crunching beneath my shoes.

A pendant hung from a broken chain—a tiny, charred birdcage.

My hand flew to my mouth.

Franco stared from me to the necklace. "Okay, do you want to tell me about this?"

"I think it belonged to Layla Maddox."

"Was Eisen bringing her here, too? Not just Abby?"

"It's very possible that he was bringing Layla here. If he was, I don't think Abby knows about it. Both Abby and Layla were given those necklaces by Emmet. After Emmet died, Abby didn't keep hers. She said she threw it away."

Slipping a zip-lock bag out from my pocket, I opened it, and Franco dropped the necklace inside it.

"What I want to know is," I said, "when was she here? Because Abby saw Layla just before she left town, and she was wearing it then."

Franco held my gaze. "So, there's the possibility that after she left to go live with her grandfather, she came back to Tallman's Valley?"

I nodded.

"If she did," he said carefully, looking around, "then she might have been the one to set this place ablaze."

I chewed my lip, trying to think. "That's an interesting thought. The necklace changes things. She really might have come all the way back to town just to destroy this building."

"Makes a lot of sense," Franco said, "because of the sick things Eisen was doing."

"But... if she hated him so intensely, why was she wearing his necklace?"

"Maybe she had another reason for coming here? But then, that doesn't explain the fire." He glanced at the zip lock bag I held in my hand. "The chain's broken. Maybe that indicated some kind of struggle."

"Yes, you're right. There could have been a struggle. But with who? The drunk Emmet Eisen? Grimshaw had the thought that there could have been a second Mr Lullaby, and that's who Layla was afraid of, and that's why she didn't come back to town. She said paedophiles sometimes operate in pairs or groups."

"A second Mr Lullaby?" Franco eyed me with a hedging expression on his face. "This is going to be one of those times that I've got to say something it kills me to say... but, could the person stopping Layla from coming back to town have been *Abby*? You told me before that Abby was angry with her. If Layla had come back to town, could Abby have followed her here—and they had a struggle?"

I pushed at that thought. "*No*. She would have told Dr Quinley."

But straight after I said that, I realised there was more of Abby's story to come. And, she still might not tell everything that there was to tell. Even Dr Quinley had indicated that she might not relate everything exactly the way it happened.

All I knew was that I was standing in a room that had nothing that Abby had told her psychiatrist about, and all it *did* have was a necklace belonging to her former best friend.

It made terrible sense that it was Abby who came here and confronted Layla. She'd hated coming here, but she still wouldn't have wanted Layla in Emmet's special place.

If so, what happened to Layla? Where was she?

I crushed my eyes shut for a moment, tremors raining down my back. When Abby had said to me that people would get hurt over this, did she mean that one of those people was herself? Did she think she might go to jail?

I stood there having a crisis of conscience. I didn't have to search for Layla. I didn't have to keep investigating Emmet's drowning—his death was a question that no one was asking. I could close the investigation. Put the genie back in the bottle.

More than that, I could simply leave the force. Walk out of this ruined funfair, go home, and tell Pete that I was leaving the job for good. In the morning, I'd inform Inspector Shintani. I knew that Franco wouldn't continue the case. He'd have his hands full with our unsolved cases. And this cold case that was never actually a cold case would go back into its box. The case would be relabelled as closed.

In my whole career, I'd never once done anything unethical. I'd done things that'd skated close to the line—in order to get a suspect to talk—but nothing too serious. But I was rattling myself to my very core by considering something now that could be considered corrupt. I was just one step away from being like every offender who'd ever covered up a serious crime committed by a loved one.

When I opened my eyes, Franco had stepped away. He was pretending to examine one of the few mirrors that was still hanging on the wall. "So, what do you want to do now?" he said quietly. "You tell me."

I took a deep breath of the damp air.

No matter what, the truth had to come out. Like the vines that were finding their way into these old buildings, nothing could stay locked up forever. Not even family secrets.

"We need to search this whole place," I said, "and see if there is anything else of Layla's lying about. There might be clues as to what really happened here."

He nodded silently.

We moved about the Hall of Mirrors, looking everywhere, and then down into the rabbit warren of hallways. There were a multitude of storage and administration rooms. Most of the rooms were in good condition for their age. The fire hadn't reached this far. I searched their floors and drawers and cupboards.

I wasn't certain what I was looking for. A wallet or some personal belongings, perhaps.

There was a set of wooden stairs on the other side of the Hall of Mirrors. Fire had half destroyed them. Police tape hung listlessly from a bannister.

Franco walked up to me from the other end of the hallway, taking in the sight of the ruined stairs. "That does not look safe."

"Not in the least," I said.

"I'm gonna chance it."

"No, you're not. I'll have to arrange some sort of scaffolding tomorrow."

"It looks sturdy. Enough."

"If you fall, I'm calling an ambulance. No way are you getting back in my car all covered in soot. Even if all you have is a sprained toe." My little joke was to cover up the mounting tension I felt inside.

"I'd better make the fall worth calling the ambos out for, then." Flashing me a smile, Franco started making his way up the scorched set of stairs.

The stairs held.

"Looks okay up here," he called. "Bit burnt, but pretty solid."

I hesitated for a moment, then followed him up there.

Franco was picking at a peeling wall with a flathead screwdriver he'd found. "I'm betting this is asbestos. It's probably everywhere. I think we need to get out of here."

"If it is, that might explain why this half of the fun house didn't burn as badly."

He pulled his scarf up over his mouth and nose. "Yep. It's asbestos city. Let's go."

"I'm just going to check out the rooms."

"They look like dressing rooms. They must have had entertainers who dressed up in clown gear and costumes, going by what's been left behind."

"I remember. They did have entertainers here. Goofy ones."

Tugging my own scarf up over my nose, I went to peer into each of the three rooms. There was nothing much in any of them. Just the costumes that Franco had indicated, hanging on hooks and clothes hangers. One room had nothing at all except for a freestanding wardrobe. A ceiling fan was dangling by its exposed wires.

I walked in and tried opening the wardrobe. It was locked.

"Gimme the screwdriver," I called to Franco.

He stepped into the room and looked quizzically at the only piece of furniture in the room. "You're thorough, Wakeland, I'll give you that."

Grinning, he wedged the screwdriver in beside the lock on the door. When the lock didn't give way, he turned the screwdriver and hacked at the lock with the other end.

The lock broke, and the door swung open.

My legs gave way at the knees at what I saw in there.

Franco stumbled back. "Oh, Jesus...."

Skeletal remains occupied the space. The legs were bent into a sitting position, the head resting on the knees. A covering of tight, leathery skin, clothing and pale hair were still in place.

35

KATE

Within a day, I had word back from forensics that the bones belonged to a teenage female. The forensic anthropologist that I spoke to was uncertain of the exact age of the girl when she died, but they estimated it as being thirteen or fourteen. The bones had not yet finished growing. The clavicles and tibia bones were immature. Cranial lines on her skull also told a story of a teenager who had not yet reached the age of eighteen. There were stress marks around her neck bones, indicating strangulation.

They'd found pieces of material around her neck.

I'd only once seen a body in which the skin and hair were preserved before. It was rare. The anthropologist informed me that the preservation was due to some precise combination of elements—such as the smoke in the air just after the girl's death and her being locked away in an airtight cupboard.

I had no doubt that the girl was Layla.

Within three days, her dental records had been checked. Her jawbone had been x-rayed when she was eleven, due to the delayed eruption of some of her adult teeth.

The body was confirmed as belonging to Layla Maddox.

A deep sadness permeated my mind.

When I started out looking for Layla, I'd expected to find her alive and well. But that wasn't to be. Instead, she'd been curled up in a tight foetal pose, deep within the ruins of the old carnival.

I left the station directly after hearing the news. The days in which I was prepared to keep working after finding out results such as this were over. Unless there was a killer to pursue immediately—which in this case, there wasn't—then I was going to give myself time to decompress.

During my career, I'd had enough of seeing murdered girls. I'd had enough of seeing murder altogether. This world was sometimes just too ugly to bear.

And this case might involve my daughter. My mind burned with the thought of it.

I drove home from work and went to find Pete. He was outside. He'd spent the day clearing away weeds. He'd now showered and was out on the deck, having a cold drink and planning on what he'd do in the garden tomorrow.

I'd already told him about the funfair and that we'd found the body of a young girl there. No one else apart from the police knew that yet.

As I stepped towards him, I could tell that he guessed I'd just had confirmation that the girl was Layla. We hugged, looking out to where the last of today's sunlight was touching the hills.

"What happens next?" he asked. "Will it be all about proving that Emmet is the one who killed her?"

"Very possibly. We need more evidence though. We also need to find out if there are other victims of his. Ever since the discovery of Layla's body, Detectives Grimshaw and Booth have been on the task, too. We're throwing all our resources at this. But we just don't know where it will lead." I took a breath. "It's going to be very, very tough on Alex and Louisa."

Pete raised his eyebrows. "Yeah. It's going to drag up a lot of hurt for them. But you can't stop the truth from getting out. A young girl was murdered. She deserves justice, even if the person who killed her is dead. She deserves for people to know what happened to her."

I nodded, exhaling heavily. "Layla does deserve that."

"How are you going to make a start with it?" Pete asked. "Put it out to the media and see if you get anyone from the public coming forward?"

"We'll feed the media some things from the case. About Layla. But Franco and I have decided to keep any possible involvement from Emmet quiet for now, until we learn more."

Pete rubbed my shoulder. "Kate... if it gets too much, I want to know that you'll hand it over to Franco and the rest of the team, right? You're still grieving the loss of your mother, and everything that happened with our little Ivy. And now Abby's revelations. I want to know that you won't let yourself fall in too deep."

"I'll take it one day at a time."

"That's the trouble. That's not what you've been doing. You've been like a bull at the gate ever since Abby told you what happened. And the past two nights you've barely slept."

I tried to formulate a reply. Whatever came next, there was no stopping.

Abby drove in through the gates.

"Pete," I said, "would you mind taking Ivy and Jasper inside the house for a little while? I need to have a chat with Abby."

He shot me a questioning glance. "You're going to tell her about Layla?"

"Yes."

I didn't want to tell him the rest of what I was going to talk to her about. I had to know if Abby had any involvement in or knowledge of Layla's last hours. If she had, then we needed to prepare ourselves for what came next.

Together, Pete and I walked down the steps of the deck.

"Who wants pears and custard?" Pete's big voice boomed as Abby unbuckled Ivy and Jasper from their car seats.

Ivy gave a little squeal of delight and ran to take Pete's hand. Pete gathered the baby into his spare arm and then walked both kids towards the house.

Abby eyed me with a confused expression. "Is something wrong?"

"Could we take a little walk?" I asked.

"What is it?"

"I'll tell you in a minute."

I guided Abby up the hill where Ivy and I had flown the kite a few days ago. A flock of sulphur crested cockatoos cawed with deafening screeches as they flew from the trees. There was only the barest amount of daylight left now, a cold breeze circling.

"Mum," Abby demanded, when we'd reached the top of the slope. "Can you just tell me what's happening?"

I stopped, nodding. "First, I want to ask you something. It's important. I know you have more of your story to tell Dr Quinley. But I want to ask you one thing right now. And I want you to tell me the absolute truth. Do you know anything at all about Layla from after the day she left Tallman's Valley? Even the slightest thing?"

I searched my daughter's face as she stared back.

"No, there's nothing that I know. I told you that, didn't I?"

"Did you know that after Layla left the valley, she returned?"

Her eyebrows pulled downward. "She came *back*? When? When did she come back? I don't understand."

I hesitated before speaking again, looking for any hint of evasion in her eyes.

Reaching for her hand, I took a breath. "Honey, Layla is dead."

Instantly, Abby shrank back from me. "No, she isn't. *She isn't....*"

I softened my tone. "Franco and I found her. She died many years ago. They think she wasn't any older than about fourteen."

Abby gasped loudly, her shoulders trembling and her eyes filling with tears. "That can't be true. *No...* She's supposed to be my age now. I wanted to see her again. I wanted you to find her... but not like this."

"I'm so sorry. This isn't what I wanted or expected, either."

Swallowing, Abby gazed at me directly through her wet eyes. "You said she came back to town? Do you mean that you found her *here*?"

I gave her a sad nod. "Abby... she was at the funfair building. Up the stairs from the Hall of Mirrors. We found her in a wardrobe."

"What?"

"I'm afraid so."

"Why would she go *there*?"

"That's what we need to find out. Honey, someone did that to her. She was killed."

Abby gaped at me as if trying to make sense of what I was saying, then she collapsed into my arms, sobbing.

I cradled her, wishing for all the world that I could have brought her different news.

I moved back to face her. "I need to ask you one more thing. There was a fire at the funfair, the night Layla died. Do you know anything about that fire?"

With alarm, I could see it in her eyes that she did.

"Abby? What do you know?"

"Just... I saw that it had been burned. Because I went there... just after I found Emmet dead in the lake."

"*Why?* Why did you go there then?"

"I wanted to get a keep sake of Emmet's."

"What was the keepsake?"

"Just a book." Her bottom lip quivered.

"Okay, look, promise you'll tell all about that next time you talk with Dr Quinley? Every last detail?"

"I promise."

"Good. Because I need to know everything. Layla's murder has changed the course of this investigation."

"Mum... when did she die? Before or after Emmet drowned?"

"There's a crime scene squad at the site who are trying to ascertain that. But it was quite possibly the same night that Emmet died."

"Does that mean that when I went there, Layla might have been there—*dead*?"

I nodded, unable to find the right words. She really might have been there at the time that Layla had only been dead for hours.

Depending on which way this case went, she might be implicated. It was a twist that I hadn't anticipated.

Horror rose in Abby's eyes. "I wish I'd known she'd come back to town. Why didn't she contact me?"

"I hope we find out. But it might be impossible to ever find out why... if the person who killed her happens to be dead now, too."

"You don't think Emmet hurt Layla before he went out on his boat that night, do you?"

"I don't know what to think."

"He wouldn't have done that. I know that all the strange things about him make him seem like he'd be capable of anything. But I've looked him straight in his eyes. He was a good person, underneath."

"We haven't jumped to any conclusions. And we won't. It's not how I conduct an investigation."

"I know, Mum. I know you."

One measure of weight lifted from my shoulders. Abby hadn't known anything about Layla's death. Of that, at least, I couldn't be more certain.

36

KATE

I stood on the doorstep of the DeCourseys' house, steeling myself.

Telling families about the death or murder of a loved one was one of the very hardest aspects of my job. And this case was intensely personal to me.

The early morning rain had stopped minutes ago, drips falling from the roof of the front porch.

Nina opened the door to me.

Immediately, her face fell. "Kate, what's happened?"

"Can I come in?"

"Yes, come on through."

I stepped inside with her. Her husband was walking down the hallway, coffee in hand. He lifted his eyebrows enquiringly.

"Scott," said Nina. "I think Kate's got something to tell us."

He glanced from Nina to me. His hair and clothing were as well-groomed as always, even though it was a Saturday morning.

Nina showed me to the living room—a space filled with white leather couches and large grey-tone artworks. She and Scott sat together, opposite me.

"Is this about Layla?" Nina asked, folding her arms low across her stomach.

"Yes, it is." I pressed my lips together in a sympathetic gesture. "You both know that Franco and I have been looking for her. Five days ago, we found a body. I've been waiting on confirmation of her identity. I'm very sorry to say that it's Layla, and she has passed away."

Nina's jaw went slack, top lip quivering. "*Dead...?* My God."

Scott put his coffee down on a glass side table, the cup clattering as his shaking hand failed to place it properly. His eyes were huge and disbelieving as he wrapped an arm around his wife. "What on earth happened?"

"We're not certain what happened," I told them. "All we know is that she died sometime in the year after she returned to live at her grandfather's house. Possibly only weeks afterwards."

"What? You don't mean...?" Nina's voice closed to a whisper. "She's been dead all this time?"

"I'm very sorry, but yes," I replied.

Nina buried her head in her husband's shoulder. Tears streamed down her cheeks, her face blotching. "I didn't expect this. Nothing like this. I thought she'd come back one day. I really did."

"That's what Franco and I were hoping for," I said softly.

"How did she die?" Scott asked in a raw voice.

I exhaled slowly. "It will take quite a while to get the final results. But so far, they're fairly certain that Layla died via strangulation."

"Oh, dear God, no," said Nina. "Who would do that?"

"Trust me, we'll be pulling out all stops to find out."

I let them both grapple with the information I'd given them so far. I'd learned that information at these times was best given as asked for, so that the families didn't become overwhelmed.

Scott shook his head, his mouth set in a tight line. "Where? Where was she?"

"We found Layla in an abandoned building. You two might be too young to know this, but there used to be a funfair on Lancaster Road in Tallman's—"

"You mean here in town?" Scott broke in. "That's where you found Layla?"

"Yes," I answered.

"So... she came back..." he said in a lost tone.

A tear ran the length of Nina's face. "I've never heard of the funfair. Why was she even there?"

"You would have been still living in Scotland at the time the carnival was closed down," I said. "We don't know why Layla was there, yet, but I'm hoping we'll be able to piece it all together very soon."

Nina extended a hand to me, her head still pressed against Scott's shoulder. "I can't even process all this right now, Kate. But thank you... for finding her. At least we know now what happened."

I held her hand. squeezing it gently. "I'll let you both know as soon as I find out any more. I'm so sorry. This wasn't the ending I expected to the search for your niece." I paused. "Nina, your father has to be told. Are you okay to do that?"

"I don't even know how I'm going to have that conversation with him," she said. "This will devastate him. And he's still in recovery after having his hip operation."

I offered a sad smile. "When I spoke to him, I could see that he was very close to Layla. I'm afraid it will have to be today though because this will be reported on the news tomorrow. We wouldn't want him to hear about this on the TV."

"We'll drive up to see him this afternoon," Scott said.

"Good," I replied. "I have a request. I'd ask that you allow me to tell Rusty—Layla's father—about Layla's death. I have my reasons."

Nina stared at me with reddened eyes. "Do you think that Rusty had something to do with her... *murder?*" Her voice faltered on the last word she spoke.

"I have absolutely no clear information linking him to that. But seeing as Layla mentioned his name in the last messages we ever have from her, I need to follow up on it." I stood. "I have to go—there's a lot to do. I'll be officially opening Layla's case when I get to the station."

Scott walked me out. His eyes were distant, but his appearance was as unruffled as it had been when I'd first stepped into the house.

"You know, I was always suspicious of those messages Layla was supposedly sending us," he said quietly. "But the Sydney police wouldn't take it any further. Kate, we'd ask for our privacy from the media. Nina isn't going to be taking the news about Layla well."

"I'll do what I can, Scott," I assured him.

I drove away from the DeCourseys' house. The rain started pattering down again as I headed to the funfair.

This time, I walked into the field through a pair of unlocked gates.

A team of forensic specialists had been fine-combing the buildings and external area since the morning after we'd found the body. This morning's rain had made the place especially damp. Small pools of water lay on the downstairs floor. The smell of wet ash and soil permeated the air.

A red-headed woman in knee-high boots and a lime-green shirt strode across the floor in my direction, kicking aside a burnt piece of timber with her foot. She was young, possibly not even thirty.

"Detective Wakeland?"

"Yes, that's me."

"I'm Jordan Smith, crime scene investigation. I understand that you made the discovery of the body four nights ago?"

"Detective Jace Franco and myself, yes."

"Nasty place for a young girl to die."

"Certainly is. Have you found anything of note so far?"

"There really isn't much. It appears that the girl and her killer didn't spend much time in here. Perhaps the two of them were in here barely long enough for the murder to occur. And then, unhelpfully, it seems that the killer torched the place to hide any trace of themselves."

"It's fortunate though that the fire didn't take off in the room in which Layla was located."

"Very. I understand that you have an intact body?"

"Somewhat, yes."

"Great news. Hope it helps you get whoever did this. We'll be bringing in an arson specialist later today to look at how the fire occurred. But I'd take a flying guess that the killer started it in the upstairs area and then left the building. Seems that in one direction, the fire got stopped by an asbestos wall and died out. But in the other direction, it found purchase on the stair bannister—and it ran along that and then into the right-hand side of the building."

"In that case, they didn't get what they wanted."

"No. The body didn't burn."

"Well, I'd better get out of your way. Let me know if anything turns up."

"There's one small thing, Detective."

"Oh?"

"In the wardrobe where the body was located, I found a piece of material that'd snagged and torn on a clothes hanger. We don't know if it's connected to the girl or not. But we'll get it analysed."

"Good work. We need anything we can get. Franco and I didn't notice the piece of material on the hanger."

Jordan sucked her mouth in. "I'm not surprised. Not when you're confronted by the sight of a body in a wardrobe. And it was after dark, right? And in *this* creepy place." She looked around for effect, raising her eyebrows.

"It wasn't the kind of discovery we were expecting, that's for sure. Good to meet you, Jordan. I'll be in touch."

I walked away, out of the ruins of the carnival.

The pitch darkness of the night we'd found Layla wasn't what was sticking in my mind. It was the too-pale colour of the dry, leathery skin still attached to Layla's bones. It was the whitish ash left behind by the burned wood. And it was the dull, colourless feeling I'd carried inside ever since finding her.

Fresh rage burned in my chest. I'd be hunting down her killer with everything I had inside me.

37

KATE

After returning to the station, I wrote up some case notes. And then had a short meeting with Inspector Shintani about Layla's murder and the change of direction in the case that involved Emmet Eisen.

I needed to go find Rusty Zamano now.

Either Franco or I had to attend court today for the preliminary court hearing of Coraline Fernsby, the woman who we were alleging had killed her fellow nursing home resident. We decided that Franco would attend court, and I'd go see Rusty.

I wanted to spring a surprise visit on Zamano—giving him no time to prepare himself.

I drove from the mountains to the suburbs of Sydney. When I cruised past his house in my car, I noted that his work vehicle wasn't there. What I knew about Zamano was that he was working as a gardener. But he could be anywhere, either cutting a lawn or chatting up some woman at a café. As Mr Maddox had said, Rusty was a slippery character.

I drove around the blocks surrounding Zamano's house. I was prepared to camp out at his home and wait for his return if I didn't spot him.

But I did spot him. He was mowing the front lawn of someone's house a few streets away.

I parked and then approached, gesturing to him to turn the lawnmower off.

He physically cringed when he saw me, switching the mower off and wiping sweat from his face with a large handkerchief.

"Mr Zamano—" I started.

Immediately, he swung into a defensive mode, rattling off a string of excuses as to why he hadn't contacted me.

I stopped him. "Please, I have something to tell you first."

"Oh yeah?"

I studied his face closely as I spoke. "This is about your daughter, Layla."

"Okay?"

"I'm afraid that she's dead."

His eyes screwed up with shock. "Dead? Are you sure it's her?"

"We're very certain."

"Oh no, not my little girl...."

I let that pass. He'd barely been a father to her.

"Mr Zamano, we'll want to call you down to the station in the Blue Mountains."

If he was the one who'd killed her, I was hoping my statement would make him splutter and say that he didn't do it. Which would be a good indicator that he *had* done it, because I hadn't yet said it was murder.

He shook his head vehemently. "I can't tell you any more than I already did."

"You were the last person that Layla had contact with."

I was driving my point home with a sledgehammer, trying my hardest to provoke him.

"I told you I don't know anything about that." His face creased, sweat running into the deep lines. "My poor little girl. How'd this happen? Drugs? Suicide? Ah, I should of been there for her. I should of...." He sighed heavily, rubbing his forehead. "I should of been a lot of things that I wasn't."

"Someone murdered her, Mr Zamano."

"What?"

"She was murdered when she was no older than fourteen. We've only just located her body."

His jaw dropped. "She didn't even get to grow up? Ah, this is my fault. I left her alone. I should of gone and got her after her mother died. It's just that... I was a big screw up. Thought I'd be a bad influence on a kid." He stared at me, anger building in his eyes. "Who did it? Whoever it was, I wanna kill them myself. My Layla was a good girl. She didn't deserve this."

If Zamano was putting on an act, then he was a damned good actor.

"I'll need to get those specifics from you now of where you were around the time that Layla returned to live at her grandfather's house," I told him.

"You can have any information from me you want," he replied. "Because if you cross me off the list, then you can go get who did this to Layla. And I did have a think about where I was back then. Her name was May Shee. I was with her for about six months before February 2010, and about a year after. I didn't remember right off, because thinking about her still stings. She's the only woman I ever loved, apart from Layla's mother."

"Okay. Could you spell her name?"

"Uh, yeah? Sure thing. M-A-Y S-H-E-E."

I wrote down the name on my phone using a stylus. "Do you have contact details for her?"

"Nah. She scrubbed me. Didn't want to know me after we broke up."

"Okay. No problem. How old was she when you knew her?"

"Good question. Twenty-six or so?"

"Could I have a description?"

"Red hair. Short. Real pretty."

"Thank you. We'll be contacting you to set up a date that you can attend the station for an interview."

"Does that mean I'm under arrest?"

"No, it doesn't. You're not under an obligation to come to the interview." I hated admitting that.

He took in a slow breath. "I'll do it. I didn't do enough when my little girl was alive. But I can do this."

I ended the talk and headed back to my car. I wasn't sure what I thought about Zamano yet. I'd been fooled by slick actors a few times before. Only, Zamano wasn't slick.

I drove to the nearest café, grabbed a cold drink, and browsed the internet on my phone, trying to locate May Shee.

It took quite a bit of looking before I twigged that Rusty Zamano might have just been guessing the spelling of the woman's name. After a few different methods of searching failed, I discovered that he'd neglected to tell me that his former girlfriend's cultural background was Chinese. Her first name was spelled M-E-I and last name was spelled X-I. Which, in Chinese, was pronounced exactly the same as what Zamano had told me.

I found pictures of Mei Xi on social media. She'd dyed her hair red at one point, ten years ago. That lined up with what Zamano had told me.

Mei was working in a bar in the city, just near the Sydney Opera House. When I called her, she was surprised to hear from a detective who wanted to know about her relationship with Rusty. But she agreed to meet with me at eleven. She had a soft, young voice that had a trace of Chinese intonation. She told me she'd come to live in Australia with her family when she was twenty-two.

I had to run if I wanted to make it into the city in time. Rushing back to my car, I drove off and into the crush of mid-morning traffic.

The bank up of cars was soon bumper to bumper. My GPS informed me that there was a traffic snarl ahead. City traffic was the worst.

A song came on the radio that my mother used to love. An old Neil

Diamond song. *Beautiful Noise.* The song made me smile. I could remember Mum humming along to it when I was a child, while I helped her bake apple pies in her kitchen. Mum's pies were still the best I'd ever tasted.

When I arrived at the Sydney Opera House, I left my car in the area designated for parking on Macquarie Street. Then I tackled the super-high set of outdoor steps that led to the shell-shaped opera house. I hadn't been doing much exercise of late, and the stairs had me puffing.

The clouds had cleared, the sun glistening on the yachts that sailed past on the harbour. An enormous cruise ship sat docked at Circular Quay.

I stood waiting for Zamano's ex-girlfriend.

A petite young woman strode towards me, all dressed in black, her dark hair in a messy but chic ponytail.

"Mei?" I asked.

She nodded. "I've got about five minutes—that's if I'm to have something to eat before heading back to work."

"I understand. I'll be quick. As I said on the phone, I'm Detective Kate Wakeland from the Blue Mountains police command. First off, I'll have you take a look at these photos and tell me if this is the guy you knew."

Taking out my phone, I brought up two separate pictures of Rusty Zamano.

She pursed her full lips. "That's him. Rusty. Okay, what's he done now?"

I switched off my phone. "How did you know him?"

She crossed her arms tightly, as if to protect herself from the memory. "I met him in a nightclub here in Sydney. I was twenty-five and as stupid as they come. Well, I must have been, because I got suckered in by him. He seemed fun, at first. He told me he had his own business. He said we could spend our lives together just travelling. It sounded romantic." She shook her head, sighing. "Yeah, right. The only business he ran was mooching on people."

"Sounds like you had a rough time with him. How long did the relationship go for?"

"Hmmm, too long. About eighteen months."

I checked the dates with her. Rusty's version matched up with hers. That was something, at least.

"Have you seen him since that time?" I asked.

She made a derisive sound from between her teeth. "No. I made sure of that. Changed my phone number and moved back to Sydney. I know exactly when I left him, too. It was my birthday. December 2010."

"Okay. Where did you go with Rusty during the time you were with him?"

"Darwin and Western Australia, mostly. We travelled about in his van. Stopped to pick up a bit of work for a few weeks here and there. And just kept moving. It was fun. Until it wasn't."

"Did you return to Sydney at all during that eighteen months?"

"No. Not once. I think Rusty owed someone some money. He stayed about as far away from Sydney as possible. Australia's a big country. It wasn't hard to stay far away."

"Yes, you're right there. So, you said being with Rusty stopped being fun. What happened, if it's okay to ask?"

"I found texts on his phone—to other women. He was asking them for money. And they were silly enough to hand it over, each thinking he was their one and only. I confronted him. He went down on his knees and begged me not to leave him. Said he was only scamming money from those women because he loved me so much, he wanted to buy me nice things."

"Oh, dear. Well, I hope your life is much better now. You deserve much better than that."

"Thanks. I'm not seeing anyone special, but I'm very happy. I've got a lot of friends. I recently bought my own unit. Life's pretty good."

"I'm very glad to hear it. Mei, could I ask you one more thing?"

"Of course."

"Did you ever see Rusty's daughter while you were with him?"

"He's got a daughter?" Her brown eyes opened wide. "That guy is a box of hidden treasures, isn't he?"

"You didn't know about his daughter? Her name was Layla."

"No, I didn't know. But I shouldn't be shocked. He only opened his mouth to lie."

I showed her a picture of Layla on my phone. "This is her. You never saw this girl while you were with Rusty?"

"No, I never did. She's pretty. I'm sorry she had Rusty for a dad."

"Now that you've seen her photo, I should tell you that you might see her on the news. She died not long after that picture was taken. She was murdered."

"Oh, my goodness! That's terrible." She frowned. "It wasn't Rusty, was it—the person who killed her?"

"We don't have any information to say that it was him. I'm just getting all the facts straight."

"Okay. I'd be shocked. He was a terrible person, but he seemed to really like children. It was one of the few things about him that was actually good."

"Thank you for talking with me, Mei. I really appreciate it." I handed her my card. "If you happen to remember anything that could be of interest, please just give me a call."

After saying my goodbyes, I walked away into the throng of visitors that was milling about in the sunshine.

Rusty Zamano wasn't in the clear yet, but so far, he was looking like a dead end.

38

KATE

I sat at my desk at the station, having a very late lunch. I was mentally and physically exhausted. This day had been intense.

I'd intended on buying something healthy to eat, but instead I'd gone for a small garlic pizza and a vanilla slice. My go-to comfort food when my energy was lagging.

With lunch done, I began investigating the owners of the funfair. The current owners needed to be informed that a body had been found on their premises.

The original owners had been Harold and Beatrix Mulden. Both born in the 1920s and both dead now. The ownership had apparently been passed on through a multitude of trusts and companies. It was a web that was giving me a headache just trying to untangle it. There were scant photos or articles online about the Muldens—and nothing at all that was more recent than thirty years ago.

I was getting an increasingly uneasy feeling that we'd found Layla on a property that had been owned by people connected to the Mulden farm. That place had had a long and troubled history. My own granddaughter, Ivy, had been abducted in December 2015 by someone who had a connection to that farm. We'd been very fortunate to get her back.

But I had no clear reason to suspect that Layla's killer had a link to the Muldens or any of the families who'd lived at the compound. And neither Emmet Eisen nor Rusty Zamano would be a member of those families.

There was just one thing that niggled at me. Emmet had chosen the funfair as a location to take Abby. He seemed to have had a fascination with things from that carnival, such as the birdcage. I remembered the birdcage from the gondola ride. It had been one of the cheesy attractions along the way. A woman dressed in a Las Vegas style sparkly leotard, bird mask and feathers had sat listlessly on that swing while the boat went by.

An image of what Abby had told me about the birdcage entered my mind.

I'd felt traumatised just hearing her story. Living it must have been a sheer nightmare for her.

I kept researching the farm and also trying to find a source for the birdcage pendants that Emmet had given the girls.

Franco walked in, munching on a Vietnamese salad roll. "How'd you go with Zamano?" he asked.

I sighed. "I could be wrong, but I don't think he was involved."

"Right. Is it possible someone was trying to frame him?"

"Possibly. Or, someone was just trying to make it look like Layla had gone off with him, so that no one would look for her. Zamano gave me the name of an ex-girlfriend who he'd been with during the time that Layla went missing. I went to talk with her. She corroborates all that Zamano said."

"Could she be covering for him?"

"I don't think so. She seemed genuine. And she didn't say much about Zamano that was good. I believed her when she told me she hasn't seen him for the past ten or so years—since December 2010."

"Hmmm. Okay. Looks like Zamano might be a no-go."

"So, what happened in court today?" I asked.

Franco shrugged. "Coraline faked a heart attack."

"Figures."

"Yeah. The thing is, she's eighty. The judge had to take it seriously. But everyone knew she was putting it on."

"I think Mrs Fernsby has been getting away with things for a long time."

"She's terrible. Hey, Scott DeCoursey was at the courthouse, too. He'd just finished defending a case. He walked up to me and demanded to know what we're doing about finding Layla's killer. He wasn't impressed I was there in court for the Fernsby case."

"Seriously? Well, what was he doing putting in a day's work when it was only this morning I told him his niece had been murdered? You'd think he would have taken a few days off for compassionate leave. Even just to support his wife."

"I never liked the guy. He's too smooth. And he never has a bad hair day."

"I noticed that."

I eyed Franco's tousled dark locks. He was the opposite of Scott DeCoursey. Franco wore his wavy hair just past his ears, and it always had a slightly wild look.

"Shintani thinks you need a haircut," I told Franco.

"He said that?"

"Yeah, he did."

"Well, it's not happening. I'm Italian. All the men in my family have proud lion's manes."

I smiled.

My phone buzzed with a text message just then.

Abby had sent a message to remind me that her next appointment with Dr Quinley was this afternoon.

I jumped up from my desk. "Have to run. It's Abby's next session with the psychiatrist."

"No problem. Wait, I got something to tell you."

"What is it?"

"I got a call from forensics just as I was leaving the courtroom.

They found that the piece of material that was snagged on a coat hanger matched fibres found on Layla's neck. And they sent through some macros of the sample of material." He showed me a picture. It was a pattern of deer heads with antlers.

"Fantastic. Might give us something to go on."

"Yep. I'll look into that while you're with Abby."

"I'll make this up to you," I said.

"You don't have to. I've got this. Just *go*."

"Thanks." I headed out. I felt bad leaving Franco to work on his own yet again.

On the other side of town, Dr Quinley's office was toasty warm. The sun streaming through the windows. It was a welcome relief from the cold day.

Abby stepped across the room and hugged me. "How did today go?"

"It was a tiring one," I told her. "How was yours?"

"I spent the day with Jasper and Dad in the garden."

"Good." I smiled.

Dr Quinley shook my hand. "Glad to see you again, Detective. Please, take a seat. Abby tells me she wants to talk about her friend, Layla, in the session today."

"We should tell you something, Dr Quinley," I said. "I'm guessing that Abby hasn't told you yet?"

"Told me what, exactly?"

"Okay," I said. "Well, we've found out something tragic, about Layla."

"Oh?"

"She's dead. She was just fourteen when she died. It was a murder."

He looked visibly shaken. "Oh, dear God. That's shocking."

"Yes, it is," I said.

He exhaled hard. "I'm sorry, I didn't expect to hear such terrible news."

He turned to Abby. "How are you dealing with this?"

197

"Not well," Abby told him. "I can barely believe it. I used to think of her and imagine that she'd be happy, having the kind of life that I wasn't."

"Are you sure you want to go ahead with today's appointment?" he asked. "We can reschedule?"

Abby lifted her chin. "I want to go ahead. I need to talk about Layla. I... I've only told you the bad things about her so far. I want to tell you who she really was. And I want to tell you the rest of my story about Emmet, too, because he's wrapped up in all this—the good... and the bad."

"All right. We can proceed with the session." He glanced across at me as I seated myself, to check that all was okay.

I nodded at him.

"Well, then, Abby," Dr Quinley said. "Let's start by focusing ourselves. Close your eyes. I want you to imagine yourself drifting. Free yourself from the things that have happened in your life recently. Feel happy for your good memories. Because you lived them. Now, I want you to reach up and choose a happy memory from your memory tree. Which memory would you like to start with?"

"I'd like to start at the beginning. On the day I first met Layla," Abby said.

"Very well," Dr Quinley responded. "Tell me about the day you met her."

PART VI

A DECADE EARLIER

39

ABBY

I was thirteen when I met Layla for the first time.

I'd been visiting my grandmother with my parents. It was Nan's birthday.

In the afternoon, when the adults were full of food and a few glasses of wine, they'd been lazing about in Nan's backyard and talking about people from the past—people I didn't even know.

Time dragged. I was nothing but fidgety and bored.

Dad took pity on me. "Abby, why don't you go for a walk? Go check out the lake or something?"

We all used to go for walks with Nan along Coldwater Lake, but her legs had been getting too unsteady lately.

I guessed that if I went to the lake, I could put in my earphones and listen to music. Whenever I was at Nan's house, my parents thought it was rude if I did that.

"Okay, thanks, Dad," I said.

Pulling on my big jacket, I walked along the garden path that led to the side gate of Nan's house.

"Make sure you've got your phone with you," Mum called.

"Yep, got it," I called back.

I stepped out onto the street. A chilly wind blew down from the mountains, blowing leaves around my legs. It was April—mid-autumn —and the trees were just beginning to turn gold.

Everything was so quiet. No one outside their houses or walking about. Dad had said that Sydneysiders wanting a weekend escape had built a lot of houses on these streets. It seemed wrong that these houses were just sitting empty, their dark windows watching me like sad eyes.

When I reached the lake, no one was there, either. The decaying reeds and the wet, sandy peat of the shoreline smelled like loneliness to me.

I popped my earphones in and listened to music on my iPod. But that didn't take away the restless feeling I had inside.

My body wanted to run.

I started at a jog. But soon, that didn't seem fast enough. My legs propelled themselves into a race. My jacket and scarf flew around me as I sped around the reeds that lined the dark sand of the shore. The wind made ripples through the heath, running with me.

The houses along the shore all stood twenty metres or more back from the lake edge, with heath and wildflowers growing in between. I kept running for fifteen minutes or more, music blasting in my ears.

I'd never been up to this end of the lake. The houses were larger, with lots of balconies jutting out from their two storey frames.

I could see the start of a tangled forest up ahead.

I raced around a bend, puffing. Two houses stood near the edge of the forest, each on large blocks of land. Their yards were open to the lake, without any fences—unlike most of the other houses I'd seen. They both had boat houses at the ends of their yards.

Out of breath now, I stopped and leaned against one of the boat houses. The forest lay to my right, dark under the cloudy sky.

I wanted to go for a wander into the forest, but I knew exactly what my mother would say. *Don't go anywhere alone where you don't have a clear line of sight in every direction.* Being a cop, Mum's directions were always very specific.

I glanced around. This part of the lake had a stretch of whitish sand that looked like a tiny private beach. I hadn't seen sand quite that colour anywhere else around Coldwater Lake. It was extremely pretty.

"Hey." A voice came from behind me—a girl's voice, with an unusual accent. "Wanna come help?"

I peered around the corner of the boat house.

A girl of about my age was gathering bits of wood. Her hair was the colour of the sand I'd just seen, tied back in a thick ponytail, wispy locks falling around her face.

I walked across. "What're you making?"

The girl looked up. "A home for the blue tongues." She smiled, showing a row of teeth that had small gaps in between them. Light freckles covered her face. "Here, hold these two bits of wood while I hammer 'em in."

Kneeling on the grass, I held the pieces of aged, roughly sawn wood. I guessed that the girl had sawn them herself.

I looked around cautiously. "Where are the lizards?" I'd seen blue tongues before that were almost as long as my arm. All I knew about that kind of lizard was that their tongues were a brilliant blue and that they had a mean bite.

Then I spotted something moving inside a large plastic container. A lizard.

"Is that your pet?" I asked.

"No, not a pet," said the girl, hammering in a nail. "They just need a safe place to have their babies. Away from the snakes." She pulled her mouth to one side as if thinking. "Blue tongues eat baby snakes though. That's a bit nasty and all, but you've got to pick a side. You got to choose who are the baddies and who are the goodies."

I shrugged. "Blue tongues are prettier than snakes."

"Yeah. And they're not trying to kill ya."

"My mum has a snake phobia, but she says they're not trying to kill us. We're too big."

The girl stopped hammering. "I know. 'Twas a joke."

"Oh, ha ha," I replied awkwardly. This girl was kind of odd. "Do you live here?" I indicated towards the nearest house.

"The one next to it. It's my aunt's house. My mum died."

"Oh... I'm sorry."

"Thanks." The girl hammered in another nail.

"Are you Irish?" I asked.

"No, Scottish."

"Oh."

"Why'd you come here?"

"It's a bit of a story. Sure you want to hear it?"

It seemed rude to say no. "Um, sure."

"Okay, well, my aunt Nina moved here from Scotland years ago. My mum was visiting Nina in Australia one time, and she met a man. They had a baby together. *Me.* They went backwards and forwards between the two countries for a while. Then my mum decided to move from Scotland to Australia for good, to live with my dad. I was nine, then. She brought me and my grandfather with her."

"Why aren't you with your dad now?"

"Haven't seen him for years. He left my mum soon after she moved to Australia."

"Oh... So, you're going to live with your aunt from now on?"

"I guess so. Until she gets sick of me or something."

I wasn't sure if that was another joke or not.

"Do you miss Scotland?" I asked.

She stared at me with clear blue eyes. "Yeah. I do. I might go back when I get old enough."

She hammered in a couple more nails and then seemed satisfied with her lizard house. Huffing with the effort, she lifted two large rocks and carried them over, placing them either side of the house. Then covered the whole lot with leaves. "This will keep a bluey safe from the snakes."

"So, which of these houses do you live at?" she asked, turning her head to me.

"None of them. My grandmother lives a few streets away. I'm just visiting. I better go. My parents will worry. They're huge worrywarts."

"You'll come back and see me, won't you?"

"Uh… maybe?"

The girl intrigued me, but she was a little strange.

"Okay, well, I'll see ya around." I turned to walk away.

"Before you go," she said, "what's your name?"

"Abby. What's yours?"

"It's Layla. Layla Maddox. We're going to be great friends. I can feel it in my bones."

I was right. She *was* strange.

"Hope the lizard likes the house we made for him."

"I think she's a girl. But I don't know for sure. It can be hers for life, if she wants. Hey, which school do you go to?"

"I go to Valley Grammar."

"Oh, that's the school my aunt booked me into. What year are you in?"

"Year nine."

"Me, too."

I grinned self-consciously, sticking my hands in my pockets. Did she expect me to be friends with her at school? How would I explain a girl like this to my group of friends? She wouldn't fit in at all.

"See you there!" My voice rose to a squeaky pitch.

Coming down to the lake today might just be my worst mistake ever.

40

ABBY

A week later, I had a change of heart about Layla.

If I was being honest with myself, the change of heart was because I was bored to tears, and all my friends were busy with their sports. My parents didn't believe in booking up my weekends with activities. I did ballet and indoor soccer after school, and softball in the winter, but the rest of the time, my parents thought I should learn to make my own fun.

Layla was down at the lake. I'd guessed that she would be. She didn't seem like the kind of girl who liked staying indoors.

She was paddling about on the water in a kayak. There were two boys there, too, in their own kayak. They looked like brothers, both with wild waves of blonde hair, about thirteen or fourteen years old.

I was instantly shy because of the boys. Layla didn't seem bothered at all by them.

"Abby!" Layla waved me over. "Come jump in the kayak with me. We'll challenge these lads to a race."

"I don't know how," I called back.

"Don't be daft. Just get in. Let's show them what we're made of."

I peeled off my sandals and ran down to the shore and then climbed into the kayak.

"Grab an oar and make yourself useful," she said.

It would have sounded rude if anyone else had said it. But not her. It was something about the way she spoke—the Scottish accent and the twinkle in her eyes.

"That's Cooper and Davey Tecklenburg," she said. "They live a few doors up. There's seven kids in that family. How lucky are they? They'd never get lonely, not amongst that lot." She sounded wistful.

In the kayaks, we raced Cooper and Davey to the spot where a lone ghost gum stood near the shore.

Layla and I got our paddles criss-crossed and overturned the kayak.

The water was ice-cold. We swam to shore frantically.

Then we threw ourselves down on the sand, laughing our heads off.

Cooper and Davey won the race—and would have won easily whether or not Layla and I had overturned the kayak. I guessed they went out on the lake all the time.

The boys paddled over to collect our kayak and they tugged it back to shore.

The four of us sat on the sand giggling and chatting.

Layla and I were shivering and soaked to the skin. The boys offered to cuddle us and keep us warm. It seemed like the most magical thing ever, to have a cute boy cuddle you, but I was too timid to say yes. Layla just rolled her eyes and told them *in your dreams*.

Layla went to her aunt's boat shed and fetched us some towels.

The boys told me they were non-identical twins. But they were still so similar. As well as sharing the same hair colour, both boys had vivid blue eyes and freckles beneath their tans. Cooper seemed the loudest of the two. I noticed him sneaking a few not-so-subtle looks my way.

Layla constantly poked fun at the boys. I was quickly realising I'd been wrong about her. She *was* unusual, but she had an energy that made you want to be around her.

It was already the most fun I'd had on any Saturday I could remember.

Just then, all four of us noticed a girl who was sitting by herself about twenty metres away. Just watching us.

"Is she one of your sisters?" Layla asked the boys.

Davey shook his head. "I seen her before. But I don't know 'er."

I squinted. "I know who that is. She's from my school. Nola Hobson."

Nola was a quiet, awkward girl. A bit of a loner who I always got an odd vibe from whenever I tried talking with her.

"We'll ask her to join us, then," said Layla, wringing water from her hair.

"No," I rushed to say. "I'm not friends with her or anything."

Layla shrugged. "Well, seems like she wants to join in." Turning to Nola, she called out. "Nola! Get yourself over here."

Nola seemed surprised. She stood, shoving her hands in the pockets of her shorts. Then she walked across to us. Her blonde hair swung in two pigtails.

"Hi, Nola," I said, trying not to sound as reluctant as I felt.

"Hi, Abby. I was just... going for a walk. It's a nice day."

Her voice was always so nervous, like she was ready to crumple into a ball and roll away at any minute.

Layla introduced herself and the boys.

Sitting gingerly down on the sand with us, Nola locked her arms tightly around her knees.

"Should have come earlier," said Layla brightly. "We were all out on the kayaks."

"I'm not allowed," Nola told us.

"That's stupid," Cooper spat. "Tell your parents to go suck on a lemon."

"I only have a mother," she told him. "I don't have a father."

"Never mind," said Layla. "I don't have a mother *or* a father. You just have to make the best of it, don't you?"

Nola didn't answer—just ducked her head and stared at her knees. She was a weird girl.

"How's the blue tongue doing?" I asked Layla. "Is it happy in its new home?"

"Yeah," she said. "I bring it food every day."

Cooper eyed her with interest. "You have a blue tongue?"

"It's not mine," Layla told him. "I just keep it safe. I've been learning about them. Reading up every day and all."

"I know something about blueys that you don't," Cooper stated. "If a blue tongue bites ya, the bite mark reappears on your skin on the anniversary of when it bit ya."

"Yeah, it's true," said Davey.

I giggled. "No, it isn't."

"Yep, it is," said Cooper in a dead serious tone. "It's like a tattoo you can never get rid of. A ghost tattoo."

"You're making that up, Cooper Tecklenburg." Layla waggled a finger at him.

Cooper stared straight at her. "Okay, time for me and Davey to put you girls to a challenge. Let's make the lizard bite all of us. And then we'll meet up again in one year and watch for the marks to come back."

Layla cringed, seeming to think hard for a few seconds. "Okay, we accept your challenge," she replied in a tone that sounded stiff and forced.

"Layla!" I protested.

She shrugged helplessly. "What can I do? On the street where I used to live in Scotland, if the kids challenged you, then you had to take up the challenge. There were no two ways about it."

All five of us walked across to where the lizard house was located.

When Layla lifted the roof off the lizard house, the big blue tongue was in there. It looked huge in the cramped space.

Cooper pointed at Nola. "She goes first."

Nola drew back. "I don't want to. What if I die?"

"Blue tongues don't have any venom," Cooper told her.

"Why do I have to go first?" Nola stared around at us.

"You don't have to," Layla said kindly.

"Yeah, she does," Cooper asserted. "That's the rule. She's the last one into the group."

"There's no such rule," I pointed out. "You don't have to agree to this, Nola." I sounded just like my mother.

But Nola wasn't listening to me. Something else had caught her attention.

"I'm in your *group*?" Nola asked Cooper timidly.

"Yep," Cooper answered. "If you cop the blue tongue bite."

Trembling, Nola stepped forward.

Cooper and Davey held the lizard while Nola knelt beside the creature. Cooper reached out and brought Nola's hand down to its mouth. The lizard snapped, biting her just beneath her thumb. Her skin wasn't broken, but it looked like a hard bite.

I expected Nola to scream or at least shriek, but she didn't. She just looked weirdly numb.

Layla said she'd go next, but the lizard refused to bite her. The boys prodded it, but it kept its mouth firmly shut. Even when Davy waved his hand in front of the lizard's face, it wouldn't snap.

"Okay, leave it alone, now," Layla cried, shaking her head at the two boys. "The poor thing has had enough of us. We're just scaring it."

"Nah," said Cooper, "It thinks it's king of the world now. It just fought off five goliaths." But he removed his hold on the lizard.

Nola's face looked chalky. She scrambled to her feet. "I... I've got to go home."

She walked away quickly, nursing her sore hand.

As the weeks went on, Nola didn't return.

Layla and I and the Tecklenburg brothers continued hanging out at the lake.

I felt sorry for Nola, but eventually, I forgot about her and the lizard bite.

All the while, Layla and I were fast becoming the best of friends.

41

ABBY

Layla walked into our school for the first time just after the April school holidays. Her long hair was pulled back with different coloured hair ties and her gap-toothed smile was on full display.

Everyone wanted to know all about her. Everyone wanted to be her friend.

I worried she'd find better friends and dump me. But Layla, being Layla, was loyal.

I spent most afternoons and weekends down at the lake with her and Cooper and Davey. I stayed overnight whenever my parents would let me.

Sometimes, the blonde, wispy-haired sisters of the two boys hung with us. We made rafts and chairs and bridges from sticks and string.

The Tecklenburgs and Layla and I were the lake kids, as wild as any creature who lived here.

The Tecklenburgs didn't go to the same school as Layla and me. In a way, that helped make them an escape from the school routine—they belonged to a completely other world.

Layla and I each had our favourites when it came to the two Tecklenburg brothers. She liked Davey. I liked Cooper. I got stomach jitters whenever Cooper looked my way.

Layla and I turned fourteen that autumn. Our birthdays were within a week of each other. The Tecklenburg girls made daisy chains for our hair. Layla's Aunt Nina bought us a huge cake to share.

The September school holidays came soon after that.

Those two weeks were the best I'd ever had in my fourteen years.

With Layla and Cooper and Davey, I did things I'd never done before. On warm days, we swung from ropes and branches into the water. And spent lazy days in swimsuits. And we laid around in the mud on the lake shore.

On cold days, we trapped turtles in yabby traps and then let them go. Watched the tiny reed warblers as they hid away in their kingdoms of reeds and the purple swamphens splashing in the shallows.

I began seeing the world through Layla's eyes. I never noticed the birds and frogs and small creatures in the way that I did now. Everything was new to Layla because she was from another country. She was always taking photos of the birds and animals. She took endless photos of Cooper and Davey and me, too. She wanted to record everything, because she said that things slip away if you don't.

On the nights when I stayed over at Layla's house, we'd sit on the shore eating ice-creams and watching the herons that only emerged from the thick undergrowth at twilight. We'd listen to the croaking of different frogs. My favourite was the Peron's tree frog. It had almost a comical face, with silver eyes and a croak that sounded like a crazy person cackling. It was pale and greyish during the day, only to turn reddish with emerald flecks at night.

But it was Layla herself who fascinated me.

Her life seemed both tragic and wild. She'd grown up in a country on the other side of the world. She was practically an orphan. She spent all her days on the shores of the lake, examining every part of it, as if there were answers to be found there.

Occasionally, Chelsea and Lianna from school would come down to the lake for a swim with us. But their weekends were usually tied up with sports. They were nothing like Layla and me.

Then came a night that Cooper and Davey challenged us to kiss them. It was twilight, the weather humid.

The boys were still thirteen years old. That seemed so much younger to Layla and me now that we were fourteen. And we'd both sprouted up taller than them.

It confused us. But I still thought Cooper was cute. He still made my heart glitch.

We agreed to kiss them.

Layla and Davey went first. Cooper and I were meant to be next.

I held hands with Cooper as we stepped away to the ghost gum tree, my palm perspiring as I tried to calm my nerves. It was at the ghost gum that we were supposed to do it.

Just as we kissed, my mum turned up and caught us. Mum wasn't supposed to pick me up for another hour, but she'd come early because Nan was ill, and she wanted to go over to the hospital.

I wasn't allowed to stay overnight at Layla's house again.

With the spring break ended, it was time to go back to school.

That was the day we met our new science teacher.

His name was Mr Emmet Eisen.

His hair was a little longer than the other male teachers, and he was *lots* younger. He wore a long-sleeved white shirt with tiny blue birds on it. And camel-coloured pants. His eyes were a deep chocolate brown. His smile seemed to curl onto his face.

All the girls in his class paid attention when he spoke.

He taught us how to read clouds. How to know when the day would remain sunny. How to know when the weather was about to turn stormy.

It seemed to me that he must know everything there was to know about the world.

42

ABBY

Layla had become an integral part of my group of friends, as if she had always been there. We all spent lunchtimes joking and laughing together. Lianna and Chelsea and I promised we'd save up and travel with Layla to Scotland when we turned eighteen.

We still spent our science lessons quietly ogling Mr Eisen.

And Layla and I learned something incredible.

Mr Emmet Eisen was the son of Layla's next-door neighbours. He'd only just returned to live with his parents after his years away at university. To Layla and me, the fact that he lived so close by made it seem that we had some sort of ownership of him. He was *our* Mr Eisen.

We'd see him sometimes, out on a deckchair, by the lake—but only at a distance and usually only when it was late. He became like another of the mysterious creatures at the lakeside who were one thing by day and another thing by twilight.

One afternoon, when Layla and I were riding home from school, Layla begged me to come to a party at the Eisens' house. The party was on this Saturday night. It would be all adults and Layla complained she'd be bored. But there was one enticingly bright spot—the party was to be a welcome home for Emmet Eisen by his parents.

I knew my parents would say no. I wasn't allowed to stay over at Layla's house anymore, so I couldn't attend the party.

Layla and I hatched a daring plan.

I'd stay at my grandmother's house and then sneak out when she was asleep. Nan was a heavy sleeper.

Still, the plan was scary. I'd never snuck out anywhere before.

I surprised my mother by asking if I could stay at Nan's house on the weekend. I said that Nan had been sick a lot lately, and I thought she could use the company.

My mother thought that was a lovely idea.

That Friday afternoon, I packed up my pyjamas and cycled down to Nan's. I watched old movies with Nan, sitting with her on her floral lounge. On Saturday, I weeded her garden and helped her bake pies.

Day turned to night. The time that I was meant to sneak out grew closer and closer.

Nan made me dinner, and then we watched TV again. I snapped a picture of myself and Nan in our pyjamas and sent it from my phone to my parents. It was proof that I was at Nan's and dressed for bed.

Nan went to bed early, just as she had on Friday night.

In the spare bedroom, I changed into my denim shorts and a butterfly halter top—which was all I had with me. I paced the floor, thinking I couldn't possibly go through with the plan.

But then Layla started sending me texts.

Abby, where are you?

Abby, get down here now!

Abby, you're fourteen, not forty. Have fun while you still can!

Venturing out from the pin-drop hush of the bedroom, I stole past Nan's room and then headed downstairs.

I was instantly terrified when I left the safety of Nan's house. It felt like the night would swallow me whole.

I walked halfway to the lake and turned back, too scared to go further.

But then Layla jumped out at me from behind a tree.

She slipped her hand into mine. "Come on, you made me wait forever."

Layla was wearing a short black dress. With her blonde hair in a high ponytail and with her face done up with light makeup, she looked so sophisticated that I suddenly felt like an awkward little ten-year-old.

"Where'd you get that dress?" I said in a way I hoped didn't sound envious.

Layla shrugged. "I went shopping for clothes with Uncle Scott, and I really, really wanted this. So, he bought it for me."

It was as if Layla had seized a big step towards adulthood and left me behind.

As we neared the Eisens' house, music claimed the night air.

We walked on the path that led along the side of the house. I held Layla's hand tightly.

Beneath party lights, people danced in their party clothes. I felt underdressed in my shorts and halter top.

She nudged my elbow. "I know where they keep the alcohol. They've got a bar inside the house. I'll sneak in and make us both a vodka and lemonade."

"Oh... I'll go with you." I'd only had a few sips of wine before.

She shook her head. "It's easier for one kid to sneak in than two. I'll be back in two shakes of a lamb's tail."

She was gone in an instant. I was left in my bubble of awkwardness and teenage angst.

An older woman called me over. She looked like she was in her forties, with buttery blonde hair, a sparkly silver dress, and no shoes. I'd seen her outside her house before.

"Ah, you're Layla's little friend," the woman said. "I've seen you down at the lake many times. What's your name?"

"It's Abby."

"Well, Abby. I'm Louisa, and this is my husband, Alex. No need for titles. You can call us Alex and Louisa. We're Emmet's parents. I think you might have met my Emmet at school?"

Louisa gestured towards a young man who was sitting by himself on a deckchair, softly strumming a guitar. The man was my science teacher, Mr Eisen.

I blushed. I hadn't noticed him sitting over there. "Oh. Yes, he's one of my teachers."

Emmet didn't look my way.

I noticed then that two of the people Louisa was standing with were Layla's aunt and uncle. I said a nervous hello to them. I'd need to escape before Layla returned with the alcohol.

"Tell us about yourself, Abby," said Emmet's father.

"There's really nothing about me you'd want to know," I said, swallowing nervously.

"Nonsense," he replied. "Tell me anything that comes to mind. What do you do with yourself, besides coming down here to the lake? Do you water-ski? Abseil? Ride horses?"

I curled my shoulders inward, uncomfortable at all the eyes on me. "I'm in year nine. At Valley Grammar. I don't abseil. I don't have a horse."

He exploded in laughter. "No horse, huh?" He turned to Layla's Uncle Scott. "Scott, this kid is horse-less."

Scott DeCoursey raised his glass of wine. "I'll drink to that."

"To horse-less children everywhere," said Emmet's father. The group raised their glasses in a cheer.

Alex grinned at me. "Interesting that you define yourself more by what you are not than by what you are." He looked around at the group. "Everyone, we have a task at hand. Abby here has called on us to tell about ourselves—but the twist is, you must define yourself by what you are not. Louisa, you go first."

"Oooh, fun." His wife took a deep drink of her wine, then nodded vigorously. "Well, what am I not? I'm not a good book clubber, truth be told. I only like book club when Dorothy Little isn't there. She always wants to stick rigidly to the book club questions provided by the publisher. The rest of us just like to have a chat. And drink wine, usually. Which Dorothy doesn't approve of."

Everyone clapped. As if this was a game they often played, and they all understood the rules. Yet, Mr Eisen had just made the game up out of thin air.

"Emmet," called Louisa Eisen to her son. "Your turn."

Emmet yawned. "Leave me out of your games."

"Come on, Emmet," said Nina's aunt. "Everyone knows what they're not, far more than what they are. Give us your list."

He locked eyes with her. "I hate... being put on the spot." For a moment, he looked almost angry, but then his eyes focused on me. He shook his head and smiled, like he'd just realised that I was at the party and I was one of his students. Getting up, he lumbered away, wine bottle and guitar in hand.

"Where's he going?" muttered his mother. "That's no fun. And does he have to use the word *hate*? It's such a strong word."

"It's the age, Louisa," said Emmet's father, with an extravagant flourish of his hand. "He's a young man. They're filled with passion and energy and rage. Everything is saturated with colour."

"That's damned sad," said Layla's Uncle Scott. "Our colours have faded. We've lost our rage."

"That's when you turn to the English poets of the 1950s," said an older man. "*The Angry Young Men* they were called. They were all angry. The women, too. Or you can seek out a bit of modern rap. Either of those is always good for some rage."

The man turned to me. "Do you have rage inside you, Abby? Some good old pubescent teenage rage? I bet you have all kinds of secrets."

"Oh, Douglas," Louisa scolded. "Sorry, Abby. This is Doug Overmire. And he's already inebriated."

"Partaking of good wine is always a good reason for wanton drunkenness," Mr Overmire stated. "Just ask my brother over there. He considers himself a wine connoisseur." He indicated towards a younger, bearded man.

The group began debating the merits of wine and old poetry and rap music.

Taking my chance, I slunk away and went looking for Layla.

But she wasn't anywhere.

I should have waited for her. But I dreaded being pulled into conversation by the adults again. I made my way towards the lake.

The water seemed mystical in the darkness, with its surface glittering from the white fairy lights strewn across overhanging tree branches.

Someone was plucking away at a guitar down by the water, just past a dark stand of trees.

The sound lured me.

I knew who it would be before I saw him.

And there he was. Mr Eisen, reclining in an old wooden boat, playing his guitar.

He raised his face to me as I walked over.

"Ah," he said, "I know who you are now. You're Abby Wakeland. From my year nine classes. Are your parents here at the party?"

"No. I'm here with a friend."

"Well, you did well to get away from that crowd. They like to poke fun, but it can get a bit much."

I smiled. "I didn't mind your dad's game. I got a bit tongue-tied, that's all. Hey, I just remembered one other thing that I'm not. I'm not good at guitar."

"Have you tried lessons?"

"Yeah. Last year. I didn't get far with it."

"Well, come over here. Show me what you can do."

As I stepped over, he swung himself to his feet. He handed me the guitar. "Okay. Showtime."

The guitar was big and cumbersome in my arms as I sat on the edge of the boat. I positioned my fingers on the frets and bashed out the beginning of *Mull of Kintyre*, which was one of the handful of beginner songs my guitar teacher had taught me.

It sounded awful. All twangs and fumbles.

I finished my song in disgrace, wishing I hadn't even told him I used to learn to play this instrument.

"I know a song that might be easier for you," he said. "Do you know *Sweet Child O'Mine* by Guns N'Roses?"

I nodded. It was an old song, from years before I was born. I'd heard it a few times on the radio.

"Okay, well I'll teach you the beginning. It's just three chords. And, bonus, you get to keep your ring finger in the same position the whole time. And then it's just a matter of counting up and down. Here, I'll show you."

Bending his head close to mine, he positioned my fingers.

The touch of his hand on mine made my fingers burn hot. All of a sudden, my lungs were straining for air.

Mr Eisen was in a world apart from me. But that world had just cracked open its doors and I saw a sliver of the view inside.

Patiently, he stayed and taught me the song until Layla came and rescued me, a bottle of lemonade swinging in her hand—lemonade that had vodka mixed in with it.

The whole time, I'd barely taken a single breath.

43

ABBY

It was later that night, back at Nan's house, that the first ever text message from Emmet came through.

I'd been snuggled up in bed, my mind a whirling carousel of images and music. And I was more than a little tipsy from the vodka I'd had with Layla.

I was sure the message would be from Layla.

But it wasn't.

It was from someone who called themselves *Mr Lullaby*.

Hope you don't mind, the message said, *but I got your number tonight.*

Who is this? I texted back.

Guess who? he texted.

Is that you, Cooper? I asked. *Are you messing with me again?*

Think again, sweet child, the message came back.

I sat bolt upright in my bed.

Sweet Child was in the title of the song that Mr Eisen had tried to teach me to play on his guitar.

Give me a clue, I texted, holding my breath.

Three chords, he replied.

My throat went dry.

Mr Eisen?

You're a good guesser, came the next message. *Did you enjoy the party, Abby?*

My heart rate quickened as I replied, *yes.*

Did he know my fingers still felt the touch of his hand from when he was helping me position them properly on the guitar?

Just wanted to check you got home okay, he said.

I'm okay. I'm at my Nan's house, I texted. I felt silly after saying that. It sounded babyish.

Good night, sweet dreams, came his last message.

After that, I couldn't sleep. His messages had shaken me from drowsiness as surely as a wind shaking leaves from autumn trees.

He was just being nice, right? I was a student of his. He was concerned. That's all it was.

But why was my heart still beating so fast?

44

ABBY

My head was bleary from the vodka I'd had with Layla the night before.

It was Sunday, the day after the party.

I had a breakfast of eggs and toast with Nan that I didn't want, and then headed down to the lake.

Layla was sitting in her backyard, her hair up in a bun and large sunglasses on her face. She was wearing a new bikini.

The bikini was orange and made of the tiniest triangles, with not much material at the back, either. Totally different to the tank top and boyshorts styles of swimwear that we usually wore.

"Where did you get that?" I asked Layla.

She smiled, waving hello. "I got it on the same shopping trip when I went with Uncle Scott." She sucked her mouth in, viewing me with bemused eyes. "How's your head?"

"Smashed."

"Mine, too."

Layla's aunt Nina stepped from the back door of the house. She wore a floral one-piece swimsuit, cork wedge sandals and a huge floppy hat. She had a tan that offset the pale pink nail polish on her fingers and toes. She perched on a banana lounge and opened a book. I'd only seen her in a business suit or casual clothing before.

She also surprised me when she whipped out a packet of cigarettes and lit one of them up. I didn't know she smoked.

Nina lowered her book and cigarette and looked across at us. "Do you kids want ice-cream? I bought a tub of choc chip in the groceries."

"I'm okay, Mrs DeCoursey," I said.

"No ice-cream for me, either," Layla told her. "I want to get onto the school running team. I need to get myself fighting fit."

"Oh." In a dismissive gesture, Mrs DeCoursey waved the hand that held the cigarette. "At your age, you can eat whatever you like. It's us older people who need to watch our waistlines."

"Sugar slows you down," Layla told her. "That's what we learned in health ed. class anyway. They're probably lying to us."

Shrugging and smiling, Nina returned to her book.

Layla and I headed down to the lake and dragged the kayak out onto the water.

Cooper and Davey showed up in their own kayak. But neither Layla nor I were in the mood for talking. We were both hungover and feeling zoned out. We just wanted to drift about, trailing our fingers in the silky water.

I felt only confusion when I looked at Cooper now. He didn't seem quite as *interesting* to me now as he'd seemed over the past months. He was a cute face with nothing much going on beneath the surface.

The boys gave up and paddled away.

I wanted to tell Layla about the text conversation with Mr Eisen last night. But another part of me wanted to keep that morsel safely tucked away. I didn't quite understand it myself, yet.

We stayed out on the lake most of the day. I kept watch on the Eisens' house. Looking for any sign of Emmet Eisen. Every word he'd said to me had burned itself into my mind.

I was being a silly schoolgirl.

But I couldn't stop myself.

I didn't spot him outside his house all day.

Layla and I made ourselves sandwiches in Layla's kitchen in the afternoon. After eating those, we changed our minds about the choc chip ice-cream. We each had a big helping of it.

Layla's Aunt Nina was still outside, having a nap now, lying on her banana lounge, the book sprawled on her chest. Her husband had joined her, lying in a banana lounge next to her. He was sleeping, too.

Scott was handsome. I'd never thought of him that way before.

Layla and I listened to music in her bedroom until the sun dropped low in the sky. I'd have to head home, soon.

I didn't want to go. I wished I could just live at the lake. Build myself a little house, just like the one we'd made for the blue tongue lizard.

We decided to go out for one last swim.

Cooper and Davey returned in their kayak. We chatted for a while, splashing each other and laughing. It was fun.

But somehow, hanging out with them didn't feel *quite* the same now. It was as if I had changed overnight. Literally. In just one night.

Layla's aunt woke and came down for a swim with us. The twin brothers slunk away, retreating to their kayak and paddling off.

Nina laughed. "Hope I didn't scare them off."

"You'd be doing us a favour if you did," I said.

"They're not so bad, are they?" Nina asked. "Or maybe they are, with all their noise and bluster. But they *are* a little bit cute."

"They're not too bad," said Layla.

Nina squeezed water from her hair. "Well, we're off to see your grandpa, Layla. We'd better go have showers and then head off."

Layla smiled. "Can't wait. I miss him."

"He misses you, too," Nina said. "Poor old guy. He's a bit lonely." She turned to me. "Do you want a ride home, Abby?"

"I've got my bike here. But thanks."

"Race you two out!" Layla announced.

The three of us swam for the shore.

Layla made it first. I knew she would. She was faster than me. But Nina wasn't far behind us.

"See you tomorrow." I gave Layla a goodbye wave.

"Oh, we're staying overnight, Abby," she told me. "We're going shopping in the city on Monday."

"But you've got school," I pointed out.

Layla shrugged. "Nina said I can have a day off."

"See you at school on Tuesday, then," I said, putting a chirp in my voice to hide my disappointment. The chirp caught in my throat. I coughed and hoped they didn't notice.

I couldn't help but feel a bit lost. Layla and Nina were more like two sisters than niece and aunt. I was certain that if my mum had been here earlier, she would have marched down to the lake and gotten rid of the boys. She surely wouldn't have described them as *cute*. And she wouldn't have given me a day off school to go shopping in Sydney, either.

The two of them strode away together, up to the house. Nina was a lot more solid than Layla, but they had a similar build. Tall, with long legs.

I decided against riding home straight away. My parents had instructed me to come straight home or to Nan's house if Layla wasn't there. But they wouldn't know.

I headed for my bike and opened up the backpack that I had strung over the handlebars earlier. I took out a hoodie and pulled it on.

Then I made my way towards the forest, shoving my hands deep into my pockets.

There were a few people in the yard of the Eisens' house. They were sitting and drinking. Maybe six or seven of them. People from the party last night, I guessed. I gave a brief wave and kept walking.

Someone was making hammering noises just past the edge of the forest.

Were Cooper and Davey in there? I didn't think so. When they made things, they usually made them in their own backyard.

I ventured in a little further.

A man was fixing an upturned boat, hammering a nail in.

He twisted around, taking out the nail he was keeping between his lips. "Abby?"

My back went rigid. I hadn't expected he'd be here. I'd ended up deciding he must have gone out.

I looked a mess, having been in and out of the lake all day.

"Oh. Hi, Mr Eisen."

"Hey. You still here?"

"Yeah. Like a bad smell."

"By yourself?"

"Unless someone's hiding in the bushes, yeah." I crunched my shoulders. "That was cringey, wasn't it?"

He laughed. "Maybe."

"Cringe is what I do best."

"Well, I don't mean to sound like a parent, but maybe it's not a good idea to go walking in there on your own."

I shrugged, trying to look casual. "It was just going to be a little walk."

"Tell you what, let me hammer in this last nail... and I'll take you for a spin in the boat. If you want, that is."

"Really? I'd like that."

He cares about me, I thought. *He made sure I got home from the party okay, and he's making sure I don't go into the forest alone.*

The idea of that made me feel warm all over.

His back muscles rippled beneath his tee-shirt as he belted the nail in. "Okay, that'll hold it. Don't worry, Abby, it's a good boat. I've had it since I was your age—how old are you?"

"Fourteen."

"Right. Well, I was thirteen when I got this boat." He grinned suddenly. "Talk about cringe. Back then, I thought it was clever to call the boat, the *Lovecraft.* Y'know, after H.P.Lovecraft. Because a boat is a watercraft and I liked reading H.P."

I didn't know who he was talking about, but I nodded anyway. It was then that I noticed the name on the side of the boat. *Lovecraft.*

Mr Eisen pushed the boat down to the lake and I climbed in.

He paddled out on the water. The sun dropped even lower,

spreading out with arms of brilliant blood orange, like it wanted to wrap us up inside its warmth.

The full moon was pale in the sky. Like the stupid little kid I was, I pointed at it. "Look, the moon's out already."

He smiled. "I've got a question for you."

"Okay?"

"What colour is the moon?"

"Oh, you're trying to catch me out. Just like a science teacher would. Okay, so the moon looks yellowish. But it only looks yellow because the sun's shining on it, right? It's actually... I don't know... the colour of rocks? Brown?"

"It's black."

"Black? Why does it always look so bright, then?"

"Because of what's around it at night. Everything is just a darker black around the moon. So, the moon stands out."

I pondered that. "If the moon were as black as space—would we still see it?"

"Not if it were so black that it absorbed all light. We could detect it, but we couldn't see it, not unless we jumped in a spaceship and went there."

"Is anything *that* black?"

He nodded. "A substance has been created that almost completely absorbs all light. The blackest substance on earth. They called it Vantablack. If I were to coat you in that, all I'd see of you is a flat, black object. You wouldn't look 3D anymore."

"Really? I could walk around anywhere at night and no one could see me? I could just... disappear. I could become, like a superhero that comes out of nowhere to stop the villains."

He laughed. "What would your superhero name be?"

"Absorber Girl. Your worst nightmare."

"I like it. Interesting that the thing you'd choose to do with it is to become some kind of hero. I could see many people choosing to do other things. Like, become a cat burglar and swipe expensive jewellery."

I shrugged. "Seems selfish to have a kind of power that other people don't, and then not do something good with it."

"Like an absolution?"

"What's *absolution*? Wait. I remember that word. They say it at the start of the movie, Titanic. People who survive the sinking of the ship look for absolution because they didn't drown. Or something. Like, they needed to be forgiven for living."

"You've got it exactly. Forgiven for living."

I felt myself relaxing, dissolving into the space around Mr Eisen.

I could talk with him. Have a real conversation. He didn't think the things I said were stupid.

He rowed around the edges of the forest and then paddled through narrow channels of water to a little cove I'd never seen before. The sand was whitish, beneath the low branches of a tree that hung out way over the shoreline.

"I like this place," he remarked. "Not many people ever go here."

"It's nice."

It felt so strange to be out here with Mr Eisen.

Grow up, I told myself. *You're not a little kid.*

He steered the boat into shore and tied it to a branch.

I stepped out.

There were six crushed beer cans in the hollow of a tree. I nodded towards the hollow. "You sure that not many people come here?"

He pulled his mouth down. "Got to be honest. Those are mine. Forgot I left them there."

"Litter lout," I said.

I set my teeth together. That was yet another cringey moment. *Litter lout* was my father's name for anyone who left their garbage around.

His laughter relieved the awkwardness. "That's exactly what I am. Come on, I'll show you around. Just don't go telling all the kids in class about this spot."

"I won't." I followed him along a short path.

To the side of the path, there was a large cement pond that had been set into the ground, surrounded by ferns. Tiny creatures swam in the water.

"Tadpoles!" I said, as I stepped near.

"Yup. I made that pond when I was about fourteen. I dug the hole, then brought over bags of cement on my boat and mixed it using the lake water. And then I made the pond. The frogs seem to like it."

I crouched to take in the details of the tiny legs that were developing on some of the tadpoles. A few sat on the edge of the pond.

A dog barked from somewhere further along the track. I whirled around then. "The dog—it might eat them." I already felt protective of the little amphibians.

"It's not a dog."

"It sounds *exactly* like a dog."

"Come on, I'll show you. It only shows itself at dusk and dawn."

We walked through what seemed like a field of ferns and palm trees.

Ahead stood a place that made me stop and stare. There was a high rock wall that stretched as far as I could see from left to right. Deep crevices ran horizontally, filled with moss and bright flowers—purple and yellow. Light green plants hung like streamers down over everything. Water run in miniature waterfalls on each level.

When I turned to Mr Eisen, he was grinning. "Pretty special, huh?"

"Did you do this?"

He made an incredulous expression. "What—me? No. That's all nature. It's always been like this."

"*So* pretty."

"C'mon," he said. "I'll show you the character that's making all the racket."

He climbed the rock wall and had me follow. "Go slow, keep quiet," he whispered.

We trod along a ledge to where a tree stood. He pointed to a thick branch.

I found myself face-to-face with eyes that looked like something out of a cartoon. Circles of canary-yellow with large black irises. The eyes of an owl. The owl itself was as tall as my forearm, with a breast of fluffy black and white feathers.

The creature stared back for a moment, barking at me, before spreading its wings and taking off towards the lake.

I startled, almost falling.

Mr Eisen caught me.

It felt strange—and right—to have him hold me at the same time.

I turned to him. "Okay, so it really does *bark*."

"Told ya."

He moved back, dropping his hold.

"It's his favourite hangout before he goes hunting," Mr Eisen said.

"Cool. What kind of owl is it?"

He shrugged. "The barking owl."

"Good name for it."

"Unfortunately, it might eat a few of your frog friends back there in the pond."

I winced. "Guess they gotta eat."

Replacing the wince with a smile, I looked back at him to show that I was okay with that. I wasn't some little kid.

The space between us went quiet.

I tried to hold my smile as he stared back at me, as if it were normal to stand in an isolated spot just centimetres away from your teacher, while you stared at each other.

A rush of pinprick needles electrified my skin.

I didn't know what would happen next or what I wanted to happen.

He sighed in an almost sorrowful way, lifting his chin and turning himself away from me. "Okay, better get you back, kid. Getting late."

"It's not *that* late."

I didn't even know where that voice came from.

Was that me? Did I really say that?

"I think it is," he said. "Any later and you won't get home before dark. Unless you pedal like a demon."

He was already walking along the ledge. His long body dropped down to the next ledge and then he climbed the rest of the way.

I stalled. I'd felt a similar buzz when he tried to show me how to play the guitar. Only this time, it'd been so, so much stronger. And this time, he'd taken me away to see a place that was special to him. Just us, alone.

God, what am I thinking? He's my teacher.

But I couldn't dispel the roar in my mind.

I followed in his tracks, my back and limbs so tense that I slipped twice and had to grab the overhanging plants to regain balance.

He was making quick strides back along the path. By the time he jumped into the boat, he hadn't looked back at me once.

As we sat in the boat together again, he rowed silently across the water.

I settled back, watching him row. Feeling strangely content.

It was only then, when he rowed around a curve in the land, that I noticed how dark the distant shore looked. The intense vermillion sky of a short time ago was surrendering to the night.

It really *was* later than I'd thought.

Normally, that would make me worry. But my mind was in a different place. I'd found a key to a secret door and stepped through.

I'd loved the lake at night when I was with Layla.

But it didn't feel quite like this.

The lake seemed raw and wild. Even the wind had a cool, secret undercurrent that was different to the warm push of air of the daytime hours. Night birds owned the lake at this time of night, making their mysterious, urgent calls.

I had the odd sensation that I was flying. Actually flying. The world had flipped upside down. The lake was the sky and the sky was the lake.

Yet, nothing had happened.

Not one thing.

Except that *I* was different.

Different blood ran in every vein of my body.

45

ABBY

That night, just after I'd had a shower, there was a message.

It was from Mr Lullaby.

Hope you enjoyed our trip on the boat, Abby.

Thank you for taking me, I texted back, so excited I could barely type.

Did you get home before dark? he asked.

Just in time, I texted. *My parents were close to picking up the phone and calling Layla's aunt.*

Parents worry too much, he said. *See you at school.*

That was it. The whole conversation.

But it left me breathless.

Over the next weeks, it went on like that. He sent me texts every few days. Just little things. Funny things. Sweet things. Like he was a friend of mine.

And then I'd see him at school, where he was strictly Mr Eisen, my teacher.

I no longer felt like just one of the other students. Because he'd singled me out.

He'd replaced the blood that ran through my veins with something else, something that felt electric.

Today, Year 9 was going on a combined science and geography excursion.

The trip was to *The Three Sisters* at Katoomba.

It was a local rock formation that I'd been to many times with my parents.

I'd changed my outfit about six times before deciding on a white denim jacket, long shirt and light blue jeans. I sneaked eyeliner and mascara onto my face on the way to school, stopping beneath a willow tree to apply it.

The weather had turned from warm to cold, as it was likely to do in the Blue Mountains in October. As if the weather couldn't decide whether it wanted to return to winter or get serious about heading towards summer.

When we entered the two buses that were waiting outside Valley Grammar, there was the usual rush for the seats at the back. Layla had saved the seat beside her for me.

Kids continued to jostle and swap seats and pull snacks out of their pockets—even though we'd been told to wait until lunch. Scents of salty vinegar crisps and chocolate saturated the air. The boys yelled out some rude things, and the girls shot back with even ruder things.

I noticed Nola Hobson sitting way up near the front by herself. She still hadn't come near us since the day of the lizard bite. I guessed that we'd scared her off.

I shivered with the early morning breeze that was blowing down the bus aisle, pulling my scarf up around my chin.

Layla dragged her scarf all the way up to just under her eyes. "Do I look exotic?"

I gave a dry laugh. "Dunno about exotic. *Psychotic*, maybe."

Layla opened her eyes as wide as they'd go. "What about... hypnotic?"

"Nah, you look, uh—" I searched my mind for another rhyming word. "You look catastrophic."

Another word came to mind. *Erotic*.

But I didn't speak it.

I didn't know why that word had come to mind, but it just hung there, as if in front of my eyes.

My gaze slid to the front of the bus, watching Mr Eisen enter and then sit next to Nola. I wished I'd sat up there by myself.

Lianna and Chelsea turned around to us, kneeling on the seats. "Hey, we've got Mars Bar share packs. What have you guys got?"

Layla opened her jacket and showed the stash she had in the inside pockets. "We've got Sour Patch Kids, Snakes, Skittles, Doritos, Freddo Frogs and cheese Twisties."

Lianna whistled. "Impressive haul."

"Impressive *jacket*," said Chelsea. "I need one like that to keep my secret stashes."

Layla grinned so widely she showed all the gaps in her front teeth. "Uncle Scott gives me fifty bucks a week to spend on whatever I like."

"Good old Uncle Scott," said Lianna.

"Layla," said Cody Green from across the aisle. "Gimme a Freddo Frog and I'll give ya a big sloppy kiss."

"In your dreams, Green," Layla told him.

Everyone within hearing distance erupted into fits of giggles.

The bus trip to our destination was short. Katoomba was not far from Tallman's Valley.

Tourist buses were already pulling into the bay at The Three Sisters. Beyond the parking bays, wide viewing platforms stretched out as far as you could see to the left and right.

The school buses parked, and the kids spilled out.

Mr Eisen and three other teachers guided us onto the main viewing platform.

Beneath the platform, the land dropped away sharply into a deep, vast valleys—an endless carpet of emerald treetops. To the far right, a skyway carriage ambled along on its metal cable high above the valley. There were walks leading off to the left and right, one of which was a set of worn, stone steps that speared straight down to the bottom of the mountain.

To the left, The Three Sisters dominated the scene—a rock formation comprised of three monoliths of stone piercing the sky, each a thousand or so metres high. The low morning sun cast the monoliths in silhouette, with golden red light glowing on their perimeter.

"Amazing, huh?" came a male voice.

I spun around.

It was Mr Eisen.

"Yeah. Makes you feel... tiny," I said.

"True," he agreed. "Incredible to think that's been here for millions of years."

Layla tapped her pen on her clipboard, smiling. "Tell us more, Mr Eisen. Mrs Horton is making us write up research on how the rocks were formed. For geography. You could save us some time and just tell us, if you like?"

Lianna half-hid her face with her hand as she mouthed to Chelsea, *"He's so hot."*

I felt a stab of jealousy.

"Aren't you girls supposed to be researching that for yourselves?" Mr Eisen teased.

"I'll give you a Mars Bar if you save us the trouble," Lianna said.

He laughed. "You girls are certainly wheeler dealers. Okay, deal. Anything for a Mars Bar. Okay, so, got your pens ready?"

We all nodded with enthusiasm.

Everyone bent their heads, ready to write. I couldn't help but keep sneaking peeks at him as he turned to gaze at The Three Sisters.

"Okay, so," he said, "the topmost layer was formed by cooling basalt. Below that are layers of sandstone, from the Permian and Triassic periods, over two hundred million years ago. Right at the bottom are rocks formed from between three hundred million to five hundred million years ago. If you want more exact figures, you'll have to look them up, I'm afraid."

I loved his voice. His cool, gentle voice. It was on its own frequency and had the power to drown everything out—even two busloads of noisy students and the hundred or so tourists who were here.

Layla clasped the railing, staring out at the scenery. "It's been here forever. I love it."

"Haven't you been before, Layla?" asked Mr Eisen.

Layla shook her head, blonde hair blowing beneath her knitted beanie. "My aunt and uncle haven't had a chance to bring me here yet. I heard about The Three Sisters, but I didn't actually know what it was all about."

"Well, I'm glad you got to see them today." He grinned at her.

Tendrils of envy crept up my body like a vine, making me shiver.

"They're majestic," he said to Layla. "No wonder they inspired stories."

"Ooh," squealed Chelsea. "Tell us the stories."

"Sure thing," Mr Eisen said. "One story tells that there were three sisters from the Katoomba tribe. They fell in love with three brothers from another tribe. That caused a big battle. To protect the sisters, a tribal elder turned the sisters to stone. Unfortunately, the elder was killed during the battle. So, he couldn't reverse the spell. And the sisters remained as stone from then on."

Layla chuckled. "Together forever."

"Yeah," he said. "Let's hope they get along with each other! As far as I know, that story was made up by a white schoolgirl in the 1930s. She was probably around the same age as you girls. There are other stories, too, from the local indigenous tribes."

"Tell us," Chelsea begged.

Chelsea's voice wasn't normally anywhere near as sweet and syrupy.

"Okay, yep, just one more," he answered, looking uncomfortable at the attention from our circle of girls. "This is a mix of indigenous Australian legends. So, there were originally seven sisters. Such as in the star cluster called the Pleiades, or Seven Sisters. The sisters were the holders of beauty and magic. A man from a different tribe to the seven sisters was chasing them across the land. He wanted one of them for his bride. The sisters escaped into the night sky, leaving behind the seven pillars. And they became stars in the sky. Their coats of crystal explained why the stars shone so brightly. Time wore away four of the pillars of rock, which is why there are only three still standing today."

"I like that story much better," I told Mr Eisen.

What I didn't tell him was that I was imagining that the girls surrounding him were those sisters. But I was the one who he chose.

During the entire excursion, wherever we went, I was watching Mr Eisen—trying to convince myself that I hadn't developed a hopeless crush on him.

46

ABBY

Emmet—Mr Lullaby—messaged me the night after the school excursion.

Hey, he texted.

Hi, Mr Lullaby.

How are you?

Tireddd. That was a lot of walking today. I stretched out on my bed.

Poor thing.

I loved what you told us about The Three Sisters, I texted. *You made it magical with your stories about the Aboriginal legends.*

The legends aren't mine, he said.

But thanks for telling them to us, I replied.

No problem. How's school in general? he texted.

Not terrible, for a change, I said. *I got picked for a play.*

Nice. What's the play?

Romeo and Juliet.

The screen was blank for a while, before he texted: *Are you Juliet?*

Yeah. Crazy, huh? Don't know why they chose me. Probably just because I have long, dark hair. I'll probably flub all my lines.

Then don't do it, he said.

Can't help it, I texted back. *I get shy sometimes and trip over my words.*

No, I meant the play. Don't do the play.

Why?

Because Romeo kisses Juliet. You don't want some skinny, pimply boy kissing you.

I replied with a *hahaha*, but internally, I was as surprised as anything by what he'd just said.

It marked a distinct change in our conversations.

We began talking every night after that.

For hours and hours.

He was Emmet, he was Mr Eisen, he was Mr Lullaby—all wrapped up in the one parcel.

He told me that I shouldn't tell anyone about our conversations. Because they'd make it dirty. And it *wasn't* dirty. It was a friendship. A very special friendship. It'd just happened, out of the blue. We were just two people who fit together like a hand and a glove.

When I saw him in person, it was down at the lake or at school. The private conversations happened only via text. At the lake, I was usually with Layla, though I wished I could be alone with Emmet.

Sometimes Emmet and I talked until dawn. I'd wake up, barely able to drag myself out of bed, and then I'd have to get dressed and ride to school.

My sleep patterns got all messed up. I started not being able to sleep at all. Emmet started sending me videos of things to help me sleep.

Lullabies.

I'd go to sleep listening to the tunes he'd chosen just for me.

Mum started getting in my face. Asking why I was tired and grumpy.

The last thing I could do was to tell her why.

Emmet's conversations with me took another turn—it happened so slowly that I barely noticed.

If I said I got a new dress, he'd ask me to put it on—snap a picture and show him. If I'd learned something new in ballet, he'd ask me to wear my dance costume and video myself dancing. Sometimes, he just wanted to watch me brushing my hair.

It just became normal.

I felt myself entwining with him day by day, like those vines in the forest that wrapped around the trees. I didn't know if it was him wrapping around me or me wrapping around *him*.

I had to keep the secret of my friendship with him all to myself. Except for Layla. Emmet said it was okay if I told her. Sometimes, he asked for photos that I'd taken of Layla and myself. That was just because he wanted to know everything that was going on in my life.

Our conversations became increasingly intimate.

He talked about us being a couple, in a relationship.

It made my heart soar.

Then came the day in November that he asked me to go somewhere private with him for the first time ever.

The old funfair.

That was the first time I went there.

That was the first time I undressed for him.

And then he gave me a gift. It was a pendant on a necklace—a pendant of a birdcage with a tiny bird inside. A bird for his little birdie.

After that day, he asked me back there again.

And I went.

This time, he asked me to undress completely.

He had a birdcage for his little birdie to swing in.

And I did it.

It went on like that. Time after time.

Sometimes I'd dance in costumes he'd bought especially for me. Tutus and dresses.

I'd dance naked, seeing myself reflected in all the mirrors. My face made up with makeup, my hair flying around me.

Sometimes, he asked me to sit on the bed, naked, and brush my hair. And do things to myself.

It was what Mr Lullaby wanted.

ANNI TAYLOR

And then I'd go to school and sit at my desk in science class, my cheeks flaming, and my head filled with unanswered questions.

I felt disconnected from everything.

When Mum asked me what was wrong, I'd snap at her. I couldn't stop myself.

At school, I'd heard talk about things that boys wanted girls to do. Sex things. The boys wanted to pull girls' hair and tie them up and choke them. It wasn't the boys saying it—it was the girls. It was everything they'd seen in porn videos. I'd seen porn like that once, at a sleepover. I'd been twelve then, and with a bunch of other twelve-year-old girls. That was what you had to do to get a boyfriend, one of the girls had said.

It'd seemed like the worst thing ever.

But if boys wanted that, then what did grown men want?

Emmet was not a boy. He was an adult. A university graduate.

I dropped out of ballet class. Something felt bad and wrong about dancing now. I couldn't dance without feeling exposed, without wanting to run and hide myself.

I dropped out of all my sports, too. I just didn't want to do them anymore.

There was a hollow space ballooning inside me. Each day, I felt it growing larger and larger. One day, it would swallow me from the inside out.

47

ABBY

The only time and place in which I felt I could exist anymore was when I was alone with Emmet at the lake. He was different at the lake. Maybe being in nature, in the places he loved, he could be himself.

Everywhere else that I went—at home and school—felt like a lie. And the times at the funfair seemed like something else entirely.

I was glad that January was at an end. School would be going back in a couple of days. The January school holidays were supposed to be fun, but they'd been anything but that.

And Mum had grounded me. The continual late nights and strangeness of the funfair had given me an explosive anger. And I took it out on her. Because she wouldn't back off when I asked her to back off. She wouldn't stop asking questions and she insisted on taking me to psychologists.

No one could help me.

I needed to find my own way out.

Ignoring the fact that I was grounded, I rode down to the lake, looking for Emmet.

Dumping my bike roughly against a tree, I made my way through the heath, to where the path through the forest began.

Emmet's parents were down at the shore talking with Layla's Aunt Nina and Uncle Scott.

They wouldn't see me behind the trees where I was. That was good, because the last thing I wanted to do was to speak to Emmet's parents. The things I knew about their son burned inside me. Like a raging fire.

I heard a voice coming from the boat house.

Layla's voice. She was shouting. *This isn't right. This isn't right. You've got to do something about it. Right now. If you don't, I will.*

What wasn't right? Pushing my hands into the pockets of my shorts, I stole across to the boat house.

Emmet was lying on the small sofa inside, an arm over his head. He was drunk—again—and not responding to Layla.

Layla stepped from the boat house, guiding me out. "Poor Emmet. He needs help."

"Does he?" I snapped angrily.

Sunlight glittered on a silver necklace inside the buttoned collar of her shirt.

I swallowed. It looked familiar.

"Yes," she said. "I was trying to tell him he needs to tell someone about—"

Reaching into her collar, I yanked the necklace out.

A birdcage pendant dangled from the chain.

My heart squeezed tight.

"Why do you have *that*?" I demanded.

"He gave it to me. He left it for me in the boat house one time."

"It was supposed to be special," I cried.

"What do you mean? The necklace is just a friendship thing."

"Why were you even in there talking to him? Emmet and I *love* each other."

"Oh no, Abby. Don't tell me that. He doesn't love you. You can't—"

Shoving her away, I turned and fled.

Layla followed me into the forest.

I stopped and spun around.

She stood there on the track, her cheeks pink from running.

"What the hell do you want?" I said.

"I want to tell you something."

"I don't want to know. Keep it to yourself."

"Abby... I'm going away."

"Away where?"

"Back to my grandfather's house. In Sydney."

"No, you're not. You're just saying that."

"Things have changed. And you don't even like me anymore."

Anger flared—a white hot pit in the centre of my chest. "You betrayed me."

"I didn't betray you. You don't understand. There are things you didn't know about Emmet. He's sick... but he wants to get better."

"I don't want to hear bad things. He is what he is. Don't talk to me, stop following me."

"No, listen to me. You need to hear this."

"I don't need to hear *anything* you have to say."

I raced away.

Dashing along the track, each of my breaths was loud in my ears.

I didn't care about Layla leaving town. Why did she even bother to tell me?

At the same time, the thought of her leaving made me feel desolate. I hated her for making me feel this way. We'd been like sisters. We'd shared every secret. *Almost* every secret. There were secrets I'd never told her. And I'd never tell her them, now.

But how did she even find out about Emmet? Had he confessed to her what he'd been doing with me? Or had he tried doing those same things with her?

I reached the place I was heading for. It was just a small sandy inlet, hidden away and encircled with ferns. Small rivulets of water ran into the lake, spanning out like hands.

No one ever came here—not even boats, because you'd have to get the boat through channels of water that were too shallow and too narrow.

This was just a spot where Emmet had showed me, once. He'd told me he liked to sit here sometimes and think.

It would become my place to think, too.

Finding a dry spot, I sat and dug my toes into the sun-warmed sand.

This was an Emmet place. The *real* Emmet. Not the dark side of him.

My head was filled with confusion over his darker side. The last thing I wanted or needed was to know any more about it. Layla could keep it to herself.

I crushed my eyelids tight. My mind was an engine that wouldn't stop running. All day long, just a relentless noise.

There was no one I could talk to about it. Especially not Layla.

Drawing out the birdcage necklace from under my shirt. I twirled the pendant between my thumb and forefinger, making the bird inside rock back and forth.

This pendant was supposed to mean he loved me.

But he'd given Layla the same pendant.

A cold despair crawled into my chest and wrapped itself around my heart.

I could feel the despair as sharply as if it were a physical thing. Like chains being dragged through my veins.

I wasn't myself anymore. I was becoming something else. I didn't know what or who.

Wrapping my arms around my knees, I rocked myself to and fro, staring out at the clouds.

The clouds were cumulus, boiling upwards. By this afternoon, they would be thunderheads, unleashing a storm.

48

ABBY

It was mid-February now.

Layla had been gone for two weeks.

Mum was watching my every move, like a hawk. I had to come home directly after school. She'd confiscated my phone. I was only allowed online on the computer in the living room, and only to do my schoolwork.

As *if* I could concentrate on schoolwork.

My mother had no idea what was going on inside my mind.

She had no idea who I was.

Being grounded had given me time to think. The things Emmet had wanted me to do weren't normal, even for an adult. Layla had said he needed to get better. But why did he even tell her that? Why didn't he talk to *me* instead? And why did he give her the same necklace?

This morning, trying to win him back, I'd worn my best red dress and I'd stolen away from my house and down to the lake.

I'd found Emmet there by the shore. Sitting on a chair, drinking wine. He'd been drunk, with a bruised face. He'd called me his Scarlet Robin. We went out on his boat, and he'd kissed me.

It'd been our first kiss.

But straight after the kiss, he'd rowed back to shore as fast as he could go, and he'd ordered me to go home.

He was so strange.

In every possible way.

I begged Mum to give me my phone back. I needed to talk to him. She refused.

I hated her, with every fibre of my being.

She had no idea what it was like to truly love someone.

She could never understand the love I shared with Emmet.

Finally, in the late afternoon, she relented.

All day after that, with my phone in hand, I waited for a message from Emmet. Something romantic.

I wanted—*needed*—to hear that he loved me.

But he didn't contact me at all.

That night, I sat at the computer, struggling through a science assignment. For Emmet's class. All I wanted to do was to write *I loved your kiss* all the way through it. And then walk up to him in class in front of everyone and just hand it to him.

I almost jumped when a message did come through on my phone.

But it wasn't from Emmet.

It was from Cooper Tecklenburg. It said: *Your stupid teacher is drunk as a skunk again and going out on his boat. What a loser.*

That was all he said.

Cooper was taunting me. He'd guessed months ago that I had a crush on Mr Eisen. What he didn't know was that Mr Eisen loved me.

The message made me worry. Emmet was drunk again on his boat? That was dangerous. I wished he'd stop doing that.

I didn't sleep all night. Thinking about Emmet. Wishing he'd message me to let me know he's okay.

First thing in the morning, I dressed for school and headed out early.

If Emmet had been drinking in his boat last night, he was probably still out there, floating around. Just like the other times.

I had to help him. Because he had no one else.

An hour later, I found him.

Dead.

Drowned.

And it was my fault.

I hadn't been there when he'd needed me most.

There was one thing I had to do now. I needed to get to the Hall of Mirrors one last time.

Rain pelted down as I rode away on my bike.

The old funfair was clear on the other side of town, in an area where the houses thinned out and vanished, and there were just empty fields.

My legs burned as I pedalled harder and harder.

Finally, I reached the chain-link fence that stood high and stern along a massive lot of land. The grass that grew high and wild on the other side of the fence was being pummelled by the heavy rain.

I rode around the corner to the adjacent street. I pushed my bike behind the *private property* sign and crawled through the hole in the metal fence.

Wet grass and ferns slapped against my bare legs as I ran across the field. Beyond the stands of tall pine trees stood the place I'd come here for.

The House of Fun.

I was out of breath as I slipped around the administration block and beneath the morning glory vine. The large purple blooms of the vine poured water down on my head.

Ahead stood the large, shuttered, flat roofed building that carried a battered old sign—House of Fun.

I froze.

It looked entirely different to the last time I'd been here.

There'd been a fire.

The roof had partly caved in. The double doors hung wide open like the mouth of a dead body, giving a view of ash and blackened walls inside.

Police tape had been strung across the doorway.

Ducking under the police tape, I walked in.

The House of Fun had looked ruined and deserted before, but now there was barely anything left of it. The wide floor that had once held the bumper cars was now littered with rubble from the collapsed ceiling. The storm had washed inside, mixing with the ashes.

The stink of wet ash and burned wood rose around me.

Emmet had told me once he'd found this place when he was a child. He used to come here to be alone. I'd never known anyone before who'd needed to be alone so much.

Coughing the ashy fumes from my lungs, I walked across the plaster and mess that littered the floor and then along a corridor to an archway. The words, Hall of Mirrors followed the curve of the arch. I headed towards it.

Emmet had fixed up the Hall of Mirrors for me before the first time I'd ever come here.

He'd thought I'd be impressed.

Instead, I'd been nothing but terrified.

Each encounter I'd had with Emmet here had been odd and disturbing.

With love and help, he would have changed.

Now, he'd never get the chance to.

Stepping beneath the archway of the Hall of Mirrors, I peeked inside.

Immediately, my eyes watered from the fumes.

All around, the mirrors were now cracked and blackened. The furniture had been reduced to sticks and rubble. Even the rafter that'd held the birdcage had collapsed. I couldn't even see the birdcage beneath the rafter and mess.

The stairs that led upwards to the changing rooms had partly been scorched. Police tape barred the way.

The left wing of the building was all still standing. Running now, I headed down the hallway. The rooms here hadn't been burned at all.

The further I ventured in, the more the light vanished.

The urge to run spiked inside my chest.

No, I reprimanded myself. I have to do what I came here to do.

My heart pumping, I felt my way along the hallways.

I needed to get Emmet's journal.

Emmet didn't know I'd seen his journal. I'd never told him. It'd been my one thing to hide from him in order to keep a sense of control. I'd planned to sneak down here one day on my own and read it. Tuck myself up in that bed and start turning the pages. I'd hoped that maybe, if I read what was inside his head, I'd understand him more. And I'd be able to help him get better.

But now, the thought of doing that made my stomach churn.

I was certain that it would be all about the awful things that he'd made me do.

He was gone now.

Forever.

I would never read the rest of the journal.

He'd been keeping the journal inside a cupboard. I'd found it once when I was looking for the bathroom and went the wrong way. It was easy to take a wrong turn in this place.

I'd seen a slim, wooden box inside an open cupboard. It was the only thing that looked new in this whole building. Stupidly—like a little kid—I'd wondered if it was yet another gift for me.

A small key had sat beside the box. I'd opened the box and found the journal.

Down this end of the building, the odour from the bathroom wafted through the dark air. The toilet had never worked, of course. That one time I'd used it, I'd had to go and get a bucket of water from the water tank outside and pour water into the toilet.

The cupboard inside the supply room was locked. I smashed it with a piece of wood. The wooden box was sitting on the shelf. I picked it up and shook it. The journal was safely inside.

I didn't know where the key was. I didn't care.

Opening my backpack, I put the box safely inside it.

I stared around now, feeling almost trapped.

Rain drummed down hard on the roof, so hard it seemed that it could crash through and flood this place.

When I stepped back outside, the rain had stopped. I rode to school and kept the journal in my backpack all day, never letting my bag out of sight once.

After school, I skipped soccer practice and rode back to the lake.

I stowed my bike and then started running into the forest. I stopped at the point where the kayaks were stacked and chose one of the lightest of them. Dragging it, I took it into the water.

It almost felt good to be paddling out on the lake. I'd been wound up as tight as a rusted clockwork monkey I'd once found at the funfair. The windup key had been stuck. All day long, I'd felt like that toy. Mechanical and tight and useless.

But now, it seemed like I was unspooling.

Twice I stopped paddling, thinking I'd heard something splashing behind me. But each time I jerked my head around, there was nothing.

My lungs felt raw by the time I found the place I was looking for.

Just beyond a mass of ferns and palm trees, a natural rock wall rose high from the ground, with bright green weeping plants cascading over deep cave-like crevices. Flowers grew in the crevices, constantly watered by the drips that ran down.

This was the place where Emmet had shown me the barking owl. It used to sit in a tree next to the wall and bark like a dog.

I climbed the wall, finding a completely dry spot where the water didn't run.

In my hurry, I slipped and skinned my leg from the shin bone right up to my knee. I barely felt the pain.

Shrugging my school bag from my shoulders, I set it down and then retrieved the narrow wooden box.

I climbed inside the dark crevice, as far as I could go before I began to feel the rock squeezing me. It smelled of soil and moss in there. I pushed the box in.

Then, taking off the necklace from around my neck, I slid that in, too.

As I tried to wriggle out again, my hips stuck.

Panic whipped up inside me.

No one would ever find me here. Not until I was nothing but bones.

Something Dad had said to me once, when I was six, flashed in my panicked mind. I'd hidden under a freestanding wardrobe of Nan's and found myself unable to move.

You got yourself in there, Abby. You can get yourself out.

That was what he'd told me.

I'd tried to back out from the cave the wrong way, that was all.

Pushing with my hands, I found a different angle and slid myself back.

Exhausted, I crawled out and onto a rock ledge and sat there. I dusted the gritty dirt from my hands. The scrape on my leg was filled with gritty dirt, too. I'd have to wash it before I went home.

From this high vantage point, glimpses of the lake peeked through the foliage.

The lake streamed quietly past, unconcerned that it had drowned Emmet Eisen last night and carried him along on its current. The lake had no care that it had held a human in its watery field of yellow bladderwort.

I knew exactly what Emmet would think of that. He'd say that the bladderwort was just doing its thing. He'd once told me that the bladderwort trapped small aquatic creatures and fed on them. He'd said it was just part of the cycle of life in the lake.

Everything fed on something else.

From the largest animal to the smallest animal or plant.

I began sobbing before I realised my face had already been wet with tears.

This had been the only time all day I could let myself sit and cry.

Once I started, I didn't think the tears would ever end.

PART VII

PRESENT DAY

49

KATE

Abby's revelations had left me reeling yet again.

It had been brutal to watch and listen to. She looked for all the world like someone who was crawling up the walls of her mind, searching for escape.

Dr Quinley began speaking to her. "Abby, I want you to walk down the hill and away from the memory tree. Your basket of memories is full now. The tree is much, much lighter. Can you sense that?"

She breathed slowly.

"Abby?" he said, "are you all right?"

Her eyes snapped open. "I feel... bad. Because of all the things I did. Why didn't I know it was wrong? And I hurt Layla so badly. And I can't make it up to her. She knew about Emmet, and she tried to tell me. But I refused to listen."

"You didn't know what you didn't know," Dr Quinley told her soothingly. "And you were just fourteen. Part of therapy is learning to forgive yourself. We still have a long road to go. For now, I want to acknowledge that you made the memory tree lighter. In place of the fruit you picked, the same memories will grow, but without judgment and fear. I will teach you how to do that over our next few sessions."

Today's session was done.

I walked Abby outside, then went to get her and myself a coffee. We sat in her car together, letting the hot drinks warm us. The wind blew gum nuts from the overhead trees across the windscreen.

"I'm proud of you," I told her.

"You have no reason to be."

"You're wrong. I have every reason."

Her expression was edged with disbelief as she turned to me. "I was so damned stupid. It's hard to even accept that I was the girl I was telling about."

"You were in the hands of a master manipulator. I hope, in time, you come to see that."

"I don't know if I can ever forgive myself. I just hope that something I told helps you to find out who killed Layla. I told Dr Quinley every little thing I could remember."

"You look absolutely drained, honey."

She was shaken, pale. I wanted to wrap her up and protect her, tell her that she never, ever needed to say another word about any of it.

But the detective in me won out.

I wanted Eisen's journal. And to get it, I would need Abby to tell me exactly where it was. If the journal was a real and accurate account of what had happened over that year, then it might tell me everything I needed to know.

"Abby, there's somewhere I need to go right now," I told her. "I'll see you back at home."

She gazed at me with her large eyes. "I know... I know exactly where you want to go."

"How do you—?"

"I'm *your* daughter, Mum. You don't grow up with a detective as a mother without starting to put some things together. You're planning on going to get Emmet's journal."

I nodded. "That's exactly what I'm planning to do."

"Well," she said. "Then let's go."

"What? No. I'll give you some paper, and I'll get you to draw me a map."

"We're wasting daylight."

"Abby, you don't need to do this."

"You're wrong again. I do."

There was a determined set to her mouth.

"You've just been through an hour of sitting with Dr Quinley. I don't think—"

"If you're not going to drive, then get out of the way, and I'll do it."

She wasn't being rude. She simply meant business.

"I'll drive," I told her.

I pulled the car out of the parking bay and into the direction of the lake.

When we reached our destination, I parked right at the end of the street, in a small area just past the Eisens' house.

Louisa Eisen was out on her balcony. She watched as Abby and I walked together along the path that led to the forest. She had her arms crossed, and she looked angry that we were even here.

The wind was whipping across the water, making patterns of ripples and whirls.

Abby strode ahead of me, looking among the assortment of old kayaks and boats that were piled up.

"We don't want to pick the wrong one. Trust me on that," she said.

I shuddered, thinking about the episode Abby had told Dr Quinley, in which the boat she'd taken out had sunk.

She met my eyes with a despondent look. "They're all wrecked. I don't think anyone's been using them since Emmet died."

"I'm guessing you're right." Crouching, I pulled at the network of grass runners that lassoed them tight to the ground. The metal boats all seemed to have holes rusted into them, and the fibreglass kayaks hadn't fared much better—all of them sporting deep cracks.

Abby scrutinised an orange kayak closely, rolling it right-side up. Two plastic oars were clipped inside it. "This one's cracked, but it's not too bad. Anyway, if we stay close to shore, we'll be okay. If it sinks, we swim."

It seemed that she was going to let nothing stop her.

We carried the kayak down to the shore. As we set it into the water, the wind battled against us.

"Let's go," Abby said.

Leaving our socks and shoes behind, we climbed in and started paddling.

It didn't take long for my muscles to start protesting the unfamiliar motion. I hadn't rowed a boat since I was in my forties. Abby was better at it, but she was young. She slipped easily into a paddling pattern, even though she probably hadn't been out on the lake since she was fourteen.

Coldwater Lake looked incredibly wide once you were out on it. An image built itself in my mind of Abby out on this lake with Emmet. It must have been heady stuff for a young teenager.

The twenty-four-year old Abby was a force to reckon with. She had a serious expression fixed on her face as she steadily paddled along the shoreline.

The wind was slowing down our progress and making paddling a chore. I could already tell my back and shoulders were going to ache tonight.

Ghost gums lined the shore up ahead. Narrow inlets led to hidden parts.

Abby steered the kayak expertly towards an inlet and kept paddling. She surveyed the scenery, as if trying to remember which way to head. "It looks different. I should have expected that, but I didn't."

I kept quiet as she took over the paddling. I sensed she was feeling her way, examining the trees and trying to find anything that was familiar.

She brought the kayak into a narrow channel. We were protected from the wind here—a welcome relief. My ears already felt frozen.

I glanced around. Birds hopped and chatted in the trees. The last spots of sunlight glittered on the ferns and palms. It really was its own little world here.

"It's very pretty," I commented.

"Yeah. I used to love coming here." She manoeuvred the boat into another even narrower channel. She pointed at a large tree. "This is where we get out. There used to be a sandy bank near that tree, but it's underwater now."

"Got it."

Abby jumped out, taking the frayed rope and tying it to a low, overhanging branch. She turned her head. "You okay? The ground under the water is a bit soft here—like quicksand. Take big steps and don't get stuck, okay?"

I nodded, climbing from the boat. My feet did indeed sink straight down past my ankles. I trudged to the shore, feeling out of my element.

Abby gestured towards what just looked like a bunch of ferns. "This way. There used to be a track here. But it's overgrown."

I started after her through the dense undergrowth.

"Wait," I said, fetching two sticks. "Just in case of snakes. We can make some noise. Scare them off."

She half-smiled, taking one of the sticks. "They're more scared of us than we are of them. Well, except for *you*."

Abby knew I had a thing about snakes. It'd amused her since she was a child. She was a lot like her father in that respect.

"Okay, okay," I said wryly. "Let's keep moving, huh?"

We continued on, rattling the ferns with our sticks as we went.

I noticed a manmade concrete pond on one side. Only, it had cracked and gone dry and become covered in moss.

Abby didn't waver from the path she was on, even though there was no longer any sign of it. She seemed to know just by the trees which way to go. There was also no sign of the crumbling, anxious person she'd been in Dr Quinley's office over the past few days.

A wall of rock blocked our way, reaching about five metres high. Plants cascaded down. Abby ran to the wall and deftly began climbing it.

I followed, scrambling up behind her.

"This is it," she told me. "Emmet's special place." She pointed to the right, at a thick tree. "There used to be an owl that liked to perch up in that tree at twilight. Sounded like a barking dog."

I exchanged glances with my daughter. No words were needed. She'd had this secret life I'd known nothing about.

I took a sweeping look across a network of large, deep crevices. "This is where you put the journal?"

"Yes." She climbed to where there was a deep space above a rock ledge. She tore away at the vines that covered it, then began squeezing herself inside the cave.

"Careful," I called.

"I know," she said, her voice echoing inside the small cave. "Snakes."

Reaching into her pocket, she retrieved her phone and switched on the light.

She moved the beam from side to side.

She wriggled back out, a look of shock on her face. "Mum... it's gone."

"Are you sure?"

"Very sure. I don't understand. No one could have found it."

She held something up—a necklace. "There was just this."

It was a birdcage pendant on a chain, encrusted with dirt.

"That might end up being helpful," I said. "Okay, do you mind if I see if I can find the journal?"

"Go for it."

Taking her phone, I used the light to look into the cave. Deep inside, it was bone dry. Unless you crawled in and looked around a corner, you couldn't see all of it. It was the perfect spot to hide something. But there was nothing there.

I hid my disappointment as I slid out and turned to Abby. "Could it be one of the other little caves?"

"No, it was this one. Next to the owl's tree."

Together, Abby and I checked the other crevices, anyway.

They were all empty.

Wiping dirt from my brow, I shot Abby a tight smile. "Well, it *has* been a lot of years. I guess kids could have climbed all over these rocks. Maybe one of them climbed inside the cave where you left the journal and found it. And then tossed it in the lake or something. In which case, the journal would be wrecked."

"I hope whoever found it didn't open the box. I never wanted anyone to read that journal. God, imagine if it was Cooper or Davey Tecklenburg—or one of *them*."

"If it helps, I think those boys were more interested in their dirt bikes and fishing than exploring the bushland. At least, that's the impression I got when I talked to that family ten years ago."

"I think you're right. If Cooper had read that journal, he wouldn't have been able to keep it to himself for a minute. He works at the same mechanics shop that Logan does, now. He's got a girlfriend and a baby. Davey went into the army."

"Sounds like they're doing well. They seemed like pretty resourceful boys."

She sighed. "Mum?"

"Yes?"

"In your opinion, do you really think some kid found the journal accidentally?"

I hesitated. Abby was asking for my professional opinion, not some reassurance from me as a mother. I shook my head. "It's highly unlikely. This spot is not easy to get to and not easy to find. I mean, it's possible. But then to crawl inside that exact crevice far enough to find a wooden box? It's still possible, but the odds are against it."

"So... what are you thinking? What happened to Emmet's journal?"

I bit down firmly on my lower lip, hating the picture that formed in my mind. "The most likely scenario, Abby, is that someone followed you at the time that you placed the journal here."

She stared back. "But no one even knew about that journal. Except for Layla... and she was in Sydney at the time I hid the journal." Abby's face crumpled in despair. "No... at that time, she was dead."

I reached for her hand at seeing the pain in her eyes. "Honey... yes, poor little Layla was dead the morning you hid that journal. It couldn't have been her. But... what did you tell her—about the journal and about Emmet? What did she know?"

"She knew that I had a relationship with Emmet. I didn't tell her a lot. I didn't tell her about the strange stuff. I was too ashamed. I could tell that she really liked Emmet. She used to talk to him a lot, down at the lake. I hated that. I told her that Emmet was keeping a journal down at the old funfair. I told her he'd been writing all about his life and about me in it, and that I was the only one he trusted to read it. That was a lie, but I wanted her to keep her distance from him."

"Okay. Well, I'll keep thinking on this and see what I can figure out."

In truth, all I had were fistfuls of loose ends.

Without the journal, I needed to find another way to tie up those loose ends and discover who hit Emmet that day, and who killed Layla and locked her body inside that wardrobe.

50

KATE

Franco had his head down, peering closely at images on his laptop. Coffee in one hand. Bagel in the other.

It was unusual to see him at work this early.

I startled him as I walked up close. "What's got your interest, Franco?"

Glancing up at me, he pointed at the screen. "It's the protest rallies of ten years back. At Close Quarters."

"Protests?"

"Yeah. I was doing some lateral thinking this morning. About Emmet Eisen. I did some digging, trying to look up any old interests of his. You know, sports clubs, hobbies. Anything that might lead to someone who knew him well—maybe even the guy he had the fight with the day he drowned."

"Okay. So, what did you find?"

"Something bizarre. Hear me out. So, okay, Eisen was involved with the group who were protesting the building of the Close Quarters development. And Eisen, for whatever reason, wasn't happy about that."

"Really?" I bent to inspect the screen. There was a newspaper image of a straggly group of about twenty people holding handmade protest signs. "Hmmm, I don't see Emmet."

He bit off a mouthful of bagel. "Look closer."

"Unless he's the size of an ant in that photo, he's not there."

"You need better glasses." Franco jabbed a finger at the screen, indicating at the wall on the other side of a chain-link safety fence.

I shot him a withering look, swiping the screen to enlarge it. There was spray painted lettering on the wall. It was difficult to make out the wording, as it was in the distance and partly obscured by the chain-link fence in the foreground. But I could see the word GOODBYE, followed by the letters L-U-L-L-A. If I tried to imagine what was behind the fencing, I could figure out what the rest of it said. L-U-L-L-A-B-Y.

GOODBYE LULLABY.

"What in the actual?" I exclaimed.

Franco sipped his coffee, an annoyingly sage expression on his face, as if waiting for me to catch up. "Now, look to the far right."

I swept my gaze across the screen. A man was walking away from the scene. I enlarged the picture again. He had a spray paint can in his fist. I could also see his face clearly in close-up. The man was Emmet Eisen.

Franco sat back, chewing on his bagel. "So, what do you make of that?"

"I'm... astounded, quite frankly. Close Quarters was bringing in a large tech facility to town. Why on earth would a science teacher protest *that*? He went to a lot of trouble to write that message, on the other side of the barrier. But why? And why would he advertise his secret name like that?"

"Maybe the guy was a narcissist." Franco shrugged. "For his own reasons, he wanted the development stopped. So, that's a message to say that he—Mr Lullaby—will make it go goodbye."

"That's possible. But it's a risky thing to do. I mean, Emmet was really putting himself out there and publicly connecting himself with that name."

266

"Except that no one noticed," Franco commented, bringing up a second picture. "This is the same scene taken on that same day. The protesters are still there. But Eisen's message on the wall is gone."

"So it is. Well, they certainly got rid of it quickly." I checked the date that the photographs were taken. "Okay, so this was just a week before Eisen died. His behaviour was growing more erratic at that time. Drinking heavily. Arguments. And this too—spray painting his secret name onto the wall of Close Quarters."

"Here's an idea," said Franco, straightening in his chair. "If we go back to the thought of Eisen being a narcissist, then he could have been broadcasting a message to Abby. Like a secret message meant only for her. The risk might have just added to the appeal of it."

"Hmmm. If so, what does the message mean? *Goodbye* means he's going away, right? Maybe he was planning on leaving town. Or, did he know he was going to die? Was the drowning a suicide, after all?"

Franco scrolled through a dozen or more other images from the protests. The pictures were taken on different days, over weeks. "Apart from that one photo," he said, "there doesn't seem to be a single other image of him joining in with the protests."

He twisted his mouth, raising his eyes to me. "I think we can agree that one thing is certain. Eisen wasn't there to protest about the building of Close Quarters. He was there for other reasons."

"I'll ask Abby and see if she can shed any light on that message. Could you send the photos through to me?"

"Sure thing. Hey, how's the shrink sessions going for her?"

"It's intense. Super intense. But she's getting through it."

"What about mama cat? How is *she* doing?"

"Mama cat is digging all her claws into the armrests while listening. It's not an easy listen by any means."

"I know you," he said. "You want someone to fight, but there's no one to fight, because one offender is dead, and he might end up being the only offender in this case. You've got nowhere to put all that fight."

"That's exactly what it feels like. I've got a ball of nervous energy bouncing around inside me. Franco, yesterday I thought I'd get my hands on a journal that Eisen wrote. But it's missing."

"Say what?"

"During the psych session, Abby told about a diary that Eisen was writing in the months before he died. Abby said she went to get it from the funfair just after she found him dead in the lake. She kept it with her all day at school—and then after school, she hid it in a small cave near the lake."

Franco made a low whistle. "She did *all that* after finding the teacher *dead*? She was just a kid. I've got to hand it to your daughter, Wakeland. She's got nerves of steel."

"You know, she really does. After his death, she found a way to put herself back together. I don't know how she did it."

The muscles beneath his eyes tensed, and he hushed his voice. "What you said before just sank in. If Abby went to the funfair that morning, then she was there literally just *hours* after the fire... which means she was there just hours after Layla died."

"Yes. It doesn't look good for her. I was going to talk to you about that. I'm fully aware that this might implicate her. But I'm confident she knew nothing about what happened with Layla."

He didn't speak for a moment, drumming his fingers lightly on the desk, a conflicted expression on his face. "Wakeland, is this the point that you should hand the case over to the team? If Abby was at the scene, even in the hours afterwards, that's dicey."

I drew a heavy breath. "I know it doesn't look good." I rubbed my temples, trying to think on my feet. "Franco, I really need to stay on this case. You know full well that it might end up going nowhere, due to the length of time that's passed. I want to make sure that doesn't happen."

He looked over his shoulder and around the office, making sure no one was in earshot. "Yeah, I know. That's true. But step back and take a good look at this. There was already a conflict of interests here. But it's just entered another level. When it comes to Abby, you're a mother first and a detective second."

"Are you telling Shintani?"

"I should."

"I understand."

"You do?"

"Of course, I do. I've been thinking about this all night long. Not one wink of sleep. This might be the event that makes me walk out the door. I could investigate on my own terms. I'll be able to do things I can't do as a cop."

"There's a lot you won't be able to do if you leave."

"I might not have a choice."

"If you leave, I can't stop you. I'll miss you in a way I'd miss no one else in this place. But you know that I wouldn't let this case drop. I'd keep pursuing it."

"I know you would. But you've got other cases. And the rest of our team is flat out, too. I can see what will happen. Eisen will be found to be Layla's killer. There's no one else. And, it most probably *was* him. He probably called her out to the funfair—perhaps using the exact same tactics he was using on Abby—and then either something went wrong, or he intended to kill her. And then he went out on his boat—as an alibi, perhaps. At which point, either he fell over the side of his boat and drowned—or someone pushed him. And if he did kill Layla, then public sympathy isn't going to be on the side of finding out if someone *did* push him."

Franco nodded. "I'm thinking along the same lines. But it will get a full investigation. You taught me well, Wakeland. You make an ass out of yourself when you make assumptions."

He managed a tight smile. "Why don't you just stay on the job and think on this for a while? I'm going to leave it a couple of days before I tell Shintani—unless you tell him first."

"I won't be telling him. Not yet."

"Okay, then we'll proceed."

I swallowed. "I feel like I'm putting you in a difficult position. You could lose your job."

"Let's just say I don't know about what Abby's been telling in her shrink sessions. You didn't tell me."

"Okay." I exhaled.

"Okay," he repeated, his eyes locked on mine. His expression was resolute, but I knew that internally, he was facing a dilemma. This wasn't fair to him.

He glanced back at the screen of his laptop. "Well, I'm going to do some more digging on this thing about Eisen writing on the wall at CQ. Might even do some legwork."

I grinned, trying to dissolve a little of the tension. "About time you did some legwork."

"Real funny. Let me know next time you and Pete are going up in the mountains on a run. I'll show you some legwork."

"Deal."

"Hey, do you know what day this is?" he said.

"No? What day is it?"

"Wednesday."

"Oh... thanks for the update. You know, your jokes really need a tune-up, Franco."

I walked away, shaking my head.

But I knew exactly what Franco's little joke was about. Today was his birthday. And he thought everyone had forgotten.

What he didn't know was that, yesterday, I'd organised a surprise party for him. Franco had messed it up by coming in earlier than he usually did. I'd planned to stall him for a few minutes. I hadn't intended on unleashing that conversation about Abby and the journal and all that had followed it. But there was nothing I could do about that now. I just hoped I hadn't ruined the mood.

I headed into Inspector Shintani's office. Squashed into that room was the rest of our homicide team and Superintendent Andrew Bigley, and a few ring ins from the missing persons and theft divisions.

Constable Ella Valletti had brought in the cake—a big, Italian-style cake with layers of chocolate mousse. I knew that Franco liked that kind.

Shintani gave Franco a call and asked him into the office on the pretext of wanting an update on one of our cases.

Franco opened the door to Shintani's office with a worried look on his face, doing a double-take when everyone jumped out with party blowers.

Despite Franco telling everyone we shouldn't have bothered, I could tell that he was secretly delighted.

It was a good party. It seemed to lighten everyone's mood.

Afterwards, when the party was done, Detectives Reagan Grimshaw and Liz Booth approached me.

"I saw the news about the girl you came to see me about—Layla Maddox," Grimshaw began. "Not a good end for her."

"No," I said. "Tragic. I'd started to worry about her, but I still hadn't expected... this."

"I feel for you," said Liz. "What an awful discovery. I didn't even know that this town had ever had a funfair."

I knew that Liz had grown up in Sydney, close to the city.

"Is it possible I could draw on your expertise on a couple of issues?" I asked Liz and Grimshaw. At this point, it was risky to talk about the case with police other than Franco—and Grimshaw was especially risky, seeing as how she was always in Superintendent Bigley's front pocket. But I needed this case solved, one way or the other. This wasn't about me. It was about Layla and Abby and Emmet Eisen.

"I have to dash back to Sydney soon," Liz told me. "But I've got fifteen minutes burning a hole in my pocket right now."

"I can make time," said Grimshaw. "Should we head to my office?"

The three of us crossed the station floor together.

Grimshaw's office looked the same as it always did—neat and orderly, just like herself. Grimshaw always looked polished. She'd had the same, sleek bobbed haircut ever since I'd known her. Her clothing always fit her large frame well.

Detective Liz Booth, on the other hand, looked like she'd flown out of her home this morning in a rush, with her ruffled hair and cardigan that was stretched out of shape. As messy as Liz looked, she had a fearsome reputation for hunting down online criminal paedophiles. Liz was one of the lead detectives in the state Child Abuse and Sex Crimes Squad.

We sat around Grimshaw's desk.

I gave them both a detailed account of the two cases I'd been working on, including the times Eisen had lured Abby to the funfair—leaving out any mention of Abby's name. Her name hadn't been mentioned to the media, nor had anything about Emmet's apparent child abuse crimes been made public. I also explained to Liz and Grimshaw all the details about the night Franco and I had found Layla —details that hadn't been given to the media.

"Well," said Grimshaw, "last time we spoke, I had an idea there could be some other guy that was causing Layla to be scared of coming back to Tallman's Valley. But, it ends up that the poor girl was dead, not scared."

"Yes," I said sadly.

"Right," Grimshaw told me, "I've been having a look into unsolved missing person cases of young girls in the district, and further afield. Nothing fits with the same timeline, but I'm still making up a list."

"I appreciate that," I said.

Liz crinkled her forehead. "The location where Layla was killed is certainly peculiar. An old funfair. So, you think the killer could be the teacher you were telling us about?"

"It's possible," I said.

"Are you going to put his name out there to the media?" Liz asked.

"Not yet," I said. "I need to tie things together better first. I want it airtight. I mean, this teacher died on the same night Layla did. His parents have been through the mill. I wouldn't want unfounded accusations to get out there."

"Makes sense," Liz said. "I wonder if you'll get other girls coming forward—about the funfair. He might have lured others there."

"You think that's likely?" I asked.

She gave a nod. "Yes. Yes, I do. Offenders with a primary attraction to pubescent girls are likely to be repeat offenders. And it wasn't anything that just happened out of the blue. There was a high level of planning involved. I'd say it was carefully planned out for months before bringing the girl he abused to the funfair. Perhaps even before he sent his first message to her. It was a long, slow grooming process he put her through, designed to reel her in bit by bit."

I glanced at Grimshaw. 'You said the same thing. About this being out of the ordinary. If I can get to the heart of why this perpetrator used the kind of props he did, maybe I can burn a trail straight to him. Even if he's dead. His props were all about birds and birdcages. The large birdcage was a fixture from the funfair when it was operational."

"I remember it," Grimshaw said. "There was always a glum looking girl swinging in it."

Liz looked from Grimshaw to me with interest. "Oh yeah? So, the perpetrator might have been someone who went to the funfair often?"

"Not if it was who we're suspecting," I said. "He was only twenty-three during the months this all happened. The funfair closed around the time he was a toddler. There's just one thing—the girl I've been speaking to said that he found the abandoned buildings when he was a kid, and he used to hang out there by himself."

"Interesting," said Liz. "If he's the perp, the old funfair must have had quite an impression on him."

I crossed my arms, thinking. "There is also the fact that the funfair was owned by the Mulden family. It would be a long shot if there was any connection. I can't even tell who owns that property now. It's all wrapped up in trusts and sham companies, by the looks of it."

"Hmmm." Liz eyed me with a pensive expression. "Would be worth looking at. I'm especially interested in the things the perp got the girl to do. Seems that he didn't want to touch her—he just liked to watch?"

"Yes," I said, "he said he wanted to take things slow with her. Thank God it didn't go any further. It was bad enough as it was."

"I'm not certain that he was telling the truth about wanting to take it slow," Liz told me. "It went on for months like that, correct?"

"Correct," I answered.

"Well," Liz said, "it's possible that he had a fetish about watching, not doing. As in, his objective was never going to be to physically touch her. I'm also interested in the things he had her do with her hair."

"You mean, the hair brushing and the clips?" I asked.

"Yep, those." Liz sucked in her mouth, pushing strands of hair back from her face. "The guy might have had a hair fetish."

I sat back in my chair. "You know, I didn't consider that. I was thinking he was trying to make her feel pretty, trying to give her things he thought a teenage girl would like. But I think you're right. He had a fetish for hair."

"Damned strange character, that teacher," said Grimshaw. "Makes you wonder if he went into teaching just so that he'd have access to girls of that age."

"It's an awful thought," I said, "but it could be true."

"Kate," said Liz, "do you happen to know if the teacher took any images of the girl—photos, videos—anything like that?"

"She hasn't mentioned anything," I replied. "The thought has crossed my mind, but I'm really crossing my fingers he didn't take any."

"I can run a face check on her if you supply some photos from when she was a young teen," Liz told me. "See if there are any matches from the dark web?"

"I'll ask her," I said. I knew Abby wanted her privacy and I doubted she'd agree.

What Liz had just said triggered a thought.

About a girl.

Nola Hobson.

Abby had mentioned her a couple of times when telling the stories to Dr Quinley.

Abby had said that Nola had come to hang out with them at the lake. But it had only been just a single time. Cooper Tecklenburg had challenged the group to get bitten by a blue tongue lizard, and he'd wanted Nola to go first.

I knew something about Nola that almost no one else did. She had suffered abuse as a young teenager, with her mother forcing her to participate in making videos with an adult man. The images had been sold online.

Nola had been one of the nursery school teachers who'd been watching Ivy and the other children on the day that five of them vanished. When questioning her over that, the story of her childhood had unexpectedly come out. She'd begged me not to tell anyone.

Could the man who'd been in those videos with Nola be Emmet Eisen? Nola had said she didn't know the man who she was forced to make the videos and images with. She certainly didn't say it was one of her teachers. But could she be blocking the identity of the man from her mind? That was possible in cases of extreme trauma.

But if Nola lived close to Layla, that meant she'd lived close to Eisen—and maybe there was something to it.

"You look like you've seen a ghost, Wakeland," Grimshaw commented.

"Oh... I just thought of something," I said. "It might or might not have a connection to this case. I'll have to find out."

A phone call came through for me.

It was Shintani, wanting to see me in his office, with Franco.

I straightened. Had Franco told Shintani about Abby and the journal, after all?

"Got to run," I said to Liz and Grimshaw. "I really appreciate you talking to me."

Liz rose. "Any time, my dear. I'd best head off, myself."

"Remember, Wakeland," said Grimshaw, "I'll be looking for payback. My time for yours."

I forced a smile that I wasn't feeling. *If I'm even still in this job after Shintani's done with me,* I thought privately.

I practically held my breath all the way to the inspector's office.

Franco was already in there, seated. He still had a small smear of chocolate cake on his chin. I guessed that Shintani had been too polite to tell him.

I sat stiffly, waiting to hear that I was being taken off the Emmet

Eisen case—and maybe kicked from the police force for failing to divulge what my daughter had done.

"Kate," said Shintani, "I've been talking with Jace, about his discoveries."

"Oh?" I replied hoarsely.

Shintani nodded. "I think it best that we release the name, *Mr Lullaby*, to the media. We will advise them that it's in connection to the murder of Layla Maddox."

My gaze skated between Shintani and Franco. *That* was all this was about?

"Okay," I said, "yes, I agree. That's a good idea."

Franco shot me a reassuring smile. "Thought this could save me some legwork. You know, let the public do the legwork for me."

I tried to smile in return, but I was still gripped with anxiety. I told myself to breathe.

"This time, Jace," Shintani said to Franco, "I think your lazy instincts have served you well. If there are any young women out there who've been contacted by a Mr Lullaby in the past, they might come forward."

In reply, Franco made a joke, but I detected a worried look swimming below the surface of his eyes.

I was walking a thin line. Whatever I did next, I had to watch that I didn't put another foot wrong.

51

KATE

The first thing I did was to look up Nola Hobson's mother—Adele Hobson.

She had been the instigator of the child abuse material. She was the one who had forced Nola into participating. I tried looking her up. I discovered that she'd gone overseas—to Thailand—and then she seemed to have vanished.

Next, I picked up the phone and called Nola. She was at a local playground with Max—a young cousin who'd recently come into her care. Max was six years old.

I drove down to Lowen Park, trying to put together the questions I had circling in my mind.

As soon as I parked and walked across to the playground area, I spotted Nola. She wore an oversize brown corduroy coat, long floral dress and boots. She had a knit cap on her head, tassels hanging over each ear.

Every time I'd seen Nola, something about the way she dressed herself always gave her the look of a large child.

She was pushing Max on the swing.

"Hello, Nola," I called. I waved at the little boy. "Hi, Max."

Max waved back shyly.

"How are you doing?" I said to Nola as I stepped up to her.

She shrugged. "There are good days and bad days. This is a good day."

"Glad to hear it."

"And you and your family?" she asked.

"We're all okay. A few hurdles. Nola, could I come and see you at some point over the next few days—alone?"

"What's it about?"

I drew a breath. "It's about the things you told me about... from your past."

"I said that I don't want—"

"I know. I understood. But something has just happened."

"What happened?"

"Have you seen the news lately?"

She shook her head. "I don't watch the news. Too many awful things."

I lowered my voice. "Okay. Well, I can't talk about it in front of Max."

"Max," she called to the little boy, "would you like to go ride your bike now?"

He nodded and raced off to grab a bike that was lying on the ground. He wheeled it towards a track that circled the playground.

"Nola," I started, "I've been searching for a missing girl. Her name was Layla Maddox."

She glanced at me in surprise. "Layla? I knew her from school. I didn't know she was missing. She hasn't lived in Tallman's Valley since she was a teenager. Probably not since she was fourteen."

"No, you're right, she hasn't. A few days ago, Detective Franco and I found her. I'm sorry to say that she's dead."

"What?"

"She was only fourteen when she died. And she died right here in town."

"I can't believe it. Poor Layla. We weren't friends... but I liked her. How did she die?"

"The only thing we know so far is that someone killed her."

She gaped at me with a horrified expression.

"It was a shock to us, too. Because of that discovery, I'd like to ask you a couple of questions. I can fit in with you. Day or night. Of course, it would have to be when Max isn't there."

"Then it would have to be now," she said. "I don't have much time. I'm either with Max or at my job. I only have one job now. The pizza place."

I studied her face with concern. "Here? Are you sure?"

"No, I'm not sure. But when you said that someone killed Layla, I'm guessing you think it could be the same man... who I knew?"

"In all honesty, I don't know. But I recently found out that you lived by the lake during that time. Abby mentioned something about a blue tongue bite?"

Nola nodded, chewing on her lip and blinking back sudden tears. "Yes, I let a blue tongue bite me. I was stupid. I thought I could be part of Abby's group if I went along with it. I got in huge trouble when I got home. Because of the bite. Because it marked my skin. My mother was angry and said the mark would ruin the photos of me. She wouldn't let me go back to the lake after that."

"Oh.... Nola...."

She whirled around in a panic then. "Where's Max?"

"He's right there," I assured her, pointing to him. "I've kept him in my side vision the whole time. You get good at doing that sort of thing in my line of work. I've almost done more surveillance missions than I've had hot dinners. I promise I won't let him out of my sight."

"Okay." Nola puffed up her cheeks and blew out a breath. "After the lizard bite incident, if I disobeyed my mother, she threatened me with letting the kids at school see the photos and videos—the ones she made me do with that man."

"Oh, no. Unbelievable. The whole thing. All of it. And I feel terrible about even coming down here to ask you questions."

"Don't. You're just trying to put the bad people away. Ask me anything. I'll answer it if I can."

"Okay. I guess the first thing I want to find out is if it was the same man. Could you describe him?"

"I think he was tall. But I was just a kid, then. He might have looked bigger to me than what he really was. His hair was brown and short. He had a beard and moustache. His eyes looked... kind. But he wasn't kind. I'm afraid that's it. That's all I remember."

"Thank you. And you don't recognise him as being anyone from your life back then—I mean, outside of the times that he came to your house? You never saw him around town anywhere?"

"Never."

"You're certain?"

"Yes."

"Okay, thank you. Now, I have a difficult question. I'd like to know if he had any interest in things like... watching you dance, watching you brush your hair—"

"Yes," she cried. "*He did.* He made me dance. And I didn't even know how to dance—my mother never put me in dance classes. And he liked to brush my hair... while singing to me."

I took a tight, shallow breath. "What did he sing?"

"I don't know. Children's songs. We'd have the awful photo shoots and videos. And afterwards he'd comfort me by stroking my hair and singing songs to me. He told me he was the lullaby man, and that he'd make everything okay."

She stared at me then, aghast. "What?"

"You sure he called himself *the lullaby man?*" That piece of information hadn't gone out to the media yet. It was going out a little later tonight. She couldn't have possibly read or heard about *Mr Lullaby.*

"One last question," I said, inhaling deeply. "Did he ever give you anything, such as a piece of jewellery?"

"He did, once. A stupid birdcage pendant on a chain. I never wore it. I threw it away."

"Oh, my gosh."

"It's the same man, isn't it?"

I nodded.

Over on the bike track, Max seemed to tire of riding his bike. He hopped off and began wheeling it over the twigs and grass, in our direction.

Nola's eyes reddened. "Last time I talked to you about this, I didn't want to do anything about it. But if he killed Layla, that changes things. That changes everything. Tell me what you want from me."

Gathering myself, I glanced upward at the dull sky.

I faced Nola again. "What I'll need are any photos of you from when you were that age. So that the child protection squad can try to find those images online—in the hope that they lead us straight to the lullaby man."

She was shaking her head. "To tell you the truth, I don't have any. My mother didn't bother taking many—apart from the images she was selling. And I destroyed all the ones that I did have. I just didn't want to remember those years."

"You don't have any at all?"

"No."

"I'll figure something out," I said softly.

I gave her a warm smile just as Max approached and hugged her around the waist.

"I'm tired." Max yawned.

"Nola, did you two walk to the park today?" I asked.

"Yes, we did," she answered. "Max's bike doesn't fit into my little car."

"It'll fit in mine. I'll drive you both back."

"You don't have to do that. You've got important things to do."

"I want to," I said. "If you like, I can take a small detour to this little café that I know that does the best hot chocolate and marshmallows in town? My shout."

Max's face lit up.

Nola looked from him to me, and then nodded, wiping a tear from her cheek.

It was late in the day when I arrived back at the station.

I returned to my desk and called the assistant principal at Valley Grammar—Evelyn Mitchell.

Evelyn had seen a news broadcast about Layla on TV last night, and she was pressing me for details, telling me she felt a responsibility to keep her students safe. She sounded peeved when I said I couldn't divulge any more information than what was currently in the media.

Predictably, when I requested the school's annual photographs of Nola Hobson from when she was in Years 8, 9 and 10, Evelyn went into overdrive, wanting to know why. Finally, she agreed to email the pictures through.

I sent the pictures through to Detective Liz Booth, asking if she could conduct a search on them online.

It was time to head home.

I switched on the radio at 6 p.m. There was a breaking news item about *Mr Lullaby*.

I imagined a shadowy man out there somewhere, listening to that broadcast. In my mind, he was sitting in a plush chair, with dozens of mirrors around him, a birdcage hanging on a chain beside him.

The image stuck fast in my mind all the way along the dark, misty roads.

I walked into my house. Pete and Ivy were in the kitchen. I gave them big hugs and kisses, then went looking for Abby. I found her in her bedroom, dressing Jasper after his bath.

Jasper smiled and gurgled when he saw me.

"Oh, let me," I cooed.

Abby handed me Jasper's grow suit. Gently, I stretched it over little legs that didn't stop kicking and tiny arms that kept trying to touch my face. I did up the snaps, then gathered him up in my arms. "You smell divine, Jasper."

Abby smiled. "He does, doesn't he? The soap has coconut and avocado oil in it."

"Mmmm, I could eat him up." I kissed his downy head. He had such a sparse covering of hair that it was almost dry already.

"Would you like to feed him and then put him down for his sleep?" Abby asked me.

"No, I don't want to put him in his cot," I said, rocking him in my arms. "I want to hold him all night long." I grinned. "Okay, okay, I'll do it. But it's hard because he's so gorgeous."

She laughed. "I can't disagree with that."

Abby had his bottle cooling on the tall boy. Taking the bottle, I went and sat on the rocking chair with Jasper. He grabbed at the bottle as I put it to his mouth.

"Where's Logan?" I asked.

"Out getting us all dinner," she said. "We're having Thai."

"Oh, lovely."

We chatted for a little while, mostly about Ivy and Jasper.

Once Jasper was done with his bottle, I carried him over to his cot and tucked him into his blankets. He gave Abby and me a sleepy, half-formed grin.

We quietly stepped out into the hallway.

"Abby," I said gently, "I want to talk to you about a couple of things. It concerns the police case. Is that okay?"

"Of course."

We walked down the hall and into my bedroom.

"The first thing is," I began, "I want you to know that a news item has just gone out to the media about the name Mr Lullaby in connection with Layla's murder. You haven't been named. And you won't be. You have my word on that. I spoke with someone else today—a girl who encountered a man who called himself the lullaby man to her. The encounters involved similar things to what you told me. Except that the encounters were filmed. I can't tell you who, due to confidentiality."

"Oh, my God."

"There may be more girls out there. We have to wait and see."

"I should have told about what was happening back then. Sounds like there were a few of us girls, all keeping secrets. And if I'd told, Layla would still be alive."

"These predators know exactly what to do to ensure that kids don't say a word. And we can't know if you telling would have saved Layla." Reaching out, I squeezed her arm. "Could I show you something? Franco found a picture today—and I'd really like to know if you know anything about it."

"For sure, Mum."

Slipping my phone from my pocket, I browsed to the picture of the graffiti on the wall at Close Quarters. I brought the wording up close.

"It says *Goodbye Lullaby*—do you see it? And to the right of the picture is Mr Eisen. This picture is ten years old, from a newspaper article about the group protesting the building of CQ."

She peered closely at the image and then raised her eyes to me. "That's definitely him. But I can't figure out why he'd write that. He always told me the name had to remain a secret. Just between us."

"Franco and I certainly can't figure it out."

"Mum, do you think the message could have been Emmet crying out for help?"

"I'm intrigued by that possibility, Abby. Really. But he did some terrible things. And if that was a cry for help, then it was a weak one. He could have done so much more to stop himself."

Her eyes glistened with tears. "God, listen to me, trying to make up excuses for him." She shook her head. "I wish I'd kept his journal somewhere a lot safer. It could have told us everything we needed to know. Did the girl you spoke to describe the man as being Emmet?"

"She can't remember his face. And he had a beard."

"Mum... Emmet never had a beard."

"It might have been a false one. Unless... there was someone else that he was doing these things with. Like a friend. Perhaps they were sharing the *Lullaby* name. I don't know. I wish I did."

"Sometimes, Emmet had friends with him at the parties, but not often. I couldn't even tell you who was who at those parties."

I chewed my lip, thinking. "You've just given me a thought. When you were telling Dr Quinley about Layla, you talked about all the pictures she used to take. I remember seeing her with a camera a few times, myself. Did she used to take photographs at the parties?"

"Yes, I'm pretty sure she did. She took photos of everything. A few times, Emmet's father or this other man called Doug told her to put the camera away. They said people don't always like having pictures taken of them, especially when they're drunk up to the eyeballs."

"Okay, I'll chase that up with Layla's aunt tomorrow." I gave Abby a hug. "Thank you for staying strong through all of this. Because of you, we found Layla. Don't forget that."

52

KATE

Nina DeCoursey was painting the inside of her boat shed when I turned up the next morning. A big dab of blue paint had stuck a tendril of hair to her forehead.

The door was open, but I tapped on it, anyway. "Hello, Nina?"

She turned, startled, paintbrush in hand. "Oh... Kate. Hi."

"Looks like I've caught you at a bad time."

"No, not at all. I just needed... something to do. Anything. It's been unbearable. If I stay indoors, I just don't know what to do with myself."

"How is your father?"

"Terrible. Telling him about Layla was the worst thing ever. He knows now that she is never going to walk in through the door and see him again."

"Heartbreaking."

"Yes, very."

"And how are you?"

"I'm just trying to deal with it. I can't even watch TV. Seeing her face on the news... it's just too much."

I pressed my lips together in sad acknowledgement of her words. "I hope Scott's been there for you."

"He tries, but...." She shrugged.

I glanced around at the new paintwork on the boat house. "You're doing a good job there."

"The old girl needed a bit of a lift. It hasn't been painted since Scott and I first bought this house. Anyway, I think I've done enough for today." She placed the paintbrush on a tray and stepped outside.

Indicating towards two deck chairs, she waved a hand. "Take a seat."

"Thanks." I sank into one of the low chairs.

She sat beside me. "I look a right mess, don't I? I've got two weeks' compassionate leave away from work, but without work to distract me, I'm just going crazy thinking about everything." She rubbed her neck. "I think I went at it too hard. I've pulled a muscle or something."

"Ouch. Well, maybe you can get Scott to finish the painting."

"Scott? The last thing he'd do is to get his hands dirty. He used to be different, but these days, all his focus goes on his job."

"Well, then maybe he can run a warm bath and get you some wine. That'll help your sore neck, at least." I smiled.

"Sounds nice," she said in a wistful tone. "Trouble is, I can't count on him to do that sort of thing either. To be honest, we're not connecting much anymore."

"I'm sorry to hear that."

She sighed, rubbing her neck again. "We've become like two people who just happen to live together. House mates, I guess you'd call us. Only last month, I tried to rekindle things a little. I had my hair coloured, wore something cute and tried to seduce him... but he didn't even notice. I think maybe... once the fire's gone out, you just can't find any sparks."

"I wish I could say something that would help." I was a little uncomfortable at her frank admission.

She turned to stare at the water.

I thought about Pete and me. The sparks had never gone out. The fire might not be roaring as it had when we were young, but the warmth was always there. Of course, I wasn't about to tell Nina that.

"Your hair looks nice that colour," I commented.

"Thanks." She smiled thinly. "It used to be a really nice golden-brown shade when Scott and I met. But it slowly went dull. Thought I'd try some caramel streaks. The hairdresser recommended it."

"It suits you."

A tear wet the side of her nose. "Scott used to love my hair. He'd run his hands through it and tell me it looked like the light on the mountains at sunset. How tragically poetic, right?"

"Very poetic."

"So, what happened? Who has he become? And who am I?" She dabbed at her wet face with her sleeve. "Sorry. I didn't mean to offload all of that on you."

"It's okay. Sometimes, we need to blow off a bit of steam."

"But you didn't come here so I could dump my woes on you. There's a reason you've dropped by, right?"

"Yes, there is. One time I was here, Scott mentioned that he'd kept an old camera of Layla's."

"A camera? No, I don't think so. He didn't keep that."

"I thought he said he did. Abby told me that Layla was always taking pictures. It's a long shot, but I wanted to see if there were any photos that might yield some clues."

"Oh... what sort of clues?"

"I'm not certain, yet. Sometimes, I don't know what I'm looking for until I find it."

"Oh. Well, I'd better go get you that camera and stop prattling on. You've got a lot of things to get on with. I hope you find something useful among the photos." She struggled up from the low chair, holding her neck. "Come inside, Kate."

Scott walked into the house from the front entrance just as Nina and I entered the house from the backyard.

He looked surprised to see me, kissing his wife and then looking my way enquiringly.

"Back in a minute," Nina said, leaving the room.

"How are you, Scott?" I asked.

He exhaled, his eyes saddening. "My head is all over the place. Can't get a grip. When I see the news, it just doesn't seem real that they're talking about our little Layla."

"It's so awful. I can hardly believe it myself."

He turned towards the hallway. "What's Nina doing?"

"You mentioned a camera of yours that Layla used to use? I just wanted to look at it."

He gazed back at me with a puzzled expression. "I've seen the first few dozen pictures on it. It's all bugs and butterflies. I'm sure you won't want to slog through that." He shrugged.

"I'd still like to see them."

"Right. Okay. I'll go get it down from the wardrobe. Nina wouldn't be able to reach."

He exited the room. The two of them returned a minute later. I got the impression that they had been having a private conversation. Possibly about me being a nosy detective. I tended to get people thinking that about me quite a lot.

Walking to the kitchen bench, Scott set the camera down.

"Great," I said. "Much appreciated. I'll take it with me to the station. We've got chargers and cables for just about every kind of phone and camera there is."

As I went to pick it up, Scott stopped me. "I'd rather you didn't. The camera is sentimental."

"Okay." I examined the camera, opening it up. "Lucky I came prepared. I've got triple A and double A batteries with me. Looks like this one takes four double A batteries."

"Would you like coffee, Kate?" Nina asked.

"I'd love some," I answered.

While Nina made the coffee, I fitted the batteries into the camera.

Scott went to fetch the cups. "I heard about a man called Mr Lullaby in the news," he said to me. "What's that all about?"

"I'll tell you honestly," I said, "we really don't have a lot of clear information yet. We're just at the initial point of information gathering.

It was put out to the public just to see if anyone knows anything that might help us."

Scott's smooth forehead creased into a deep frown. "But do you know for certain that a Mr Lullaby even exists?"

"We have a fair idea," I said.

"I just hope it doesn't impede you from finding the guy who did that to Layla," he said. "You know how it is. The public latch onto an idea and then embellish it. The lullaby man thing sounds like the beginnings of a modern boogey man tale."

"I know what you mean, Scott," I said. "But we didn't make that decision lightly."

"I understand," he replied. "I just want him found. He shouldn't get away with this."

"Trust me, we'll do our best to find out his identity," I said.

Nina poured out three cups of coffee, and then sat at the kitchen bench. She picked strands of hair from the drying splotch of paint on her forehead.

Scott turned the camera on. "Okay, prepare for the creepy crawly parade."

The camera had a large LCD screen at the back of it. I watched as Scott set the camera up to slowly flip through the images. I dug a set of high magnification reading glasses out of the police shoulder harness that I wore inside my jacket. I wanted to be able to see even the tiniest detail.

As Scott had said, there were a lot of animal pictures. I sipped my coffee, watching the lengthy display. I was prepared to view every last photo.

Layla had been a big fan of close-up shots, it seemed. There were lizard faces with alien-looking eyes. And the pebbled skin of green tree frogs. And moths, spiders and ants—showing their various eyes and antennae and even the miniature hairs on their legs. She really had loved them all.

"Seen enough?" said Scott. "I just liked to keep these because they're Layla's."

"I'll keep watching. They're lovely photos," I commented. "I never realised there were so many different creatures here at the lake."

"Yeah, me either," he said. "Hate to think of them all creeping around out there while we're sleeping."

"It's just nature, Scott." Nina shook her head at me.

After a run of about three hundred photos of insects, birds and animals, I was surprised to see a series of photos of Abby.

Just like with the insects and amphibians, these photos of Abby were in extreme close-up. A nose or an eye or a mouth, all taken as gag images.

There were also photos taken when Abby hadn't been aware there was a camera on her. There was Abby crouching on the shore and touching the water with her fingers, her dark hair blowing in the wind. And Abby in a swimsuit, bathed in sunset colours, with a brilliant orange sky behind her, standing in a boat out on the lake. And others.

I hadn't ever seen photos of Abby in which she looked so... free. It was as if a window had opened up, giving me a view all the way back to a decade ago.

"Pretty girl," Scott remarked. "I'd forgotten. Seems so long ago now that she and Layla and the other kids spent so much time together at the lake."

"Like a lifetime ago," Nina agreed.

The gallery of old photographs kept scrolling. I recognised the Tecklenburg boys in some of the photos. Once or twice, I noticed a lone girl sitting by herself far from the other children. Nola Hobson.

I watched intently as several self-portraits of Layla showed up. Some were happy, showing her gap-toothed smile and startling blue eyes that had dark outer rings around the irises. In other self-portraits, she looked so sad and serious that I wanted to reach inside the camera and travel back all those years in time, and just hug her. She was staring so closely at the camera lens that it was as if she wanted to understand herself.

"Layla was so lovely," said Nina wistfully. "I don't think she knew.

The boys were certainly all interested in her. But she was more interested in her frogs and lady beetles."

"Gorgeous," I said. "I'd like copies of these images."

"Of course," Scott told me. "I'm betting there are a lot more creature features to follow. I'll put the pics on a memory card for you."

"I've brought my own storage cards, thanks Scott. Force of habit. I always bring batteries and cards when I know I'm going to be looking at images on cameras. I've found it useful more times than I can count. Would you mind if I keep looking at the photos, though? If I have a question about something, I can ask you both right now."

He sipped his coffee. "Yeah, no problem at all." He set the camera up to start scrolling again.

The photos now were all taken at night. Of night birds and reflections of the moon on the lake. Then came a run of pictures at an outdoor party. Abby was in these pictures. She looked *so* young. The party was being held in the stretch of land between the Eisens' backyard and the lake. People in party clothes danced and drank wine. Fairy lights were strung through the trees. just beyond the Eisens' yard. I could almost hear the music and laughter. This was one of those parties I'd never known about.

I kept looking through the gallery of photos. There were often series of night-time party pictures interspersed between the wildlife and daytime photos now.

"Could we hold here, please, Scott?" I touched the edge of the screen. "I'd like to look at these two photos again."

In the first photo, Scott and Alex Eisen were standing with an older man. The older man was pouring Abby a drink. In the next photo, the older man had walked away from the group, and was now standing next to a tree. Emmet was there with him, looking as if he were having an argument with the man, his arms raised in the air in an aggressive manner.

"Who is this?" I asked.

"That's Doug Overmire," Scott told me. "He's someone Alex knew. Some big shot financier."

"Do you know anything about the argument these two seem to be having?" I asked.

"Emmet was getting drunk and shouting a lot back then," said Scott. "It wasn't anything unusual."

I nodded. "Okay. Did Overmire come to the get-togethers often?"

"Yes, he was there all the time," Nina said. "He had a big personality. One of those guys who thinks a lot of himself."

"Do you happen to know what his connection to the Eisens is?" I asked.

"Not sure," she replied. "You'd best ask the Eisens that, Kate."

I sighed, downing the last of my coffee as if it were a stiff drink. "I'm not their most favourite person since I started this investigation."

Nina nodded. "That's natural. I can understand it. They don't want the good name of their son tarnished. His memory is all they've got now."

"Yes, true," I agreed. "But from my side of things, I have a job to do."

"I'm sorry if I'm overstepping," Nina said, "but I'm really worried about Louisa. She seems like someone at the tipping point to me."

Scott put an arm around his wife's shoulder. "I'd agree with that. I've seen her from our kitchen window, just pacing the shoreline. Like a lost puppy or something."

I glanced at the DeCourseys. The two of them looked like any close couple, Scott's arm still around his wife. I wondered if it annoyed Nina that he was putting on a show, pretending that they were a loving couple when they weren't. After I left, would she push him away? Or cry and demand to know why he didn't hug her when they were alone?

I wished Nina hadn't given me that little insight into their relationship earlier. Some things I was better off not knowing.

Inserting my memory card into the camera, I saved the entire roll of pictures.

Then I steeled myself for what came next: talking to the Eisens again.

53

KATE

I ended up not having to go and knock on the Eisens' front door. As I was leaving the DeCourseys' house, Alex and Louisa approached me. They didn't look at all happy.

"Detective Wakeland," said Alex, "could we have a word with you?"

"Of course. I actually need to talk with you both as well."

Louisa crossed her arms tightly. "Oh? What's it about *this* time?"

"Should we go inside?" I asked.

Louisa shook her head, pressing her mouth into a hard line. "No one can hear. And I will not go sit inside my house—with the memories of my dead son all around and then have his memory rubbished."

"Louisa..." I was momentarily lost for words. This conversation was not going to be easy. And the conversations were only going to get worse in the future when they found out exactly what their son had done.

"We just saw the latest news update on Layla Maddox," Alex informed me. "About the *lullaby man* thing."

I raised my eyebrows. "Yes, we have good reason to think there is a connection with a man who went by the name, Mr Lullaby."

Alex's expression darkened. "Really? And where did you get that name from?"

"I'm sorry, I can't tell you that."

"I know exactly where you got it from," said Alex harshly. "Emmet wrote a silly slogan on a wall once. Something about a lullaby. *That's* where you got it from."

"No, we didn't," I assured him.

Alex shook his head. "Do you expect us to believe it's just a coincidence that its being splashed all over the news right now? Our son, writing that slogan on a wall? You guys fed it to the media. This is all some campaign to make Emmet look guilty."

I lowered my tone. "Alex, that's simply not true. And we didn't inform the media about the slogan Emmet wrote. Perhaps the reporter who took the photos that day remembered it. Or some other reporter went searching. I'm afraid that the media will go looking for any angle they can. From our side of things, all we're trying to do is to discover what happened to Layla."

Louisa's mouth turned down. "Of course you are. Layla deserves that much. But you can't go after Emmet. He's not the one you want. He's not—"

Her shoulders shook as she broke off.

"I assure you that we haven't leapt to any conclusions," I said.

"Don't give me your *haven't come to any conclusions* speech, Kate," she told me. "You know full well what conclusions other people are going to come to. This damned lullaby man thing is all anyone is talking about. And now there's the graffiti linking Emmet to it. You knew full well this would happen. Emmet lived right next door to Layla, after all."

I held up the palms of my hands. "Please. I'm not going to defend myself here. I have a job to do."

"Our son did nothing wrong," Alex growled. "And what's all this going to achieve anyway? He's dead. You've got no one to put in jail. I would have thought you'd have better things to do with your police hours than this."

"I knew from the very start that there was bad intent behind opening Emmet's case," said Louisa. "It was never about finding out if he was murdered, was it? It was only ever about this insane thing about Emmet having something to do with hurting young girls. A bait and switch if you ask me."

"I'm going to ask that you calm down," I said quietly. "I want you both to listen to what I'm telling you. I have no information that links Emmet to Layla's murder. I'll be making a statement to the media as such."

"It won't help now." Louisa's bottom lip quivered. "We won't even be able to live in this town anymore. We'll have to leave the house that Emmet grew up in ever since we moved to this country."

"Well, I hope that it doesn't come to that," I said.

But I knew the truth. Families of murder suspects or murderers were often forced to move away from their hometowns. It was unfair, but people were often tainted by the actions of their family members.

There was little I could do to dispel the tension. Any parents who were in the shoes that Alex and Louisa were in right now would be terrified about what was coming next.

"There's something you could tell me that might help," I said. "You can tell me what that slogan Emmet painted on the wall was all about? That would clear things up instantly."

Alex glanced at his wife before turning a direct gaze on me. "We don't know. Emmet was having problems at that time. We don't know why. He was depressed. He was having treatment. He was trying to get better—"

"Don't tell her all of that, Alex," snapped Louisa. "She'll only use it against us."

I softened my tone. "I won't use it against you. Look, let me assure you that reopening your son's case was genuine. If someone's actions directly led to Emmet drowning that night, then that matters. I had no idea that this investigation would lead to a search for Layla. Finding her dead was as much a shock to us as it has been to everyone else."

"Why were you searching for her, then?" Louisa demanded with an icy glint in her eyes.

"I hoped she might have some information—about Emmet. But whether or not I was investigating Emmet's death, the fact that Layla was missing would have eventually been noticed, and we would have found her. And events would have unfolded in the same way."

Alex lifted his chin. "You said you came here to talk with us? What was that about?"

I nodded. "It's about a man who used to attend your parties. Doug Overmire. I've seen a photograph in which Emmet looks as if he's having an argument with him. It was at a party that was held one night at your house. I'd like to ask if you know what that argument was about?"

Alex shook his head. "An argument? We don't know what you're talking about. And who showed you that photograph? The DeCourseys? Fine friends they've ended up being."

"I asked to see the photographs, Alex," I said. "Could you tell me more about Mr Overmire himself, then?"

Alex stared at me coldly. "He's just someone I used to do business with. He was one of the major backers of the Close Quarters development. I bought into it as well, and that's how I came to know him."

"Okay, thank you," I said. "I'll let you know if I need anything else from you both."

"We're not answering any more questions," Alex told me. "This is all having a terrible effect on Louisa. She's having panic attacks where she can hardly breathe. What I'm saying is, don't come back."

I exhaled a taut breath. "Let's hope I don't have to, Alex. I'm very sorry about the effect upon you both. I know this isn't easy—on anyone. I'll be in touch."

I walked back to my car. I felt awful, but I couldn't allow myself to be railroaded by the Eisens. There really was nothing I could do except to continue doing my job.

54

KATE

After grabbing a quick lunch, I headed to the station.

Franco and I sat down for a catch-up session. I told him where I'd been this morning and about Doug Overmire.

"Sounds like a tense morning," he remarked.

"Very. What about you?"

"Me? Fielding calls from the public about the *Mr Lullaby* item that went out to the media. We're getting the usual noise to signal feedback. All noise, no signal. I've also been trying to find a source for that piece of material that was snagged on the coat hanger—I've got our whole team working on it. But that pattern is not proving easy to track down."

"Should we put it out to the public? Someone might know what it is."

He shook his head. "Shintani think it's best if we hold that back. If the killer ends up not being Emmet, then we need to keep some things up our sleeves. That's his line of thought, anyway."

"Okay. Makes sense."

A text came through on my phone. It was from Detective Liz Booth. She'd found matches for the photos of Nola Hobson. She was close to the Blue Mountains right now, seeing about another matter.

She said it would work well for her to meet within another hour, if that was okay with me.

Great news, I texted back to Liz. *Give me five minutes and I'll see if Nola can join us.*

I called Nola. I didn't tell her exactly what Detective Booth had found—it was best to tell her face-to-face. Nola said she couldn't make it down to the station. She had no one to pick Max up from school. I asked if she'd be happy to allow Abby to pick Max up when she went to get Ivy. And then Ivy and Max could play together. Nola agreed to that. I then made a hurried call to Abby.

Everything was set up.

I prayed we'd find some answers this afternoon.

When I looked back at Franco, he had a concerned look on his face. "Wakeland, you're breathing a bit fast."

"Am I?"

"Yup. Slow down. You're going to give yourself a heart attack."

I took a measured breath. "It's just been... such a rough few days. Ever since we found Layla. And then talking with the Eisens earlier really put me in a spin. It's like they think I'm framing their son deliberately."

"Well, you're not framing him. You're a good detective. Remember that." He exhaled audibly. "I've got to go out on site this afternoon—for the Boylson murder case. Will you be okay?"

"Yeah. I'll get myself under control. Might go to the gym and run my anxiety out before the meeting. How are you doing with the Boylson case? I'm sorry that I've been leaving you on your own with it."

"It's fine. We know that old man Boylson killed his wife. It's almost at wrap up stage."

"Good. Might see you back here later on?"

"Yeah. See you then. And take it easy."

I headed away to the floor where the police gym was located, then took my sports gear out from the locker and got changed. I spent the next half hour going hard on an elliptical trainer. After a hot shower, I was back in my clothes and feeling better.

Franco had been on point. Sometimes, you needed someone to tell you when you were stretched so thin you were about to snap.

I met with Liz in the interview room. She briefed me on everything I needed to know before seeing Nola.

Nola Hobson came in twenty minutes afterwards.

"Nola, please take a seat," I said. "This is Senior Detective Liz Booth. She's very experienced in all matters to do with child exploitation. As I said to you in an earlier conversation, I've brought her in on this because of that expertise."

"Hello, Nola." Liz shook her hand. "I'm glad to meet you. I want to thank you for allowing us to do this. Very brave."

"Thanks, Detective Booth," Nola answered. "But I don't feel very brave."

"You can call me Liz," said Booth. "No need for labels. And it *is* brave of you."

"Have you found... anything?" Nola asked.

"Yes, Nola, we have," Liz told her. "We found *you*."

Almost immediately, tears began spilling down Nola's cheeks. "You found *those pictures? Those videos?*" She said those last words with revulsion, her arms drawing across her stomach.

Liz nodded, giving her time to digest that piece of information.

"What about *him?*" Nola said, her eyes opening wide. "He was in those images. Do you know who he is now?"

"I'm afraid not," Liz told her. "He was very cautious. He made quite certain to keep his face out of the camera. We couldn't see much of him at all. And the lighting was on you, not him. I'm sorry."

"So... this was all pointless," Nola said. "If you can't see his face, you can't find him."

Liz gave her a reassuring smile. "The perpetrator often isn't in the images. But we still find them a lot of the time. Now that we've located the images, that's half the battle."

Nola turned her face away. "It feels bad... that someone else has seen them. I'm sorry. I'm trying to be adult about this. I don't know if I *can* be. It feels like I've been... exposed. All over again."

"Nola," said Liz softly, "if it helps at all, I've been involved in hundreds of cases and I've seen everything there is to see. What I see is pain. I see the pain inflicted on these kids. And I know that's what Kate saw, too. *Pain.* We had to look through many images and videos to find you. All children who have suffered more than any child should ever have to."

Nola pressed a handkerchief to her face. "Are you sure you found *me?* Not some other poor girl?"

"Yes, we're sure," I said. "Are you okay to view them?"

She nodded.

I placed a computer tablet in her hands. A gallery of images began playing, each image remaining on the screen for a couple of seconds before the next appeared. The pictures were disturbing to me, and I couldn't even imagine the effect upon Nola right now.

They showed a terrified young girl and a man, though the man kept most of his body out of sight.

Nola recoiled and then nodded. "It's me," she said tightly. "And it's *him.*"

I took the tablet and stopped the auto scroll function. "Are you all right?"

Her bottom lip quivered. "No matter what I do in life, there is always going to be... *this.* Me, in those porn photos. Forever more. No matter how much you and Liz try, you won't be able to get rid of *all* the photos and videos. People out there have seen them. They've seen *me.* Like that."

"Listen to me," said Liz firmly. "It's *not* porn. It's nothing to do with pornography. It's not in the least sexual for the child. It's abuse of the worst kind. You're the victim. This man and your mother were the perpetrators. The people who upload and watch the images are the abusers. I need you to reframe the way you're thinking about this. Can you do that for me?"

Nola inhaled a shuddering breath. "I'll try."

"Good girl," said Liz. "The people who download and view such images are scum. Don't waste time thinking about them. Leave that to us, okay? We're going to go after this guy hard. We'll be like rabid dogs on his trail. And when we find him, we'll nail his nuts to the wall. Okay, sweetie?"

Liz Booth had a colourful way of talking. Her language matched the field she worked in. What child abusers did was shocking, exposing children to things they never should be exposed to.

Nola's shoulders relaxed as she exhaled. Then she unlaced her fingers from the white-knuckled ball they'd been in. "Good. That's exactly what I want to happen."

Liz's little speech had worked.

"What about my mother?" Nola asked. "Are you looking for her?"

I nodded. "We've got international police on her trail. She booked a flight to Thailand years ago. She never came back to Australia. We'll keep looking until we find her."

"She should be in jail. Not out there free as a bird," said Nola darkly.

"I agree," I said. "For now, what we're going to do is try to follow these images back to their source. Of course, that won't be easy. As you can imagine, people who upload this material keep themselves well hidden. So, we're going to try to set a trap."

"What kind of trap?" Nola asked.

I looked across to Liz to prompt her to answer that question.

"We're going to pretend to be a collector of that kind of material," Liz told Nola. "We'll be asking where we can find more. So as not to raise suspicion, we'll choose three or four different girls. Then, we wait and hope for contact from Mr Lullaby."

"Will that work?" Nola said doubtfully.

"It's not a guarantee," Liz conceded. "But it's just one method that we use. We're going to try this first, because it's the simplest. The biggest problem we're facing is that it's been ten years since these images first came online. Trying to track such old images can be problematic. We also have to tread carefully. We've got online profiles that we've been using for many years, and we'll be using those to make contact with paedophiles online."

"What happens about those other girls whose photos you'll be pretending to want more of?" Nola asked. "Will you find out who they are and help them?"

Liz sighed, pressing her lips together grimly. "That's the problem. We have files and files of children who we can't ID. We do what we can. The police work together across countries and we all have the same objective. To rescue any kids that we can and track down the perpetrators, no matter what country the bastards are hiding out in. But ID'ing the kids can prove challenging. Kids can look very different from year to year as they grow older. Sometimes they're made to wear wigs. Or the lighting is too dark on their faces. I wish we could find them all and gather them up and get them out of their situations. It's heartbreaking."

Nola went silent for a few seconds. Then she looked from Liz to me. "So, what's next?"

"What comes next," I said, "isn't pleasant. We'd like to have you view all the images and tell us if they spark any memories. Anything you remember about the perpetrator can be useful. Can you manage that?"

"I'll try."

Liz and I sat there with Nola for the next half hour. Nola watched the videos and looked through the photos, tears on her face and horror stamped plainly in her eyes.

It was one of the saddest points of my career.

When it ended, Nola looked up at us, dabbing at her eyes with her handkerchief.

"Kate told me you can't remember anything about his face," Liz said, "apart from the fact that he had facial hair. But do you remember anything more now?"

Nola shook her head.

"Okay, well," Liz said, "we've got one small thing. For a split-second in one of the videos, he wasn't careful enough, and he got his hand and watch into the frame."

"I remember the watch, now." Nola shuddered.

Leaning across, I studied the picture. It was a vintage sports chronograph watch—high end, by the looks of it. It seemed familiar.

I tapped on one edge of the image. "Could I get a copy of this, Liz?"

"Sure thing," she said, then turned to Nola. "Did you happen to see what kind of car he drove?"

"No," Nola replied. "I was never allowed out of the room when he was there. My mother would take me into the room just before he arrived, and she'd make me stay there until after he'd left."

Liz settled back in her chair, quietly observing Nola for a moment. "Kate also told me that after the video sessions, he'd sing you nursery rhymes and brush your hair. Can I ask what he sang to you?"

"Just... nursery rhymes. *Rock-a-bye Baby*. And *Hush Little Baby*. Sometimes, he'd tell me bits of stories. I—" She crushed her eyes shut. "I'm trying to remember. It was so long ago... and I've tried so hard to forget...."

"Take your time," I said gently.

Liz and I exchanged a long, thoughtful glance. I understood that Liz was silently telling me that we didn't have anything she could use yet.

A minute passed, perhaps two.

"He... quoted from books a lot," Nola said finally. "I can only remember two of them. *The Little Mermaid*. Lots of stuff about mermaids. Silky, long mermaid hair. And... being naked. And there were Hemingway novels. More quotes about hair. About taking women's hair in and out of pins. And... kissing..." Opening her eyes, she looked across at us. "I'm afraid that's all I've got. There's nothing else."

"That's helpful," Liz commented. "I have one last question for you. And it's the most difficult one. Again, take all the time you need. So, in all the videos and images that I could find, I didn't see him *touch* you... apart from brushing your hair and putting clips in it. If it's okay, could you describe what he did?"

Nola stared at her. "That was everything. He'd stand there, naked, watching, while I posed and danced."

Liz chewed her lip, appearing to consider what Nola had just told her. "He never... touched you?"

Nola shook her head. "No. Just the hair stuff."

"Thank you," Liz said quietly. "That tells me a lot."

I rested my gaze on Nola. "Thank you *so* much. From both of us. I know this was so hard for you. And I promise you, Liz and I will go to every length to find this guy. From this moment on, we're on his trail, okay?"

She nodded, drawing in a deep breath.

55

KATE

With the interview done, I walked Nola out to her car.

"If you remember anything else, or you just need to talk, I'm here," I reminded her. "Are you feeling okay after everything we just put you through?"

She swallowed, swiping away a tendril of blonde hair from her eyes. "Yes. I'm glad you're looking into this. I thought I wouldn't be. But he doesn't deserve to get away with it. And neither does my mother."

"No, they really don't."

I saw her off and then returned to the interview room.

As I walked in, Liz pointed at a cup of tea on the table. "Made you one. Too late in the day for coffee, right?"

"Thanks." Grabbing it, I nursed it in my hands, trying to mentally unpack the interview.

Liz sipped her tea. "That was rough on Nola, poor girl."

"Yes, awful. So, what was your take?"

She crossed her arms, frowning. "Well, it certainly looks like the guy who abused Nola liked to watch and not touch—apart from brushing her hair. He appears to be very sexually aroused by hair.

Layla and Nola were both blondes with long locks. What about the third girl you mentioned?"

"She had long dark hair when she was fourteen." It felt wrong that I still wasn't disclosing Abby's name to anyone except for Franco. But I had little choice.

"Okay," said Liz. "Well, the fetish doesn't extend to hair colour, then."

"Do you come across hair fetishes much in your cases, Liz?"

"No, I can't say that I have. Trichophilia is rare. I mean, it's just a fetish, and such fetishes are usually completely harmless. They're not pathological."

"Do you think the murder of Layla is likely to be connected to the hair fetish?"

"It's hard to say. I wouldn't place bets on it, but it's not totally out of the question. There have been cases of men with hair fetishes killing girls and women in the past. There was one case in Italy. Women had been reporting someone cutting their hair on buses. Then it was discovered that a serial killer with trichophilia was at play. He would kill his victims, then cut off their hair and mutilate them, then place their hair in their hands."

"Wow. Horrific." I gulped my tea.

Liz began scrolling through her phone. "While you were walking Nola out, I looked up some of the things she told us—about *The Little Mermaid* story and Hemingway. Well, there's a lot about hair in *The Little Mermaid*. Here's a quote for you, 'And then he kissed her rosy mouth, played with her long waving hair, and laid his head on her heart, while she dreamed of human happiness and an immortal soul'".

"Okay, that certainly fits."

"And here's something interesting—Hemingway had a hair fetish."

"Really?"

"Yep. It was apparently well-known. But, in his case, his fascination was nothing terrible. His interest was in the hair of his wives. Cutting, styling, pinning—that kind of thing. And it spilled over into his writing."

"You know... at the parties that Layla and the other girl were attending during that time, the adults would often quote from books, including Hemingway. And the mermaid quote just reminded me of something. At the old carnival, along the gondola ride, there was a mermaid. I'd forgotten about her. So, there was a girl in a birdcage and then there was a mermaid."

Liz eyed me with a pondering expression. "Sounds like the guy had a serious fascination with that gondola ride."

"Yes. I need to figure out why. How did Emmet develop such an intense interest in a funfair attraction that was way before his time?"

"It's a puzzle all right." Liz drank the rest of her tea, then checked her watch. "Yikes. It's getting late. Better run. Traffic will already be a nightmare."

"I don't envy you. I can't stand city traffic these days. I don't know how I lived that life for so long."

"As much as I complain, I couldn't live anywhere else. I secretly love the noise and bustle." She flashed a smile.

Liz hurried out the door, almost bumping into Franco as he walked in.

Franco sat down heavily. He had an odd look on his face.

"What's up?" I asked him.

"I just came back to the station," he said. "And I saw something odd —Louisa Eisen was coming out of Bigley's office."

"What?"

"Exactly. What's she doing here?"

I crossed my arms. "Probably complaining about me."

"That's what I was afraid of. She certainly gave *me* a dirty look."

"But why is Bigley taking up the cause? He's the superintendent, for the love of—"

My phone beeped. It was a text message.

From Bigley. He wanted to see me.

Franco shot me a supportive look.

I made my way down to the other end of the station, to Superintendent Andrew Bigley's office.

He was in there sitting behind his ostentatious desk, his *ship-inside-a-bottle* ornament having pride of place.

"What is it, Andrew?" I didn't sit.

"Mrs Eisen just came in to see me."

"Oh?"

"She didn't lodge a complaint—yet—but she wanted to discuss, ah, recent police tactics. *Your* tactics, to be precise."

"And she came to *you* with that? Isn't that something that should go through the usual channels?"

"I play golf with her husband. It was more of a friendly chat. Anyway, Kate, she seems to feel that you've been harassing them."

"Harassing them? You know me. I don't go around harassing people." I paused. "Not without very good reason, anyway. And I've been as kind as I can be to the Eisens."

"She seems to think you've been following her around. Stalking her, in fact."

"Really? Do you believe I'd do that? Like I've got nothing better to do with my time?"

"She said she saw you and your daughter hanging about her house."

"No. We went for a walk on the track that runs alongside her house, and then into the forest. We were next to her house for mere seconds."

"Well, maybe try keeping a wide berth."

"I will if I can. But I might still need to talk with the Eisens again."

"I had a meeting earlier with Shintani. About Emmet Eisen. Look, the coroner's report was sound. The drowning was accidental. I know that Shintani agreed to reopen the case, but I have to wonder if that decision was the right one? It's putting Alex and Louisa through needless grief."

"I had new information, Andrew."

"I heard the information. It all rests on the say-so of a teenage girl. Not only that, but it's based on her recollections from a decade ago."

"Since when do you keep up on the day-to-day decisions of our homicide department, anyway?"

He sucked in a long breath. "I keep an eye on things. And, I have to say, I don't agree with Shintani's decisions lately, including putting the Mr Lullaby name out there to the media. We need to give the public a sense of running a tight ship. That we know which course we're sailing. But now, they think there's a Mr Lullaby on the loose. Not a good look for us, is it?"

"It's not a made-up name, Andrew. It's very real."

"Whether it's real in the minds of former teenage girls or not—is it necessary? All I'm asking is that you put the focus on finding the killer. Rely on the evidence at hand. Steer your course that way. Consider putting the case of Emmet's drowning back into its box."

"You know that Emmet is a possible suspect, don't you?"

"Yes, of course I know that. I'm not saying you shouldn't pursue that line of investigation. If Emmet Eisen ends up being the killer of Miss Maddox and he was also abusing young girls, then the truth must come out. Just tread carefully and keep a tight rein on what messages go public."

"Okay. Noted. If that's all, I'm going to head off now. It's been a long day."

I exited his office as fast as I could.

Franco was packing up as I walked back to my desk.

"Bigley up to his old tricks?" he said.

I nodded. "Always beating the same drum. About appearances. And running a tight ship."

"Bigley and his nautical references, huh? He never seems to run out of them. Walk you out?"

"Yeah. Let's get out of this place."

Franco and I left the station.

Louisa's car was parked around the corner. She was sitting at the wheel.

"What's she doing?" Franco kept his voice down, even though she wouldn't be able to hear.

"Probably still fuming about me. But there's nothing I can do to change the situation."

"Anything you got to do with the Eisens in the future, I'm taking it on."

"You don't have to do that."

"Yeah, I do."

"I've dealt with worse."

"Doesn't mean you have to deal with this."

"Thanks. I really appreciate it. I warn you though, things could get very ugly."

Shrugging, he opened the car door of a police vehicle.

"You're taking this tonight?" I asked. "Not your own car?"

"Yup. I've got a case to go to first thing in the morning."

"Okay. I'll see you tomorrow."

A faint screech came from down the road as Louisa drove away.

56

KATE

Pete had bought a huge box of vegetables from a local market. I helped him sort and store them away in the cupboard. Then I started prepping dinner. Making dinner was a welcome distraction from the noise inside my head.

Ivy ran to show me a picture she'd drawn at school. Abby chatted to me about Jasper saying his first word. Abby thought the word he'd said was *Ivy*.

That brought a tear to my eye.

Inspector Shintani called as I was peeling the potatoes.

There were only two reasons Shintani would call me at night. A large breakthrough in a murder investigation or a fresh murder. Murders tended to happen in the night-time hours.

"Kate," Shintani said. "Franco has been in an accident."

I gasped. That was nothing I'd been expecting. "An accident? Oh, God. How is he?"

"He's okay. Under sedation. He had to have a minor procedure. Apparently, a car came flying out at him at a T-intersection. Hit him on the front driver's side. They didn't stop afterwards."

"A hit and run?"

"Yes. But they did apparently call an ambulance, saying they'd just hit a police vehicle."

"I'm going to run down to the hospital."

"I knew you would. Give him my regards."

"Pete," I called, "I need to go. Franco's been hurt."

He rushed into the kitchen. "Hell. What happened?"

"A car accident. Hit and run. It doesn't sound serious, but I just want to know what he saw—before he forgets. Easy to forget things after an accident."

I drove straight down to the hospital.

The corridors had that familiar hospital smell of hand sanitiser.

Franco was in the recovery ward, in a room by himself. He was sleeping, a bandage around his left wrist and hand.

Tiptoeing in, I carried a chair over to his bedside.

As I was settling myself down in the chair, Franco mumbled something.

"I didn't mean to wake you," I said. "What did you say?"

He gave a crooked smile, eyes fluttering heavily. "I said, haven't you got better places to be?"

His words put me instantly at ease. If he was still joking, he was okay.

"You're right, I do," I shot back. "Unlike you, just lying about relaxing."

"Eh, I thought I needed a break. I heard you get fed and bathed here."

I grinned widely. "What's the damage?"

"Fractured wrist. Sore head. The prognosis is that I'll live."

"Glad to hear it. How'd the procedure go?"

"Good, apparently. They wheeled me straight in. My wrist was fractured in two places. The head scan showed my brain is okay— though some will disagree with that. A pre-emptive *shut up, Wakeland.*"

"Ouch, your poor wrist."

"It's not hurting yet. Will probably hurt like hell once the drugs wear off."

"I hope they keep you dosed up. I don't want to hear your complaining." I winked at him. "Hey, I'm really glad it wasn't worse. From what I heard, a car came flying at you and hit you on the front driver's side?"

"Yeah. Maybe I'll remember it differently in a couple of days' time, but it seemed to me that the other car was stopped, ready to enter the street. Then they saw me and accelerated."

"Oh, no. You think it was deliberate?"

"Yeah. I didn't see who it was. The car was silver. An SUV."

"Okay. Gotcha. Any other details?"

He shook his head, then groaned a little from the effort. "I think I smacked my head on the window. I can't recall anything else. It's a blur."

"That's understandable. Sorry about your sore head."

"Yeah, me too. I'm thinking this person could be someone with a gripe against the police, maybe?"

"That's feasible. They didn't stop afterwards, but someone did call an ambulance and said they'd just hit a car. So, someone with a gripe but also a conscience?"

"It's hurting my head just trying to figure that one out."

"I'd better let you have some rest."

"Thanks for stopping in, Wakeland. Sorry I was too groggy to talk when you came in earlier. They gave me a heavy-duty pain killer when they were fixing my wrist."

"You must have really been away with the fairies, then. I wasn't here earlier."

"Are you kidding me? You were standing right there, just inside the door."

"It was probably a doctor or a nurse."

"Nope. They weren't dressed like a doc or a nurse. She was wearing a jacket and a long skirt. I know skirts aren't your style, Wakeland, but bear with me. She was tall with short blonde hair, cut like yours."

"Hmmm, interesting. So, do you know anyone who looks like that?"

"Don't think so. My family is Italian. No tall blondes among them. Anyway, I don't think any family or friends even know I'm in the hospital yet. So, who would it be?"

"Franco, I just had a bad thought. Did you happen to notice what Louisa Eisen was wearing when you saw her at the station earlier?"

He frowned as if thinking hard. "Can't remember. Too fuzzy." He opened his eyes wide as he followed my train of thought. "You think it could have been Louisa?"

"I'm not certain. But what if she thought I was in the car with you? The last time she saw us, we had both walked to your car. I'm going to go chase this up."

"You don't have to. Leave it to the CIU."

"Try and stop me." I shot him a smile. "Hey, do you want anything? Drink? Food? Call your mother? Plump your pillow?"

"Nah. I'm feeling a bit woozy. And don't call my mother. She'll have an army of relatives down here in a flash for a bedside vigil. I just need to zonk out."

"Okay. Have a good rest. And get better quick."

Heading out of the hospital, I called the Collision Investigation Unit. In a conversation with them, I learned that they'd had a couple of reports about the accident from the public, but the two witnesses had only given the same details that Franco had. The car had been a silver SUV. Neither of the witnesses had been close enough to tell exactly what type of car it was.

Could the hit-and-run driver have really been Louisa? I didn't think she'd do something like that. And was she the woman Franco had seen in his room?

Although she was a few years younger, Louisa could resemble me in the eyes of someone with blurry vision, as Franco's had been. She had a tall frame, like mine, and her hair was similar. My hair was straighter and more of an ash shade, but the differences were not extreme. Silver SUVs were common, but Louisa did have one and she had been in the area. And of course, she'd been angry with me.

Please don't let it be you, Louisa.

With a sinking feeling, I became almost certain that it was.

When I tried calling her, I just got her message bank.

Without the option to talk to her via phone, I drove to the Eisens' house.

Alex was outside as I arrived, collecting the mail. I didn't see Louisa's car parked under the carport where she normally kept it.

I parked and then hurried across to him. "Alex, is Louisa at home?"

He gave me a sharp look. "No. She's not, actually."

"Do you know where I can find her?"

"Detective Wakeland, would you mind leaving us alone for a while? What you're doing amounts to stalking."

Taking out his phone, he began filming me. "Here we have Detective Kate Wakeland back at our house, yet again. She was only here just this morning. We've started proceedings to put in a complaint about her conduct. And lo-and-behold, she's back here, again. Are you here to intimidate us into withdrawing that complaint, Detective Wakeland?"

"Alex, please don't do this. Put the phone away."

He kept filming. "No, I won't."

"I really do need to talk with Louisa."

"She's gone away. You can talk with her when she gets back. Better still, don't. She's had enough."

"She's gone away? Where?"

"You don't give up, do you? My wife just needed some time away. I don't need to tell you where."

"Actually, you do. We have an unconfirmed report that Louisa was involved in an accident at Katoomba." It was a lie, and my lie was being captured on film. It was a big risk to take.

His voice faltered. "My wife wasn't involved in any accident. She's fine."

"The other person isn't. He's in the hospital."

His arm dropped away, and he switched off the phone. His mouth hung open as he stared at me.

"Alex," I said, "did you notice any damage on the front of your wife's car before she left?"

"There was no damage that I saw."

I believed him that he hadn't noticed the damage and that he didn't know about the accident. Perhaps Louisa had made sure he didn't see any dents.

"I'm afraid I might have to put out an APB if I can't find her," I told Alex. "An All Points Bulletin."

"Please don't do that," he said in a contrite tone. "Look, she's gone down to the South Coast. To Vincentia. We've got a holiday property there. Like I said, she felt like she needed to get away." His voice faded out. I assumed he was realising exactly why his wife had gone away in such in a hurry.

"Alex, I assume that once I leave here, you're going to try calling Louisa to alert her. Please understand that I'm not saying for certain that it was Louisa who was involved in the accident. If you talk to her, please tell her the best thing for her to do is to find somewhere safe to pull off the road and wait for the police to arrive. When the police get there, they'll ascertain whether her car has been in an accident."

"I'll jump straight in my car and head down there."

"It's best that you leave it to the police."

Alex hunched his shoulders. "I'm worried about her. My car's currently being fixed at the mechanics. But it should be ready any minute now."

"Okay, look. You can drive down there when it's ready. Just give us a head start, all right?"

I walked back to my car, my head swimming.

Only one thing was clear. I needed to follow Louisa down to the South Coast. If she was desperate enough to ram a police car, then she might be desperate enough to harm herself. I didn't want that on my conscience.

Or, she might even decide to remove the bumper bar from the front of her car and dispose of it. Then there'd be no evidence of the accident.

If it *was* Louisa, why did she do it? Was she really that upset with me, or was she trying to stop the investigation? I'd gotten an odd feeling from her since the day I'd first told her I was reopening the case.

I needed to find out answers to all those questions—tonight.

57

KATE

I raced upstairs to my bedroom and began tossing items into an overnight bag. The dinner I'd prepared earlier was in the oven, cooking.

Pete walked in, fresh from a shower with a towel around his waist. "Kate? You're going away?"

I paused, my back and shoulders sagging. This day had exhausted me, but there was no stopping now. "Yes. I'll be back tomorrow."

"What's happening?"

"Franco's in the hospital—a car accident."

Pete's eyes were large with concern. "Is he okay?"

"Yes. Thankfully. Just a fractured wrist. It was a hit and run. Pete, I've got good reason to think it was Louisa Eisen. I just went to her house to talk with her. And you know what? She's gone. Her husband said she needed to get away for a while... so she's headed to their holiday house."

"Whew! Crazy stuff. I'm glad the accident wasn't worse. I got to admit, it does sound suspicious that Louisa has left town all of a sudden. Pretty coincidental."

"It really is. I tried calling, but her phone's turned off. Pete, I need to see her car before she has a chance to have it fixed."

"Where's the holiday house?"

"The South Coast. Apparently."

"*The South Coast?*" His eyebrows shot up. "You're driving all that way *now?*"

I nodded. "It's not just the accident... but why she did it. I'm worried that she's hiding something."

"You think it was deliberate?"

"I can't be one hundred percent certain. Wait... no, I *am* certain. Pete, I have to go. Please give the kids kisses for me."

"Who's going on this little road trip with you? Obviously not Franco."

"It's just me. It'll be fine."

"No. That's not happening. You're not going alone. You haven't been sleeping well. I see you tossing and turning during the nights."

"This is a police matter. It's just work."

"And one member of your team is out of action. So, I'm stepping in. I'll drive while you sleep." He pressed his teeth down on his lip. "I like driving. You need sleep. A perfect match, am I right?"

"Okay. All right. You've convinced me. And... thanks." I shot him a smile that was meant to be warm, but I guessed that it just looked tense.

Pete went to his wardrobe and dressed himself quickly. He threw a tee-shirt and shaving gear into a bag. "Okay, I'm ready."

We stood in the room, facing each other.

I worried about Pete joining me on a police mission. Things were likely to get messy. Louisa had been increasingly unstable—especially now if she really had deliberately crashed into a police car. Once we got to our destination, I had to keep Pete out of it.

"Let's go," he told me. "We'll grab dinner on the way."

"What about the dinner that's in the oven?"

"I'll tell Abby to get that sorted. All the hard work's done. She'll just have to keep an eye on it."

After briefly explaining to Abby what was happening, we headed out the door.

The sky was settling into a deep purplish-grey hue as we drove from the mountains and onto the highway.

Sitting in the front passenger seat, I pulled a thick blanket up around my shoulders. Immediately, warmth entered my bones and my head felt fuzzy.

Pete glanced at me. "You look sleepy."

"I am," I admitted. "So much for me being on the job."

"And you were about to take off on your own."

"I'm a safe driver. I won't drive if I've gone past the point where I can stay alert." I stretched. "I'm just allowing myself to switch off."

"Yeah. But you've spent a lot of years pushing yourself like that. Sooner or later, it's gotta be time to slow down. Hey... you know what? It's been years since we went on a road trip somewhere."

"You're right. It really has been years. Our lives have been on hold for a long time."

"We have to start remedying that. Make a list of places. And just go. Remember all the places we've talked about going? India. Ireland. Hiking the redwood forests in California...."

"I remember. Sounds good to me."

"It does?" Pete chewed the side of his lip as he drove. "Because, you know, your career...."

"I know—it gets in the way. One day soon, I've got to make the call and walk out of there for good."

"When? I mean, I know you couldn't leave when Ivy was missing. But once the two cases with Layla and Emmet Eisen are over, can you see yourself leaving?"

"I want to. I do. But I also feel like I'm not quite finished."

"I get it. But *I* want you. I want us to be able to do things together. We've got the cottage and the land now—and that's great. We got brave. Not long ago, we were both thinking of downsizing, remember that? Well, I'm glad we bought the property instead. We have to keep being brave. Take a leap. Go off and have some adventures."

"You're right. So very right. I just...."

I hesitated as I tried to form words in my head—words that hadn't even come to the surface yet. Shadowy thoughts. Whispers. Blurry images.

"Pete... I don't know how to say this without you thinking I'm going a bit crazy...."

"Whatever it is, you know you can tell me."

"Okay... but it's hard. I don't even know how to explain it to myself. It's just that I can't help but feel that something isn't right with our town. Something at its core."

Pete went silent for a few moments.

"Something at the *core*?" he said. "What, you mean like a bad apple or something?"

"Yes."

"What's at the core?"

"I don't know, exactly. That's what's been keeping me awake at night. I've got the sense of something big—and terrible—but I just can't manage to make the connections."

"Honey, do you think maybe things lately have been getting to you? It can't have been easy to find Layla in that awful place. I don't know how I'd handle that myself."

"Yes, that was... horrific. But this is something more. I sit and picture water flowing through the reeds of this town. Things keep banking up, and the water is not flowing as it should. It's not just about Layla and Abby and Emmet. It's about a lot of things. Things that go way, way back."

"You mean... something that's organised? Organised crime?"

"Not exactly. Because the intent of organised crime is to make a profit, right? That kind of crime leaves trails that you can follow. It's predictable. This is different. But like I said, I can't explain it."

"Have you talked to Franco about this?"

I shook my head, staring ahead at the road. "Franco likes his cases concrete. He's a good detective—one of the very best. But he doesn't place a lot of value in the things you can sense but can't see. So, I can't really discuss this with him. He'll just scratch his head and say, *tell me when you've got something I can do something about, Wakeland."* I gave a dry laugh.

Pete returned the laugh. "That sounds like Franco."

I inhaled the dry, warm air of the car's interior. "If I leave the force now, I can't do anything about it. I can't fix it."

"You can't fix everything, Kate. You can't fix the world. We've got a long drive ahead. Why don't you have a sleep? Just forget everything for the next hour or so."

I began to feel myself drift, the low hum of the motor in my ears.

The night swooped down, the purple-hued sunset giving way. At home, the dark seemed to lumber along, crawling up and over the mountains and pooling in the valleys, with glints of sunlight staying stubborn on the higher ranges.

Here, there was just the black, straight line of highway ahead.

58

KATE

I woke as Pete was driving through the long road that snaked through Kangaroo Valley. I knew the road well. For endless kilometres, there were fields and hills.

It was another hour from here before we reached Vincentia. We'd been on the road for two hours so far.

I tried calling Louisa again. No answer. Then I tried Alex. He said he was on his way.

I dozed off again, only waking this time when Pete's booming voice announced that he was starving. We'd reached the coastline.

We stopped off at a restaurant to buy some dinner that we could take back to the car and eat quickly.

"How are you feeling?" Pete asked. "Did the nap and food help you feel more awake?"

I grinned. "Yep. That and the ocean breeze. Totally awake."

"We'd better find a motel."

"Pete, I need to go find Louisa now."

"I'll come too."

"You can't. I'm here as a detective. I need to do this alone."

He exhaled heavily, running his hand through his hair. "Can it at least wait until morning?"

I shook my head. "It has to be now."

We drove around until we found a motel at a place called Sailors Grave Beach. Leaving Pete to book in, I headed off.

The GPS told me that the Eisens' holiday house was near a heavily wooded area named Greenfield Gully. I made my way there, to a street where the houses were sparse and there was a forest on the opposite side.

The Eisens' holiday house was a cute little single-storey home with a letter box in the shape of a surfboard.

All the lights were off.

Damn. Where was she?

The bracing sea air hit my face as I stepped from the car, making me shiver.

Before walking to her front door, I peered through the garage window.

Louisa's car was in there. The silver SUV.

Good. She was here.

The garage was a barn-like weatherboard building that stood by itself. Getting inside proved to be easy. There was no lock on the side door.

Switching on the light on my phone, I checked the stainless-steel bumper bar she had on the front of her car. It was dented.

I snapped a series of six pictures.

Sending the pictures off to online storage, I headed for the front door of the house. A porch light flickered on.

I rapped lightly on the wooden door.

She didn't answer my knock. But she had to be in there. Where would she go at night without her car?

"Louisa! It's Kate. Kate Wakeland. I'd just like to talk with you."

A minute passed before I heard trudging footsteps inside the house.

Louisa's pale face was filled with fear and uncertainty when she cracked the door open.

"Hi... I'm guessing you know why I'm here."

"What do you want from me? I needed some time, and I can't even have that. You just keep chasing me."

"I'm sorry that it's felt that way to you. From my side of things, I've tried to go easy on you and Alex. Louisa, did you drive into a police car earlier today?"

Her eyes darted away. "I don't know what you're talking about."

I showed her a photo of her car's bent bumper bar.

Her shoulders lifted and bunched inward, her lips sucking in tightly. "Am I going to be arrested?"

"Not at the moment. I want to talk with you. Inside?"

"Fine."

She let me into the house.

From what I could see in the dim light, the interior was decorated in a style typical of holiday houses—pale wooden floors, old furniture painted white, and collections of shells in wicker bowls.

A few tea candles flickered here and there.

The TV was on but the sound was off. An oil heater provided a comforting warmth to the air.

"Mind the rug," Louisa said. "It's easy to trip on. I didn't want to put on the lights. Because then the neighbours will know that I'm here. And I didn't feel like talking to anyone tonight. Anyway, have a seat. Can I get you a coffee or tea?"

"No, thanks, Louisa." I sat on the worn leather couch.

She sat opposite me, knees together, hands on her lap, shoulders still high. The TV screen made shadows move across her face.

I couldn't imagine why she'd thought it a good idea to come all this way on her own and sit here in almost complete darkness. She must have known the police wouldn't be far behind.

"So, you came all this way to talk to me because of the accident?" she said in a quiet tone.

"*Was* it an accident?"

"In truth, I don't know what it was. How is Detective Franco doing?"

"He's recovering. A broken wrist. You went to see him in the hospital, didn't you?"

She nodded. "I'm glad it wasn't anything more serious. Kate, what's going to happen now?"

"I'm afraid I can't tell you what a court will decide. There might be extenuating circumstances. It was you who called the ambulance, wasn't it?"

She nodded.

"The crash investigation unit will arrive first thing in the morning. The best thing to do is just to wait here for them. Don't go anywhere, okay?"

Her voice became wobbly and thin as she spoke again. "I never could have thought my life would pan out this way. It used to be a good life. A happy family. I don't know how so many things went wrong. I feel... persecuted. My son died, and then Alex's business went bad... and now... *you*. You've been coming around with your questions... and then yet *more* questions. I'm sure that for you, it feels like a whole decade has passed since Emmet died. Because, it has. But for me, it's been but a blink of an eye."

She began sobbing, silently at first, but then a low, lost sound came from her throat.

I exhaled a tense breath. "I wish I didn't have to pursue this case. Please believe that."

"My son was a good person, Kate. He might have had a few... different things about him. A few quirks. But everyone does."

"What kind of quirks?"

She looked away, pulling at her cardigan and crisscrossing it tightly over her chest.

59

KATE

It was time to ask Louisa Eisen about her son.

"Louisa," I began, "did you know that Emmet and my daughter had some sort of relationship?"

I hated calling it a relationship, but I wanted to tread lightly and keep her talking to me.

She looked at me aghast, then bent her head. "Not exactly. Sometimes I'd see them talking alone or out on Emmet's boat. I could tell that Abby had a crush on him. She was very attractive. And tall. When she wore makeup at the parties, she looked more like a sixteen-year-old. It did worry me. But I never thought that Emmet would—" She breathed out slowly. "If only Abby had been older. I think the two of them would have made a nice couple."

Internally, I shuddered at the thought. I hadn't told Louisa about the strange and terrible fetishes of her son. It was going to hurt her a lot when she did find out. And if her son had killed Layla, she would be even more devastated. For now, I wanted her cooperation, and I couldn't do that by laying everything out on the table.

"Did you ever talk about it with Emmet?" I asked.

"Yes, I did. I told him it could be seen by others as... inappropriate."

"And what did he say?"

"He'd say that he couldn't stop Abby from coming down to the lake."

"What about the times he took her out on his boat?"

"He admitted that it could have been inappropriate, in retrospect."

"You said that Emmet had some quirks? Could you tell me about that?"

She pulled her lips in. "He was a loner. Preferred his own company. He only ever had one girlfriend, and that was only for three months, if that. But he seemed to like Abby's company... too much."

"Okay." I drew a steady breath, pausing. "Now, about that graffiti that Emmet wrote on the wall at Close Quarters. Do you know why he wrote, Goodbye Lullaby?"

Louisa shook her head. "I have honestly no idea. As I said, my son had quirks. All I do know is that he and Alex had a big argument over it at the time."

"About what, exactly?"

"Alex was just telling Emmet to grow up and be a man. That's my Alex. The typical type A personality. That's just who he is. Alex was always a go-getter. Whatever he does, he's completely driven. Emmet was more of a dreamer, a passenger in his own life. That annoyed Alex no end."

"So, Alex had been annoyed with Emmet in general during that time?"

"Yes. Emmet was drinking too much, and he was depressed. Alex and I couldn't understand why."

Wind rattled the windows of the old holiday house. A draft circled my shoulders. I guessed that repairs hadn't been carried out on the house in a long time.

I leaned forward. "Louisa, could I ask you about something?" Taking out my phone, I scrolled through the picture gallery until I found the photo of a vintage chronograph watch. It was the watch that had been on the wrist of the man who'd been in those videos with Nola Hobson.

Turning the screen to her, I showed her the photo. "Have you seen this watch before?"

She peered at the image. "No?"

"Are you sure? Emmet never had a watch like this?"

"He had an old watch his grandfather gave him before we left Germany. But that isn't it."

"Okay. Thank you."

I'd hoped she'd say *yes*. Then we could have moved this case along swiftly.

"What's all this about, Kate? Asking me about the lullaby thing, and now about this watch. Please, you need to back off. And, to be honest, I can't think of a single reason why you and your daughter needed to go for a walk right near my house. It's not like there aren't dozens and dozens of nice walks around our area. It did feel like harassment, as if you two were trying to put pressure on me."

"That's not why we were there at all. It was a police matter."

"With your daughter? Didn't seem like a police matter to me."

I was about to admit things to Louisa that almost no one else knew. And once Louisa knew, I wouldn't be able to keep it under wraps much longer.

"I needed Abby to come along," I said, "because she's the only one who knew where she put a certain object, ten years ago. That object was Emmet's journal."

Louisa stared back at me silently.

"Just after Emmet died," I explained, "Abby went to get the journal. She didn't want anyone finding it and reading it, but she also didn't feel like she could throw it away. She was a child, and she did what a child might do. She hid the book."

"That was Emmet's property," Louisa exclaimed.

"You knew about the journal?" I said in surprise.

"Yes. It was his therapist's idea."

"Okay, so the journal was therapy?"

"That's right. Alex asked around and found someone for him. Emmet refused at first, but then he agreed. You know, sometimes, I

330

thought that if I crept into his room and read the journal one day, I'd understand what was going on inside his head. I did read a couple of pages one time. But then, he died. After that, I didn't want to read it." Her mouth twisted. "Abby didn't have the right to run and hide his journal where she did."

"Louisa?"

"Yes, on the day Abby hid the journal, I followed her."

Tension wound up inside me. "It was you who took the journal from the little cave, wasn't it?"

She nodded. "Abby looked very suspicious that afternoon. Emmet had only just died that morning. I knew that his classes of children had been told. But there was Abby, after school, sneaking off on a kayak, looking over her shoulders. I had to wonder what she was doing. So, I followed her. I took out my own kayak, being careful to stay out of sight. I saw her take the box out of her schoolbag and put it in the cave. I knew exactly what the box was and what was inside it. She stayed for a while, crying. I cried with her, though she didn't know I was there. When she finally left, I went and retrieved the box."

I didn't know whether I was more stunned that she'd done that or that I hadn't considered the possibility that it was her who'd followed Abby that day.

"Why did Abby think she had a right to it?" Louisa cried. "Did she break into my house to get it—from Emmet's bedroom?"

"No. That's not where she got it."

"Then, where, for goodness' sake?"

"I can't tell you that right now. But it wasn't from your house."

"Oh, so many secrets." She shook her head mournfully. "Everyone has secrets. It's not the secrets that destroy us. It's when people hide them away...."

I gazed at her directly. "What did you do with the journal?"

"It's gone. Destroyed."

I couldn't help but inhale a loud breath. "*Destroyed?*"

"Yes. I took it home and burned it. That journal contained Emmet's private words. Abby didn't have the right to keep it. As his mother, it was my duty to ensure it remained private." Her shoulders trembled. "Whatever he did in life, he paid the ultimate price already. He's dead."

Silence fell in the space between us, with the deft blow of a hammer.

Internally, I felt desolate.

"Louisa—you said you read a couple of pages of the journal?" I said in desperation. "Would you mind telling me what you read?"

Her expression turned bitter. "He spoke about your daughter. He liked her... a little too much. If I'd known, I would have banned her from coming to our parties. But I didn't read the journal until just days before he died. It was too late."

My back went rigid as I listened. "Didn't Emmet's words make you worry... about his state of mind?"

Her face looked pinched, drained. "Of course. But I didn't know what to do. He was already talking to a therapist." Tears streamed freely down her face. "And then after he died, I had to endure whispers about him. And the autopsy. And our house broken into and Emmet's things desecrated. We were left with nothing... just nothing."

"Your house was broken into? When?"

"About four days after Emmet died. It was during when our family and friends were all out on the lake on boats—having a special remembrance for Emmet. It was a brazen daylight robbery."

"I had no idea."

"Honestly, at the time, it was the least of my concerns. Alex and I didn't make a big deal of it, because we were both pretty numb."

"We were broken into around that time, too. And it was Abby's room that got upended the most. That's got me a little suspicious, now."

Louisa straightened. "You, too? Well, that's odd."

"Yes, it is. They took some of my jewellery and a watch belonging to my husband. We thought it was an everyday robbery. But now, I really have to wonder if the only reason they stole those things was to make it look that way."

"So, what are you thinking? That it was the same person?"

"Possibly. If so, then they were looking for the journal."

"This is all too much. Who could it have been? And what interest did they have in Emmet's words?"

"Louisa... I'll tell you something about where the investigation is headed. We're looking at the possibility of Emmet having had a friend in the year leading up to his death—a friend who he later fell out with. We think this friend pushed Emmet around on the day of his death. That explains the bruises. The fight seems to have been about Abby. We think the friend knew about the journal and was worried that something in it might implicate him."

"Implicate him in what?"

"Having interactions with underage girls."

"Oh...."

"Now, we're not certain of any of this. But it's what we've pieced together so far."

"Kate, would you please tell me where Abby found my son's journal? I have the right to know."

"Okay, I'll tell you. Louisa... Emmet kept his journal at the old funfair."

She looked faint, her cheeks hollowing. "The funfair? You don't mean—"

"The same place where we found Layla, yes."

Louisa jerked herself up from her seat. She began pacing the floor. "No, no, this is wrong. This is all wrong."

"I'm sorry."

"I think I'm going to be sick." She hurried away, swallowed up by the darkness in the corridor.

I heard water being turned on in a bathroom, old pipes groaning and protesting.

She returned to the living room, a haunted expression on her face. I tried to speak to her, but she didn't reply.

I raised my voice. "Louisa, please switch on your phone so that Alex can get through to you. I think you might need to talk with him right now. He's on his way."

"I'm fine."

She wasn't fine at all.

"I'll wait with you until Alex gets here."

"No, I don't want you to. You're the one who dug all of this up. If not for you—and your daughter—all this would have stayed in the past. Where it belongs. I'm very sorry about Nina's niece, of course, but she's dead, and no one can change that now. I don't know why I let myself sit and talk with you. I was stupid. Please leave, Kate."

I nodded. "If that's what you want."

She locked eyes with me. "Get out."

She was talking like someone who was in shock. I left her house and returned to my car. The whole encounter had been so tense, it'd left me shaken, too.

I knew two things, now.

I knew that Louisa wasn't hiding anything, apart from having knowledge of the journal and a few pages of its contents.

And I knew that the journal had been destroyed.

60

KATE

I drove towards Sailors Grave Beach, where Pete and I had booked the motel. Losing my way, I stopped to check the GPS.

Vincentia was a small place, but I wasn't familiar with it and it was easy to get my directions mixed up. I was on Berry Street. I'd come through a row of houses and now there was only bushland on either side.

Okay, wrong way.

But instead of turning around and heading straight back down the road, I found myself just sitting, an image of Louisa's anguished face in my mind.

I hated leaving her alone. After learning that Emmet had been keeping his journal at the funfair, all kinds of thoughts must be whirling through her mind.

I sent Alex a text: *How far are you away? I think Louisa really needs you right now.*

About forty minutes he texted back.

Forty minutes wasn't long. But it could seem like an eternity to Louisa. I hoped she wouldn't go do something rash, like drive away and crash the car again. Something else worried me, too. Louisa had thought

I was stalking her. But what if someone actually *had* been stalking her? It wasn't likely, but still, it made me nervous that she was here all alone.

I called Pete.

"Kate, you're taking longer than I thought you would," he said. "Is everything okay?"

"I'm a little worried about Louisa's state of mind. I'm just going to stay and watch her house and make sure she doesn't leave. Until Alex gets here. He said he'll be forty minutes."

"You're gonna be sitting in the car by yourself all that time?"

"Yeah. I'll be okay. I've got my blanket."

"Come pick me up. I'll wait with you. You've already gotten your police stuff out of the way."

"You don't have to do that."

"If you don't pick me up, I'm walking down there myself."

"Okay, okay. I'm coming."

I swung the car around and went to the motel. Pete was waiting out the front. He jumped in and I drove back to the street where Louisa's holiday house was. I parked a short distance away, where she wouldn't notice my car, not even if she came right out of her house and looked.

Pete wrapped the blanket around himself and me. "Going to be a long wait."

"Yes. Can't tell you how many hours I've spent doing this kind of thing. Just... waiting and watching."

"Hell of a job."

"Yep. Who'd do it?"

"Oh, just some crazy lady who wants to save everyone."

I laughed. "Hey... Pete... I've been wanting to tell you something. This has been such a difficult year for our family. On top of a rough three years. You've been an absolute rock through all of it."

I could tell I'd caught Pete off-guard with that comment. I knew that I'd been rushing around and not always noticing things that were going on within our family. But what I'd said was true. Pete was always the steady presence in the household.

I hugged him.

The two of us then sat chatting about family things and about Pete's garden.

"I want to try planting vanilla beans," he told me. "Going to need a glasshouse for that."

"Well, we've got the space for it now."

"Yeah, hard to get used to the fact that we have loads of land now. I've got all kinds of ideas running through my head, and I—"

He stopped short. "You said Alex wasn't here yet, right?"

"That's right."

"Well, there's a man at the side of the house—wait, dammit, I think he might have just climbed out of a window."

"Wait here." Drawing my gun, I exited the car.

The man raced away up the street.

"Stop!" I yelled. "I'll shoot."

I fired a warning shot, adrenalin surging through my limbs.

The man vanished into the forest. In there, he could go in any direction.

I spun around as someone raced up behind me. It was Pete.

He grasped my arm. "I'll go get him. I run faster than you."

"Pete, no. He could be dangerous. Stay put. I need to check on Louisa."

But Pete was already off and running.

I raced in the other direction, to Louisa's house.

The front door was locked.

With my gun still drawn, I ran around to the side of the house. Curtains ruffled in the wind, blowing outward from an open window. That must be where the man had exited the house. I didn't want to access the house that way in case I disturbed any fingerprints.

The back door was also locked. The French doors had just a flimsy lock between them. With two hard kicks, I had the doors open.

I rushed inside.

On the kitchen bench top, a kettle lay on its side, water leaking and pooling on the floor. Pieces of a ceramic cup were scattered about.

Louisa must have been pouring herself out a cup of coffee when the man disturbed her. Watery footprints led into the living room.

Carefully stepping around the splashes of water and footprints, I moved into the living room.

A figure lay sprawled face down on the floor beside the sofa.

Louisa.

I hurried across and knelt next to her. I checked her pulse and then adjusted her head to test her breathing. Her lip was split and bloodied. Running a hand over her scalp, I felt for any lumps. There was a large, bone-like mass on the back of her head. The intruder had either hit her from behind or she'd done this while falling.

I shouldn't have left her alone.

The man must have been watching the house, and he'd ventured inside only once I'd left. I'd probably surprised him when I returned. I guessed that he'd heard my car as it came up the street.

Louisa murmured, a low moan coming from her throat. As she woke, she recoiled from my touch.

"Louisa, it's me, Kate."

"Kate..." Her voice was hoarse and fearful. "There's a man... is he still here?"

"No. He ran off. Did you see who it was?"

She shook her head. "He wore a balaclava."

"Did he say anything?"

"No, no words. Nothing."

"Just rest, okay? I'm going to look around."

"Please... stay with me."

"Let me help you up."

I assisted her to the lounge, then fetched her some tissues from a tissue box she had on the nearby coffee table. "Hold these to your lip. It's bleeding."

She nodded gratefully.

"I won't go far," I told her. "I just need to check that no one else is in the house."

I called for an ambulance and police backup while I headed down the hallway.

Switching lights on as I went, I checked all the rooms. They were a mess. The man had thrown things everywhere.

To the left was a small sunroom. Every book in the wide, wall-to-ceiling bookcase had been torn out and strewn on the ground.

I looked in Louisa and Alex's bedroom next. Drawers and cupboard doors hung open. Louisa had a gold watch and earrings on the bedside table. The man hadn't touched them. That told me that he wasn't a thief who was looking for expensive items.

I ran back to Louisa.

"Can I see your hands?" I asked.

She held up both hands, gazing at me in confusion. "You don't think I did this to my own house, do you? There really *was* a man in here."

"I know. I saw him. I just wanted to see if you still had your wedding rings or any others. I see that you do. And the watch in your bedroom wasn't taken, either. I don't think the intruder was looking for the usual things."

"Then what was he looking for?" She wiped at her lip with the tissue. "And why did you come back?"

I sat beside her. "I was worried about you. You told Superintendent Bigley that I've been stalking you. And, well, I haven't been. So, I thought that maybe someone has been doing that. Where were you when you thought you were being stalked?"

"When I went for walks in the forest near my home, mostly. And then when you turned up with Abby, I thought you were getting more brazen."

"I'll make a wild guess, Louisa. The man who came here is the one who's been stalking you. And whoever he is, he's looking for the journal."

Her eyes widened. "Surely not. It's been ten years...."

"That's true. But the two cases have been in the news lately—about Emmet and Layla. I'm guessing this man knows that we're close to finding out things he doesn't want known. And for some reason, he thinks you have the journal. Did you tell anyone that you had it?"

"No." She rubbed the back of her head, feeling the large lump that was there. "Except... Alex and I have had a couple of get-togethers recently. I've admittedly been getting pretty drunk and shooting my mouth off—about the police. About *you*. I really don't think I mentioned the journal... but perhaps I did?"

"Yes, you might have let something slip."

She grimaced. "Who *was* that man? Following me. Breaking into my house. What the hell does he want from me? My blood? The journal is all I have left of my boy."

A rush of pinpricks sped down my back and arms. "Louisa? That sounds a lot like—"

She turned her head to look away from me. "Yes," she said flatly. "I still have it."

I drew a sharp, deep breath. "Right. Okay...."

"I keep it in my safe deposit box in town," Louisa told me, her voice still leaden. "Alex doesn't know about it. I've been paying for it for all these years."

The wails of an ambulance and police cars wailed in the distance.

"Can I have the key to the safe deposit box?" I asked boldly.

She hesitated, staring at me. Then she nodded. "I guess it's time. No matter what's in the pages of that thing... I'll still have the good memories of my Emmet."

As an ambulance parked in the driveway, I told Louisa I had to go. She was in good hands now.

I needed to go find Pete.

61

KATE

The police arrived just after the ambulance. I gave the team clear instructions: while they were searching for the intruder in the forest, they were not to shoot. They could mistake my husband for the other guy.

Ten minutes later, they found Pete, but not the intruder. The intruder was long gone, it seemed. I guessed he'd planned out what to do if he were disturbed. A neighbour had heard a car screeching away on another street, which could easily have been the intruder—if he'd exited the forest on that street.

Alex pulled up outside his holiday house. He looked dazed at he viewed the surrounding scene. Police and ambulance vehicles. And neighbours everywhere who'd come to see what the commotion was about.

I explained to him what had happened tonight.

"Where's Louisa now?" he asked anxiously.

"She's inside, resting," I told him. "The paramedics were able to treat her here. Apart from a nasty bump on her head and a cut lip, she's okay."

"I'll go in and sit with her," he said.

"Alex, I need to let you know something."

"What is it?"

"Louisa has told me she's been keeping Emmet's journal in a safe deposit box here in town. I'm going to be picking it up."

He eyed me strangely. "Emmet had a journal?"

"Yes. We'll need to keep it for a while. But we'll return it to you and Louisa after that."

He nodded and then turned and walked into the house, still looking dazed.

At least I hadn't left him entirely unprepared for what was about to come.

I requested that two police escort me to the safe deposit box. I wasn't taking any chances.

I pushed the key into the metal box and then opened the tiny door. Inside was a wooden box. Locked. I rattled it. There was a book inside.

It was hard to believe I was holding it in my hands. I was itching to open up the box and start reading, but the journal needed finger-printing first. I had to wait.

I transferred the box into a secure vault at the local police station, and then Pete and I returned to the motel and crawled into bed.

"How're you feeling?" Pete asked me.

"Wrecked. I feel bad that I left Louisa alone. It took me too long to put the pieces together."

"You couldn't have known that the guy would chase her all the way here."

"I didn't know that for certain, no."

He kissed my head. "Well, then stop beating yourself up."

"You shouldn't have gone after him. He could have hurt you."

"I guess that nabbing that guy just seemed like something I could actually *do*. All the stuff lately—about Abby and then Layla—those are things I can't do anything about."

"I'm glad you're okay."

We watched TV until we both fell asleep.

The morning sun was on our faces when we woke again. I'd slept later than I'd meant to.

"Got to run!" I jumped up and started dressing.

Pete sat up, yawning. "Hold on. Can't it wait for a few minutes? We're at the beach. I kind of thought it'd be nice to take a walk?"

I hesitated, then took a breath, nodding. "Let's go."

Pete threw some clothes on, and we walked together down to Sailors Grave Beach.

The beach was a small curve of some of the whitest sand I'd ever seen, densely ringed by trees. The early morning sun gave a rose-coloured glow to the ocean.

Pete was a few steps ahead of me. He twisted around. "Hurry up, slow poke."

"I hurt my foot kicking a door in last night."

"If you asked anyone else how they hurt their foot, it wouldn't be *that*." Shaking his head, he grinned. "My wife, the detective."

I limped over to him.

"Should have told me it was busted," he said. "We didn't have to walk all this way."

"It's not broken or anything. I'll live. Anyway, after the day I had yesterday, it's very nice to see this." I gestured at the sunrise. "I think I needed it."

Pete slung an arm around me. "We need to see a lot more sunrises like this one, in different parts of the world."

"Yes, we do."

We took a brief wander along the sand.

Four hours later, I was back at Tallman's Valley police station.

Inspector Shintani and I sat at the meeting table. The box containing the journal sat on the table. Everything had been finger-printed and inspected by forensic specialists, with the contents of the journal photocopied.

Franco was a last-minute arrival, walking in with his hand in plaster. He'd insisted on coming straight back on duty after being released from the hospital.

Shintani opened the lid and then lifted the journal out.

The journal had a plain cover.

He then plucked three locks of hair from the box. The locks were all tied with ribbons. Two blonde, one brunette.

Immediately, I felt sick to the stomach.

"Okay," said Shintani. "We have some reading to do." He handed out a photocopy to each of us and kept one copy for himself.

Shintani then raised his dark eyes to me. "Good work, Kate."

I nodded in acknowledgement then began reading.

62

JOURNAL EXCERPTS

September 2nd

The girls are down by the lake again. Practising their ballet.

They are beautiful.

Perfect and innocent.

But my days in this room are so damned dark.

I've been holed up in here for weeks, watching the lake from my bedroom window.

I want to end it, just end it right here.

My doc is making me write this journal. Said it would help.

I didn't want to get a head-doctor. Can't think of anything worse than sitting across from some guy in a suit who's pretending to look interested while watching the clock with one eye. But my parents wouldn't let it go.

I shouldn't have come back here.

This is a mistake.

September 6th

I want to call the school and tell them I can't start.

The doc said I'll be fine.

I need to face my fears.

October 17th

Started teaching at Valley Grammar.

The kids are okay.

The girls sure do giggle a lot.

My parents keep trying to drag me into their social life.

They're worried about me spending so much of my free time alone.

I'm not alone. I've got the birds and the animals along the lake to keep me company. What else do I need?

October 20th

My parents held a welcome home party for me—them and their collection of odd-bods and friends.

I didn't want to be there.

I shouldn't have come back to Tallman's Valley. If I could go back in time, I would have taken off overseas. Not for a gap year, but for a gap decade.

Why did I end up at university studying science? What possessed me to become a teacher?

The doc says he thinks he knows. It's because I needed to go back to school and do it all again. All my teenage years. To somehow make it better, make it different. Heal from the past.

October 22th

Before we came to Australia, we lived in Soltau, Lower Saxony, Germany. It was right near the Heide theme park. My parents took me there with my cousins all the time to go on the rides. The park's Colossus ride was the fastest and highest wooden rollercoaster in the world. A heady boast for young children, as my cousins and I were.

Those were the best years.

November 15th

Woke up thinking about Canada.

It was so real, like I was there again.

When I was ten, my parents took me on a trip to Quebec.

We stayed in a cabin. A real Canadian cabin made of red cedar.

We went out and helped when they were tapping the sugar maples for sap. It was the end of the season, they told us, so the sap was dark. They graded the sap by how much light could pass through.

I was fascinated.

There was the golden shade that allowed seventy-five percent of light to pass through it. And then Amber and Dark and Very Dark. Very dark sap would allow only twenty-five percent of light through. The syrup was a rich, golden brown. I had it every morning, on my stack of pancakes, this golden-brown magic.

My ten-year-old mind had trouble grappling with the fact that this stuff had been tapped from a tree. My mother walked out of the cabin that first morning after we'd been tree-tapping and found me crying. I couldn't adequately explain why.

It was the sheer beauty of it. The colour of the sky that afternoon and the cold snap of the air on my face. And nature all around—giving things to us for free. The wood the people had chopped down for the cabins and the maple syrup. It was all too beautiful.

At age ten, I didn't have the words.

I still don't.

November 16th

Abby Wakeland hangs around like a lost puppy. I think she's lonely. She might have a crush on me. I have to tell her to go home sometimes.

If I were fourteen, I'd have the biggest crush on her.

She reminds me of maple syrup. The dark kind. I get the feeling that she only lets a little light through and holds the rest back. She's also got magic. The magic of being fourteen.

November 11th

My mother saw me writing in this journal. She looked a little too interested. I'll keep it in the boat shed from now on.

December 20th

Pre-Christmas drinks with the parents and their friends.
Fuck my life.

December 21st

I like Abby Wakeland too much.

The doc made me understand that I crossed the gulf from boy to man at age thirteen on the narrowest and shakiest of bridges. It's not really Abby I'm attracted to—it's just the idea of her.

One minute, I was just a thirteen-year-old kid. And the next, something happened that made me grow up fast.

I remember myself when I turned thirteen. I remember that boy.

Hoping I'd get the game I wanted for Christmas. Throwing sticks and climbing trees with my friends. Pulling pranks and wanting to be the best at skateboarding down at the park. Sneaking looks at cute girls in class.

But all that changed.

December 27th

I can't trust anyone.

Is everyone in this damned world hiding something twisted about themselves?

I caught him taking photos of Layla and Abby at the lake in their bikinis. With a long zoom lens. I thought I'd noticed him staring at them at the parties before.

He was whispering to himself, *Come fly to Mr Lullaby, little birdies.*

That guy is damned sick in the head.

January 7th
   GOODBYE, LULLABY.
   GOODBYE, LULLABY.
   GOODBYE, LULLABY.

63

KATE

There weren't many journal entries.

But there were enough to gain an insight into the workings of Emmet's mind.

I was stunned. But not in the way that I expected to be stunned.

In the journal, Emmet had sounded like a vulnerable, sensitive young man. He'd written *nothing* of his monstrous acts.

He'd mentioned an inappropriate attraction to Abby. And he'd talked about some man taking photos of Abby and Layla and calling himself Mr Lullaby. But even that wasn't until the end of December.

I hated to even think it, but was Superintendent Bigley right? Had Abby embellished her stories? Was it possible she'd convinced herself it was all true when she was a teenager, and now, as an adult, she'd come to believe it?

Shintani was the first to break the silence. "I don't know what to make of all this, Kate."

"Me neither," I admitted.

He drew an audible breath. "It's difficult to say this—"

"Just say it, Jiro," I told him. "I know that I might have blind spots."

He frowned. "Could the girl partly have been... fantasising? About her teacher?"

"In all honesty, I don't know what to think," I replied.

"The second thing is," he said, a stern look entering his dark eyes, "the journal named the girl. It's your own daughter, Kate."

My hands curled into tight balls on the table. "Yes."

"Before Kate says anything," Franco broke in, "*I knew.*"

Shintani eyed us coolly. "This is a serious matter."

I tried not to show the desperation I felt inside. "Yes, I'm aware. But I assure you, I've led this case just as I would any other case."

"Yet," Shintani said, "it seems we have some fairly baseless accusations against Emmet Eisen."

"I can't explain that." My mind reeled with all the things Abby had said. How could so much of it be made up? Or, had Emmet just failed to tell the truth—in his own journal?

Franco ran his hands through his hair, his fingers catching and tugging on his wavy locks. "Wakeland did everything right. Because of her, we found Layla Maddox. And it's been a proper investigation into what might have happened the night Eisen died."

Shintani looked unconvinced. "What you're saying is, this wasn't a revenge plot. Now, while I might believe that—and I do—it's not proper procedure. It can look very bad in the eyes of the public."

"This year alone," Franco said, "Wakeland's done an awful lot for the reputation of the police, and—"

"Franco," I took a breath, "it's okay. I knew this might all go wrong when I started this investigation. Whatever happens from now, I'll take it on the chin."

Ignoring me, Franco kept his gaze on Shintani. "Here's a suggestion. To clear this up, we can conduct a police interview—with Abby. Wakeland can be there, but I'll be the one asking the questions."

Shintani turned to gaze out of the meeting room window before looking back at each of us. "Okay. Go and do that. Just... keep it away from here. Then report back to me."

My first instinct was to push back at this. I wanted to protect Abby and not put her through any further trauma.

But if it had been any other young woman we were talking about, I'd have wanted to interview her.

Also, Shintani had just handed me a lifeline that I couldn't refuse.

I nodded. "Thank you."

Excusing myself, I went to call Abby.

As I'd predicted, she was hesitant and confused.

We decided to hold the interview at my house. We had a barn that had an old wooden table inside it—Pete had been using it to pot up seedlings. Today, it would serve as an interview room.

My mind was in overdrive as Franco and I drove to my house. I dusted dirt from the table with an old towel and fetched some old wooden stools. Franco placed our files and laptop computer on the table.

Pete kept Ivy and Jasper with him in the house as Abby walked to the barn. She was subdued and nervous as she stepped inside and closed the door.

Had I lost her trust? I'd sworn that I'd protect her during all of this. But now, her words were about to be questioned and dissected.

"I'd get you a coffee or tea, but the facilities here are terrible," Franco joked, trying to lighten the mood.

Abby pressed her lips into a hard, unsmiling line.

Franco flicked his gaze to me. "All righty. We'll get started."

The three of us sat at the table.

Abby picked at a loose thread on the sleeve of her top, looking down.

"Abby," Franco began, "thank you for agreeing to this. Are you okay for this session to be filmed and recorded?"

"Yes," she said so softly I could barely hear it.

"As you know," Franco said, "we've been reading Emmet Eisen's journal. We've gotten to the end of it. And his account and your account do not quite match."

Abby looked from Franco to me, startled. "What do you mean?"

Franco nodded. "I'll tell you. Emmet does talk about you, but not in the same way as you've been describing."

Her face creased with shock. "What did he say?"

"Not a lot," Franco said. "He says he liked you. But he didn't write anything about the late-night conversations. No watching you dance at the funfair. No... *lullabies*."

"I don't understand," Abby said. "Are you saying I made those things up?"

Franco held up the palms of his hands. "No. I'm not saying that."

Her eyes flashed with a cold anger as she turned to me. "Mum? You sat there and listened to those sessions with Dr Quinley. Do you think I was lying?"

"Of course not, Abby," I said quickly. "We're just trying to work out why there is such a different account of things in Emmet's journal."

She shook her head. "In other words, I'm lying."

"Abby," said Franco calmly, "you understand, better than most people, what detective work is all about. It's about getting down to the bedrock. We need your help to do that."

He pushed across a copy of Emmet's journal to her. "This is it. His journal."

Snatching it up, Abby began reading. She flipped through pages, reading bits here and there.

Finally, she raised her eyes to Franco. "This is all wrong. He talks about me like I'm a kid. He didn't see me that way. I swear to you that he didn't. And it's not true that he was trying to stop me from hanging around him so much. It was *him* asking me down to the funfair. It was *him* watching me through the mirrors. It was *him* who gave me the birdcage necklace. That was all *him*."

"We're not sure what's going on," said Franco. "We've been through the whole journal. We didn't find a single mention of the funfair or the mirrors or the birdcage."

I leaned forward. I wasn't supposed to talk, but I'd just picked up on something that confused me. "Abby, did you say that he watched you *through* the mirrors? You mean, he watched you *in* the mirrors, right?"

She stared back at me. "There were mirrors that were two-way. He watched me through them."

Franco widened his eyes at me before turning back to Abby. "Tell us about that. Why was he watching you through two-way mirrors?"

"I don't know," she answered. "That was just the way he wanted it."

Abby hadn't mentioned the two-way mirrors before. Was she embroidering her story right before my eyes?

"Abby," said Franco, "we can check if those mirrors are still there. The forensics group is still going through everything. The two-way mirrors might be smashed and burned, but they'd still be able to find fragments of them."

"You don't believe me, do you?" Abby drew her mouth in.

"It's not a matter of not believing you," Franco told her.

She was close to crying. "Yeah, I know. The bedrock, right? Emmet's words in his journal are apparently the bedrock, and mine are just fantasy, floating up there in the clouds somewhere."

"Stay with me," said Franco. "I'm just trying to establish the scene. I know it's upsetting. It's upsetting me, too, just asking you this stuff. Believe me." He sighed. "All right. Now, did he often sit behind the two-way mirrors when you were there?"

"Always," she replied.

I listened closely, shaken by her latest revelation.

Franco raised his thick eyebrows. "*Always?* So, you're saying he spoke to you from *behind* the mirrors, every single time?"

"Yes."

"Did he show himself?" Franco asked.

"No. He just liked to see *me.*"

"That was a big room," Franco commented. "Did he shout at you from behind those mirrors?"

Abby crinkled her eyes, gazing back at Franco strangely. "Shout? No... he spoke to me the way he always did."

Franco frowned deeply. "And how was that?"

Abby picked up her phone, showing it to Franco.

"You mean he spoke via phone?" Franco asked. "Like, with the loudspeaker on?"

"By text," Abby told him.

"By text?" Franco asked. "*Every single time?*"

She nodded.

"Abby," I breathed, "did you actually ever *see* Emmet at the funfair?"

She went silent. I could sense thoughts racing through her mind.

"Abby, did you *see* him there?" I repeated.

"No," she answered finally. "He never let me see him."

"I need to get this straight," said Franco. "You never saw—or heard —Emmet at the funfair?"

She shook her head. "He told me he was taking things slow with me. Trying not to frighten me. He also said it was the way he liked it. It turned him on."

Thoughts whirled in my head until I felt sick.

I touched her hand. "Tell me something... all those times you spoke to Emmet on the phone, all those conversations that went until the small hours—how many of those were actual verbal conversations, and how many were text conversations?"

For a moment it seemed that she didn't understand the question. And then it was like she was struggling to put something together in her mind.

Her face paled as she told us, "They were all text conversations. *All of them.*"

Franco gaped. "So... we don't know for certain if a single time that you spoke to Emmet by phone or went to the funfair that you were actually talking to Emmet at all?"

Abby wrapped her arms around her middle, rocking herself and shaking her head. "No, it *was* him. It *was*. How could it not be?" Abby kept shaking her head, her eyes huge. "He always knew about the conversations we'd had—and I mean the face-to-face conversations. How could he fake those? He couldn't!"

"A skilled manipulator can manage that," Franco told her. "I'm not saying that's what happened here, but we're going to have to consider it."

"Honey," I said to Abby, "someone could have gleaned that information from you. When you spoke via text, this other person could have gotten you to tell them all kinds of things. You were just a child. You wouldn't have even realised it was happening."

She sat back in her chair with a stunned expression. "I don't understand this at all. It was so... real."

I swallowed, a lump hardening in my throat. "What was Emmet like when you were with him—I mean *actually* with him? Face-to-face."

"He was always nice," Abby answered in a trembling, hushed voice. "Like an old-fashioned gentleman or something. Only once he told me to go home—that was on the last day I saw him. He never spoke to me about the things he did during the text conversations. And he was nothing at all like how he was at the funfair."

Leaning my head back, I exhaled, staring at the ceiling. "Why didn't I guess all this before? I didn't even ask you the right questions."

"Mum, you weren't even asking me the questions, remember? I was just telling my story to Dr Quinley. I just... told it the way I saw it in my mind. Not in a million years, would I have ever thought to question whether it was Emmet or not. The relationship between us started off in text and it just continued like that. It seemed so real."

My eyes grew wet. "Of course it seemed real. Because text conversations *are* real. That's how teenagers talk. Via text. You're not to blame for someone doing this to you. Like Franco said, they would have been a skilled manipulator."

"But then, why," Abby questioned, "would Emmet's journal have been at the funfair? How did it get there?"

"I can't answer that one," I said. "But we'll find out."

"My mind is spinning in circles," Abby breathed. "I just can't believe this.'

Franco gave Abby a reassuring smile. "I think we're done for today. We got down to the bedrock."

64

KATE

Abby, Franco and I sat in silence for a few moments, each of us trying to come to grips with the thought of Abby having been fooled by some stranger.

Abby's phone beeped.

She checked her phone. "Oh... that's a reminder—for my next appointment with my psych. I'll call and make up an excuse as to why I can't go."

"Maybe it's best you keep up your appointments, Abby," I said. "Especially this afternoon. You might need to talk things through."

"But you need me," she said, "to work out what happened."

Franco shook his head. "You've already helped us way more than anything we could have expected. You should go, kid."

"I'll come with you, for support," I told her.

Abby stood. "No. It's okay. You stay with Franco. You guys need to find out what happened to Layla."

"Are you sure?" I said. "I feel terrible now."

"Mum, I'm sure. I just sat through a police interrogation. I can sit through a session with my psych." She managed a small grin.

Taking in a long breath, I watched her leave.

I couldn't shake the sense that I'd let her down. I'd listened to her sessions with Dr Quinley as a parent would, caught up in the horror of it. I hadn't thought hard enough about all the small details of what she was telling.

I walked to the house to make Franco and myself some coffee—and to tell Pete what had just happened. Carrying the coffee and a plate of nibbles, I returned to the barn.

Franco and I recalibrated what we knew, and what we needed to do next.

The person who'd been trying to steal the journal was most likely the person who'd fooled Abby. And they were also likely to be Layla's murderer.

Whoever they were, they'd know we were now racing to uncover their identity.

"It was seamless," Franco said. "This person catfished her. The catfisher was watching Abby and listening to her conversations. And the rest he was just filling in. He pretended to be Emmet Eisen and made it all real in her eyes."

"Yes," I agreed. "It was seamless. She really believed it was him. I've heard of catfishing. But to be honest, I don't know a lot about it."

Franco sipped his coffee. "My years on the fraud squad came in handy."

"I did the fraud squad, too, before I went into homicide." I shook my head. "But that was way before the tech revolution."

"Yeah. Social media changed the world. Some of these catfishers are serial offenders, and they get good at what they do. They can make you believe anything. Your mind will fill in the blanks and make excuses for them. The catfisher could be anyone. Old man. Teenage girl. A guy sitting in his basement in another country."

"You think it could have all been for kicks? To destroy Abby in every which way that they could?"

"I don't know. Sometimes, you get a sick individual who wants to do that. There have been women who've done that to their own friends. But usually, it's a stranger targeting someone for money."

"Okay, so, all we know with any reasonable certainty is that this was a case of a catfisher."

"Yeah," agreed Franco. "But we have a problem. Nola's Mr Lullaby and Abby's Mr Lullaby are the one person, right? Yet, he showed himself to Nola but not to Abby."

I knew that Franco was playing devil's advocate. It was a system we'd used for years to try to cut through a puzzling case in the quickest way possible.

"Nola was forced into it by her mother," I answered. "She was alone, cut off from everyone. She had no one to turn to, and he knew that."

"Sounds feasible. Now, we've got two more problems. One, Emmet was keeping locks of hair in the box the journal was kept in. And, two, the journal was found at the funfair. How do we reconcile those two things with Emmet being innocent?"

I swallowed a mouthful of hot coffee, thinking. "The catfisher placed the locks of hair in the box. He also picked up the journal and took it to the funfair. Emmet said in the journal he wasn't keeping it in his room anymore, because of his mother's prying eyes."

Franco tilted his head. "But Abby knew it was at the funfair. How'd she know that?"

"She said she'd seen it there before. She thought that was where he always kept it. I don't think either the catfisher or Emmet knew she'd seen the journal."

"All right. So, the catfisher stole the journal on occasion and took it to the funfair. How and why?"

"Can't answer the first question. But as for the second, maybe it helped him to believe he really *was* Emmet."

"It sounds like the catfisher knew a lot of things. He knew about the journal. He must have known quite a bit about Emmet, too. And, recently, he might have overheard a drunk Louisa Eisen talking about the journal."

"So, he must have been someone close to the Eisens."

"That's what I'm thinking." He looked through the case file, studying all the pictures that Layla had taken of the parties. "There are three guys who are in just about all the photos."

Franco wrote down a short list of three people:

Alex Eisen.

Scott DeCoursey.

Doug Overmire.

"I'd hate to think it was any of them, but I'd especially hate to think it was Alex."

"We've got to throw a spotlight on everyone."

"Yes, true."

"Okay," he said, "if I look at the events of last night in detail, we've got Alex following his wife down to the coast. But... do we know for certain where he was at any one time? You've noted here that he was travelling on the highway, half an hour away from Vincentia, when he last texted you. But could he have already been there?"

"I guess so. He said his car was being repaired, but I don't know that for certain. But if he found out about the journal recently—and he wanted it—why wouldn't he just ask his wife? Why stalk her and then break into his own holiday house?"

Franco shrugged. "If the journal implicates him, he'd have good reason to want it destroyed. Maybe Alex knew that Louisa wouldn't agree to hand the journal over. After all, she'd been holding onto it for a decade."

"Okay. But what about the day their house was burgled? Alex was on a boat with Louisa and others all day that day—it was a remembrance for Emmet."

"Right, so Alex Eisen both fits and doesn't fit."

"I strongly lean toward him not fitting."

"Yep," Franco said. "Onto the next cab off the rank—Scott DeCoursey. What do we think about him? You've spoken to him more than I have. The only interaction I had with him is when he approached me in court that day. Sounded angry."

"He is a bit of an unusual guy. Unemotional and efficient. Nina confided in me about their relationship. She said he thought he wasn't even attracted to her anymore. She described him as cold. Having said that, he was close to Layla. So he says. When Nina was cleaning out Layla's room, Scott kept Layla's camera and a few of her things. I remember when Abby was a teenager, she used to complain that Layla's Uncle Scott bought Layla clothes and gave her money. Abby thought she was missing out, because her parents didn't lavish money on her like that."

"Hmmm." Franco rubbed his chin. "So, Scott DeCoursey might be attracted to young girls and not women? Anyway, he's a strong contender."

"I guess he is."

"That leaves Doug Overmire."

"I started doing some research on Mr Overmire," I said, "but time hasn't been on my side these past few days. What I know is that he's a financier who lives in the city. He's financed large projects in a number of different countries, generally all tech related. He's married with two children. Emmet had a verbal disagreement with him at one of the parties. As you can see in this picture—here." I pointed at the relevant photo.

Franco nodded. "Would be good to know what the problem was."

"I know that Overmire put up most of the money for the Close Quarters development. And then we know that Emmet scrawled graffiti all over it." I gasped. "*Goodbye Lullaby*—was that a message for Doug Overmire?"

"It fits." Franco furrowed his brow. "That really fits."

Franco swung straight back into devil's advocate mode. "But what interest would a financier from Sydney have in a funfair ride from little old Tallman's Valley? How the heck would he even know about it?"

Switching on the laptop computer, I did a little more research into Doug Overmire. "Oh... look here. He lived overseas with his wife and family from 2007 to mid-2009. In San Francisco, USA. That means he can't have been the man in the Nola Hobson videos. It wasn't him."

"Okay, looks like we might have to rule Overmire out, too."

We sat in silence for a short period.

I squeezed my eyes shut. "What if we reverse engineer this? As in, we don't try to fit someone to what we've got—we start from what we've got and work outward?"

"Okay, let's do that. Let's take a good look at that gondola ride."

We began researching the carnival, trying to find information. There were a few grainy pictures online from old print newspaper articles, and a sprinkling of sentimental photos on people's blogs. None of it was of any use.

"I've got an idea," Franco said. "I remember that a retired journalist started up a site where he was posting old photos from the years he worked at one of the Blue Mountains newspapers. Good quality pictures—not like what you get in print newspapers."

"It's certainly worth a try."

Franco browsed to the site, and then began scrolling through the photographs. The website was filled with pictures from yesteryear.

As Franco had said, the photographs were great quality. But it wasn't anything like looking at the results in a modern search engine. It was more of a case of guessing dates and years and then looking through photo after photo in the hope of finding something relevant.

After half an hour of searching, we came across a batch of photos from the Tallman's Funfair.

There was a note from the journalist that said he'd tried to get the information as accurate as possible. He said that the family who'd run the funfair were notoriously private and had rarely appeared at the carnival. The names of the family members he'd listed had mostly come from what he'd overheard.

"Hey," I said. "This says it's a picture of Harold and Beatrix Mulden and their daughter, Henrietta Mulden." The picture was from 1975. Henrietta looked about thirty.

"Check out the flared jeans on Henrietta," Franco said gleefully. "What a blast from the past."

"I was twenty in 1975. I was proud of my flared jeans, I'll have you know."

"I'd pay good money to see a picture of your flares."

Grinning, I kept looking through the website, trying to find some more recent photos of the funfair. I found a batch that were dated 1989.

"Look at this," I said, "there's the old gondola ride. See? There's a boat going around on the water—and there's the big birdcage in the background, with the girl on the swing."

Along the course of the manmade 'river' there were other large objects, such as a big, open clam with a mermaid girl inside it. A bored young man sat next to a lever—obviously the operator of the ride. I zoomed in on him, but his face was slightly turned away from the camera.

Franco examined the picture. "I know I went on that ride a couple of times, but I can barely remember it. I was a teenager back then. Jeez, is that what passed as entertainment in those days?"

"Yep. It was all about large objects, then. All over Australia. Giant fruit, giant farm animals, giant crustaceans even."

A grin cracked across his face. "Gotta give the people what they want."

"Those 1989 photos must have been taken just before the funfair closed down," I remarked. "It closed thirty years ago, just after the Mulden farm was raided by police."

"Were you part of that raid?"

"Nope. I was in Sydney. State homicide squad. But what I do know is that there were several families who lived on the farm, and most of them didn't register their children's births. Investigators didn't know which child belonged to which set of parents. The children went to orphanages or foster homes, and they were given new names. And the adults who hadn't been convicted of any crimes mostly changed theirs. Which makes things really, really hard."

Franco browsed through some of the photos from 1989. There was one photograph of Henrietta Mulden and a group of five people who I assumed were her children—all standing outside the *House of Fun*.

I peered with interest at the photo.

The journalist had listed their names and ages:

Doug Mulden, aged twenty-eight.

Gordon Mulden, aged twenty-five.

Maude Mulden, aged sixteen.

Polly Mulden, aged nine.

Elsie Mulden, aged seven.

I zoomed in on the photo, bringing their faces up close.

I know those people.

They were the much younger versions of themselves, but I was good with faces.

Doug Mulden was now Doug Overmire—the financier. He was close to bald now, but back then, he had long, bushy hair in an eighties' style.

Maude Mulden was now Adele Hobson—Nola's mother. She wore a straw hat and a long floral dress. She was currently in Thailand.

Polly Mulden was now Madeline Brightwaters. She was currently in jail.

Elsie Mulden was now Penny Foster. She was also currently in jail.

I squinted at the fifth young man. He was holding out the palm of his hand to the camera, in a gesture to both hide himself and stop himself from being filmed.

His eyes looked so familiar.

But who was he?

"Franco, let's look at the gondola ride pictures again," I said.

Franco returned to the batch of gondola photos.

I zoomed in on the ride's operator. I still couldn't see his face, but he was the same man as in the photo with Henrietta Mulden. His hands were perched on his upper thighs, in the way young men often posed when sitting. He wore a watch on his right wrist. A vintage sports chronograph watch.

Franco sucked in a breath. "Oh, man. That's it. The watch. That's him, isn't it? *Mr Lullaby*. He's Doug Overmire's brother. That would have been why Emmet was having arguments with his father and with Overmire. He told them about Mr Lullaby, but they didn't want to know. All he knew was what he wrote in his journal. It wasn't much—

maybe not enough to go to the police with. So, he wrote the message on the wall at Close Quarters—a message they couldn't ignore."

I nodded mutely, my mind racing.

"Let's get Overmire on the phone," Franco said. "And we'll make him tell us who his brother is."

"Wait. I don't want him tipped off. I've seen him before. Give me a minute to remember."

In a hurry, I scrolled to the photo in which I could see the man's eyes just above his hand. "I know those eyes," I said. "*I know them.* And I know that watch. I just can't place them."

A terrible thought grabbed hold of me as I realised exactly who the man was.

"What is it, Wakeland?"

"Oh, Dear God..." I cried, jumping up. "We need to go. *Now.*"

65

KATE

The truth was staring me in the face. I knew the identity of Mr Lullaby. But I needed to be certain.

While Franco drove, I sent the pictures of the gondola ride operator to Nola.

Within a minute I had my answer.

Yes.

Yes, those were his eyes.

My breath roared in my ears as Franco and I sped across town to the Close Quarters precinct.

We raced across the cool, marble floor of the reception area and up to the third floor.

As we entered Dr Quinley's office, the receptionist had her head down, typing. She raised her face, casting a curious eye over us. "Can I help you?"

Franco placed a hand on the counter. "We're Detectives Wakeland and Franco. Is Dr Quinley in right now?"

The receptionist gave a fluid nod. She was very young—a different receptionist to the one I'd seen in here before. "Yes. He's seeing a client. If you give me your card, I'll have him call you back."

"No, thank you," I replied. "We'll be seeing him *now*."

She pursed her lips. "I'm afraid you can't do that. You need to make an appointment."

"We're making that appointment right now," I said.

Franco and I headed away, the receptionist's thin protests following us down the hall.

Without knocking, I opened the door to Dr Quinley's room, and we walked in.

Abby and Quinley were lying side-by-side, in his zero gravity recliners. I'd expected she'd be finished with her session by now. Her session had run over time.

She had her eyes closed, hands clasped across her waist, murmuring. Quinley was lying on his side, arm under his head, watching her intently.

Quinley jumped to his feet. "Kate! What on earth? You can't interrupt a session."

Abby, shaken from whatever memory or thought she'd been telling Quinley about, sat bolt upright. "Mum? *Franco?*"

"Abby," I said in a measured tone, "would you mind waiting outside?"

She fetched her handbag from the floor. "I don't understand. Have I done something wrong?"

"No, honey, this isn't about you. Just go sit in the waiting room. Detective Franco and I need to speak with Dr Quinley. We'll be out soon."

Abby headed out, clutching her bag.

The receptionist, who'd been standing in the doorway, seemed to think the better of trying to stop us, and she slunk away.

Franco shut the door behind her.

Quinley leaned against his desk, crossing his arms. "This is all very extreme. In fact, I find your behaviour downright disturbing."

"And yet," I remarked, walking up to him, "you look so calm."

"I'm in the business of being calm," he answered. "Unlike the two of you, who seem to think you have the right to barge in here."

I stared at him, loathing stirring up inside me. "Did you really think you could stay hidden forever, *Mr Lullaby?*"

Quinley's jaw went slack. But he recovered quickly.

"I'm afraid I don't have the foggiest of what you're talking about," he said.

Inwardly, I shook with rage. I'd expected him to bluster and try to cover himself. This unnatural composure of his was unnerving.

"We have you on film," I said, "in a series of child exploitation materials that were filmed with a young girl named Nola. And we know that you lured Abby to your mother's old funfair, while you sat behind a two-way mirror, never allowing yourself to be seen."

His eyes darted away. He walked across to a window, putting a hand against the glass, staring out at the overcast sky. He wasn't wearing the chronograph watch today. I'd only seen it once—on the first day I'd met him.

His jaw muscles pulled taut while his chest sank inward.

I could guess this was the moment he saw his entire career disintegrate.

"Dr Gordon Quinley," Franco said, "you're under arrest for historic child sexual abuse offences."

The sound of footsteps had me pivoting around.

Abby stood behind me. I hadn't even heard her open the door.

Her skin was ashen, her eyes flashing with a cold blaze. "Dr Quinley? Please... tell me that wasn't *you.*"

He looked back at her blankly then returned to gaze out the window.

His silence loomed large in the room.

I wished I could have protected Abby from this moment. The look of betrayal on her face cut into my soul.

I walked across to her. "Abby, I'm so sorry—"

She put up a hand to stop me, her eyes fixed on the doctor. "I thought I remembered your voice. But I told myself that was my mind playing tricks. I only saw you a couple of times at the Eisens' parties.

But you looked very different. Your hair was brown, not grey. And you... you had a beard. You were always hanging back, away from everyone—in the dark. I barely noticed you..."

Her voice grew shaky. *"You* were Mr Lullaby."

66

KATE

Dr Quinley flexed his fingers, then placed his hands on the police inter-view table. "I'll be using my right to remain silent."

I leaned across the table and faced him squarely. "You don't have the right to remain silent. Not for an indictable offence you don't."

"I don't believe you," replied Dr Quinley, still keeping his veneer of cool composure.

He'd come down to the station without fuss, but we hadn't been able to squeeze more than a few words out of him. I was still grappling with the fact that the psychiatrist who'd been treating Abby for months was the *Mr Lullaby* who'd abused her as a teenager.

Franco drummed his fingers on the table, sighing. "Let's put it this way, Quinley, why would we go ahead with something that won't stand up in a court of law?"

His upper lip twitched. "Tell me what crime you imagine I've committed?"

I settled back in my chair, gathering strength. "Where do you want us to start? Child sexual abuse? Involvement in Emmet Eisen's death? The murder of Layla Maddox?"

The mention of Layla's name produced a visible reaction. He

recoiled, his shoulders hunching. "I had nothing to do with Layla's murder. Or Emmet's regrettable death, for that matter. More to the point, you're going to have to pinpoint which of those accusations is the indictable offence. I need parameters."

I pressed my lips together grimly. "You need parameters? Strange that you didn't impose any on yourself. You're Abby's therapist. And all along, the person who caused her the trauma was *you*. You were Mr Lullaby."

"Perhaps the therapist needed a therapist," Quinley conceded in a well-oiled voice. "Perhaps there was some wrong-doing. I've been under a great deal of stress with work and family life for many years."

He'd just admitted that he was Mr Lullaby.

I was struck silent. He'd admitted it so casually, as if it were nothing.

Franco could see that I was stretched thin by Quinley's words, and he jumped in.

"So, you called yourself, Mr Lullaby?" Franco asked him.

He didn't reply.

"Well, Dr Quinley," Franco said, "I'll answer your earlier question. The indictable offences for which you were arrested concern the grooming and abuse of minors and the production of child exploitation material. And we have strong suspicions that you're guilty of other offences, too."

Quinley rubbed his hands together slowly, reminding me of a fly rubbing its front legs together. "You have to understand that I was a victim of circumstance. It was all in good faith that I took on Emmet Eisen as my client—"

"Emmet was your *client*?" I exploded.

Franco shot me a kind of glance I knew well. It was to tell me to cool my jets.

Quinley's brow creased into deep ridges. "You didn't know?"

"No," I snapped. "But it makes terrible sense now. Louisa told me that Alex asked around for a therapist for Emmet. Of course, *you* were in the Eisens' social circles. You stepped up and offered your services, right?"

"I contacted Emmet online and offered my professional services, yes. The therapy was all conducted online."

I crossed my arms. "It was your suggestion that Emmet write a journal. It says so in Emmet's entries. And then you kept taking the journal... to the funfair."

Quinley licked his lips. "It was simply part of Emmet's therapy. He'd write things down and I'd read them. That's how I helped him."

Franco was shaking his head. "No. It wasn't part of his therapy, was it, Dr Quinley? It was all for *you*. You got off on Emmet's descriptions of the young girls. That's why you were reading his journal. That's why you wanted him to write it."

I stared at Franco. He'd made a connection that hadn't even occurred to me. It made perfect sense.

"It's not my fault," Quinley insisted. "I became enticed—seduced, if you will—by Emmet's descriptions of the young girls down by the lakeside. During that whole summer, the more he spoke of Abby and Layla, the more entranced I became. I was helpless."

I eyed Quinley with an uncompromising gaze. "I can guess that you drew those descriptions out of Emmet. Basically, you catfished him. You pretended to be his therapist. Instead, you were using Emmet for your own ends."

Dr Quinley looked back at me silently.

"In the journal," I continued, "Emmet talks about a man who was taking photos of Abby and Layla—a man who he said betrayed him. *You* were the man taking the photographs. *You* were the man who betrayed Emmet. You were meant to be his doctor. But you just used him."

Quinley brushed a hand dismissively through the air. "That journal was filled with fantastical imaginings. Emmet was quite a fanciful young man."

"On the contrary," I said, "what Emmet said in his journal all sounded very believable."

"I'm going to wait for my lawyer," Quinley responded.

Prickles of white-hot anger shot down my neck. "We'll be waiting. And let me tell you, we won't be impressed by your claims of victimhood."

Franco nudged my elbow, a gesture that didn't go unnoticed by Dr Quinley. A facial tic flicked the edges of his mouth upward. Quinley obviously thought he had the upper hand.

I walked out of the room, caught up in the sensation of tumbling into a deep, dark pit.

Franco closed the door after we were both out of the room, sending a constable to sit with Quinley.

After grabbing coffee, we headed back to our desks.

I couldn't sit. A fierce energy bristled through me. I stood sipping at the piping-hot coffee and barely feeling its burn.

Franco pulled at his collar—a thing he did when he was having trouble forming his words.

"Blurt it out," I said.

He let out a short breath. "Things got messy in there. You threw everything at him at once. Too early, Wakeland, too early."

"I know. I just—"

"You just wanted to murder him with your bare hands. Anyone can see that."

I gulped a mouthful of coffee. I had to back off. More than anything, I needed to calm the turbulence in my mind.

I took a breath. In... out. Then another breath.

"When the lawyer gets here," I said evenly, "I can't do the interview."

Franco nodded soberly. I could see it on his face that he already knew that—he was just waiting for me to say it.

"Don't worry," he assured me, "I'll be your voice. Let's sit down and go over everything. And then I'll be ready for him."

"We'd better start by calling Liz Booth. We need some advice." I pulled out my phone and called her.

"What's up, Kate?" came Detective Booth's voice.

"Liz, I need your thoughts on something." I outlined what we knew about Dr Quinley and his child abuse offences.

"Well done on finding out the identity of that monster. Unbelievable. Do you know for certain that he was the one who produced and distributed the child abuse images and videos?"

"He was *in* the videos," I replied.

"Yes, but it was just the guy's wrist and watch, in just one frame. He might claim it was someone else. Or, he might claim that he just innocently walked into the room and accidentally got filmed. I've heard it all. You'd be shocked at what some of these abusers can get away with, with a good lawyer. A lot of the rest of the offences could come under grooming. Which is still a serious offence. Depending on what he's done, he could get a fairly light sentence. We need to make sure that doesn't happen. Are you about to hand this case over to me?"

"Soon," I said. "For the moment, he's ours. There are two possible homicides he's had a hand in. Franco and I don't know how this is all going to unpack yet. I'll let you know when we're finished with him."

I said goodbye and then drained the rest of the coffee out of my cup.

The constable we'd left with Quinley came to inform us that the lawyer had just walked into the station. The lawyer had requested some time alone with his client.

Franco and I used the time to plan out how the interview would go.

At the same time, as the next two hours ticked on, I felt every muscle in my body flexing and tensing, over and over again. I hated the wait.

Finally, we received word that Quinley and his lawyer were ready.

"Pin him to the wall," I hissed to Franco as we stepped into the hallway that led to the interview room.

I intended watching the interview from the observation room next-door.

A tall figure in a business suit stood in the hall, looking like he'd stepped from the pages of a men's fashion magazine.

Scott DeCoursey.

I marched up to him. "Scott, please don't tell me you're taking on this case?"

"I am, indeed."

"Well, I'll let you know that we have some very compelling evidence against Dr Quinley. Why did he choose *you* if I may ask?"

"I've defended a few of his clients in the past. People have been sent to him for psychiatric analysis due to crimes they've committed. He's then passed them onto me to defend in court."

"Nice system," Franco remarked wryly.

Scott shrugged. "It's just business."

"I still don't get why Quinley would choose you," I said. "You're a friend of the Eisens."

"Not lately," he replied. "We've had a falling out. They think we've been talking about them to you. Quinley knows that."

"But, Scott," I said, "there could be a connection between Quinley and Layla's murder. Are you sure you still want to do this?"

"I'll consider myself warned," he said steadily.

Shocked by Scott's non-reaction, I tried to decode his tone. He sounded like someone who had everything under control. What had Quinley told him? Something was making Scott think his client was innocent of that charge.

As Scott walked into the interview room, I twisted around to Franco.

Franco gave a confused shake of his head, stepping behind Scott.

I headed into the observation room, having no idea what was coming up next.

67

KATE

I settled into a seat in the observation room. Through the two-way mirror, I watched Franco sit on the opposite side of the table to Dr Quinley and Scott DeCoursey.

"Dr Quinley," Franco began, "in our preliminary interview, you admitted to using the name *Mr Lullaby*. You used this name when communicating with young teenage girls, in the years 2008, 2009 and 2010. Is that correct?"

"I suppose so," Dr Quinley said stiffly.

"Okay," Franco continued, "in this interview, when I refer to *Mr Lullaby,* I will be referring to you. And when I refer to *you*, I might be referring to Mr Lullaby. Do you understand?"

"Yes. Understood," said Quinley.

Franco took out a pile of photographs from the file he'd brought in with him and placed them on the table. He gave Quinley a picture of the birdcage necklace. "You gave these birdcage pendants to Abby Wakeland, Layla Maddox and Nola Hobson. Why did you do that?"

Quinley rolled his shoulders in an offhand way. "They were just little gifts. Pretty things. I'd see the young girls at the parties, and I thought they might like them."

He was trying to get Franco off-guard already.

Franco lifted his gaze to the two-way mirror and then back to Quinley. "Abby says that you insisted that she wear it. In fact, she said you told her it made her yours."

Quinley gave him a helpless look. "Well, I think she must have been conjuring up things in her mind."

"Let it go, Franco," I whispered to myself. "Stay on track."

It was so hard being on this side of the mirror. I wanted to rush into the interview room and play hardball. Franco wasn't used to doing that. He usually played the quieter, more empathetic detective in interviews while I put the pressure on the suspect. Both Franco and I were out of our comfort zones right now. But no other detective knew the case the way Franco and I did. With me out of the running, that just left Franco.

I cast a dark glare at Quinley that he couldn't see. "Ironic, isn't it?" I muttered under my breath, "I'm the one behind the two-way mirror now—watching *you*. Just like you watched my daughter."

Franco passed Quinley another photograph—this one from the funfair in its heyday. "You operated the gondola ride at the Tallman's Funfair when you were in your twenties, correct?"

Quinley nodded.

"You gained an interest in birdcages and mermaid hair there, didn't you, Dr Quinley?" asked Franco.

"I guess I did," Quinley admitted.

"There were three locks of hair inside the box where the journal was kept," Franco said next. "I assume the locks were from Nola, Abby and Layla?"

He gave a wincing sort of shrug. "They were just keepsakes."

"You were taking the journal to the funfair frequently, weren't you, Doctor?"

"Yes. It was part of Emmet's therapy. He was supposed to write an entry each day, and I was meant to take his journal with me to read each week. But, typical young man, he barely wrote in it. He wasn't very good with his therapy."

"You took it just before Emmet died, at which time, you placed the three locks of hair in the box. Correct?"

Quinley nodded.

"But, you didn't have time to read it on that occasion, did you?" Franco speculated.

"No," said Dr Quinley. "I was feeling very ill at that point in time. I didn't know why. I later realised that I'd been ill for days with appendicitis."

"Right," said Franco. "So, you didn't read it. And then, after Emmet died and you returned to the funfair to fetch the journal, it was gone. You were afraid of what was written on its pages. You searched the houses of Abby Wakeland and Emmet Eisen in the days afterwards. You didn't find the journal. Ten years later, you overhear a drunk Louisa Eisen saying she'd kept a journal belonging to Emmet. You begin stalking her. Am I correct, Dr Quinley?"

"Not quite," he said. "I didn't overhear Louisa. I'd been giving her therapy. Yes, she was mostly drunk on those occasions. I was a friend of the Eisens. I simply offered a little help."

"You offered help in order to find out if she had the journal," Franco pressed.

"Yes," he hissed.

"You heard that the case of Emmet Eisen's drowning was being opened up again, and you started to feel desperate, didn't you? You'd already been trying to pry information from another of your clients—Abby Wakeland. But when that went nowhere, you turned to Louisa Eisen, right?"

"Yes. Right."

Franco studied his notes for a moment then raised his eyes to Quinley. "You gave Layla a necklace with a birdcage pendant, which she thought was a gift from Emmet. How did you manage that?"

"I left it for her in her aunt's boat house. I spoke to her later, via text, as Emmet. I told her I had a surprise for her."

"Okay. Thank you. I'll move onto the next thing. You asked both

Abby and Nola, at different times, to remove their clothing and dance for you. Correct?"

Scott DeCoursey tapped his chin with his index finger. "Do you have evidence of those things, Detective Franco?"

"Yes," Franco answered. "We have video evidence in the case of Nola Hobson. And we have Abby's witness statement."

"In other words," Scott said, "you have physical evidence for Nola Hobson only. And we might find even *that* piece of evidence flimsy."

Franco passed them the photo that showed the man's wrist with the chronograph watch and a fourteen-year-old Nola.

"Is this all you have?" DeCoursey blew out a breath in a dismissive gesture.

Franco ignored his question. "It's clear that this is Gordon Quinley."

"Even if this did turn out to be my client," said DeCoursey, "it proves nothing. It's possible he thought this was a girl of age eighteen or older. The lighting is quite dark."

I sensed that the evidence that Franco and I had gathered had begun to evaporate. I was certain about what Quinley had done. But I knew only too well how serious offenders escaped jail time due to inconclusive evidence.

"Why did you lure Layla Maddox to the ruins of the funfair, Dr Quinley?" Franco asked boldly.

I gasped. Franco had just gone for the jugular. A surprise attack that Scott DeCoursey wouldn't have been expecting him to make on his client.

Quinley shook his head. "I did no such thing."

"I propose that you did," Franco said. "I propose that you targeted Layla in the same way you targeted Abby. But then Layla found out that you, and not Emmet, were Mr Lullaby. Feeling afraid, Layla returns to Sydney to live with her grandfather. Two weeks later, Emmet accuses you of being Mr Lullaby. You have a fight. He falls, bruising himself. Later, you follow Emmet out onto the lake, and you push him into the water."

Quinley kept shaking his head all the way through Franco's speech. "That's not what happened at all."

"I haven't finished," Franco told him. "After you made sure Emmet drowned, you turned your attention to Layla. You kidnap her from her grandfather's house. You take her from Sydney back to Tallman's Valley, to the old funfair. Once there, Layla struggles, the necklace snaps and falls to the ground. In the struggle, you don't notice this. You then wrap a length of material around her neck and tighten it until she is dead."

Scott slid a weary look in Franco's direction. "Are you finished, yet, Detective?"

"No," Franco told him, drilling his back into the chair. "Dr Quinley, after setting fire to the funfair, you use Layla's phone to send a message to Layla's aunt. You then return to Sydney, and you leave a note in Layla's grandfather's house—a note that you forced Layla to write before you killed her."

I kept my eyes on Quinley while Franco outlined his scenario. He had his hands flat on the table and a hostile expression on his face. When I flicked my gaze to the unflappable Scott DeCoursey, I noticed that his face had paled.

Had Franco's description of what might have happened to Layla horrified Scott? Or had Franco said something that'd made Scott think twice about Quinley's innocence?

With Scott staying silent, Quinley took over the reins, performing a long, weary blink. "Are you quite finished, Detective?"

Franco shot him a tense stare instead of a nod.

"I'll give you another scenario," Quinley said. "Layla ran off to her grandfather's, and then she returned to Tallman's Valley for reasons known only to herself. And then someone, regrettably, killed her. Meanwhile, I was in a hospital bed having my appendix removed."

I digested his words, blood rushing in my head.

"You were *where?*" Franco breathed.

"Would you like me to draw you a picture?" Quinley said with a triumphant look in his eyes.

"Do you have proof of your hospital stay?" Franco asked.

"My client does have proof," Scott answered. "He had his receptionist email through records an hour ago."

Franco frowned. "What time did you arrive at the hospital, doctor?"

"Midday," Quinley answered.

Internally, my belief that Quinley was guilty of Layla's murder had just developed deep cracks. If Quinley had been in a hospital at midday, he couldn't be responsible for Emmet's death, and neither could he be Layla's murderer.

Franco lifted another photograph from his pile—of the graffiti on the wall at Close Quarters. He also took out photos of Emmet arguing with his father and Doug Overmire. "Can you tell us about this?"

Quinley sighed. "Emmet had somehow found out about my online identity—Mr Lullaby—and he wanted to go to the authorities. But the problem was that my brother, Doug Overmire, was the largest financier of the Close Quarters development. Alex Eisen had also invested a considerable amount of money in it, and he couldn't afford to lose his money. So, Alex was worried that if Emmet made trouble for Doug's family, that Doug would pull his money out. Alex insisted that Emmet wait until the first stage of development was complete."

"And the graffiti message?" Franco asked. "What was that all about?"

"*Goodbye Lullaby* was a threatening message to *me*," Quinley stated. "Childish. He was volatile by this point. I'd stayed overnight at the Eisens' house, after a party. In the morning, I felt ill. It was the beginning of my bout of appendicitis. Emmet confronted me, started shoving me around. I pushed back in self-defence. Emmet fell. Emmet had already been drinking—it wasn't hard to make him keel over. Then I drove myself back to Sydney and then straight to a hospital."

Franco was listening intently. "Did you arrange to have Emmet and Layla murdered from your hospital bed, Dr Quinley?"

An incredulous look came over Quinley's face. "Why would I do that? I had no bad feelings towards Emmet. And Layla was a beautiful young girl. Lovely, tanned skin. Wheat-coloured hair that skimmed the small of her back and shimmered in the sunlight. It's a crime to destroy beauty."

Scott stared at his client with a look of disgust.

"That's an oddly specific answer," Franco remarked.

"It's an odd reply to an odd question," Quinley said contemptuously. "We've established that I couldn't have killed Layla or Emmet. So now you're trying to fabricate some story about me paying someone else to do the job. *From my hospital bed*, no less."

Scott sprung to his feet. "Detective Franco, could I have a word with you, outside?"

Dr Quinley glanced at him in surprise. "I don't think you should be having private conversations with detectives, Scott."

"It will only be a minute," Scott replied in a sharp tone. "I need to clarify an item of police procedure."

Franco nodded at Scott with a puzzled expression on his face, and he headed outside with him.

68

KATE

The next moment, there was a light rap on the door of the observation room.

It was Scott, indicating for me to come outside. I walked with him and Franco to a room further up the hall.

"Scott?" I said. "What's the problem?"

He swallowed. "I'm going to come clean with you both. I only took on this case for Layla's sake. As soon as Quinley called me and told me what it was about, I had to do it. If he'd called some other defence lawyer, I know exactly what would have happened. We defence lawyers are in the business of clouding the truth. If Quinley had been any other client, there is no way I'd have allowed him to answer the questions that he just did. I'd have shut him up, quick-smart."

"I was having a lot of trouble understanding why you'd take this on," I said. "Now I know."

Hints of anguish showed in Scott's expression now. "I wanted to be the first one to interview him. Offenders are more likely to let their guard down with their lawyer." He chewed his lip. "He's not the one who killed Layla. At least now, you know that, and you can go out and find the guy who did."

Franco cast a quizzical glance Scott's way. "Are you still going to represent Quinley—on the child exploitation charges?"

"Nope. Wild horses couldn't keep me on this one. I'll let him know tomorrow I can't proceed. I'll tell him I've got schedule conflicts. Do you two need this interview to continue?"

"Yes," I said. "We do."

"All right," Scott said, his dark eyes flashing. "I'll go back and keep up the charade—if I can stomach it. Hope you can squeeze something else out of him you can use."

The three of us stared at each other. We were all playing a dangerous game. Everything could unravel in the blink of an eye.

Scott and Franco headed back to the interview room.

I returned to the observation area and kept watching through the mirror.

Franco sank into his seat heavily. He was playing the role of a defeated detective right now. "Okay," he said to Quinley, "it seems that Mr DeCoursey is unhappy with my line of questioning. I've got to keep this focused on the known offences."

Quinley nodded, his expression not giving anything away.

"Dr Quinley," Franco started, "it must have been a strange experience for you, knowing that both Abby and Layla loved Emmet, and not *you?*"

The question seemed to crumple Quinley instantly. "They were young girls. Little birds still in their nests. They didn't know what love was, yet. In any case, Layla didn't have feelings for Emmet."

"What makes you think Layla didn't have feelings for him?" Franco probed.

"Because the person she had a crush on was actually Detective Wakeland's daughter, Abby," he replied.

I couldn't hide my surprise. Was Quinley trying to throw Franco off-track?

Franco didn't skip a beat. "What made you think that?"

"She told me," Quinley said. "In one of our text conversations. And I finally worked out why I'd been unable to form a connection with her.

It was because she had no interest in Emmet. I couldn't be Mr Lullaby to her. But she did ask me for advice on how to deal with her feelings for Abby. Of course, being that I'm a psychiatrist, she'd inadvertently come to the best possible person."

"I'd have to question Layla not having feelings for Emmet," said Franco. He passed Dr Quinley a photocopy of the love letter we'd found in the boat shed. "We think this is a letter that Layla wrote to Emmet."

Dr Quinley scanned the letter, his brow rippling in deep furrows. "This makes no sense at all. Layla said none of this to me. It's like someone else entirely wrote it."

Franco crossed his arms tightly across his chest. "Like who?"

"You're the detective," Quinley muttered through gritted teeth. "You figure it out."

"We'll keep moving," Franco said, a note of uncertainty catching in his throat. He picked up another photograph from the pile—this time of the close-up shot of the piece of material that had been snagged on the coat hanger. He slid it across to Quinley. "Can you tell me anything about this?"

Picking it up, Quinley peered at it closely. "No."

Dr Quinley had no discernible reaction to seeing the sample. I'd hoped to see some kind of unease from him at least.

But if he'd been recovering in hospital after surgery, it was almost impossible that it *had* been him.

Scott leaned to take a look. "What's this? Something you think Dr Quinley gave to Layla?"

Franco turned his attention to Scott. "Maybe."

"The answer is *no*, Detective Franco," asserted Quinley. "Why would I give such an ugly scarf to such a lovely young girl? Deers with antlers? Perish the thought."

"Ugly?" Scott exclaimed. "Hold up. Those are Persian Fallow Deers." He raised his eyes to Franco. "Where did you find this?"

"Locally," Franco answered.

Franco wasn't meant to be questioning Quinley about the subject of murder, and I could tell that he was treading carefully.

"Well, I can clear up the mystery," Scott said. "This is from a scarf. It's my wife's. I'm guessing you found it snagged somewhere down by the lake?"

I felt my chest sinking. I'd hoped the material would end up being something important, rather than being an article of clothing that Nina had passed onto her niece. If the material was from a scarf, it made sense that pieces of it were found around Layla's neck. That was, after all, where one would wear a scarf.

"Tell me about the scarf," Franco asked flatly.

"Sure," Scott said. "The scarf came from Iran. My grandfather is Iranian. Just before Layla came to live with us, Nina and I went to visit my family over in Osku, Iran. I bought Nina the scarf there. It cost a bomb, but I loved it on sight. It's hand stamped."

Franco went silent. I guessed he was trying to reroute his direction. He cleared his throat. "Okay, we'll check that with your wife."

Dr Quinley stretched his spine and shoulders. "Seems that you keep running into dead ends, detective. "All you've got in your hands is a dreadful, expensive scarf and the private journal of a long-dead teacher and a letter that Layla didn't write."

Scott picked up the letter, then wrinkled his brow. "I have to agree with Dr Quinley. This doesn't look like something Layla wrote."

"Because of what it says or the handwriting?" Franco asked.

Scott shrugged. "Both."

"We couldn't find any other sample of Layla's handwriting," Franco told him.

"I think I can clear one of those things up." Scott reached down and picked up his briefcase. "You just reminded me of something I'd forgotten. I still have a Christmas card she wrote me."

I held a breath, shifting to the edge of my seat.

Franco raised his eyebrows high. "You got the card here?"

"Yeah," Scott said. "As far as I know, anyway. She popped it into my briefcase the last Christmas before she left."

"And you kept it all this time?" Franco asked.

Scott slipped his hand into a leather side pocket inside his briefcase and retrieved a card. "I thought it was sweet what she wrote in it. It was the kind of thing you'd keep. Anyway, I'll show you."

He handed it to Franco.

I squinted to see better.

All I could see was the front of the card depicted a cartoonish Christmas scene.

Holding the card gingerly on its edges, Franco opened it.

He read it out loud. I knew that was for my benefit.

Happy Christmas, Uncle Scott, from Layla.

If I could pick a dad, I'd pick you.

Franco eyed Scott. "Did you ever show that to Nina?"

Scott shook his head. "It'd break her heart. She wanted a relationship with Layla. But it just didn't happen. The two of them were forever at loggerheads. Like two bulls."

That was the opposite of what Nina had told me.

Franco set the card down next to the letter. "It's not a match."

I inhaled a shallow, open-mouthed breath. Layla didn't write either the letter or the note.

But who would go to the trouble of trying to make us believe that Layla was in love with Emmet—and for what reason?

My heart raced as I stared through the two-way mirror at the love letter, Scott's Christmas card and the photo of the scarf.

Layla's killer had to be in those three things. There had to be connections right there.

What if the person who wrote that love letter didn't write it to fool anyone? What if they were genuinely in love with Emmet?

My mind went to a dark place.

There was one person who fitted. Just one person.

It hurt me to think it could be them. But the evidence was lying right there, on the table.

I watched Franco switching his gaze between the three items as well, and I knew he was making the same calculations I was.

Dr Quinley glanced from Franco to Scott, his mouth dropping open. He'd figured it out as well.

Franco rose to his feet. "This interview is done."

Scott didn't speak or react.

He remained in his seat with a dazed expression.

But it was almost as if his perfectly aligned features had slid ever so slightly out of place.

69

KATE

Rain hammered down as Franco and I drove away on the dark roads.

Neither of us spoke.

I had no idea what we were going to say when we reached our destination.

Storms brewed in my mind.

We parked outside Nina DeCoursey's house.

Her car was in the driveway.

Lights were on in the house.

Jumping from the car with umbrellas in hand, Franco and I headed towards the front porch.

A surprised Nina opened the door to us, dressed in a skirt and jacket, without her shoes. *"Kate... and Detective Franco?* Oh no, do you have more news for me?"

Closing my umbrella, I placed it against the exterior wall. "Could we come in, Nina?"

"Of course. Come through." She kept talking as we followed her in. "You just caught me. I came in from work just ten minutes ago. I had to go see a pregnant teen who's been stealing from her employer. I think I can get her off the hook, but boy is she ungrateful."

She headed into the kitchen. "Can I get either of you a drink? Coffee? Coke?"

"No, thanks, Nina," I replied. "We... we have some questions for you."

"Oh? Well, of course. Anything." She offered us a warm smile. "I'm so grateful for all the work you've both been putting in on this. I'm still coming to terms with everything, but I'll get there."

She glanced at Franco. "I heard about the hit-and-run. I'm so glad you're out and about again. I knew Louisa was having a rough time, but I never thought she'd do something like that."

"Thanks—I'll survive. Could I get you to take a look at this?" Franco pulled out a photocopy of the love letter from the plastic folder he had under his arm. He placed it on the kitchen bench.

"What is it?" Nina asked, but her gaze bounced away from the piece of paper. "Are you sure I can't get you a coffee? I'm feeling like one."

I pointed at the photocopy. "This is a romantic letter that we found ten years ago, in Emmet Eisen's boat shed. Remember I told you about it?"

Nina's mouth formed a small circle. "Wow, I wasn't expecting to actually *see* it. Layla wrote it, right? What a shock. A bit of warning would have been nice, guys."

"I'm sorry," I apologised in a brisk tone. "It's been a very long day. I've lost my subtlety."

"I've just had one of those kinds of days, too." Nina poured water into the kettle and then put it on to boil. The crockery rattled on the shelf as she fetched herself a cup.

"Okay," I said, "going back to the letter, did you write it?"

"What?" She whirled around. "Me? Write that to Emmet? I don't—"

"Nina," I said, "it's okay. We can clear this up quickly. If you didn't write it, then just show us a sample of your handwriting."

She stared back at me. "Well, I... I don't have anything at hand. Everything is digital these days. I haven't handwritten anything in donkey's years." She laughed thinly. "I'll find you something over the next few days. But I'll tell you, Layla had very similar writing to me. You could tell that we were related, I'll tell you that." She attempted to smile, but it came out more as a grimace.

"We've got a definite sample of Layla's writing," I told her. "It's very different."

High spots of colour bloomed in her cheeks. "You did? I thought that you—"

"Scott still had a Christmas card Layla gave him," I said.

"He did?" Her voice went faint and she sank onto a stool. "Look, yes... I wrote it. It was stupid. Totally stupid. I wasn't myself at the time. Scott wasn't paying much attention to me. And Emmet was pursuing me. It just... happened."

"Emmet pursued you?" I raised my eyebrows questioningly. "It sounded as if you were trying to convince *him*."

"I wanted to rekindle a former relationship we'd had," she admitted. "He didn't."

She was starting to tell us things. It was time to give her a little push.

"Thanks for telling us," I said. "Did you know that we have Emmet's journal?"

She blanched. "*Journal?* There's no journal. It was destroyed."

That confused me. I didn't think she'd even know there *was* a journal. Had Louisa told her about it?

"No, it wasn't destroyed," I said cautiously. "Louisa was keeping it in a safe deposit box, in the town where her holiday house is."

"You mean... she had it, all this time?"

I nodded. "But she didn't read it, apparently. But *we* did, today."

Nina's head dropped low, and she clutched her forehead. "Oh, God. *Oh, God.* Did he write about... *him and me?*"

"I'm afraid so," I answered, but I didn't know, exactly, what she was so worried about. Was it just because she'd had an affair with Emmet? She had much, much bigger concerns than that.

Tears rolled down her face. "I didn't mean for it to happen. You have to believe that. I really didn't. Yes, he was thirteen when it started. But he was a very mature young man. He seduced *me*, you know. But I just didn't know how to refuse him."

Franco stared with stunned eyes from Nina to me.

I swallowed, my throat drying. Emmet had only been *thirteen* when the relationship started? That would have been the year the Eisens moved to Tallman's Valley.

My stomach turned.

This was a very different scenario than the one I'd thought. It had not been a relationship at all. Nina had abused Emmet when he was just a child.

Instantly, so much about Emmet fell into place. Emmet's depression and losing his way in life. The way he'd holed himself up in his bedroom when he'd returned to live at his parents' home after being away at university.

I could guess what happened after his return. Nina had started hounding him again. She'd written him the letter, begging him to love her and to be with her.

The kettle boiled. Nina poured herself a cup of coffee with trembling fingers. She gulped a mouthful, leaning her back against the counter and facing away from us.

I had to use every bit of strength to keep my voice steady. "Nina, Emmet told about his last day—the day he died—in his journal. But I'd like to hear *your* version of events."

That wasn't true, except wanting to know what she knew. But I wanted to force her to tell the rest of what she was holding back. My breath felt cold in my lungs as I waited for her reply.

She didn't turn back around to me, but she nodded her head. "Okay, I'll tell you. That morning, I went to see Emmet. He was sitting on a deck chair down by the lake. But Abby—she got there before me. And she went out on his boat with him. I was beside myself, wondering what the hell the two of them were doing alone together. I went into the boat house and wrote him that letter on some notepaper. Then I left it there for him. From my house, I watched him row back to shore.

Abby ran off. She seemed upset. Emmet went to the boat house. I walked across and asked if he'd read my letter. He picked it up and screwed it into a ball, and he threw it at me. Right at my face. Can you imagine? I loved him like crazy, and he was treating me so damned poorly. He looked *awful*. His face was all bruised. He said he'd been in a fight earlier—with some older guy who he thought had been trying to seduce Layla and Abby."

"Then what did you do?" I prompted.

"Well, I told him I'd calm him down. Get him some alcohol. So, I went back to my house, grabbed some beer and bourbon, and took it back to him. I sat drinking with him, making him happier. I tried to get him to see reason, you know? He was older—he wasn't a kid anymore. There was nothing stopping us from being together now. I couldn't understand why he wouldn't even entertain the thought. He fell asleep for a long while. But when he woke, he just walked straight out of there, taking the remaining alcohol with him. He took his boat out again, and just paddled away. I forgot about the letter... until the next morning. I was drunk, too, you see...."

Nina returned to sit on the stool, wiping her face—which was now streaked with tears and mascara. "I never saw him again. Ever...."

Anger flashed in Franco's eyes.

I felt it, too—fury at what Nina had done to Emmet. I remembered something Abby had told Dr Quinley in one of her therapy sessions. Abby said Emmet had looked strange that day—that his pupils were dilated. Emmet had probably been suffering from a concussion from the fight he'd had earlier. Nina would have seen his eyes. She'd known he'd been in a fight. Yet, she went ahead and plied him with alcohol. Because she'd been trying any which way to force him into a relationship with her.

I believed her when she said Emmet had paddled away alone. We had a witness statement to say as much—from Cooper Tecklenburg.

I could guess what had happened from there. Emmet had taken his boat out for the second time that day—just to get away from Nina. At some point, when he was out on the lake, the effects of the alcohol and the concussion had resulted in him falling from the boat. Had he been on dry land, he might have survived.

Nina was sitting there taking long, quiet breaths. I could see it in her eyes that she thought this was the end of it. That we'd found out what we'd come here to find out. She had no idea that Emmet's journal had told us very little.

"Thank you for telling us the truth," I said. "We have a couple more things to show you."

She waved her hands across each other in a gesture of refusal. "No, no more. I can't. That's enough. I feel terrible as it is. I had some lapses of good judgment. Tell me who doesn't?" She exhaled audibly. "I'm guessing my career is done. I won't be able to work with children again. Serves me right. I shouldn't have allowed Emmet to—"

Ignoring her, Franco put the next picture on the kitchen countertop —a photo of the piece of material with the deer antlers.

Nina took a quick look and then turned away. "I've no idea what that is. Should I know?"

"Nina," I said. "Please look closer. Is it from an article of *your* clothing?"

"Mine?" Twisting around, she glanced at the picture again. "*Oh*. Well, I'm not certain, to tell you the truth."

"Your husband said this scrap of material is from a scarf of yours," I said pointedly.

"Scott? Did he go down to the station to tell you all of this? He's... turned against me?"

"No, that's not how it happened." I decided not to give her any more explanation than that.

With a guarded look in her eyes, she pushed her hair back and peered at the photo. "Oh, it's just *that*. Yes, that was a scarf of mine. I think I gave it to Layla. She liked it."

"Please try to remember," I said. "Did you give it to Layla or not?"

"I'm not certain," she attempted to explain. "I haven't seen it in a long time. That's why I'm thinking I must have given it to her. And that's why I'd forgotten it."

I felt as if an ice-cold breeze had just circled around me. I recognised the way Nina was talking. It was the same way many offenders before her had spoken to me—with all the vague recollections and denials and backtracking.

Before I'd come here tonight, I'd hoped that there was something I was missing—some part of the story that would leave Nina at least partly innocent.

But, so far, the only part I'd been missing had been the part in which Nina had forced herself on the thirteen-year-old Emmet Eisen.

Franco placed another picture on the countertop, as if he were laying out a deck of cards.

It was a copy of the note Layla had supposedly written to her grandfather.

"Nina," Franco said. "I think you know what this is."

She read it quickly, her back going rigid. "That's... Layla's note. I threw it away. I don't know why he kept it."

I examined the creases that showed up on the photocopy. It told the story of a note that had been crumpled up in a fit of anger. "Can I ask why you threw it away?"

"I was damned cranky with her at the time," Nina said. "Going off with her father as she did."

Nina was sticking with the script. But she had to know that it no longer made any sense.

"Nina," I said, "Layla didn't go away with her father. And she didn't write the note. She died before it was written. We know that the person who wrote the letter to Emmet also wrote that note."

At first, Nina's face turned hard and bitter, her jaw and cheeks drawn tight. But then her mouth dropped loose, her eyes growing huge and distant.

She was ready to talk.

70

KATE

She knew that we knew what she'd done.

The only things we didn't know were the logistics and Nina's reasons for doing what she did.

We'd take her in for a formal interview down at the station, later. But to do that, we'd need to arrest her. And we didn't have quite enough yet to arrest her with.

I glanced at Franco, giving him a nod. He understood the nod. It was best that he took the reins. Layla had been my daughter's best friend. I had too close a personal involvement to go any further.

Franco placed his phone on the kitchen counter and pressed *record*. "Nina, do we have your permission to record you? As you'd know, anything you say can and might be used against you in a court of law."

She nodded woodenly, like a mechanical doll. "Yes."

"Nina DeCoursey," Franco began, "tell me what led up to Layla Maddox leaving town and what happened on the night she died?"

Nina gazed straight ahead. "Layla found out about Emmet and me. It was at one of the parties at Alex and Louisa's house. I'd gotten Emmet off to a quiet spot, and I kissed him. I was very tipsy... and throwing caution to the wind. Emmet reacted badly. He told me I'd ruined his life by going after him when he was a kid. Layla overheard us. Later, she and I had a huge fight about it. I told her to leave if she thought so poorly of me—just get out of my house. She wasn't welcome here anymore. We hadn't been getting on, anyway. She was so wilful. She told me she was going back to live with her grandfather. I thought that was the best thing for everyone. I mean, I took on a very big burden when she came to stay with me. And I did the best I could. But this... it was too much. She didn't have the right to get in my face and call me a... *child molester*."

Nina rubbed her face, as if she were scrubbing it, leaving faint red fingernail marks on her cheeks. "Layla returned to live with her grandfather. And everything would have been just fine if she'd stayed there. But two weeks later, she came back. It was night-time. She came to my house and stole her bicycle from the shed. Scott was still at work. I went out and asked her what the hell she thought she was doing. She refused to tell me. I was suspicious. I mean, why did she return?"

Nina seemed to realise she was clawing at her face and she stopped, twisting her fingers together instead.

"I went after Layla in my car. She ended up at the strangest of places. A big old empty lot of land. Of course, I know what that place is now. I didn't then. I followed her in. She ran across the field and inside one of the buildings. It totally creeped me out. What on earth was she doing? And then it got even stranger. The place had a bed and furniture in it. And mirrors everywhere. And a silly birdcage on a chain. Layla ran through the rooms as if she were trying to find something. I showed myself and demanded to know what she was up to. She marched right up to my face. She said Emmet was keeping a journal here. And she was going to take it to Abby's mother. Right now. Tonight."

"And then what happened?" Franco asked Nina.

"Well, I didn't know Emmet was keeping a damned journal, that's for sure. I got angry. Told her she couldn't do that."

"What did Layla say then?" he asked.

"She said I couldn't tell her what to do. She said that Emmet was refusing to tell anyone what I'd done to him, but *she* would. She said that once she had the journal, everyone would know."

"And then?" Franco prompted.

Nina's knees began shaking. "It's a bit of a blur. She pushed me, told me to leave. I pushed her back. She hit me—right in the face. I pushed her again. Hard. She fell back against one of the mirrors. Smashed her head. The mirror shattered. The next thing I know, she's on the ground, knocked out. I panicked. Here I was, in this Godforsaken place, and I'd just done that to my own niece. What was I going to do? Call an ambulance? If I'd done that, everything would have come out. *Everything*. And that would mean my job gone. My husband gone. My whole life gone. Once Layla woke up, she would have told them about Emmet."

Nina shivered, rubbing her arms. "I was angry at Layla, but I didn't hate her or anything. I wasn't in a rage. I was just... *terrified*. From that point on, I wasn't myself. The next thing I know, I'd taken my scarf off and I'd gone over to Layla, and I'd wrapped it around her neck. And I'd pulled it. Until she stopped breathing. When I realised what I'd done, I was in shock. I remember feeling just so cold and numb and scared. I couldn't believe I'd done that."

"Then what did you do?" Franco asked.

"Well, I had to hide what I'd done," Nina replied. "I just wanted to fix it. Pretend it never happened. I dragged her up the stairs and put her in a cupboard, and I locked it. Then I went searching for the damned journal. But I couldn't find it. I started to think Layla had lied about it. That she'd lured me out to the old carnival just to taunt me. I thought the best thing I could do was just to burn the whole place down. Layla was already dead. It wouldn't hurt her. And if there really was a journal, it'd burn, too. I gathered up some old plasterboard and papers, took out my lighter and set the pile alight. Then I ran out of there, back to my car. And I let it burn."

Franco and I met each other's eyes. We'd just heard the story of Layla's murder, in every awful detail.

Right then, I did something I'd never allowed myself to do, not in any police interview I'd ever attended.

I let a tear run down my face, unchecked.

Things could have played out so differently that night.

If only Layla had come to *me* first, she would still be alive.

But it had all started way before that.

If only Emmet had told about Nina.

If only Nola had told about her mother.

If only Abby had told about the funfair.

But none of them told—because they'd only been children.

One thing I'd learned in my job was that the world looked very different to a child. They were so easily silenced. And then afterwards, they often became so wrapped up in shame that they wanted to lock everything away.

With a sad realisation, I knew why Layla had wanted to fetch the journal before coming to me. She was a young girl who was almost alone in the world. And the family she'd lived with—her aunt—had thrown her out of the house. Layla would have been afraid that without proof, she wouldn't be believed about what her aunt had done to Emmet.

A timeline formed in my mind, everything locking into place, scenes forming themselves like a movie.

At a party near the end of January, Layla overheard Nina and Emmet's tense conversation. Layla discovered that her aunt had abused Emmet when he was a child. After Layla confronted Nina, Nina told Layla to leave. Layla returned to live with her grandfather.

Two weeks later, it was a hot day in February.

Dr Quinley had stayed overnight at the Eisens' house after a party. He woke with stomach pains on Sunday morning—pains that he would later discover to be due to appendicitis. Emmet, already intoxicated, confronted him about taking photos of Abby and Layla, and a fight ensued. Emmet most probably sustained a concussion when Quinley pushed him to the floor. Dr Quinley then drove himself to Sydney and to a hospital.

Perhaps an hour after that, Abby snuck out of her house to see Emmet, who was then sitting down at the lake. Emmet—perhaps trying to evade what he saw as a lovelorn teenager—took his boat out on the lake. Abby invited herself along.

Nina, incensed by the sight of Abby and Emmet together, went to Emmet's boat house and wrote him a letter.

When Emmet returned from his trip on the lake, Nina cornered him in his boat house. He balled up her letter and threw it at her. In a desperate, last-ditch attempt to seduce Emmet, Nina went to fetch alcohol from her house. She plied Emmet with beer and bourbon.

At midday that day, in Sydney, Layla had lunch with her grandfather. She then made the fateful decision to travel back to Tallman's Valley and expose what Nina had done. I could guess why—during the short time I'd known Layla, she seemed to try to help those who she thought needed protecting, whether they were people or animals.

Layla went to Nina's house to fetch her bike. Layla had probably been certain that Nina wouldn't hear or see her taking the bicycle out from the garage—but Nina had. Nina followed her to the funfair. And killed her. Then Nina set the funfair ablaze. I guessed that Nina then drove back to her house and showered before Scott returned home.

Fire fighters put out the fire and secured the building.

During this night, Abby was at home, still grounded. She was especially restless and agitated. I relented and allowed her the use of her phone. Cooper Tecklenburg sent a message to Abby to taunt her that the teacher she loved was fall-down drunk yet again, and he'd gone out boating.

Sometime during that night—perhaps even while the

funfair was still burning—the heavily inebriated and concussed Emmet Eisen slipped into Coldwater Lake and drowned.

The next morning before school, Abby went looking for Emmet at the lake. After finding him dead, she rode to the now burned-out funfair to retrieve his journal. She hadn't had the barest inkling that her friend Layla was dead inside a cupboard upstairs.

Franco and I were called out to the lake a little later that morning, after Louisa Eisen found her son's body. We also picked up Nina's letter from the boat house.

That afternoon, after keeping the journal in her schoolbag all day, Abby hid the journal in the little cave in the forest. Louisa Eisen, who had followed her, retrieved her son's journal and kept it.

That was it. The whole, awful timeline.

For the past ten years, there had been only one event from that night and morning that I'd been aware of—Emmet's death. I'd been completely in the dark about all of the other events.

Franco handed me a handkerchief.

I dabbed at my wet cheek.

Franco turned to Nina. "Nina DeCoursey, I have to inform you that you're under arrest for the murder of your niece, Layla Maddox."

71

KATE

Spring turned to summer in the valley.

The lakeside filled with people who'd come to say their last good-byes to Layla.

Layla was finally laid to rest, her ashes spread on the water. The lake was a place she'd loved, among her beloved animals and birds.

Brolgas and swamphens and swans paddled at a distance along the shore.

I was proud of Abby as she managed to stand in front of everyone and talk about her friend.

Layla, Abby said through her tears, *we give your ashes to the lake. We'll always see you here, in the sunsets and sunrises. We'll always hear you here, in the bird calls and the wind in the trees. We'll always find you here.... because you never really left us.*

Of all the speeches today, that was the one that'd made me cry.

Layla's entire class from Valley Grammar had come to the ceremony. She must have made quite an impression during her short time there.

The nine members of the Tecklenburg family came, too, and

dropped flowers in the water. Davey Tecklenburg had made a plaque for Layla, to hang on a tree.

A surprise appearance had been Layla's father, Rusty. He'd looked stunned and grief-stricken the whole time. But it was a case of far too little, far too late.

Scott DeCoursey brought Layla's grandfather down from Sydney, wheeling him down to the lake in his wheelchair.

Scott held it together during all the speeches and during when Layla's ashes had been spread on the lake, his expression steadfast. But afterwards, he retreated to his boat house and sobbed his heart out.

I found him there when I went looking for him.

"Scott...?" Not knowing what to say, I simply hugged him.

He pointed at an empty spot on the wall. "There... right there."

"What's there, Scott?"

"Nina painted over it. Layla drew love hearts all over the wall, back when she was thirteen. Inside the love hearts, she wrote things like, *Scott loves Nina* and *Abby loves Cooper*. I remember that now. Little things are coming back to me."

I winced. "I remember the day I found Nina painting the boat house."

"She was making damned sure no one found any of Layla's writing." His eyes filled with pain. "She found it hard having Layla in the house, right from the start. I could tell she didn't like it when Layla and I joked with each other or played board games. I used to take the kid clothes shopping—because Nina didn't. The poor kid had the same clothes she'd come to us with, and she was growing fast."

"I didn't suspect any of that."

"You know what was sad? Layla didn't really care a lot about the clothes she wore, but she intentionally chose clothing for herself that she thought Nina would like. Nina had a lot of glittery clothes she'd wear to the parties, and she spent a lot on swimsuits and shoes. Layla tried to copy her, in an effort to make Nina approve of her."

"That *is* sad. Goodness, the way Nina spoke about her relationship with Layla, I really thought they were the best of friends."

"Nina hid it well. She took Layla shopping just once—and she made a really big show of it. Gave Layla a day off school and wrote a note to the school to say she'd needed to supply her niece with clothing. As if it was some grand gesture."

"I'm glad Layla had you in her corner."

He shook his head mournfully. "I didn't do enough. I thought Nina would get used to Layla being around. I should have known better."

"You didn't know. How could you have known? Scott, I'm a seasoned detective, and I never suspected Nina. Not until you told me about the scarf."

"But I knew Nina. You didn't. She was a strange person in many ways. During our whole marriage, she'd be loving one minute and then ice-cold the next. I ended up not knowing how to react to her. Because I kept getting hurt." He dragged his fingers through his hair, ruffling his perfect waves. "But I had no idea about what she'd done to Emmet. Not a clue."

I remembered something. "Do you think that when Emmet was asking you about historic child abuse offences that time, he was actually talking about *Nina?*"

Scott stared at me. "You know, you're right. You're damned right. During that conversation, Emmet kept casting hard glances at Nina. I didn't know why. But he was hard to read. He'd always been... intense. It must have been around that time that she was writing him love letters. She never wrote *me* a love letter in her life. I didn't even recognise her damned writing when I saw it. She never handwrote anything."

Reaching out, I squeezed his arm. "I feel for you. Do you have family you can turn to at this time?"

"I don't have much family. I think that's why I was secretly delighted when Layla came to stay with us. I considered her my family. I'd never seen much of her before that. Nina hadn't been much into family things. When her sister, Kirsten, came out to live in Australia, Nina basically gave her the cold shoulder."

"Wow. Sad."

"Yeah."

I turned to look out of the boat house window. "Speaking of family, where's Layla's grandfather?"

"I left him with Abby."

"Okay. I'm going to go see how both of them are doing."

Scott raised his eyes to me. "Today wouldn't be easy on either of them. I'll stay here awhile. I need to clear my head."

I found Abby and Mr Maddox sitting together under the ghost gum, swapping stories about Layla. Abby had brought over a stack of Layla's photos to show him, too.

I'd had the best of Layla's photos printed, all in a large size, and then laminated them. They were on display today. It'd been the best way Abby and I could think of to show who Layla had been. We'd wanted everyone to see the world through Layla's eyes.

"How are you, Mr Maddox?" I asked.

He viewed me through watery blue eyes. "Wishing I could go back in time, Detective."

"Me, too." Bending, I gave him a hug.

I noticed then that Louisa and Alex Eisen were standing on the shoreline—a short distance away.

Louisa was out on bail after her hit-and-run offence—due to attend court soon.

I'd sat Alex and Louisa down the day after Nina was arrested, and I'd explained everything that had happened. We'd surmised that a concussion as well as the large amount of alcohol that Nina had given Emmet had resulted in him losing consciousness and falling into the lake. But we'd never know exactly how it had happened. At the point the Eisens heard that Emmet was innocent of any wrongdoing, their relief had been almost palpable. I knew though, that Alex would carry the grief of what he'd done the rest of his life—he'd tried to silence his own son purely because it suited his business dealings.

A young woman approached Abby, her eyes sad and reddened.

Nola Hobson.

Abby rose from her seat beside Mr Maddox. At first, she and Nola seemed a little awkward with each other, not knowing what to say. But then they hugged, crying on each other's shoulder. I hoped they'd become friends. It seemed fitting that ten years after the lizard bite incident—in the exact same place that incident had happened—Nola and Abby would finally become friends.

In the weeks prior to today, I'd assured Nola that we were going to track down her mother, no matter what it took. DS Liz Booth and her entire squad were already on the job. Adele Hobson needed to be in jail—along with Gordon Quinley and Nina DeCoursey. We were also going to look closely at Doug Overmire. We still weren't sure of his part in this. Had he known what his brother Gordon was doing, and he'd turned a blind eye? That would all have to come out in court—so far, he'd refused to talk.

Abby stepped away with Nola. I took a seat beside Ernest Maddox, and I began listening to his stories about Layla and her mother Kirsten.

Ivy, who'd been down at the shore looking at the ducks with Pete, Logan and her baby brother, came skipping up. Putting an arm around her, I drew her in close as she listened to Mr Maddox's stories about Layla, too.

When the ceremony was over and everyone had returned home, just two people remained at the lake.

Abby and me.

We needed the quiet, the empty shore.

The day was completely still. Not a breath of wind. Only the calls of the lake birds slipped through the silence.

"She really is still here, Mum," Abby said. "I can see her."

"I can see both of you here. Hang onto the happy times, honey. All of the other things will fade away, in time."

"I hope so, because I don't ever want to see Dr Quinley's face again —not in my mind, not anywhere."

A flock of rainbow lorikeets darted and wheeled above us, as if painting the canvas of sky with strokes of colour. The air filled with their noisy chatter.

Abby raised her face, squinting into the sun. "I've been seeing those birds ever since I can remember. I mean, they're everywhere. But I never stopped to really look at them—until I met Layla."

I reached for her hand, squeezing it. "Feel like a walk?"

Wiping a tear from her eye, she nodded.

72

KATE

From the deck of our cottage, Pete and I watched the sunset fade and turn to a velvety night.

The stars seemed cold and silvery. Even though of course they were neither of those two things.

The temperature dropped so low that my cheek felt like ice when I touched it. But I didn't want to go inside yet and neither did Pete.

He stood behind me, his arms over my shoulders and a thick blanket wrapped around the two of us.

The events of the past weeks had turned all of us inside out. Left us raw and bleeding.

All the things we hadn't known.

I could see Abby and Logan through the window, with Jasper in Logan's arms and Ivy on Abby's lap. The four of them in front of the fireplace. It was a lovely little family scene that gave me back hope for the future.

The funeral today had been rough on Abby. It'd been rough on all of us.

Over the past weeks, other girls had come forward about *Mr*

Lullaby. Just like with Abby and Layla, Dr Quinley had pretended to be someone else to them.

He wouldn't be hurting any girls now.

It wasn't just girls he'd hurt. He'd hurt Emmet, too. He'd taken him on as a client purely so that he could hear all about the young girls at the lake. Instead of helping Emmet, he'd twisted his mind, insisting on hearing more and more details about Abby and Layla. For a sensitive young man who'd been trying to heal from past abuse and find his way in the world, Dr Quinley had been the worst possible person he could have confided in.

We'd been able to obtain the records Dr Quinley had kept during his sessions with Abby and Emmet. I'd discovered something I didn't know. Dr Quinley had known about Nina's abuse of Emmet when he was just thirteen years old. Because Emmet had told him during the therapy sessions. Quinley had kept that fact from us due to a patient confidentiality clause. Deceased patients were still entitled to strict privacy of their records. Dr Quinley hadn't wanted to be struck off by the registrar. Apparently, he still imagined he would be absolved in court of wrongdoing, and he'd be allowed to keep his psychiatry practice.

He was delusional.

Pete kissed my temple, pulling the blanket close around us. "You okay, Kate? You're very quiet."

"It's not quiet inside my head. So many thoughts spinning around in there."

"I thought so. It's all been a whirlwind. The funeral was a nice goodbye for Layla, at least. Did you see the black swans out on the lake? It was like they came just for her."

"Yes, I noticed the swans. I hope she's at peace, now. We found her. And we found out who took her life. I just wish it didn't happen, that's all."

My eyes were filling with tears again.

"I know, honey. I wish the same. I felt the sorriest for her grandfather today. He looked in poor health, too. Awful thing to have happen near the end of your life."

"Yes, poor old guy. It probably would have been better if he thought she was still alive, out there living her life. But now, he's lost his whole family. One daughter to cancer, one daughter to jail... and his grand-daughter murdered."

Pete nestled his head against mine. "Maybe we can do something for him—bring him out here sometimes? As if he's our own family, even? If he wants, that is."

I half-turned around to Pete. "What a lovely thought. I'll ask him."

"Was Scott close to Layla's grandfather?"

"I don't think so. I get the idea that Nina kept them at a distance from each other. She was very... *possessive* with people. I spoke with Scott after the funeral."

"Strange woman."

"Yes. She must have been so difficult for poor Layla to live with. But Layla must have felt she had no options and nowhere to go."

"Too many kids out there in that situation."

"Yes, you're right. Far too many."

"Layla was loved though, Kate. Take strength in that. Her mother and grandfather loved her. And then her Uncle Scott and Abby. We treated her like a daughter, too, whenever she was at our house. She was loved."

I found myself crying yet again. "She really was."

We fell quiet for a time.

I tried to feel restful, to find my own sense of peace.

But I couldn't find peace.

Something still stirred beneath the surface.

"Pete... I can't stop thinking about the apple."

"The apple?"

"Do you remember, on the car trip to the South Coast—"

"Right. Yeah. You said you thought there's a rotten core. And you were talking about this town."

"Yes. Like a core of people who are connected. And they're not *good* people."

"Kate, you're seeing our town through the eyes of a detective who's seen the worst of it. But look at what else is here. Lots of space to move around. Clean air. Forests. Mountains. The people."

"I know. We've got all that and more. We do. But people like Dr Quinley and Adele Hobson didn't come out of nowhere. They were all born and bred in this town. On the same farm."

"They were a bad bunch all right. But, honey, you know better than anyone that ordinary people can do terrible things. Like Nina DeCoursey."

"That's true. Anyone can take the wrong path. But you're talking about individuals. I'm talking about something else." Anxiety welled inside me. "Do you know what? The records of the police raids of the Mulden compound are very sketchy and incomplete. So many missing records. The people who lived there are barely even listed. It's not right."

"You can't do anything about that. What you *can* do, tonight, is to feel a sense of achievement. You've made a big difference to a lot of people this year, including our own family. Hold onto that, okay?"

"I'll try."

"Kate... would you do something for me?"

"What's that?"

"Let the world go on without you. Take a step back—from everything. Don't let this thing about the Mulden farm get to you. Let's just enjoy... *living*."

I tugged the blanket up higher. "I promise I won't let this take over our lives."

Internally, I was making a second promise:

I'm going to find my way to the rotten heart of this town.

READER'S NOTE

I hope you enjoyed
THE LULLABY MAN

Book 3 THE SILENT TOWN
(Coming in 2021!)
DS Kate Wakeland will strive to uncover the shadowy undercurrents
of her town.

BOOKS BY ANNI TAYLOR

Find my books on Amazon here:

ANNI TAYLOR

Domestic psychological thrillers

THE GAME YOU PLAYED

STRANGER IN THE WOODS

Detective Kate Wakeland

ONE LAST CHILD

THE LULLABY MAN

THE SILENT TOWN

Dark psychological thriller/horror

THE SIX

POISON ORCHIDS

ABOUT THE AUTHOR

Anni Taylor lives on the Central Coast north of Sydney, Australia, with her wonderful partner, amazing sons and a little treats-wrangler dog named Wookie.

Her first thriller, THE GAME YOU PLAYED, and her subsequent thrillers, have all been chart-toppers in their categories. Anni enjoys nothing more than diving into writing the next dark story!

Find out more about her books here:
annitaylor.me

Made in the USA
Monee, IL
20 September 2021

78438247R00245